*Pride Publishing books by Jason Wrench*

**Single Books**
Twelve Days of Murder
Till Death Do Us Wed

# TILL DEATH
# DO US WED

JASON WRENCH

Till Death Do Us Wed
ISBN # 978-1-83943-771-7
©Copyright Jason Wrench 2022
Cover Art by Kelly Martin ©Copyright February 2022
Interior text design by Claire Siemaszkiewicz
Pride Publishing

# TILL DEATH
# DO US WED

# Dedication

This book is dedicated to my family, who has been with me through all my adventures and misadventures over the years. Without their amazing support, I would not be the person I am today.

# Acknowledgements

First, I want to thank everyone at the Office of Letters and Lights for their continued support to budding novelists everywhere through National Novel Writing Month (NaNoWriMo). Second, I want to thank the people involved in the Poughkeepsie area NaNoWriMo group. You're all the best! Without your continued support, this novel would never have happened. And to my NaNoWriMo buddies, thanks for the support, the write-ins and the splendid memories. Third, I want to thank The Ninja Writer's Guild for providing me a safe space to write and stay accountable. Last, I want to thank my editor at Pride Publishing, Jamie Rose, for her patience and guidance through this journey.

# Chapter One

Frank stared around the pink office, wondering if a bottle of Pepto Bismol had accidentally spilled. He watched the perky blonde woman sitting in front of him, doing his best to pay attention. It wasn't exactly how Frank liked to spend his Saturday mornings. But it was Aaron's big day, so he'd promised to grin and bear it.

"With Central Park wedding locations, we are definitely somewhat limited. For example, the Bow Bridge only allows for ten guests and the Belvedere Castle Terrace only allows thirty. The North Garden, Southern Garden, Wisteria Pergola and Cherry Hill each allow for up to one hundred. What size are you two thinking?"

"Eloping," Frank muttered.

"Twenty-five to fifty," Aaron said, shooting Frank a sideways glance.

"I'm joking," Frank reassured, patting Aaron's leg and giving it a squeeze before turning to the woman. "Whatever Aaron wants, I want him to have."

NYPD Detective Frank Schultt and FBI Special Agent Aaron Massey had met the previous year during a serial murder spree. The Twelve-Day Killer, as dubbed by the media, had terrorized NYC over the holidays. Aaron and Frank had put their lives and careers on the line hunting the bastard down. In the process, they had found each other.

Frank glanced over at the man he loved. *God, where would I be without him?* He reached up and rubbed the back of Aaron's neck gently. From the top of Aaron's head with his dark brown quaff haircut and his Caribbean ocean-blue eyes, to his lithe but fit body, Frank took in this man sitting beside him who was going to be his husband. Frank was still stunned at his good fortune in landing the affection of such an amazingly intelligent and gorgeous man.

Realizing his thoughts had drifted, Frank brought his attention back to the woman sitting in front of him, who was rattling on about Central Park weddings. He glanced down at her nameplate, *'Amber Wethersfield'.* The woman was in her late twenties. And judging by the giant diamond on her wedding ring, her husband was definitely wealthy. Frank glanced across the pink office looking for personal items and was surprised by the lack of photos. *For a woman who sells marriage, where are the pictures of her happy day?*

"So, do you have an officiant for your wedding lined up? If not, I have a list of great people who work with LGBTQIA+ people."

"Huh?" Frank blurted before he could catch himself.

"Officiant...the person who will oversee the ceremony and the exchange of your vows," Amber offered.

"No, you listed off a bunch of letters," Frank said.

"Oh." Amber perked up. "Lesbian, gay, bisexual, transgender, queer-questioning, intersexed, asexual and others."

*Dear God, that sounds like a gay BLT.* Frank was about to make the snide comment, but a quick glance from Aaron told him that he'd better hold his tongue. Instead, Frank just nodded his head and gave a thin-lipped smile.

"Actually, we have a few people in mind," Aaron noted. "Frank knows a judge who volunteered her services, and we have a couple of other names in the hopper as well."

"Oh, good," Amber said. "You'd be amazed at how many people totally forget the officiant until the last minute. I even have a license I got from an online church because I've had to step in at the eleventh hour when something went horribly wrong. I just don't enjoy being in the wedding party, because it makes it harder for me to run things behind the scenes."

Frank leaned back in the chair and watched as Aaron and Amber discussed the wedding. This wasn't Frank's first. He'd been married, but his husband had been murdered in a liquor store robbery on Christmas Eve over six years ago. As much as Frank loved Aaron, there was still a vast hole in his heart that had been left by Adam's death. But Frank loved Aaron and was going to make sure their wedding day was every bit of glitz and glamour that Aaron desired.

"Well, if you have questions," Amber said, bringing Frank's attention back once again, "just let me know.

You have my email, cell phone, home phone and office phone numbers, so never hesitate to reach out. I look forward to working with both of you on your big day."

Amber stood up from her desk to usher the couple out of her office. She pushed herself up, exposing her pregnant belly.

"When's the due date?" Aaron asked.

"Mid-March. But I swear she's ready to come out any day."

Frank stared at her belly and just thought, *Are you sure there's only one in there?* But once again, he held his tongue.

"Don't worry. I won't miss your big day. When I'm out on maternity leave, my assistant will take over the day-to-day preparations, and he'll be in constant contact with me. When I had my first baby, we were texting right up until they told me to push."

"Well, it was really nice meeting you," Frank said.

"Likewise. And I just have to say, you two make such a cute couple."

"Thank you," Aaron said. "I think he's a keeper." Aaron gave Amber a little wink before turning to leave.

As Frank followed suit, Aaron's hand rested in the small of Frank's back. Frank leaned into Aaron in response.

"Earth to Frank!" Aaron said as they exited onto the sidewalk. The February chill immediately caught Aaron off guard, and he lifted the collar on the trench coat to protect his neck.

"Huh, what?"

"I said, "*Earth to Frank.*" What's going on inside that head of yours?"

"Overwhelmed, I guess."

"How so?"

"The whole wedding planning is just bringing up some memories."

Aaron squeezed Frank. "I hadn't thought about that. I forget that you've done this before."

"Yeah," Frank said, scrunching his forehead. "It's surreal. Don't get me wrong, I'm excited to be marrying you. I hope you know that. It's just that it brings up memories of Adam."

"I get it," Aaron said. "I would be surprised if it didn't, to be honest." Aaron hesitated for a second before adding, "Just know...I will never try to replace Adam. I know what you two had was special—"

"What we have is special too."

"I know," Aaron acknowledged. "I just want you to know that I love you and would never try to change you...warts and all."

"God, I hope I don't have any warts."

"We all have warts. Some have them physically and others have them metaphorically."

"Sure thing, professor," Frank teased.

After dealing with the Twelve-Day Killer, Aaron had taken a teaching position part-time with the John Jay School of Criminal Justice. He was technically still on the FBI's payroll, but his utility as an undercover agent had taken a hit after the amount of press the Twelve-Day Killer had received. And with the forthcoming publication of his new book about the case, Aaron and Frank both knew a fresh round of press attention was right around the corner.

"So, we didn't have breakfast after the gym this morning," Aaron said. "Shall we have a quick brunch before heading back to the apartment to get ready?"

"Do we have time?" Frank asked, glancing down at his watch. "It's already ten a.m. What time is the car picking us up for the reading?"

"The reading's at two o'clock, so the car is scheduled to pick us up about one-fifteen."

"I guess we have plenty of time. Any suggestions on where we should eat?"

"How about 9Ten?" Aaron asked, referring to one of their favorite diners.

"Lead the way."

\* \* \* \*

Frank ordered the 9Ten Tsoureki French Toast, a Greek sweetbread topped with powdered sugar and maple syrup, and Aaron ordered the Topped-Out Waffle with organic scrambled eggs and Black Forest ham. At ten a.m., the diner had slowed from the early morning rush, but it was still a bustling establishment. It sat on Seventh Avenue between Fifty-Seventh and Fifty-Eighth, so it wasn't exactly in a high-traffic tourist part of Midtown, which was one reason Frank and Aaron enjoyed going there.

"So, are you ready for your reading this afternoon?" Frank asked.

"As ready as I'm going to be, I guess."

Aaron's new book, *The Twelve-Day Killer*, his follow-up to the international bestseller *Blood Money*, was coming out the next week, so his agent and publisher had scheduled a reading at Barnes & Noble to build buzz—not that the book needed it. The book was already sitting atop several bestseller lists, based on preorders alone.

"Decided which part of the book you're going to read?"

"I'm still debating, but I'm definitely leaning toward how we met."

Frank and Aaron had met at a crime scene. Frank had found Aaron's demeanor extremely suspicious, so Aaron had catapulted to the top of the list of Frank's suspects. Frank had later found out that Aaron's suspicious behavior resulted from his being undercover on a human-trafficking case for the FBI. At first, Frank had loathed Special Agent Aaron Massey, but Frank and Aaron had quickly realized that they liked each other and had eventually fallen in love during the case.

The waiter, a very attractive Greek man in his mid-twenties, approached the table and set down their breakfast. *Damn! He could be a model*, Frank thought. Frank caught the slight uptick at the corner of the man's mouth as he set Aaron's plate down in front of him.

"Flirt much?" Frank said under his breath as the waiter left the table.

"I beg your pardon," Aaron said, stabbing a piece of waffle into his mouth.

"Not you," Frank reassured. "The waiter. He was practically drooling on you."

"Frank," Aaron said with a bit of an exasperated sigh, "he wasn't flirting. Besides, I don't think he's even gay."

Frank narrowed his eyes skeptically but decided not to pursue that line of thought any further. *Keep it together, Frank! Jealousy is not sexy.*

Frank quickly changed topics, "So, how are things in your class?"

With a new topic on the table, Aaron spent the rest of their breakfast talking about his new group of students and how much he was enjoying teaching. Frank wolfed down his French toast, smiling and nodding his head at appropriate times. The couple of more times when the waiter approached the table, Frank did his best to keep it together, but he instinctively wanted to growl at the man and tell him to back off.

# Chapter Two

"Aaron, we're going to be late. The car service called. They're downstairs waiting," Frank bellowed as he downed the last of his coffee.

"I'm putting on my tie."

Frank walked back to the bedroom of the condo to see if Aaron needed help.

"Dammit!" Aaron yelled from the bedroom.

"What's wrong?"

"I stubbed my toe on the box next to the dresser."

"How many times have I told you to get that sucker unpacked?"

"I know… I know."

Frank rounded the corner to see Aaron sitting on the edge of the bed rubbing his foot. "I thought you only needed to put on your tie?"

"Well, tie, shoes and jacket."

"What am I going to do with you?"

"Love me?" Aaron said, looking at Frank with his best innocent puppy-dog face.

"Now, if I can just get you house trained."

"Hey!"

"Who's a good boy?" Frank joked as he rubbed Aaron behind his left ear. Aaron responded by panting like a dog getting the best belly rub of his life. "Okay. Get your shoes on and let's get moving." Aaron bent over and finished putting on his shoes then his tie. Aaron stood and slipped into his coat before checking himself out one last time in the mirror. Frank stood behind, engulfing him in his arms, whispering, "You're going to do fine," before straightening Aaron's tie.

Aaron turned around and stared into Frank's eyes. "Thanks. I needed to hear that. I don't know why I'm so nervous. I've spoken before groups hundreds of times."

"True, but this is the first major reading from your new book. It's only natural you're going to have some butterflies fluttering around in your stomach."

Aaron took a deep breath in and let it out in one big huff. "You're right. If nothing else, I at least look damn hot in my new suit."

"That you do." Frank leaned in, kissing Aaron. "That you do."

"Okay, let's get out of here."

"Did you put Bully in his crate?" Aaron asked.

"Oops, I knew I forgot something."

"Did you at least walk him earlier?"

"Aaron, yes, I walked him. He went to the bathroom and everything. He's good for a few hours." Frank went into the living room to find Bully in his usual spot at the base of the couch. He grabbed a treat from the treat box, which immediately got Bully to raise his head from his sleeping position. Bully's tail wagged back and forth furiously. Frank pointed toward the crate in the kitchen, and Bully got up, did a quick stretch and headed right into it. Frank bent and handed the pup the treat before latching the crate shut.

Frank and Aaron had adopted a three-year-old English Bull Dog that they'd named Bully when they had moved into their new condo. Thankfully, Bully had been crate-trained, so having him in their new place was easy. As a whole, Bully was probably one of the most laid-back dogs Frank had ever seen. Not much seemed to frazzle the little guy.

With Bully safe in his crate, Frank headed toward the front door. Aaron was waiting with Frank's overcoat in hand, and Aaron helped Frank shrug into it before opening the door. The two walked in silence to the elevator, pushed the button and waited for it to arrive. The elevator was empty, so they entered and leaned against the back wall as they made the quick trip to the lobby.

After exiting the building, Frank looked left, then right, staring for the black sedan sent to take them to Barnes & Noble on Fifth Avenue. *Gotta love the perks of rolling in style with a bestselling author.*

"There it is," Aaron said.

Frank turned his head, saw the sedan and quickly followed Aaron, who was already heading in that direction. When they got near the car, the driver exited and opened the door, greeting them. "Dr. Massey, Detective Schultt."

Frank paused for a second. "How d'you know it was us?"

"They gave me an advance copy of the book with Dr. Massey's photo on the back cover. As for you, I knew you were his plus-one."

"Simple enough," Frank said. "No big mystery on that." Frank lowered himself into the sedan and buckled his seat belt. Aaron reached over and grabbed Frank's hand as the car took off into traffic. "You're going to do fine, Aaron."

"Keep saying that. I need to hear it."

"Why are you so anxious today?"

"I don't know. I didn't do many of these for *Blood Money* because of my position with the FBI. Now that I'm a desk-jockey and working primarily at John Jay, I feel like I have a lot more riding on this."

Frank gave Aaron's hand an extra squeeze. The two rode in silence for the next ten minutes as their car wove in and out of traffic.

* * * *

Frank stood in the back of the bookstore's makeshift audience area and watched as the event's host introduced Aaron.

"I am so proud to introduce our distinguished speaker this afternoon. Special Agent Dr. Aaron Massey is a forensic psychologist who works for the Federal Bureau of Investigation's acclaimed Behavioral Analysis Unit and is a visiting assistant professor at the John Jay School of Criminal Justice. He is the author of the international bestseller *Blood Money*. His follow up book, which is based on the case he worked on last December, *The Twelve-Day Killer*, skyrocketed to the top of *The New York Times* bestseller list within twenty-four-hours of it being released for preorders. Please join me in an enormous round of applause for Dr. Aaron Massey."

Aaron stood, and one of his winning grins spread across his face as he took in the seated audience while shooting a wink in Frank's direction. Frank noticed a pillar off to the side, so he made his way over and leaned against the concrete surface. Since Frank and Aaron had closed the Twelve Days of Murder the previous December, their lives had been a roller coaster. First, the dramatic conclusion of the Twelve-Day Killer at St. Patrick's Cathedral on Christmas morning was an international sensation. Thankfully, Frank's department and the FBI had done an excellent job of shielding Frank from a lot of the mass media hysteria that had followed. Unfortunately, Aaron hadn't been so lucky. As the author of a previously published international bestseller, Aaron had once again become a media darling.

After dating for nearly a year, Aaron and Frank had decided it was time to stop the constant back and forth between their respective apartments. They bought a new place on West Fifty-Fifth between Columbus and Tenth Avenue. Upon moving into the new condo, Frank had popped the question, and Aaron had agreed to marry him.

Frank leaned against the pillar watching the crowd sitting on the edges of their seats as Aaron read from the book. *Who can blame them? Look at that smile, those eyes, that fantastic, well-toned body.* Frank suddenly daydreamed about the amazing sex he'd had with Aaron the previous evening. Frank was enjoying himself, lost in his memories, when suddenly his cell phone rang loudly.

"Shh-h!" an older woman said as she swiveled her head and looked at Frank.

"I'm sorry," Frank said, politely looking at the woman. He then looked at Aaron and mouthed, "Sorry," before heading outside into the February cold. "Jasika, what's up?"

"Hey, Frank, sorry to call. I know you're at Aaron's thing at Barnes & Noble."

"No biggie. Not exactly my scene. What's up?"

"Not too much. We caught a fresh case—a dead body at the Sofitel," Jasika said as she walked over to Frank.

"Oh really," Frank said, looking at his partner and cutting off the call. "And you felt the need to call me, even though you were practically here?" he asked as he hung up his phone and placed it back in his pocket.

"Well, I didn't want to cause a commotion by walking in on Aaron while he was reading!"

"Thanks, I think. I'll let him know. Be right back." Frank headed back into the building, meandering through the stacks of books until he found the location of Aaron's presentation where his reading was in progress.

"It was the beginning of another day undercover. I'd gone to talk to the store manager when I heard a blood-curdling scream from across the store. I raced over to find my 'coworkers' at Children's Welfare International standing in a circle. In the middle of it, I saw the first image of the Twelve-Day Killer, a severed hand sticking out of a mitten attached to our tree. My first instinct was that my cover was blown."

Frank watched Aaron pause for effect as he looked up from the copy of the book laid out on the podium in front of him. The previous night Frank had listened to eighteen different variations of this same passage as Aaron asked him to rate the dramatics of each one. Honestly, Frank hadn't been able to tell the difference from one to the next. However, he had read Aaron's body language well enough to provide Aaron the feedback he had wanted.

Frank caught Aaron's eyes, held up his cell phone and mouthed, "Gotta go," as he pointed to the exit. Aaron nodded his head in understanding. Frank turned on his heels and headed back the way he'd come. In the distance, he could still hear Aaron talking about his immediate reaction, and how Detective Jackson Kelly had showed up at FAO Schwarz and immediately thought he was a suspect.

Of course, 'Detective Jackson Kelly' was the name Aaron had used for Frank in the book after Frank had begged Aaron to make him as anonymous as possible. Aaron had argued that anyone with Google and half a brain could see through the fake name. Frank hadn't been ready to have his life and his case written about in a book, much less in the avalanche of press that was sure to follow when the book was released. To Frank and Aaron's surprise, none of the advance reviewers had questioned the fact that Aaron had included a pseudonym for Frank.

Frank exited the building, the smell of garbage, urine and street meat filling the air. "Ahh...fresh air," Frank muttered to no one in particular.

"Yep. Nothing like the smell of trash day on a winter afternoon," Jasika replied, looking at the stacks of trash lining the curb.

Thankfully, the Barnes & Noble store where Aaron was conducting his public reading was just one block away from the Sofitel. At Forty-Fourth, Frank and Jasika crossed Fifth Avenue going west. Frank saw the police lights ahead and the all-too-familiar yellow tape hanging around a crime scene.

# Chapter Three

Every detective has their own way of approaching a new crime scene. Some say a silent prayer for the victim, while others try to step into the killer's shoes before getting to the facts. Frank preferred to depend on the experts he worked with at the NYPD. Specifically, he always checked in with the medical examiner he usually worked with, a Latina named Mariella Ramos. Mariella had joined the ME's office right after Frank had earned his shield, so they had rocketed through the ranks together. The woman was thirty-eight years old, and at five-foot-two-inches, she was a force of nature not to be messed with.

"Hey, gorgeous, it's about time you showed," Mariella said from her position, crouching next to the victim's body.

"Aaron had a book reading around the corner at Barnes & Noble."

"Ahh, well, baby, you tell him if he ever calls me a 'sharp-tongued temptress' in one of his books again, I'll be happy to castrate him using a spork!"

Frank laughed as the woman looked at him and winked. After forcing the mental picture of Mariella wielding a spork from his mind, he responded, "What? Is Carlos jealous of you hitting on all the sexy gay detectives and FBI agents in the city?"

"Of course not! He loves the attention. It's my mother. She's jealous!" To which they both laughed. Frank had met Mariella's mother once, but she was a powerfully charismatic woman in her own right, which explained Mariella's personality and sense of humor. Although Frank's mother was commonly referred to as the 'Ice Queen', Mariella's mother was a community organizer in the Bronx with ties to numerous community outreach organizations within the Latinx community.

"Okay, now that you two have gotten your flirt on," Jasika said, "what do we have here?"

Mariella turned the body over, and Frank saw the face of a woman in her late fifties or early sixties. The hair was stark white but cropped in a way that kept the woman's bangs out of her eyes and hair off her ears and above her neckline. The short haircut was almost military style but still had a distinct femininity to it. As for the victim's clothing, she wore a fitted blue suit with a silk maroon blouse underneath. The woman wore a wedding band on her left ring finger.

"Earth to Frank," Mariella said. Frank quickly snapped out of his own assessment of the body, returned to reality and focused on what Mariella was saying. "As I was explaining, the victim is a female in her late fifties or early sixties. The suit looks expensive and was probably not made in the USA, but then so many aren't these days," Mariella continued.

"What happened?" Frank asked.

"The doorman" — Mariella gestured to a young man in a bellhop uniform talking to a uniformed officer — "told me that a Lincoln Town Car pulled up, the victim got out and as the car drove away, she just fell to the ground."

"Then what?" Jasika questioned.

"We have little to go on other than that. Although the car service she used wasn't cheap, the driver told us the reservation was actually under 'Jane Doe'."

"Really?" Frank responded. "Great. Well, at least we have a name."

"And before you ask, pretty boy," Mariella started, "the driver had a pickup time for the customer but no flight number on file."

"So, why were we brought in?" Frank asked. "The woman could have died from several causes. What makes you think it's not natural?"

"Honestly, Frank, something doesn't seem right here. From all indications, the woman was in great physical health." Mariella lifted the woman's shirt to show them her stomach, which was clearly toned, although not sculpted like younger people. *Many women would kill to have her abs*, Frank thought to himself.

"Okay, so what causes an otherwise-fit woman in her late fifties or early sixties to keel over?" Jasika questioned.

"See? That's the problem I'm having. From all indications, there is nothing physically wrong with her externally. One thing that is a bit odd is the bleeding around her eyes." Ramos bent and gestured for Frank to do the same. She then peeled back the eyelid and showed Frank that the victim's eyes were almost completely blood red around the iris. "Admittedly, this could be one-thousand-and-one different things and

26

not even related to her death. Obviously, I'll know more during the autopsy. But presently, something on the surface doesn't feel right." She then held up a small tube with a scraping of a flaky substance and handed it to Frank.

"What's that?" Frank asked.

"This is why I called you in. Although I can't declare the cause of death at the scene, bystanders said the woman seized after she fell, and this substance bubbled at her lips. Again, I'm not saying anything about the cause of death, but something is clearly not right here."

"Are you thinking poison?" Jasika asked.

"Again, I'm not one for conjecture, so meet me at autopsy around five, and we'll open her and see what we can discover."

"Hey, can we make it six-thirty? I see Dr. Weintraub at five." Frank had been seeing a department-required psychologist since he had engaged in a series of very destructive behaviors following the murder of his first husband, Adam Bosque. Frank had kind of fallen apart after Adam's death and had found himself swirling in an ever-increasing pit of despair, which included risky, unprotected sex and drug and alcohol abuse. During the height of his chaotic life decisions, Frank had stumbled upon a liquor store robbery. The perpetrator had raised his weapon, and Frank had shot the robber where he stood. But he hadn't just shot the robber… He had unloaded his entire clip into the man. Although the shooting had been declared a 'good shoot' by Internal Affairs, his chief had told Frank to get his shit together or face being out of a job, which is why he'd started seeing Dr. Weintraub.

"Okay," Mariella responded, "it's a date. I'll bring the corpse, and you bring your *hard* gun!" she continued in a seductive voice, causing all three of them to laugh.

Frank turned to Jasika, asked her to double-check with the responding officers and see what they learned from original witnesses. Turning back to Mariella, he asked, "Where are the Geek Twins?"

The Geek Twins, as Frank called them, were criminalists who worked with Mariella on her cases. Their actual names were Al-Rashid Nasab and Colin Richardson. Both had master's degrees from respected universities in forensic sciences before joining the Office of the Chief Medical Examiner or OCME.

"Richardson's inside with hotel security, and Nasab is at some training in a new technique for preserving contact fibers at a crime scene." Frank looked at her with quizzical eyes, so she continued, "You may not realize it, but criminalistics isn't exactly like you see on TV. Trace fibers rarely lead to an actual suspect because they disappear so quickly. In fact, research shows the typical body loses ninety-five percent of trace fibers within five hours after someone's death. Most of the fibers on a body are contact fibers and have nothing to do with our victim or her killer, assuming there is one." Mariella continued her impromptu lecture on forensic science, pointing out several fibers on the current victim while she picked them with tweezers and placed them in paper evidence collection envelopes. She picked up one fiber, noting it could be from the car company or the airplane. "Even if it contains fibers that are related to car or airplane seats, the fibers themselves could just as easily be from someone who had previously sat in the car or on the plane. Fibers don't get us anywhere most of the time."

"Then why bother?"

"Because forensic scientists must look for the one-in-a-million chance the fiber they've collected is unique and specific to the killer. For example, in a very famous case from the late nineteen-seventies, a man named Jeffrey Robert MacDonald had been convicted of killing his pregnant wife because fibers from his pajama bottoms had been found under his wife's body and underneath her fingernails. The killer had claimed he had had torn his pajamas in the living room earlier that night. No evidence of the torn pajamas had been found anywhere in the house except underneath the victim and beneath her fingernails. In that rare case, the collected fibers had helped seal the deal and had put MacDonald behind bars."

"Okay, I give in. I believe you," Frank pleaded, raising his hands in surrender. "Go-o, fibers!" he said in his best cheerleading attempt. Mariella looked at him with a smirk then back at the body. "I'm going to go find Richardson and see what's going on inside." He turned on his heels, walked over to the Sofitel entrance and through the revolving door. Just inside the entrance on the right-hand side of the lobby, he found the concierge desk and luggage check. About ten feet farther into the building, Frank eyed the check-in desk. Even though it looked like the desk had six unique stations, there was only one person staffing it. The hotel atrium had a fairly tall ceiling and marble floors. His loafer heels clicked on the floor as he walked over to talk to the young woman staffing check-in.

The hotel clerk smiled and said, "Good afternoon, sir. Checking in?" Frank flashed his gold shield before asking if the clerk had a reservation for a Jane Doe. "I'm sorry, Detective, but I'm not allowed to give out that information. Our Chief of Security may be able to help you, though."

"Actually, one of my colleagues is with your security department now. Can you point me in the right direction?" The clerk told Frank to come around to a side door, allowing Frank to get behind the desk. After getting directions, Frank proceeded to the end of the hall and to the last room on the right. Frank walked down the hall and rapped twice on the door labeled 'Security'.

"Who is it?" called a voice from the other side of the door.

"Detective Frank Schultt, NYPD." The door opened, and a balding, heavyset man in his mid-fifties opened the door.

"Harvey MacMahon, Sofitel Head of Security. I was telling your crime-boy here I used to work at the Fifth Precinct in Chinatown before I took a bullet to the knee."

"How are you enjoying private security?" Frank asked.

"Could be worse," MacMahon admitted. "At least it pays the bills and keeps my wife off my back about not working." The man chuckled at his own joke before continuing, "So, Detective, I was copying the outdoor security feed for your boy to an external hard drive. Anything else I can do for you?"

"Any chance you can tell me if you have a reservation for a 'Jane Doe' today?" Skepticism flashed across the other man's face. "I know… It's the name the victim gave her car service, so she may have used it here, too."

MacMahon strolled over to a computer terminal and rapidly hit a few buttons. Frank saw the moment of surprise on the other man's face before he said, "Yep, a Ms. Jane Doe was supposed to check in today around noon. According to our logs, she was flying in this morning and needed the early check-in after her international flight."

"What credit card did she use to make the reservation?" Frank continued.

MacMahon turned back to his screen, furrowing his forehead as he typed. Frank noticed immediately when MacMahon had his eureka moment. "According to this, the reservation was made internally from management at our corporate office in Paris."

"What does that mean?"

"Honestly, I couldn't tell you. Someone pretty high up in the Paris offices had to have completed this one. It could be anything from a family relative to a government official. We don't see too many of these, but they do come in occasionally."

"Interesting... So our victim is probably French. That should at least help narrow the flights we're looking for."

Frank turned to Colin Richardson, who was sitting in a chair on the opposite side of the small room watching the interaction unfold. "Richardson, I need you to check all international flights coming into JFK from France. She arrived at the hotel around noon, so that would mean she probably landed between nine and ten this morning—depending on how long things took at customs. See if there was a 'Jane Doe' listed on a passenger manifest. I'm going to bet there wasn't, but it's worth a shot. Maybe that new intern of yours can cross-check people on the flight with TSA records. There's got to be something that will help us identify the victim."

"Got it! I'll have the information for you at autopsy, assuming TSA and the airlines help without a court order."

Frank scrunched his head and rolled his eyes slightly, understanding the hurdles both TSA and the airlines might throw up. Neither were known for their willingness to be open and transparent with local law enforcement. "By the way," Frank started, "we're meeting at six-thirty at the ME's office."

"See you then—or at least talk to you. I'll probably be at our lab processing the hotel security footage and other trace evidence found at the scene."

Frank then turned back to the head of security. "Mr. MacMahon, thanks for your help."

"Any time, Detective. Always willing to be of service."

Frank turned and headed out of the door. He walked down the short hallway, opened the door and once again said thank you to the clerk who'd helped him earlier. As he exited back into the central atrium area, Jasika was coming through the rotating doors from the street.

"What's up?" Frank asked.

"Not much. Basically, the witnesses outside weren't reliable."

"How so?"

"Everyone saw something different."

"Not surprising. Eyewitnesses are notoriously unreliable."

"However, a couple of eyewitnesses mentioned a doctor coming through the crowd to help the victim. The doctor pronounced her dead and took off."

"Was the doctor a man or a woman?"

"Well, the witnesses don't remember. Some said it was a white woman dressed in a green sundress—"

"Yeah, that's likely. Who in their right mind is going to be wearing a green sundress in this freezing weather?"

Jasika just nodded in agreement. "Another witness said it was a man in a gray pinstriped suit. Yet another said it was a Black woman in a trench coat. Basically, the witnesses are all over the place with their descriptions. Hopefully, the security video will give us a better idea of what happened."

"The joy of witnesses," Frank responded, rolling his eyes. He glanced at his watch and noticed it was quickly approaching four forty-five. "I've gotta jet. I need to be at Weintraub's by five."

"Not a problem. I can wrap things here. Call me when you're done. I'll check out a car from the motor pool, swing by to pick you up then we can head out to autopsy together."

After exiting the hotel, Frank said goodbye to Mariella, who was overseeing the loading of the victim into the OCME transport van. He turned West, heading away from the Sofitel on Forty-Fourth Street. He nodded to a couple of patrol officers who were holding back the spectators trying to get a closer look at the crime scene.

Frank lifted the yellow crime tape and ducked under, hoping to make a quick escape from the scene.

"Frank!" a female's voice yelled. "Detective Schultt!"

He turned around and looked back toward the crime scene to see if someone from there was calling his name. Not seeing anyone, he turned around and scanned the crowd. Then he found her, Jenny Mace, a television reporter elbowing her way through the gaggle of onlookers with a cameraman in tow.

Instead of reaching toward him with a microphone, which is what Frank braced for, Mace reached out and pulled him into a hug. *Now we're hugging?* "Jenny-y." He let the "y" hold on for a few seconds too long. "How

33

are you?" Frank asked, noticing Mace looked perfectly put together in full makeup, even in the bitter cold.

"I'm doing great. Just as an FYI, I'm going to be leaving WNTV at the end of the month. N-Cubed hired me to run their new hour-long crime show five nights a week. They were so impressed with my reporting on the Twelve-Day Killer that they wanted me on their line-up."

"N-Cubed?" Frank asked, not knowing what Jenny was talking about.

"It's the new National News Network. They're positioning themselves between the liberal CNN and the conservative FOX News. You know, 'Be a Voice for Moderate America'. That's our tag-line."

"Well, good luck with that. Not sure if CNN is that liberal, but good luck anyway."

Completely missing the sarcasm in his voice, Jenny continued to tell Frank about how she was hired and all her new show's inner-workings. "Oh, I'll totally have to have Aaron and you come on and discuss the Twelve-Day Killer during my first week on the air."

"That's more Aaron's department." Frank glanced at his watch. "I have a meeting in a few minutes, so I need to be heading in that direction."

"Perfect!" Jenny stated, before turning to her cameraman and barking, "Roll it." Jenny pulled Frank into a side embrace, locked her arm through his and began her introduction. "I'm standing with famed New York City Police Detective François Schultt. You may remember him as the lead detective who caught the notorious Twelve-Day Killer last December while working with international bestselling author and FBI Special Agent Dr. Aaron Massey." She then pulled herself slightly away from Frank before asking him,

"Detective Schultt, I hear there's been a murder outside the Sofitel. Any comments?"

"The medical examiner assigned to this case has not determined the cause of death, or even if there was a murder. Although the woman's death today definitely raised some interesting questions, as of right now the NYPD is not investigating this death as a homicide."

"Cut!" Jenny barked. "That was perfect."

"How did you get here so fast?" Frank wondered aloud.

"Oh, the station asked me to cover the series of muggings around Rockefeller Center. When we had wrapped there, we heard the call on the police scanner and came over. We've been hanging out for a while, hoping to see who had been assigned to the case. And lucky us, it was you! My favorite detective."

*Really, I'm your favorite detective? A year ago, you almost got me fired.* Thankfully, Aaron had taught him a thing or two about working with journalists, so he kept his internal monologue from crossing his tongue. Once again, he glanced at his watch. "Jenny, I've got to go. I have five minutes to jog four blocks." Frank took off in the opposite direction at a slow jog without waiting for a response.

# Chapter Four

Frank caught his breath when he entered the professional building's lobby where Dr. Weintraub's offices were located. He took the elevator to the sixth floor. When he exited, he caught a glimpse of himself in a mirror that hung on the wall. He looked a little disheveled and sweaty, having run a few blocks to get to his appointment. He straightened his clothing, noticed the sweat stains under his armpits and hoped his suit jacket would cover most of it.

Once he looked quasi-presentable, he turned toward Dr. Weintraub's office and walked into the waiting area. Seeing no one there, he rapped twice on Dr. Weintraub's inner office.

A voice from beyond the door said, "Just a second." He could hear her talking to someone in hushed tones.

*Probably on the phone*, Frank rationalized.

Moments later, he heard her get up from behind her desk and walk to the door. As she opened it, she informed Frank that he was late. One thing she didn't put up with was tardiness. Frank quickly explained what had happened and how he had been caught by Jenny Mace, who had been determined to keep him hostage.

"Okay, I'll forgive you this time, Detective, but keep track of time in the future." She gestured for Frank to take a seat on a large, overstuffed couch as she sat in a leather high-back armchair to the left of the sofa.

"Cold enough for you?" Frank asked.

"I've been inside since nine a.m. I've been in my cozy office with my space heater under my desk, so I couldn't tell." She eyed Frank up and down before commenting, "But from the looks of you, I would have guessed it was a bit warmer outside."

"I left the crime scene in plenty of time to leisurely walk here, but then Jenny got ahold of me and wouldn't let go. She somehow thinks we're friends now."

"Why do you say that?"

"Well, this is the same woman who tried to single-handedly kill my career last December with her guerrilla 'gotcha' journalism tactics. And today, she acted as though we were best friends, hugging me when we saw each other. Honestly, it was borderline creepy."

The conversation was informal for a few minutes as Frank and Dr. Weintraub caught up. Frank provided a quick overview of the previous week's events. He told her about work, Jasika and his relationship with Aaron.

"Speaking of Aaron, how are things going between you and him?"

"Umm... Well, I think they're going okay. I mean, we haven't had any fights or anything. I feel something isn't progressing the same way as it did with Adam."

"Well, you are a different person now, so you shouldn't expect things to be the same."

"I guess I understand, but I feel like there is some kind of disconnect really keeping me from fully committing to this relationship. Sure, we're engaged and all, but I still feel like there's a block between us." As soon as the words left Frank's mouth, he knew what the problem was. It was him. Over the next twenty minutes, Frank felt like a silly schoolgirl who couldn't give up on her first crush. He knew Aaron was terrific, but every once in a while, something would happen that would bring memories of Adam flooding back.

"Frank, Adam was your first love. Let's face it. You lost him in a horrific manner. You shouldn't expect to get over him. He's always going to be a part of you. The question is, how can you let Aaron *also* be a part of you?"

"I know what you mean, but I feel like I should be able to get over Adam to let myself fully commit to Aaron. We've only been dating for over a year and just moved in together."

"How is that working out?"

"Honestly, I think things are going pretty smoothly. It's definitely easier on both of us since we're living squarely between both of our jobs. Not commuting from Aaron's old condo to the precinct has made life easier. And although I'm ecstatic we're engaged, I worry some other shoe is going to drop and everything is going to blow up in my face."

"Frank, you need to learn to take this relationship for what it is and enjoy the small moments. Don't fret the larger decisions. When the time is right, those decisions will seem natural for you to make."

Frank listened to what the doctor had to say but didn't take it to heart, because his mind was already racing to his next series of thoughts. "Aaron also increasingly wants to know information about my childhood."

"Learning more about one's romantic partner is a normal part of relational development. What seems to be the sticking point?"

"My parents."

"Oh," Dr. Weintraub noted. "This is the first time since we've been seeing each other you've brought them up."

Darlene and Gaétan Schultt, hadn't exactly been the greatest parents. When Frank had been in high school, they had shipped him away to the Leysin American Switzerland boarding high school because both of them had been too busy with their lives to worry about their son. Frank hadn't minded his boarding-school education. In fact, he was glad he'd had the experience, because he had ultimately met his best friend Logan Cunningham, who was a real-estate attorney in NYC, during his days at Leysin.

After high school graduation, which his parents hadn't bother attending, Frank had returned to the states and gone to Yale, where he had majored in business—the heir apparent to the Schultt Pharmaceuticals Empire. As his parents' only child, Frank had had it drilled into him since birth to either become a chemist like his mother or a businessman like his father. During his years at Yale, he had realized that he hated business, had no desire to work in the pharmaceutical industry or work for his parents. It was also during his undergraduate years Frank had come to terms with his sexuality. After graduating from Yale, Frank had told his family he was gay, and his parents had immediately disowned him. The blowup happened when Frank had told his father he was gay.

Those had been the last words Frank had ever said to his folks.

After that, Frank had felt adrift and had traveled around the United States, taking in everything life offered. He had taken a couple of odd jobs here and there before finally moving back to his old stomping grounds of New York City. Although his parents practically ran the high-social scene in New York, Frank had stuck to the parts of the city his parents would have never been caught dead entering. After deciding he wanted to go into law enforcement, he had enrolled in the New York University's Master's in Criminal Justice program. Upon graduation, he had joined the academy, and the rest had been history.

"Frank, where did you go right then?" Dr. Weintraub asked.

Shaken out of his own jog down memory lane, Frank responded, "Just remembering how I got here." He paused before adding, "Did you know my father died in April?"

"Yes, I read about that in *The New York Times*."

Frank wasn't surprised that Dr. Weintraub had heard about his father, the socialite philanthropist. He was a little surprised that she'd never mentioned it to him before, so he asked, "Why haven't you raised that issue during our sessions?"

"Frank, you know that's not how this works. I cannot push you to disclose information to me. You need to be open and ready to have these conversations. I figured when you were ready, you'd open the door and let me peek in — like you're doing now."

Over the next fifteen minutes, Frank broke down his relationship — or the lack thereof — with his parents for Dr. Weintraub. The entire time he talked, Weintraub scrawled across the page, taking copious notes. "Thankfully, I had an amazing support network of both friends and acquaintances who took me under their wings. Do you by chance know Judge Janice Kahl?"

"I know of her, but I don't know her personally," Weintraub responded.

"She and her partner, Polly, were there for me when I came out. Judge Kahl was in my parents' circle of friends as a corporate lawyer in those days. Although my father always called her that 'dyke lawyer', he'd still respected her and knew not to cross her. When I returned to the city, Janice and Polly let me live with them for about six months while I grounded myself. I honestly think it was the late-night discussions I had with Janice that led me to a career in criminal justice."

After making some further notes on her legal pad, Dr. Weintraub looked up and asked, "Do you still keep in touch with them?"

"Not as often as I would like, but I have dinner with them at least once a month. Janice still has run-ins with my mother at various social functions. It may have even been Janice who first dubbed my mother 'The Ice Queen'."

"Why do you call her that?"

"Trust me... If you ever meet my mother, you'll know why. That woman has no personality, no sense of compassion. The only person who can actually put up with her besides my father is her personal assistant. I've left a few gay bars in the city when that guy has come into them. He once tried to hit on me right after I'd been disowned. Thankfully, I haven't spoken two words to that fucker in over a decade. Sure, I see him in public from time to time, but I avoid him at all costs."

"You clearly have a lot of hostility for your mother's assistant? Why?"

"I know it's not his fault, but he's the one piece of my past I can't shake. So, he gets the brunt of my disdain because I see him out socially as if nothing ever happened. I realize his job is to do what my mother tells him to do. I don't see how a gay man can stay employed by the very woman who threw her gay son into the street without a second thought. And that, Dr. Weintraub, is why I call her 'The Ice Queen'."

Dr. Weintraub's pen was in overdrive as she jotted down the new information. As she finished writing, she glanced at her watch and said, "So, back to our regular time on Tuesday?"

"I'll be here. And I promise I won't be late. And again, thanks for seeing me on a Saturday."

"Not a problem. I completely understand that the job comes first. And, Frank, if you're ready for it, maybe you could bring in Aaron. I think it could be good for you *and* for him to open up in a safe environment. Just tell him what you've told me. Help him understand where you're coming from. From what you've told me about him, I bet he would jump at the chance to look inside that brain of yours."

Frank looked at Dr. Weintraub skeptically and was about to dismiss her outright but opted for a different tactic instead. "I won't say no, but I won't commit to anything at this point. I will think about it. And if I think I'm ready, I'll mention the idea to Aaron and we'll see."

"That's all I'm asking you to do." She ushered him out of her office. After leaving, Frank headed back toward the elevator. Both a sense of relief and one of anxiety about bringing Aaron to his therapy sessions occupied his mind as he rode the elevator down and exited the building.

# Chapter Five

Upon exiting Dr. Weintraub's professional building, Frank pulled out his phone and said, "Call Jasika."

She answered quickly.

"Detective Torv."

"Jasika, just finished with Weintraub. I'm about a block from Viva La Coffee. Can you get a pool car and meet me there in ten?"

"See you then."

As darkness engulfed the city, the temperature had dropped rapidly. Frank pulled up his coat's collar to help keep the chill off his neck as he walked toward his favorite coffee shop. Thankfully, it wasn't far and the foot traffic at six p.m. wasn't very heavy, so he got to the shop in just a couple of minutes.

Walking into Viva La Coffee, Frank noticed that the place was practically empty except for a couple in the corner making googly eyes at each other and a college student hunched over a laptop next to the front window. Frank made his way to the counter and ordered a couple of coffees. After finishing his order, he paid and went to wait for his drinks at the end of the bar. *I'm not sure if I'm ready to let Aaron into one of my therapy sessions. I don't know what's wrong with me. I shouldn't be holding anything back from Aaron at this point. For fuck's sake, we're engaged.*

"Frank," the barista spoke.

Hearing his name, Frank shook himself out of his internal monologue, grabbed the coffees and thanked the young woman. He slipped cardboard sleeves around the cups before heading over to doctor the coffees to both Jasika's and his liking. Jasika's coffee received two Splendas and an eighth of a cup of skim milk. Frank dumped some coffee into the trash to get all the skim milk into the cup. As for his coffee, he took it straight black with a smidge of half-n-half—not enough to alter the color drastically, but enough to take the edge off an overly bold roasted bean. Once both cups were travel ready, he popped the plastic lids in place. Frank exited the building right as Jasika pulled up in a dark blue sedan. He placed his coffee on the roof before opening the door. He leaned into the car and handed Jasika her coffee before reaching up to grab his cup.

"For me?"

"Of course. I wouldn't want my partner to be uncaffeinated before we see an autopsy."

Frank slipped into the passenger's seat, putting on his seatbelt with a swift movement.

"So, how was head shrinking?"

"Don't worry. My ego is still one-hundred percent intact."

"Good to know."

"Any other developments at the Sofitel?" Frank said the hotel's name with his worst French accent.

Jasika shot him a sideways glance and rolled her eyes while Frank took a sip from his coffee. "Well, if you must know, the video looks like a bust. We watched the scene, but there was nothing to see on the first go-through. Richardson is taking it back to his lab for analysis. Maybe he'll see something after watching it one-hundred times. We also sent a couple of patrol officers out to JFK to see if we can get the Department of Homeland Security and the TSA to release the videos of customs, but that will probably take a judge's order for them to hand over anything."

"Did you check out the flight manifests arriving from Europe this morning?"

"Surprisingly, the airlines didn't put up much of a fight this time. Richardson texted me right as I was getting into the car that he received the manifests, so I haven't looked at them yet. Richardson said he'd have his intern start poring through them first thing in the morning." At a stop light, Jasika pulled her cell phone out of her suit jacket, waited for the face recognition software to identify her, then handed it to Frank.

"You know, you're not supposed to hold your phone in your hand while driving," Frank said as he accepted Jasika's phone.

"Bite me."

Aaron had convinced both Jasika and Frank to let his publisher buy them new iPhones. Jasika had taken to the phone like a fish to water, but Frank was still trying to figure out all the random features the blasted thing had. Thankfully, one of the few apps he had learned to use was text messaging, which hadn't changed too much from the old crackberry he'd had for the past decade.

Frank swiped up, unlocking the iPhone for his viewing. He quickly found the text message Jasika had mentioned and read it out loud. *"Flights were a bust. Four came in from Europe. Three had layovers in Paris before heading stateside. The two US-based airlines are giving us manifests, but British Airways and Air France are routing our request through their home offices. No Jane Doe yet. More soon, Rich."*

"Well, that's *useful,*" Frank noted. "He basically said we have a couple thousand passengers arriving this morning, and none of the leads are overly helpful."

"It was a long shot," Jasika responded, keeping her eyes on the road and honking her horn at a cabbie who'd pulled out in front of her while cursing under her breath. "God, I hate Midtown traffic."

"That's why I prefer to walk or cab it. When you're walking, you don't have a care in the world. And in a cab, you can close your eyes and pretend you're somewhere else. So, how's Ginny doing?" Ginny was Jasika's four-year-old daughter.

After working in narcotics, Jasika had met a guy who she had thought was on the up-and-up. That was until one day, a few weeks after their daughter's birth, she had caught him during a drugstore snatch and grab. Frank had always wondered who had been more surprised in that moment—Jasika for seeing her boyfriend robbing a drugstore or her boyfriend, Travon Smith, for getting caught by his baby-mama. Travon was now serving his time at an upstate minimum-security prison near Fishkill, NY. Thankfully, Jasika had a good support network and didn't have to raise Ginny alone. Jasika often talked about how different her life would be if her mother weren't around to help raise Ginny.

"Funny you should ask. Travon is asking for visitation privileges with our daughter. I talked to my lawyer. She thinks we can fight it in court. At the same time, I realize it's often in an offender's best interest to have a family visit—just as long he's very clear that *we* are over and there are no chances of us ever getting back together."

"Sounds like a smart move to me," Frank said. "You say the word, and I can arrange for you to get a sympathetic judge."

Frank and Jasika had become partners right after Ginny's birth. Frank had ensured Jasika navigated the NYC legal system with the help of Janice Kahl. Judge Kahl had placed a few phone calls, and almost overnight, Jasika had received full custody of Ginny, and Travon had lost his rights. Upon his release from jail, Travon would be expected to pay child support. Even now, Jasika received the random check from the NY State Penal system for child support garnished from his wages working in the prison laundry facility. Although the checks did not help Jasika much, Frank periodically had called one of the correction officers he knew there to ensure Travon worked and that the checks were disbursed

As they approached the OCME office, Jasika found the underground parking structure entrance where personnel and visitors could park. Since it was after five p.m., no attendant guaranteed that only people there on official business could park. Jasika found a choice spot near the elevator bay. After exiting the car, the two walked into the building and meandered through a maze of corridors they knew all too well.

# Chapter Six

The sound of a surgical saw squealed in the small surgical theater. Frank let out a guttural throat sound announcing Jasika and his arrival. Mariella looked up from her seat atop a stool on the other end of her autopsy room.

"It's about time you two showed. I was wondering if I was going to have to dissect Ms. Doe on my own." She put down the surgical saw on the rolling tray next to the table where a Black man in his mid-to-late sixties lay with his chest cracked open. She stripped off her apron, facial mask, gloves and hairnet from her body before stuffing them all into a biowaste container near her desk.

"Who's the deceased?" Jasika asked as Mariella handed them a clipboard.

"First things first... You two, sign the logbook then get suited up. No one goes near one of my bodies until all T's are crossed and I's dotted. I won't have you two bringing any stray evidence into my pristine lab." She handed them each a set of scrubs and an autopsy kit to make sure that no contamination happened while guests were there. To the lab's side were three changing stations. Frank picked out one of the stations and walked in.

"What? You're not going to undress in front of me, lover boy? You know I've always been curious to see if you're wearing boxers or briefs."

"You assume I'm wearing anything under these pants," Frank responded with a wink before sliding the curtain full across the changing room doorway.

Mariella barked out a laugh and continued to talk. "As for this victim? Black male in his mid-sixties found in an alleyway on Forty-First Street between Eighth and Ninth Avenues."

"The Port Authority?" Frank asked as he quickly stripped and put on his scrubs, apron, face mask, hair net and surgical gloves.

"Who gets a gold star in Geography?" Mariella cooed from the other side of the changing area like she was talking to her favorite puppy. "Frank does... Yes, he does."

For a half-second, he glanced at his Under Armour boxer briefs and thought to himself, *Sorry, Mariella. You'll never get to see these!*

"The Port Authority Police found the victim a little before five p.m. Since I was already out and finished picking up your body, I agreed to pick up Mr. Doe. I was just getting a jump start on that autopsy when you walked in. Physically, I couldn't find a cause of death, so I need to open him up and find out what killed the gentleman."

"Any ID on him?" Frank heard Jasika ask.

"Nope. No wallet, cell phone or watch. But the victim was dressed in a Brunello Cucinelli cashmere suit, which cost the man more than my mortgage payment."

Frank opened the door to his changing room. He watched as Mariella looked up from her desk. "Do I look good in these, or do they make my ass look fat?" Frank asked before twirling in his OCME smock.

"Honey, you could bounce a quarter off that ass! But while I personally would love to stand here and discuss your butt for hours, my husband has reservations for us at nine, so I need to get moving."

"I'm meeting Aaron for dinner around nine, too. We should totally double date. Maybe our future husbands could flirt while we play footsy under the table?"

"Aaron can only wish he'd land a hottie like my hubby," Mariella said. The sound of Jasika sliding the curtain across her changing room rod caught Frank's attention, so he swiveled his head in her direction.

"What's your working theory on the other case?"

"Isn't one dead body enough for the two of you?" Mariella joked, shaking her head from side to side. "Curiosity and the dead cat and all. Anyway, I'm leaning toward death by natural causes, then someone stole the man's possessions after he died. But I'm just going to perform the autopsy and let the Port Authority Police Department conduct their investigation."

"Excuse me," a voice interrupted. Frank, Mariella and Jasika all stopped to look at the new woman who had entered autopsy. An average-sized blonde entered the room with her hair pulled back in a tight bun. Frank noticed her six-inch red leather heels and her navy-blue pantsuit were definitely out of place and a little rich for the morgue.

"And who are you?" Mariella questioned.

"I'm Belle Popova. I'm the new Assistant District Attorney. I caught the Jane Doe case."

"Interesting..." Mariella observed. "ADAs don't always show for preliminary autopsies. You know, since I haven't ruled the cause of death yet."

"Let's say there are a lot of eyes already looking at this one. An otherwise-healthy woman comes off an international flight and dies before she gets to her hotel. I don't see this being accidental or natural. Of course, Detective Schultt's performance on the evening news had the Mayor's office asking the DA's office to get involved in this case early."

"Well, fuck," Frank muttered.

"Don't worry, Detective," Popova continued. "You were about as pitch perfect as the PR people at city hall would have asked for. But in the future, do try to stay away from cameras. It's clearly becoming a thing with you."

Frank wanted to defend himself, but the tightening grip on his forearm from Mariella caused him to bite his tongue.

"Well, at least you have some decent suspicions going into this one." Mariella handed ADA Popova the sign-in clipboard and a set of scrubs and pointed her toward the changing rooms. "Please sign in here, then you can change over there."

As soon as Popova was out of sight, Frank turned to Mariella and Jasika. "I was ambushed by Jenny Mace as I was exiting the crime scene."

"You don't need to explain to me," Mariella said. "I saw the whole thing go down. You were cornered and handled yourself as well as could be expected. It's not your fault the vulture was already flying around, looking for her next kill."

The slight scraping sound of the curtain being pulled back on the dressing room made Frank turn his head in the direction of the changing room as Popova exited. He immediately noticed that the heels had been replaced with a pair of tennis shoes. *Well, at least she's not a rookie.*

"Shall we?" Popova asked as she motioned toward the other table occupant in the room. Without saying a word, the group walked over to the autopsy table. Mariella folded back the sheet covering the victim's body. She had already performed a preliminary autopsy, which had included collecting trace evidence, washing the body and taking hundreds of pictures along the way as she dictated in precise detail every step she took, likely all to ensure the autopsy would be admissible in a court of law.

"As ADA Popova said, the victim was in pristine health, which validated what I thought at the crime scene," Mariella said. "Let's get started." Mariella flicked the 'on' switch for the audio recording device. "The Autopsy of Jane Doe is being conducted by Dr. Mariella Ramos. In attendance are Detectives Frank Schultt and Jasika Torv of the NYPD, and Assistant District Attorney Belle Popova."

With the formalities out of the way, Mariella walked around the body methodically. Periodically she'd stop so the other three could examine something that struck her as unusual or just slightly off. Mariella pointed out every slight skin imperfection, even when she deduced that they were normal. She often had the whole group look at the victim's body using a large magnifying glass that swiveled above the table. Mariella cataloged everything she saw to ensure that nothing was overlooked—not even the smallest detail. Jasika,

Mariella and Frank had conducted enough autopsies together to form a seamless system.

"After taking in the victim's external body," Mariella said, "I do not see a clear cause of death. With that said, I found one mark that is out of the ordinary." She motioned for the other three to come in closer as she lifted the woman's right hand and held it under the magnifying glass.

On the back of the woman's hand was a round bruised area with what appeared to be a tiny injection hole that had coagulated over. "I didn't see this mark at the crime scene or when I prepped the body for autopsy. The bruising didn't happen until she'd been in here for at least an hour. I'd checked out the hand multiple times before finally seeing the needle mark."

"That hole is ridiculously small," Jasika said.

"True that!" Mariella continued. "However, if this woman was injected with something, even a small hole is all that is needed."

"Are you saying this woman was poisoned?" Popova questioned.

Mariella held up her hand before saying, "Let me finish my autopsy. Then I'll be able to say definitively one way or the other. But once I crack her open, I have a pretty good idea of what we're going to see. ADA Popova, have you been through an autopsy before? I don't want you losing your lunch all over my decedent."

"I worked as an ADA in Columbus, so I've been through many autopsies in my career."

"How did you end up here?" Frank asked.

"Husband took a job at New York Presbyterian Children's Hospital. He's a pediatric oncologist."

"Well then," Mariella said, "let's continue."

Mariella pulled a scalpel off the rolling dissection tray and cut a 'Y' shape, starting at the victim's shoulders and intersecting above her sternum before slicing to right above her pubic region. Mariella then pulled out a surgical saw to cut through the victim's ribs. With the ribs cracked, she used a retractor to open the victim's chest cavity. Mariella swiftly probed inside the victim's body, making comments into the digital recorder. Once she surveyed the victim, she began pulling out various organs. She noted the weight of each one before putting them into separate specimen containers.

Frank noticed immediately that something was amiss when Mariella sliced into the stomach. The small pouch erupted in blood, spattering all four of them.

"And that, my friends, is why we wear protective gear during an autopsy," Jasika commented as she wiped the blood from her face shield using a towel that Mariella had handed her. Mariella, on the other hand, weighed the stomach as if nothing had happened.

"Stomach weight is within normal boundaries. I need to dissect the stomach to see what was going on inside, though." Mariella turned to Jasika and asked, "Can you take a few photographs for me? I want to get a few close-up shots as I dissect."

"Sure thing," Jasika said as she reached up to pull down the digital camera that hung above the autopsy table.

"Gloves!" Mariella scolded. "Don't touch my baby with those blood-stained ones you have on. Put on new ones. Who do you think you are, Lady Macbeth?"

Jasika quickly disposed of the blood-covered gloves before grabbing a new pair out of a box and putting them on. Jasika then reached up and grabbed the digital camera to begin helping Mariella photograph things.

Frank eyed Jasika, remembering how she'd reacted during her first autopsy. It had been shortly after they had become partners and they had received a double-murder call — mother and unborn child. Having just given birth, Jasika hadn't been ready for the sight of a pregnant mother impaled through her stomach. When Mariella had shown them the X-rays, Jasika had passed out and hadn't made it to the actual autopsy.

"Look at this," Mariella said, urging Frank and ADA Popova to come closer to the dissection dish. Mariella pinned back the stomach wall. "See how this surface is ragged? It's supposed to be smooth. I can say with certainty now this woman died because she bled to death internally. I didn't pick up the bleeding at the crime scene because all of it was happening within her stomach, so there would have been no outward signs of bruising as the blood was all pooling in here and not next to her skin." After making sure Jasika took photographs of the stomach from various angles and checking each picture as it was taken, Mariella set about examining the victim's other organs.

Frank watched Mariella's reaction as each new organ revealed more damage. Finally, when Mariella found many of the capillaries in the deceased's lungs had ruptured, she turned to Frank. "Let me be straight on this one. I don't have the foggiest idea at this point what actually killed her. Any of these systems incurring this kind of damage could take down a completely healthy adult. Having all of them rupture simultaneously like this is new to me."

"Are we looking at a virus?" Jasika questioned with a hint of nervousness in her voice.

"I have no reason to believe we are. There are no known viruses that do this specific amount of damage in this fashion. Honestly, if I were a betting woman, I'd put my money on a human-created toxin. I'm going to call a friend at the CDC and find out if she knows anything about this specific combination of trauma, because I'm completely at a loss here."

Frank looked at Mariella, who stood there looking at the various dissected organs around her before ADA Popova asked the question everyone was thinking. "So, you're telling us this was not natural? We're looking at murder? When do you think you'll have an official cause of death?"

"Sorry, ADA. I'm still not ready to say it was murder. You know how this goes. Until I get the tox screens back, I don't want to say anything with absolute certainty. If it were between the three of us and the victim, I don't see how this was natural. But I'm going to have to call in the Chief ME on this one. I know you're new here and all, but I'm damn good at my job, and this one is definitely different."

"No worries, Dr. Ramos. I was told about your reputation for excellence before I came over. I was also told about both of you," Popova said, looking at Frank and Jasika.

"I hope it was all good," Frank said, half joking.

ADA Popova cocked her head to the side and seemed to study him for a second in the same manner Mariella had looked at the skin imperfections under the magnifying glass just moments before. "Not always, Detective Schultt. Not always," Popova said flatly. "*But*, everyone in the office is impressed with Detective Torv's and your close and conviction rates."

"I don't know how I should take that," Frank said.

"Let's say I think you're competent until you show me otherwise."

Frank stared blankly at the ADA, not sure how he was supposed to respond. Frank glanced sideways at Mariella, who glanced at her watch.

"I hate doing this to Carlos, especially on a Saturday night, but I'm going to have to cancel my dinner date with my husband. Between your Jane Doe and my other John Doe, it's going to be a long night." She headed toward her desk, peeling off her gloves and surgical apron before picking up the phone. Frank didn't need to hear the other side of the conversation, but he could tell Carlos was not happy getting stood up by his wife for dinner. When the call was over, she hung up the phone and looked at the three of them. "Well, that was fun. I have a lot of paperwork to do here. I need to wait for the Geek Twins to get here for sample collection. There's no reason for you three to kill your Saturday nights because I have to. We'll have results to you first thing on Monday morning. Enjoy the rest of what's left of your weekends."

Frank, Jasika and ADA Popova quickly stripped out of their PPE, putting their street clothes back on before heading out of the door. Mariella was already typing at her computer when the three emerged and didn't even respond when Frank tried to say goodbye. They exited the building into the parking garage. Popova wrapped a bright red scarf around her neck as they all braced themselves against the cold that filled the underground parking structure.

"Can we drop you off anywhere?" Jasika asked.

"I have my own transportation," Popova said. "I'm sure we'll being seeing more of each other soon." With that, she headed off in a different direction from Jasika and Frank.

As soon as Popova was out of earshot, Jasika said, "Well, that was fun. It took every ounce of control I have not to pummel that woman when she gave us her uppity look."

"Yeah, if she's introducing herself to everyone that way, she is definitely not going to be on anyone's Secret Santa list. Anyway, I need to call Aaron and see what he's up to." He pulled out his phone, spoke Aaron's name and it immediately started ringing.

"Hey, babe," Aaron answered. "I was just ordering Chinese food at the place down the street from the condo. I can always get a table and wait for you to get there."

Glancing at his watch, Frank said, "Sure, sounds like a plan. I should probably be there in about twenty minutes." Frank turned to Jasika. "Would you mind dropping me before taking the car back to the lot?"

"Not a problem, but on one condition—have some fun tonight. I have a horrible sense this case is about to get complicated," Jasika said with no sense of irony in her voice.

Speaking back into his cell he said, "I'm on my way. Love you, too." After hanging up the phone, he looked at Jasika and asked, "Complicated? How so?"

"I don't know. After what we just witnessed, I don't think all the shoes have dropped yet. Something still seems odd about the ADA showing up like that."

"Maybe she's overly thorough since this is her first case in the 'big city'?"

"Or maybe she's read Aaron's book and wanted to get a look at... Remind me. How did he write it? Oh yeah, '*Detective Jackson Kelly was drop-dead gorgeous. He was built like a brick shithouse, and his firm bubble ass looked like it was ready to burst from the tight pants he was wearing.'"*

"Dear God, how long have you been waiting to use that one?"

"Partner, if you have the ass-ets, flaunt 'em." Jasika giggled. "I've been holding on to that one for almost two months, ever since Aaron let me read the page proofs. I hadn't found the right time yet to drop it into a conversation."

"And my pants weren't that tight! None of my pants are that tight! Any other nuggets of wisdom you got out of the book you feel like sharing?"

"No, but that scene of you and Aaron in his condo made me feel dirty."

"Dirty?"

"Yeah, it was like spying on my brother's sex life. Some things, your partner should never have to read."

This time, it was Frank that chuckled before saying, "You're a mess."

The two got into the sedan. Jasika started the car and pulled out of the garage before pointing the vehicle uptown toward the Chinese restaurant and the precinct. Jasika drove while the two chit-chatted about a range of topics until she deposited Frank at the Chinese restaurant where Aaron was waiting.

"Hug Aaron for me," Jasika said. "Tell him I'm sorry I had to miss his reading today. But, you know, at least one of us had to handle the phones."

"I will. Hug Ginny and your mom for me. I'll see you at nine a.m. on Monday, all bright-eyed and bushy-tailed. Enjoy your Sunday. Do something fun." Frank got out of the car and stood on the stoop watching Jasika pull away before he headed into the restaurant.

# Chapter Seven

Frank walked into the restaurant, hearing the wind chimes above the door as he entered the place. It took his eyes a moment to adjust to the dark lighting. The hostess looked up and asked how many, but Frank spotted Aaron and told her that his party was already seated. She smiled and went back to busying herself at the hostess stand.

"Glad you got us a table. This place is hopping tonight," Frank said as he approached the table. Aaron looked up as Frank leaned in for a kiss.

"Yeah, even for a Saturday, this place is busier than normal," Aaron said after they both came up for air.

"How was the rest of your reading?" Frank asked as he took off his coat and hung it on the hook next to the booth.

"It went well. Penny was thrilled with the turnout."

"She was?"

"Yep! With presales already beyond expectations, she's predicting the book will stay on top of the charts for a number of weeks once it's officially released."

Aaron told Frank about the rest of the reading. Even though the book wouldn't be released to the public for another week, the publisher had surprised Aaron by having fresh-off-the-press copies for his book tour launch that afternoon. He'd spent two hours autographing copies and taking pictures with fans.

"You have fans? Little teeny-boppers looking at you as their matinee idol?"

"Hardly. Mostly middle-aged women who love all things real crime. I had a few ask me if I was still dating 'my detective'."

Frank raised his eyebrows at that one. "And did you let them down easy?"

"I did. I told them we were still madly in love and recently engaged. I got to show off my platinum engagement band and everything." Just then, the server appeared with their meal. "Hope you don't mind that I ordered your usual."

"Not at all. It's nice that you know me so well."

"Also, I've been dying to tell you about the good news I heard."

"Oh really? What?"

"There is already a bidding war on the film rights to *The Twelve-Day Killer*. Isn't that nuts?"

Frank drank a sip of his wine, trying not to scowl. "'Nuts' is definitely one way to put it."

"Frank, I know this publicity stuff is not your forte. Hey, all the press killed my career as an undercover agent, but it has done a few amazing things for me as well. If it weren't for my public persona, I never would have met you."

"True, but I don't want to be in the limelight. And, you know, a movie would push us right back in the media spotlight." Sensing Aaron felt a little deflated by his comments, Frank added, "We'll have to make sure the contract is written in a way that gets Ben to play you in the movie!"

"What? You want your best friend's boyfriend to play me? An ex-soap star?" Aaron responded in mock shock. "I was hoping to get someone young, sexy and gorgeous. I thought Sean Connery would be great for the NYPD detective role!"

Frank took a noodle and flung it at Aaron, saying, "Fuck you!" Aaron dodged the pasta and just grinned. "I may be old, but I ain't *that* old! Besides, he's no longer with us. I think he died."

After laughing for a few seconds, Aaron grew somber once again. "Frank, I know a giant Hollywood movie would be hard on you, but it is kind of out of our control. The publisher owns the rights to the book, so they can sell it to anyone. With our luck, it will be turned into a Lifetime movie."

"Hey, then we wouldn't have to worry about anyone actually watching it!" Frank replied.

"So, you heard about my afternoon. What sent you scurrying away when your hot bestselling author fiancé was reading?"

"The only thing that takes me away from you — Jasika and a dead body."

"Should I be jealous?"

"Of Jasika or the dead body?" Frank grinned. He spent the rest of the meal breaking down what had happened at the Sofitel, Weintraub's and the ME's office. He thought about telling Aaron about Weintraub's idea of having Aaron come to one of his sessions but held off until the time seemed better. "So, that was my day," Frank concluded as he finished his meal. "Be right back. Gotta go to the little boy's room real fast."

"I should have a witty comeback to that, Frank. But we're in public, so I'm not even going to touch that one."

Frank left himself open for a snarky comment as soon as the words had passed his lips. He leaned down and whispered into Aaron's ear, "If you're lucky, maybe I'll let you touch little Frank later and you can help him grow into big Frank." He stood back up, not waiting for a retort from Aaron.

He walked through the restaurant and found the men's room opposite the door that led into the kitchen. The room was dark, so he flipped the switch and locked the door behind him. *You need to tell him about Weintraub's request. Why didn't you ask him? What is wrong with you, man?* Frank finished his business, washed his hands and stared at himself in the mirror. *Why won't you let him in completely? He's your fucking fiancé, and you're still holding back? This will never work if you don't learn to let him in.* Frank sighed, giving himself one last look before unlocking the door, switching off the light and heading back to the table.

He slid into the seat and stared at Aaron. The look on Aaron's face worried Frank, so he asked, "What's wrong?"

"Amber's on bed rest because of the baby."

"Amber... Amber who?"

"The wedding planner."

"The one we saw this morning? *That* Amber?"

"Don't give me your 'that Amber' look. I know that look."

"Sorry... I forgot her name. I knew it was one of those country-club-type names like Buffy, Tiffany or Amber."

"How you keep up with all the clues in your day-job amazes me."

"I'm great with dead people?"

"Anyway, Amber won't be able to finish our wedding. She was put on bedrest today for the rest of her pregnancy by her OBGYN. She has already sent back the deposit check and hopes we're able to find another planner soon."

"Wait a second! Didn't Amber mention an assistant? I thought the assistant could see things through?" Frank asked.

"Yeah... I asked that same question. According to Amber, her assistant had hopped on a plan to Brazil with some guy he'd met at a club. He had texted her his resignation from the airport. But don't worry. Amber provided a list of names of others she respects who could handle our event."

"Event? You make it sound like a grand opening or a movie premiere."

"You know what I mean. Besides, the list of wedding invitees Amber and I had compiled has a ton of celebrities."

Frank knew Aaron was trying to get a rise out of him, so he just arched a single eyebrow instead before saying, "There's no need to freak out. We've got like, what? Six weeks to throw something together?"

"Frank, you can't just 'throw' this type of event together. There's a reason we hired Amber. She handled the President's daughter's wedding. She's used to managing these types of large-scale nuptials."

"Large-scale? You know I'd be just as happy running to city hall with you tomorrow. We could call our best friends. You bring Judi and I'll invite Logan…" Frank let this thought hang in the air.

Aaron squinched his face and gave Frank his most determined look. "Not. Going. To. Happen," Aaron said flatly. "You're not getting out of the wedding that easily. I'm going to see you in a tux. We're going to say our vows. And I'm going to get my first kiss."

"We do that every day, many times a day."

"You know what I mean. This wedding isn't just for us. It's for our family and friends."

"And I'm sure a few of our frenemies will show up, too," Frank added, trying to lighten the mood. Aaron sharply tilted his head to the side as he narrowed his eyes. "Don't worry. I'll be there," Frank promised. "Just tell me the date and time, and I'll put it on my calendar." Aaron glared at Frank. "I'm joking. I'm joking." Frank reached out his hand and grabbed Aaron's. "I know how much this wedding means to you. And we'll do whatever we have to do to make sure it's the most amazing wedding of the season—even if that means I have to pull out a clipboard and start bossing cater-waiters around. I know losing Amber upsets you, but we'll get through this…together."

Aaron took a deep breath in and let it out. "Dear God, I'm becoming a bridezilla."

"Nah… Well, maybe a little."

Aaron stuck his tongue out at Frank. "Hmm… Sexy…" Frank said with a wink.

"You wish, Detective. No wedding planner, no sexy time."

"Sexy time? Who calls it that?"

"I did, right then. So, no sexy time."

Frank reached his foot under the table and rubbed it against Aaron's calf while giving him one of his most smoldering looks.

"Check, please?" Aaron yelled, catching the server's attention.

* * * *

After dinner, Frank took Bully out for his evening walk before coming back into the condo. Usually, Frank would end his day by washing away his world, but right now, he wanted to throw on his pajamas and lounge around with Aaron and Bully and enjoy a peaceful evening. He quickly stripped out of his suit and hung the pants and coat back into the closet. *It still has one more wear in it before it needs the dry cleaners.* He tossed the shirt into the clothes hamper before hanging his tie on the rotating tie rack that Logan had bought him a few Christmases before. Standing only in his boxer briefs, Frank went over to his dresser, applied an additional layer of deodorant and put on a pair of jogging shorts and a fresh T-shirt with the words 'Yale Alumni' emblazoned on the front.

Aaron lay down on the bed with Bully curling up next to him as he turned on the eleven p.m. news on WNTV. Frank turned around, looked at the bed and Aaron lying back wearing only a pair of boxers and a white T-shirt. *God, he's hot!* At that moment, he flung himself on top of Aaron and pinned him at the shoulders before kissing him deeply.

Before Frank knew what had hit him, Aaron had thrown his bodyweight upward, and Frank suddenly found himself pinned underneath Aaron with Aaron sitting slightly above Frank's pelvis. Both of them became hard, and they kept kissing. Frank used his muscles to arch upward under Aaron's weight as their lips connected.

*"I'm standing with famed New York City Police Detective François Schultt. You may remember him as the lead detective who caught the notorious Twelve-Day Killer with international bestselling author and FBI Special Agent Aaron Massey,"* Frank heard the TV say in the background. *"Detective Schultt, I hear there's been a murder outside the Sofitel. Any comments?"*

*"The Medical Examiner assigned to this case has not determined the cause of death, or if this is murder, so there is no murder investigation at this point. Although the woman's death today definitely raised some interesting questions, as of this moment, the NYPD is not investigating this death as a homicide."*

Aaron rolled off Frank and looked at the television — both of them suddenly becoming less energized. The view suddenly switched to an image of Jenny Mace sitting behind one of the station's anchor desks. "Currently, the medical examiner's office has not ruled on this death, but they're telling me they are expected to release the cause of death on Monday."

The male anchor nodded his head with his perfect hair and copy-paper-white teeth, "Thanks, Jenny. We look forward to finding out more about the surprising death outside the Sofitel." The anchor then looked at the camera and said, "And in other news, the New York Kennel Club held its annual pet picnic in Central Park today." The camera switched to an image of a group of pet owners on picnic blankets. Aaron picked up the remote and turned it off.

"So, you forgot to mention you saw your *best* friend today?" Aaron said, knowing all too well the animosity Frank had for Jenny Mace.

"Well, at least this time she didn't make me look like an idiot on television."

"Frank, I don't think you've ever looked like an idiot on television." With that, Aaron leaned over and gave Frank one more deep kiss before turning off the lights.

# Chapter Eight

Frank opened his eyes to find a fifty-pound bulldog looking down at him. Bully tilted his head to the side with his tongue hanging out.

"Good morning, Bully," Frank whispered as he reached up to scratch the dog behind his ears. "Just let me throw on some clothes and I'll take you outside."

With that, Bully turned, walked to the edge of the bed and walked down the ramp Aaron and Frank had installed to make it easier for him to get on and off the bed.

When they had first gotten Bully, Frank had been determined to keep the pup off. But it wasn't too long before Frank had been the one picking Bully up and placing him on it every night. Frank had even found a doggy ramp online and ordered it. When the ramp had appeared one day, Aaron hadn't even said a word. He'd just shaken his head back and forth and laughed.

Frank glanced over to see if Aaron was stirring, but he was very much asleep. Frank slipped out of bed and threw on a pair of sweats, a hoodie and sneakers. Once he was dressed, he crept out of the bedroom and into the kitchen area where they kept Bully's harness. Bully was already there, waiting for Frank, his little tail wagging back and forth furiously. Frank grabbed Bully's harness from on top of the refrigerator, placed it on the dog and grabbed the poo-bags they had in a counter drawer. After double-checking to make sure he had his keys and iPhone, Frank set off to let Bully do his morning business.

The streets on Sunday mornings were pretty quiet, so there wasn't a lot of foot traffic going on. While Bully was sniffing the few local grass patches near the apartment, Frank pulled out his cell phone and texted his best friend Logan to see if he and his partner wanted to do brunch. Within a couple of seconds, Logan responded and said it sounded like fun. After a few back and forth texts, they agreed to meet at The Liberty at one p.m. for drag brunch.

With brunch plans settled and Bully empty, Frank went back to their apartment. He opened the door and heard the shower running. Instead of interrupting Aaron, Frank set about feeding Bully. Once the pup was gobbling down his breakfast, Frank went into the bedroom, took off his clothes and entered the bathroom.

The steam in the bathroom immediately hit Frank. He pulled back the shower curtain and stepped in. "Want company?"

"I was almost done, but now that you're here..."

Frank stepped into the shower and pulled the curtain closed behind him. As the water flowed from the shower, Frank lifted his arms and placed them around Aaron's neck. Frank gently urged Aaron's face to his as their lips met.

Immediately, Frank's lower half was standing at attention as he pressed himself into Aaron's abs. A light whimper escaped Aaron's lips, which only caused Frank to grind into Aaron harder.

"What do you want?" Frank whispered into Aaron's ear before nibbling on the earlobe.

"I want you in me. Then I want to return the favor."

Frank flipped Aaron around and grabbed the waterproof lube they kept in the shower for these occasions. Aaron leaned forward a bit and braced himself against the back of the shower. Frank positioned himself behind Aaron. Despite the warm water raining down on them, Frank could feel the shuddering of Aaron's body in anticipation.

\* \* \* \*

Forty minutes later, Aaron and Frank were dried off and sitting at the kitchen table in the living room having their morning coffee.

"So, drag brunch? Sounds like a Ben idea," Aaron said, looking up from the Arts and Leisure section of *The Sunday Times*.

"I would bet you're right. I'm sure he knows someone in the cast." Aaron watched as Frank scrunched his face, a puzzled look flashing. "Do drag brunches have casts? I don't know what the right terminology is for that."

"I think 'cast' is probably a safe bet," Aaron said. "And knowing Ben, I'm sure he's been in some show with one of the *cast* members at some point or another."

Benjamin Hiller was a daytime soap opera actor who also worked on and off-Broadway. Although Ben's soap opera career had always done well, his stage work had so far been a huge bust. If there were a flop getting revived, Ben was always the first one to sign up, much to his agent's distress.

"What does one wear to a drag brunch?" Frank asked.

Aaron sat there for a second pondering the question before answering, "Honestly, I haven't the foggiest idea. I would go with Sunday casual. You know, nothing with holes in it, but not formal."

"Well, that leaves the options wide open. Should I put on my Sunday leathers?"

"Only if I get to wear a rubber gimp suit," Aaron joked back.

"As tempting as that is," Frank said, "I'm betting chinos and a sweater is probably the best bet."

"I don't even know if chinos are necessary. I would just wear a pair of jeans. I mean, it's drag brunch, not the Rainbow Room."

Aaron spent the rest of the morning catching up on a few home 'to-dos' before getting dressed in a pair of slim-fitted jeans and a blue Ralph Lauren sweater with a teddy bear knitted into it. Once Aaron put on his blazer, he looked like he was mimicking the teddy bear.

Frank went with a simple black button-down shirt that stretched tightly across his chest and a pair of dark blue jeans.

"Looking good," Aaron noted. "What brand are you wearing?"

"Well, Tim Gunn, if you must know, I'm wearing the finest apparel from Old Navy...I think."

Aaron rolled his eyes and let out a sigh. "Are you sure you're gay?"

"Hmm... Ask your sore ass that question," Frank replied.

Aaron slapped one of his butt cheeks. "Yep, the ass says you're definitely gay. Your fashion sense, on the other hand, says you're a straight frat boy."

"Do I look hot?"

"Of course."

"Then does it matter what I'm wearing? Especially when you'd rather I weren't wearing anything."

"Touché."

\* \* \* \*

The Liberty was packed. Thankfully, Logan had called ahead and gotten them reservations, because there were no walk-ups being seated. The hostess wormed her way through the maze of tables and sat the men at a four-top.

"Your waitress will be right with you," she said, depositing a stack of menus.

The dance music permeating through the small restaurant was giving Frank a headache. He enjoyed hanging out with Ben and Logan, but this was definitely not his scene. He'd gone through his club-kid phase. Heck, he'd spent more time at clubs than he honestly wanted to admit. He glanced down at the menu and decided he wanted The Liberty Burger because it seemed pretty straightforward. There were a few specialty brunch items on the menu, but a burger just seemed like it would hit the spot, especially after his morning workout in the shower.

"So, what's everyone getting?" Ben asked, looking up from his menu.

"A burger," Frank said.

"Why am I not surprised? You are a meat and potatoes kind of guy," Ben said, before continuing his grilling. "And you, Aaron, have you decided?"

"I'm thinking of going with the grilled salmon salad. I haven't had salmon in a while and a salad just seems like a smart move today."

Ben turned to Logan, who started speaking before Ben even got the chance to ask. "I think I'm going to follow Frank's idea and go with the burger."

"You are like two peas in a pod."

"There's a reason our friendship has lasted this long," Logan said.

Just then a six-foot drag queen in stiletto heels that probably made her at least six-foot-four-inches sauntered up to the table dressed like a nineteen-fifties waitress. "Howdy, folks, I'm Anita Waffle, and I'll be your waitress this afternoon. What can I get for you?" Frank wasn't sure if the southern accent was part of her character or heritage.

The waitress began with Ben, who answered, "I'm still deciding. Come back to me last."

Without skipping a beat, the waitress went around the rest of the table and finally came back to Ben, who had decided on the fig-jam pizza.

"Okay, y'all, I'll get that order put in for you right away. As you can see, we're busy, so it may be a bit. If you need anything until then, just holla."

"So, how goes the wedding planning?" Ben asked as soon as Anita had stepped away.

"We met with the wedding planner you recommended yesterday," Aaron said. Frank tuned out the conversation as Aaron and Ben spent the next ten minutes going into all the details Amber had given them the day before. Frank kicked back and just took in the surrounding scene. He recognized a few guys he'd met over the years, but he hadn't spent too much time in the gay scene for a while, so he felt more and more like the old guy hanging out with all the millennials and Gen Z cool kids. On the plus side, he realized he was definitely dressed appropriately, if not over-dressed. Some of the brunch-goers looked like they'd stepped right out of their pajamas and into the restaurant. At the prices they were paying for a drag brunch, he would have expected people to want to be a little more put together.

"Ladies, Gentlemen and Those Who Have Yet to Decide," a drag queen said over the microphone. "I'm Kitsch Kitsch Bang Bang, everyone's favorite drag aunt, and I want to welcome you all to The Liberty for drag brunch. The show will start in about ten minutes, so get those dollars ready. Please remember to tip your waitresses, but just the tip." A round of laughter filled the bar.

*Wow, it wasn't that funny,* Frank thought. *I guess the people in here are sloshed already.*

As soon as Kitsch Kitsch Bang Bang finished speaking, their server Anita Waffle came to their table with their lunches. After she put the plates down, she rested her hand on Aaron's shoulder, asking the table, "Anything else I can get y'all? I need to get ready for my performance, so I'm going to be unavailable for about ten minutes."

*You can get your hand off my fiancé's shoulder.* Frank said nothing, but the muscles in his jaw tensed. Frank looked down as Aaron put his hand on Frank's leg and squeezed him gently. *Even without looking at me, he knows what's going through my head.* With that simple gesture, Frank felt the air letting out of his sail, and he relaxed as he picked up his burger and took a first bite.

For the next ten minutes, the table was pretty silent as everyone dug into their food. Ben talked a bit about the musical he was in, and Frank once again found himself tuning out the conversation. He figured he'd get dragged to Ben's show at some point, whether or not he wanted to go. It's not that he didn't enjoy attending the theater, but it just wasn't necessarily his idea of a rip-roaring good time. He'd much rather go to Yankee's game, eat fattening ballpark food and drink beer. Aaron had gone with him a couple of times during the previous season, but Aaron wasn't that interested in baseball. Frank figured it was because Aaron had grown up over in the United Kingdom as a diplomat's kid, so he was exposed to things like rugby and squash, whatever those were.

"Ladies, Gentleman and Those-In-Between, I give you Anita Waffle," Kitsch Kitsch Bang Bang yelled into the microphone.

The lyrics, "*At first I was afraid, I was petrified,*" burst into the restaurant. *Well, at least she chose a good, old standard.* Anita danced her way around the room and ended up at their table. Aaron had moved his chair so he could watch the show. As she approached their table, Anita performed a death drop. Then she was on her hands and knees crawling toward their table. Before Frank even knew what had happened, Anita was simulating oral sex on Aaron as the crowd hooted and hollered. Even Ben was in on it as he pulled out a dollar, creased it in half and held it toward their waitress. Anita jumped to her feet, grabbed Ben's dollar then put one of her feet between Aaron's legs and hoisted herself up, holding onto Aaron's shoulders as she lip-synced the last "*I will survive*" as the audience burst into applause.

Anita climbed down from the chair and leaned in between Aaron and Frank before yelling, "Thanks for being a good sport," over the applauding crowd.

*Good sport, my ass. That was a violation of New York State Penal Code 130. That's a Class A Misdemeanor, buddy.* Frank stopped himself from saying anything out loud, however. Instead, he stood without saying a word and headed to the back of the restaurant where the bathrooms were located. He wormed his way through the crowd and found the men's room just as a different drag queen was coming out of the ladies' room. He went into the restroom, walked over to the urinal and relieved himself before zipping back up and going to the sink to wash his hands.

"What was that?" Logan asked as he entered the restroom.

"What was *what*?"

"Frank, don't play games with me. I thought you were going to deck the drag queen. Then she could have been Anita ER."

"Well, did you see how she was all over Aaron? That's *so* not cool."

"She's a drag queen. They're inappropriate. It's what you get when you go to a drag show. You should know that."

Frank looked away from Logan and stared at himself in the mirror, willing himself to calm down. "I know. I know. I just... I don't like it when people are so brazenly hitting on my fiancé."

"Jealousy doesn't look good on you, Frank. You know you have nothing to worry about." Logan walked over to the urinal and kept talking. "If you keep acting like an ass every time someone hits on Aaron, you're going to drive him away."

"How the hell am I supposed to act, then?"

"Like an adult," Logan said as he finished, zipped up and headed to the sinks to wash his own hands. "He's engaged to you — not Anita Pancake or whatever her name was. You just need to chill. Okay?" Frank let out a frustrated breath but nodded his head. "Now, put on a smile and let's get back to brunch. At this rate, Aaron and Ben will have eaten our fries."

"Yeah, I worried about my fries as soon as Aaron said he was having a salad."

\* \* \* \*

After lunch, the group walked over to the Union Square Green Market and did a bit of shopping. Thankfully, Aaron had thrown a fold-up bag in his pocket before they'd left the apartment. The two hadn't discussed going to the market afterward, but they often went there on Sundays when the weather was good, so it made sense that they would go today.

"Wow, you came prepared," Frank remarked.

"I was a Boy Scout once," Aaron admitted.

"Until some brat got scared," Ben added.

Aaron laughed. From the look on Frank's face, he didn't get the reference at all. "Theater reference," Aaron said. He watched as Frank just nodded his head.

"Are you sure you haven't had your gay card revoked?" Ben asked. "Come on. It's a *Rent* reference. Everyone's seen *Rent*."

"Not everyone's seen *Rent*," Logan chimed in. "I know every theater queen has seen it, but not every gay man in the city."

With that, their small group set out to search for good deals on fresh produce. Aaron reached out and grabbed Frank's hand, drawing him closer.

"You okay?" Aaron asked.

"I am. I'm just overthinking things, as usual."

"The drag queen?"

"How d'you guess?"

"I know you, Frank," Aaron said, giving Frank a reassuring squeeze. "I know you have a bit of a jealous streak, but I'm yours and nobody else's."

Frank wrapped his arm around Aaron and drew him even closer. "I know. I'm sorry I'm such an ass. I just don't want to lose you."

"Oh my God!" Ben suddenly blurted. "Aaron, look at your crotch."

Aaron quickly glanced down, noticing a lipstick ring right in the center of his pants. *Well fuck!* Frank dropped his arm from Aaron's shoulder and pushed ahead of the group. Even looking at his backside walking away, Aaron could see Frank's clenched fists and straining neck muscles.

"Want me to talk to him?" Logan said, sidling up to Aaron.

"No. He just needs to shake it off," Aaron said, still watching Frank walk away. "If there was one thing I could change about him, it would be this damn jealous streak. Was he like this with Adam?"

"Not really," Logan said.

"I'm sorry about that," Ben said, joining the conversation. "I should have kept my big mouth shut."

"It's okay, Ben," Aaron said. "You know how protective Frank can be. He means well, but it can get old some days."

Aaron watched Frank get farther and farther away. "Anyway, I better catch up with him. See you to two at the gym in the morning?"

"We'll be there," Logan said.

Aaron gave Ben and Logan hugs goodbye before turning around and hustling after Frank.

# Chapter Nine

*Buzz... buzz... buzz.* Aaron rolled over and looked at the clock sitting across the room. *Dear God, it's already five.* He pulled himself out of bed and walked into the bathroom. Thankfully, the room had a nightlight, so he didn't even need to bother turning the light on to take a leak first thing in the morning. After peeing, he looked at himself in the mirror, trying to blink himself awake. He washed his hands then brushed his teeth. By the time he began flossing, Frank stumbled into the bathroom, turning on the lights, his eyes still half-closed, wincing at the light as it filled the small room.

"Morning, sleepyhead," Aaron responded in a slightly too-chipper voice. Frank grumbled back some sign of admission that he realized Aaron was alive and standing in the same room as him. Aaron was getting used to Frank's non-chipper morning persona. The smartest thing to do was to give Frank about fifteen minutes to wake himself. Frank wouldn't be utterly awake until he'd jogged on the treadmill, but Aaron could get him out of the house in about ten minutes and still meet Logan and Ben at five-thirty. Aaron often wondered how Frank had ever gotten up in the morning before they'd started dating.

Aaron finished flossing and gargled with mouthwash, spit it out and left the bathroom so Frank could get ready. Aaron walked back into the bedroom and went to the chest of drawers, pulling out his gym clothes and an FBI cap he wore so he didn't have to shower before going to the gym. He dressed quickly, grabbed his suit hanging behind the door along with his gym bag that contained his dress shoes, socks, underwear, T-shirt and shower gear. *God, I'm so glad I put this together the night before. I'd hate to see what I'd end up wearing if I did this when I'm still half asleep.*

He strolled into the kitchen with his gear in tow and turned on the Keurig he'd bought Frank for Christmas. Frank would never have asked for one. Still, he'd become friendly with Aaron's Keurig before it had died a slow, miserable death, so it made sense to buy a new one for their condo. Aaron selected a couple of Death Wish K-cups and brewed their first coffees of the morning. As the second cup was finishing, Frank came into the room, and Aaron handed him his initial caffeine of the day.

Aaron looked at Bully in his crate, who had lifted his head to see what was going on. "Don't worry, Bully. Rose will be by in a couple of hours to feed you breakfast and let you out." When Aaron and Frank had adopted Bully, they'd realized their schedules could be a bit hectic, so they'd used a dog walking app to find Rose. After about a month, they had taken the dog-walking relationship off the app, and Rose had become Bully's permanent dog walker slash caretaker. She came in two to three times a day, making sure Bully was fed and walked. When Aaron and Frank had an early morning or needed to stay late at work, they would shoot her a quick text, and she'd take care of all his needs. Rose had been an amazingly reliable Godsend for Bully.

With caffeine running through his system, Aaron followed Frank as the two headed out for the day. They bypassed the elevator and headed down the stairs to the street because walking down the flights was a good warm-up. Once outside in the freezing cold, Aaron grabbed Frank's hand, and they walked the two blocks toward Club H, the gym where they were members. Aaron swiped the membership card on his key chain as he walked in the door before heading to the locker room to secure his belongings.

"Good morning, gorgeous people!" came a booming voice from behind them. Without looking, Aaron knew Logan had just joined them.

Aaron turned around to give Logan a hug asking, "Where's Ben?"

"That bum is still in bed! Now that he's back in a show, he rarely ventures out of the house before noon these days."

"How's the show going?" Frank questioned. "Meant to ask him about it yesterday, but I got a bit distracted."

"Honestly, I haven't seen it yet. It's still in previews. Ben won't let me see it until it opens tonight."

"Tonight?" Aaron asked. He then turned to Frank and said, "I guess that means we need to get tickets to see the show before it closes."

Logan looked at Aaron, perplexed. "Why do you say that?"

"Oh, Logan, you haven't heard?" Frank responded. Logan stared at Aaron and Frank with a blank look on his face. "Let's talk about this while jogging. You'll need some endorphins to get through this one."

The trio headed out of the locker room, found three empty treadmills and started their warm-ups. Aaron placed his iPhone and headset inside a small cubbyhole under the console and a water bottle in the circular slot up top before starting the machine. Out of the corner of his eyes, he watched the other two follow suit. As they all warmed up, Aaron informed Logan about the lousy press Ben's new show was getting. In fact, *The New York Post* theater writer had said it was probably the worst show in history and that none of the leads could actually act.

"Greaattt..." Logan began. "I can't believe Ben hasn't told me about that."

"From what I've read on Twitter about *Bobbi Boland*," Aaron responded, "the cast was told not to look at any outside information about their artistic endeavors for fear it would interfere with the director's process," saying this last part in a voice resembling of an English aristocrat.

"Basically, the show is going down in flames faster than the Titanic sunk," Frank added. "I hate admitting it. I watched a clip on YouTube, and well... How do I say this nicely? I hope Ben has a movie in the works, because he may not have a career in theater after the show opens."

"Ouch," Logan responded as he picked up speed on the treadmill. His breathing had already slipping into a runner's rhythm. "Well, at least I'm prepared. Dear God. Well, shit."

The three chit-chatted for a few more minutes about other rumors from the show that were surfacing on the Internet. Logan finally asked Aaron how he knew so much. Aaron had to admit that he had created an RSS feed about the show because he was curious. Before Aaron knew it, he had a full-on obsession with the show. "I mean, come on. Who in their right mind thought we needed a revival of *Bobbi Boland* on Broadway? The original play never even opened the first time."

*Bobbi Boland* was one of those infamous flops in Broadway history. It had been initially mounted off-Broadway in 2001, and the producers had tried to bring it to Broadway in 2003 with Farrah Fawcett. The show had only seven previews on Broadway before closing. In fact, the theater writer of *The New York Post* likened the show to *Moose Murders*, which Ben had also been in a revival of the previous season.

"Well," Logan said slowly, "I have to admit I didn't think it was a smart career move for Ben. He needs to stop doing revivals of notorious flops on Broadway." Turning toward Frank, he continued by saying, "But you know how he is. He sure didn't listen to me...or his agent...or his manager."

"Yes, I do. What's next? He going to take on the title role in *Lestat*?" Frank joked.

"Look at you, knowing your Broadway theater history," Aaron chided.

"I had a few dates with a guy in the ensemble. I was forced to see the show and pretend it was good. I think I fell asleep in Act Two, and a quarter of the people around me never returned after intermission."

"Ouch!" Aaron interjected. "It was that bad?"

"Let's just say they recorded a cast album that was never released," Logan replied. "And before you ask, I didn't see the show. I worked on the original union contract negotiations for the firm."

"Aaron Massey!" a voice screeched from across the gym. "Oh, my God!" A gorgeous young man with black hair and a perfect set of teeth came bounding toward him.

"Jonathan?" Aaron replied, bewildered. "Frank and Logan, this is Jonathan Fetty. We dated several years ago before he picked up and move to Los Angeles."

Out of the corner of his eye, Aaron caught Frank giving Jonathan a quick up and down before putting on his best fake smile. Feeling this conversation would lead to a lot of questions, Aaron decided to speed things up. "Jonathan, what brings you back to New York?"

"Aaron, dear," Jonathan said in a sultry baritone voice. Although the words he said hinted at femininity, the way the words came out of his mouth sounded like a lumberjack reading an audiobook. "My publisher, your publisher, brought me back to the city to take on several higher-profile clients."

"Great," Aaron replied. "Well, call my agent, Penny, and maybe we can have coffee some time. You, me and my *fiancé*, Frank."

Jonathan turned toward Logan and replied, "So you're his new boyfriend?" Jonathan glanced and Aaron and mouthed the word 'hot'.

"Actually, no," Frank corrected. "I'm his *fiancé*."

Jonathan smiled and greeted Frank. Then looking Logan up and down, Jonathan mouthed to Aaron, *single?* Aaron shook his head no, and Jonathan said, "Too bad." Aaron saw Frank roll his eyes in Jonathan's general direction.

"Anyway, Aaron, it was soooo good to see you," he said, reaching out and touching the side of Aaron's face as he ran. "We'll definitely have to keep in touch."

Jonathan winked at Aaron, making it very obvious before saying goodbye.

Logan upped the speed on his treadmill before asking, "You dated *that*?"

"Yeah," Aaron started, the words dripping with his own bewilderment. "He was young and more naive back then — but then weren't we all?" Out of the corner of his eye, he watched Frank pull out his earphones and turn on the television mounted to the front of the treadmill. *Great, he's pissed!* Within a few seconds, Logan followed suit and began running to his music. Being the last one of the three open for conversation, Aaron gave in and pulled out his iPhone, selected his exercise playlist and kicked it up a notch.

Thirty minutes later the three friends finished their early morning runs and headed to the showers. Aaron always felt like a hot, sticky mess right after working out, and he couldn't wait to feel the warm water rushing over his naked body. As he turned the corner to head into the locker room, Jonathan was getting out of the shower. Aaron purposefully averted his gaze and headed right to his locker. He spun the combination on his lock. With a snapping sound, the lock gave way, and he opened the compartment and unpacked his shower gear. He pulled off his sweaty tank top and was about to pull off his shorts and jockstrap when someone tapped his shoulder.

"Yes?" Aaron's eyes went bug-eyed as a stark-naked Jonathan stood in front of him. Before Aaron could react, Jonathan pulled Aaron into a bear hug. Without thinking, Aaron shoved Jonathan away as a scowl crossed his face. "Dude," Aaron scolded. "This place may be gay friendly, but this isn't a bathhouse." *What the fuck?*

"Oh, Aaron, you're such a prude these days. And speaking of bathhouses, remember that one time…" Jonathan trailed off with a wistful smile on his face.

To his left, Aaron noticed Frank had clenched his fists, and his jaw was set so tight that he was practically grinding his teeth to dust. *If I don't get rid of Jonathan, Frank's going to lay him out!*

"Hey, Jonathan, not to be a *prude*, but I do have to get to work. So, I wish I had time to catch up, but now I've got to get in and out of the shower."

Jonathan, clearly not taking the hint, replied, "Okay, I'll let you off the hook today. But we'll definitely have to get together…and soon. Bring what's-his-name if you want to."

"The name's Frank," Frank groused.

Jonathan looked dismissively at Frank. "Sorry… I suck at names. I barely remember the names of the people who matter in my life."

Before Aaron could stop him, Jonathan reached out and kissed Aaron on the cheek. Aaron stared slack-jawed as Jonathan spun on his naked heels and headed off to another part of the locker room. Out of the corner of his eye, Aaron saw that Frank was about to say something, but Logan placed a hand on Frank's shoulder and shook his head no, warning Frank to keep his anger in check. Frank grunted before heading off toward the shower.

Aaron grabbed his gear and followed Frank, selecting the shower stall next to him. The warm water washed over his body instantly. He turned his back toward the stream, allowing the warming sensation to start at the top of his neck and trickle down his spine. Next to having an orgasm, this was the single most spectacular feeling Aaron knew. He stood in the shower, letting the water flow over his body before picking up his face wash. He then picked up the container of shampoo and squeezed out just enough to provide his short hair with the requisite lather. With freshly cleaned hair, he doled out a dollop of shower gel onto a washrag before cleaning the rest of his body.

Stepping out, Aaron grabbed the towel hanging there and dried his hair vigorously before patting the rest of his body. Once he was sufficiently dried, Aaron flung the towel over his shoulder and walked back to his locker. Frank was already there fully dressed and tying his shoes when Aaron got there and started spinning the combination.

"Exhibitionist much?" Frank said, eyeing Aaron's naked body.

"Usually you enjoy the sight of me naked," Aaron responded, realizing Jonathan had done a number on Frank. "Frank, Jonathan means nothing to me anymore. He's an old friend. An eccentric friend, but he's just a friend. Heck, I haven't seen him in years. I don't even know if he still qualifies as a friend."

"Whatever," Frank replied, throwing his coat over his shoulders. "Tell Logan I'll meet him at the Greek diner down the street." With that, Frank grabbed his gear and walked away. Aaron watched Frank pause for a second before turning around to come give him a kiss on the cheek before leaving.

As soon as Frank had left, Logan appeared at Aaron's side, digging into his own locker. Logan had one towel around his waist and was still drying his hair with a second one.

"Where's Frank?" Logan asked.

"He took off. Told me to tell you he'll be at the Greek diner."

"Okay," Logan said as he pulled out a pair of boxer shorts. "Wanna talk about it?"

"Jonathan?"

"Yeah."

"Nothing to talk about. I dated him like six years ago. We broke up and were still on friendly terms when he picked up and moved to Los Angeles. I wasn't even torn up by the breakup. I'm so beyond over him it's not even funny. Honestly, he's probably the single most selfish person I've ever met, and that was before he went all Hollywood." Aaron slipped into his boxers and slacks before applying his deodorant and throwing his white T-shirt over his head. He then tucked the T-shirt into his boxers and reached for his pressed button-down shirt.

"Aaron, don't worry. You know Frank has a jealous streak. Just think about his insane reaction yesterday to the drag queen. It's because he loves you. Don't worry."

"I'm less worried about our relationship than I am that Frank's going to finally snap one day and actually hurt someone who flirts with me. Frank needs to get a grip. It's like he doesn't trust me at times."

"It's not you he doesn't trust," Logan interjected. "It's other men around you he doesn't trust. I think he's just over-protective. Subconsciously, I think he feels the need to protect you in a way he never felt the need to protect Adam. Between Adam's murder and the serial killer who tried to kill you, I just think Frank's internal mama-bear instincts are on hyperdrive these days."

Aaron glanced over at Logan, who was buttoning up his white button-down shirt. "I just wish he'd remember that I'm an adult who actually knows how to take care of myself. I'm a trained FBI undercover agent."

"He knows that," Logan said, winding his tie around his neck creating a Windsor knot. "He just loves you, is all. And I think that love scares him more than he lets on."

Aaron let out a slow breath of air. "I know you're right, and I needed to hear that." Aaron reached up and straightened Logan's tie before they grabbed their belongings and left the locker room. Outside, Aaron and Logan hugged before Aaron caught a cab and Logan headed to breakfast with Frank. Once inside the cab, Aaron looked at his watch, which now read seven-thirty. *Still two-and-a-half hours before class starts.*

# Chapter Ten

Frank sat in a corner booth in the Olympus Diner a block away from Club H, sipping his coffee. *What is up with that guy!? I've never seen a more blatant asshole in my life. How dare he!* Frank replayed the events of that morning repeatedly in his head, trying to figure out if Aaron had somehow encouraged the asshole. Wanting to find anything else to concentrate on, Frank scanned the diner to see if he recognized anyone.

The older man at the table next to him paid his check and left the restaurant. Frank glanced over at the dirty dishes still strewn across the table and noticed the guy had left his copy of *The New York Times*. Frank grabbed the paper before the server could come by and bus it.

He flipped through the first section and learned a little about a new conflict happening in Gabon, some country in Africa that he'd never heard of before. Then he rapidly flipped through the rest of the paper. He found a short one-inch article about the death outside the Sofitel. Thankfully, the article stuck strictly to the facts and provided no extra information about the case other than that a death had occurred. He flipped through the entertainment section and read a brief article about Aaron's book reading from the day before. The journalist was smitten with Aaron because it read more like a romance novel than an objective detailing of the reading itself.

He sipped on his coffee and kept flipping through the section. He turned the page and almost spit out his coffee as he gagged for a second. There on page nine of the entertainment section was a picture of Jonathan Fetty.

"Whoa there, cowboy," Logan said as he approached the booth and slid in on the opposite side. "Don't kill yourself."

Frank practically threw the paper at Logan before he even sat. "I just met this asshole, and already I can't seem to escape him."

Logan read the accompanying article while Frank stared at him, waiting for some kind of reaction. After completing the story, Logan looked up and said, "It was a picture of Fetty with one of his clients at a movie premiere. From what I can tell, he's a pretty high-class literary agent with an impressive list of authors. Now that he's back in New York, you're probably going to see more of him."

"Maybe I can arrest him," Frank said. "You know, police find drugs on people all the time."

Thankfully, Logan took this last idea as a joke, but Frank wasn't nearly as sure he'd meant it as one. Before he could offer this bit of insight, a server approached the table and asked for their orders. The server was clearly just doing her job, which meant she was half-aloof and not paying real attention to either of them.

Magically though, fifteen minutes later, their breakfasts appeared exactly as they'd ordered them.

Logan was an oatmeal and one egg kind of guy. Frank wanted something a little syrupier, so he had gotten a short stack of pancakes with sausage. The two quickly dug into their breakfasts, clearly having worked up an appetite at the gym.

"Let's face it, Frank," Logan said. "You looked like some kind of jealous teenage girl with the tantrum you threw in there. I was afraid you were going to knock the guy out when he hugged Aaron."

"Well, how would you respond if some hot naked guy came over and hugged Ben while you were standing there?"

"Hmmm... Depending on the night, I might ask him to come home with us."

"Seriously, Logan."

"Okay, sure, I would be a little peeved, but I would trust Ben." Frank cocked one of his eyebrows at Logan, showing he didn't entirely believe him. "Come on, Frank. Ben and I—just like you and Aaron—have sexual histories. Eventually, those histories are going to come up. Let's face it. There are parts of this town where your exploits a few years ago are legendary. I mean, you'll never be able to go back to the New York Bondage Club after that one scene you made there."

"Point well taken. But I feel skeeved out by that guy."

"And just to clarify, I have been in similar situations with Ben."

"Really?"

"Ben is a former soap opera star. His female and male fans often throw themselves at him when we're in public. At first, I wanted to rip each adoring fan off him and growl like a pit-bull. Hell, if I could have hiked up my leg to mark my territory, I would have."

"I didn't realize you were into watersports," Frank said dryly.

"Hardy-har-har," Logan responded, deadpan. "Anyway, over time, I got used to the fans and realized I could trust Ben. He knew how to deal with them. It's an occupational hazard of sorts. You get shot at by bad guys, and Ben has middle-aged men and women throwing their panties at him."

"I'd rather someone shot at Aaron than have a naked Jonathan Fetty clinging to him."

"I get it. I really do. This Fetty guy was a bit crazy."

"Crazy Fetty... I think it fits."

Logan grimaced and just shook his head. "As I was saying, ultimately it's about trust. And that's something you need to figure out...and fast."

Frank stabbed a piece of pancake, making sure to swirl it around on the plate to soak up as much syrup as possible. He sat in silence for a few moments before Logan asked about the reviews of Ben's show.

"Is it that bad, Frank?"

Frank pulled out his iPhone and quickly searched for *The New York Post* website. Once he was on the site, he found the article written by Daryl Davenport, the theater writer. Unlike traditional theater critics, Davenport reported on what was going on backstage at various shows before the shows ever opened or even had a chance of opening. Frank scrolled through the list of entries from Davenport, found the one in question and handed it over to Logan.

Looking up from Frank's iPhone, Logan read out loud, "*Benjamin Hiller, the former soap star, has a voice that reminds me of the sound female raccoons make while in heat.*

Ouch!" Logan responded before handing Frank back the phone.

"I warned you," Frank said sympathetically. "Have fun tonight! Just remember that Ben won't be able to complain if he's going down on your cock!"

"Frank!" Logan scolded while stifling a laugh. "I'm sure it's not as bad as that. Besides, that Davenport is notoriously known for exaggerating the behind-the-scenes drama in her columns. There's a reason she's not a critic."

"Maybe so, Logan, but she's single-handedly prevented shows from ever getting a footing."

Logan looked at Frank and nodded his head in agreement. But before they could continue that conversation, the server appeared with their check. And since there was a line of people waiting for an empty table, Frank and Logan opted to make a quick escape. Outside the diner, they hugged and said their goodbyes. Logan headed south toward the business district, and Frank started walking toward Midtown to his precinct.

# Chapter Eleven

After making a quick pit-stop to Viva La Coffee to get a couple of coffees for Jasika and himself, Frank arrived at work a little after nine a.m. Jasika was already in the office, busying herself with paperwork from Saturday. Frank walked in and immediately hung his suit coat over the back of his office chair.

"Dear God, how cold is it going to get today?" Frank asked as he sat down at his desk.

"According to NOAA, with the windchill, we could be looking at temps of eleven below zero," Jasika replied.

Frank made some kind of grumbling noise as he lowered himself into his desk chair and turned on his computer. While waiting for the computer to boot up, he checked his voicemail. He found a message from Mariella concluding that the official cause of death was poisoning, and that he should contact Nasab for information on the specific pathogen. Next, he had a phone call from Richardson saying something about the video, but Richardson must have been on the train when he'd called because the message was choppy and there was a lot of background noise competing with his message. Last, he had one from Logan reminding him to take a breath and not overthink what had happened that morning in the gym. *God, he knows me too well.* By the time he'd finished listening to his messages, his computer had finished booting, so he pulled up his email.

"Richardson left a message for me to call him, and I figured we could kill two birds with one stone by calling the Geek Twins at their offices," Frank said to Jasika, who was already putting information on their whiteboard. She put down the marker and walked back over to her desk. Frank hit the speakerphone button and dialed Richardson's direct.

After two rings, the familiar voice answered, "Richardson."

"Hey, Richardson, is the other geek with you?"

"*Oi*, other geek! Get in here!" In a few seconds, both Richardson and Nasab were on the phone.

"Hey, Nasab, missed you yesterday at the crime scene. Heard you were in a fiber workshop. Sounded fascinating," Frank said, barely stifling a yawn as he said the last part.

"Funny, funny there, Frank. You may not appreciate the finer skill involved in collecting fiber evidence, but one day that evidence may actually help you catch a bad guy!"

"Nasab, I've been doing this how long? And never used fiber evidence to actually solve a case. I prefer good old-fashioned detective work."

"You mean detective work that involves DNA analysis, fingerprint analysis and computer forensics?" Nasab countered.

"Exactly. Just like my grandpappy used to use."

"Frank, your grandfather was in pharmaceuticals," Richardson said.

"Touché! Anyway, so what do you have for us this morning?"

Richardson went into a detailed analysis of what they'd found on the video. As expected, there were no clear shots of the female who claimed to be a physician. However, they had missed a few things when looking at the security tapes at the Sofitel. Richardson sent Frank a link to an email, which Frank opened. Immediately, Frank and Jasika could see what was happening on Richardson's computer. Richardson walked Frank and Jasika through the video. First, he stopped when the woman came out of nowhere wearing a hat tilted toward the security camera. Next, Richardson forwarded a few frames, and they could see the woman pull her hands out of her pockets and she was wearing latex gloves. The next frame surprised both of them. When the woman stood, she was now holding a briefcase and quickly walking away.

"Did you pull other security tapes?"

"Well, I didn't have a warrant, but they were all helpful. At every turn, the woman is completely obscured. It's almost as if she knew where each security camera in the area was. The doorman at the Sofitel remembered the victim getting out of the cab with a metal briefcase. He remembered it because most women prefer leather softback briefcases."

After a few minutes of discussing the implications of that, they quickly realized that they had way more conjecture than actual evidence. Nasab joined the conversation and mentioned he could definitively say what toxin killed the victim.

"This toxin was like nothing I'd ever seen before. At first, I wondered if she had been exposed to a naturally occurring toxin on either the plane or elsewhere. However, after talking to Mariella about the autopsy and the sheer amount of damage done to the victim's body, I decided it was probably a combination of toxins the victim had been exposed to. And I was right." Nasab quickly explained he found three unique toxins all within the victim's system—*daphne mezereum, C. majalis var. majalis* and *physostigma venenosum.*

"And for those of us who failed high school chemistry?" Jasika questioned.

"All three of them are plants," Nasab added. "The flowers daphne, lily of the valley and calabar bean. Now here's the interesting thing... This specific strain of lily of the valley is only available in Europe, and the calabar bean is found primarily growing in the wild in Western Africa."

"In other words," Frank began, "there's no way this happened naturally."

"*Nada!*" Nasab responded. "I can say this is one nasty combination of toxins, though. Basically, if you try to treat for daphne or lily of the valley, the calabar bean will kill the victim and vice versa. The combined effect of these three toxins basically attacks every major system in the body—brain, heart, kidneys, lungs, stomach, etc...."

"Fuck," Jasika said. "This was a well-planned, premeditated murder."

"Anything else?" Frank wondered.

Almost in unison, Nasab and Richardson responded, "Nope!"

"Any chance your new intern started looking into the plane manifests?" Frank asked.

"She has narrowed the list a bit, but it's still a pretty slow process. Homeland Security hasn't been overly helpful. We're hoping that now it's officially ruled a murder, they'll be a bit more forthcoming," Richardson explained.

"Sounds good. Let me know as soon as anything pops." Frank hung up the phone, stood, walked over to the whiteboard and added the additional information.

"Jasika, start tracking down any places in New York where someone can buy that combination of flowers and plants. Maybe we'll get lucky and find a potential source for flowers — or at least a possible combination of locations. I'm going to go through passenger manifests myself and see if anything jumps out at me. But honestly, I have no idea where to go on this one."

# Chapter Twelve

After discussing the reality of forensic psychology with a group of twenty-year-olds who all wanted to work for the FBI's Behavioral Analysis Unit because of the television show *Criminal Minds*, Aaron was ready for a break. He looked at his watch and it showed eleven-thirty. *Hmm, I don't have to be back to the office until two.* Realizing he had a good chunk of time, he decided to surprise Frank and Jasika by taking them out to lunch.

"Dr. Massey," a voice called after him.

"Yes?" Aaron responded, turning around to see who the voice belonged to.

"You may not know me, but—"

"Trevor Murray, sits in the back left hand side of the room, got an eighty-five on the first exam and a ninety on his first paper. Your parents' names are Jerry and Jacqueline Murray from Poughkeepsie, NY. And, I might add, I know you fabricated part of your entry essay. You never made it on that trip to France during your junior year. You signed up for it but didn't go."

"Wow! How did you know all that?" the kid said with a pure look of shock.

"Trevor, my job is watching and knowing people. And I've checked out all my students. Gotta make sure none of you are domestic terrorists."

"Still, I can't believe you remember that."

"Thank my parents for a photographic memory. Anyway, this wasn't about me. What can I do for you?"

"I know this may sound goofy," Trevor acknowledged as he pulled out a copy of *Blood Money*, "but would you mind autographing this book for my mother? She's a huge fan of it. That's probably why she convinced me to take this course."

"Sure, not a problem," Aaron said as he pulled out a pen from his jacket pocket. "So, this course wasn't your idea?"

"Nah, my goal was to go into chemistry, but my mom thinks criminalistics is a much broader field. This class is one of the introductory courses to the major, so I thought I'd check it out and see how things went."

After autographing the book for Trevor, he closed the cover and handed it back to the kid. "Well, all I can say is don't go into it if you don't love it. The pay is mediocre, the hours are long, relationships are hard and your life is filled with a lot of death, destruction and disease. You need to have a pretty thick skin for this work."

"Wow. Maybe John Jay should put that in its brochures. I'm sure they'd recruit lots of people with that slogan," Trevor said as he laughed.

"Don't get me wrong," Aaron responded, feeling the need to self-correct. "I love my job. I just don't want anyone going into it without fully realizing what the realities are. If you want to talk more about career options, come by during my office hours before class next week and we can talk about all the options a degree in criminology can provide."

"Thanks… I'll do that," Trevor responded, sliding the autographed book in his backpack and heading off in the other direction.

He thought about hailing a cab because of the weather, but the Midtown Precinct North was maybe a ten minute walk from the school, so he buttoned his jacket and wrapped his scarf around his neck. Aaron replayed that morning's lecture, processing what had worked and what hadn't worked with his students. He'd taught before at Quantico, but he'd never had a group of twenty-year-old college students staring at him blankly in a lecture hall. *It's definitely a novel experience.*

Before he knew it, he was walking into the precinct. He said hello to the desk sergeant, a woman he'd met a few times in passing at the station. She had him sign the visitor's log and buzzed him right through. Their desks were empty, but Jasika suddenly appeared, heading back to hers.

"Hey, Aaron," Jasika said, throwing her arms around him in a friendly embrace. "Did Frank know you were coming?"

"Nah, I thought I would surprise you by taking you both out to lunch. I know how you two get when investigating a murder. You forget to eat!"

"So true! Well, Frank is in a meeting with Hays, requesting additional help on this investigation."

"What's up with the case?"

"Nothing yet! We don't know who the victim is. We do know she was poisoned with some weird concoction of plants."

As Jasika told Aaron about the poisoning and the effects Mariella had found from the plants on the body, his mind started whirling. Aaron hesitated a second before asking, "Dear God, I hope I'm wrong, but what was the combination?"

"What are you thinking, Aaron?"

"Nothing yet, but tell me the combination."

"It was a combination of..." Jasika hesitated, glancing down at her notes for the exact combination of plants. "Calabar bean, lily of the valley and daphne."

*It couldn't be? Could it? She's never been on US soil before.* "Was the victim from Africa or of African descent?" Aaron asked.

"No. Why?"

"The combination reminds me of the signature of a hitwoman I ran into when I worked with Interpol. They called her Daphne because she always killed with daphne and left a petal somewhere on the victim's body."

"Let me see." Jasika thumbed through the printed-out reports from Mariella and the Geek Twins, looking for any sign of a flower petals. "Well, that's odd. There were a half-dozen daphne flower petals in the victim's suit coat." Jasika slowly raised her head from the stack of printouts to look Aaron in the eyes. "You know something."

"We need to talk to Hays and Frank now," Aaron noted.

"Let's go."

Aaron and Jasika wormed their way through the bullpen toward the chief's office. Jasika knocked on the door and waited for a reply.

"Come in."

"Hey, Chief..." Jasika said.

"What's the Fed Boy doing here?"

"I dropped by to take Jasika and Frank to lunch. Jasika mentioned the odd combination of toxins — "

"Detective Torv, you should not be discussing an ongoing case with a civilian."

"Sorry, Chief."

"Chief Hays. I'm sorry for interjecting myself here," Aaron said, slipping into his FBI voice, "but it's actually a good thing Detective Torv mentioned this to me, because I have critical information that will further your investigation."

"Give it to me, Fed Boy."

"When I worked as an FBI legal attaché in Lyon, France, I worked closely with Interpol. One case we spent a lot of time investigating was a female hitwoman we called Daphne. Her signature was the exact combination of toxins your victim died from yesterday. From the looks of it, Daphne is here in New York."

"Interesting…" Chief Hays said, steepling his hands underneath his chin. "What can you tell me about this Daphne? How do you know it's not just a copycat?"

"Let me answer that second question first. There is information Jasika just read to me from the autopsy report that was never released to the public. As for what we know about Daphne, that's just it. We never had much to go on. We had a few pictures of her, but she was always concealed, seeming to know where every camera was. She's very methodical and doesn't take chances. Last I heard, Interpol never had an exact body count, but they had estimated she was easily responsible for twenty-five to forty hits Interpol officially knew of. And those were her totals from a number of years ago, so I can only imagine what that number may be now."

"Damn!" Frank let out under his breath. "How have we never heard of her?"

"Honestly, Frank, she has never operated in the US, as far as we could tell. And back when I was in France, the more we tried digging into her, the more of a giant mystery she became. I can reach out to an old contact at Interpol to see if they have any recent information."

"Okay. Do that and let us know, myself included, as soon as you know something definitive," Hays responded.

"Before I do that, what can you tell me about the victim?"

Aaron watched as Frank looked to the chief for permission. Hays gave Frank a single head nod. "Here's what we know so far," Frank explained. "The victim flew in yesterday on an international flight. We're still trying to figure out which one she came in on. The airlines weren't exactly helpful yesterday, and DHS has been a bit of pain too."

"Okay," Aaron said, pondering the information as he processed it.

Frank opened a folder he had on the table before saying, "Here's a photo from the crime scene."

"Fuck!" Aaron said, his face blanching as he looked down at the face of a woman he knew all too well. "That's Danielle Tebbutt."

"Who?" Frank and Jasika asked simultaneously.

"Danielle Tebbutt. She's the Head of Directorate Training of the National Police in Paris. She was coming to a conference this week on international policing at the United Nations. We were supposed to have lunch this week."

"That would explain the odd reservations at the Sofitel." Aaron watched as Frank turned to look at him before he began explaining. "The head of security had a reservation for a Jane Doe. Someone in the corporate office in Paris made the reservation, so we've been working under the assumption that our victim was a French national. Her status also explains why we didn't have her prints on file, but I'm kind of surprised we didn't trip any alarm bells overseas when we tried running them," Frank noted.

"Unless someone tried running the prints through Interpol's automatic fingerprint identification system—AFIS—I doubt anything would have been red-flagged. And even if it was, it would probably travel through formal channels through the embassy system, which is notoriously slow," Aaron explained.

"Okay," Chief Hays said, taking over the conversation. "I want you, Fed Boy, to call your contact at Interpol and get any information my detectives can use."

"Chief Hays," Aaron started, "with your permission, I would like to see if the FBI will let me consult on this case since I have the expertise and some background with the hitwoman."

"Not sure I like the idea. You have a tendency of bringing more media attention than I want my detectives to see."

"I promise I'll stay out of the camera line and work behind the scenes to ensure the flow of information from sources I have internationally."

Hays thought about it for a second before saying, "If the Bureau says it's okay, then I'll allow it. But if I see you discussing this case on the television just once, you are out of here." Hays turned and looked at Frank. "And I don't care if you two are engaged. If he slips once, I'm holding you responsible. I don't want another media circus."

"Got it, Chief," Frank said.

With that, they left Chief Hays' office and continued into the bullpen.

"I'm going to call my contact at Interpol." Aaron glanced at his watch and did some quick international time conversion before continuing, "It's about seven p.m. there, so I should be able to catch Pasquale at home. Fingers crossed."

Pulling out his cell phone, Aaron scrolled through his contact list until he found the one for Pasqual Bosc and hit the call button.

"Aaron, to what do I owe the pleasure this evening?" Pasquale asked in a thick French accent.

"Hello, gorgeous. How are things in Lyon these days?"

"The same. More criminals, more cases."

"Sounds like the US."

"Yes. But we have fewer gun-toting cowboys in the rest of the world."

"Touché."

"But I'm guessing you didn't call for quick wit and banter. How can I help you?"

"It's about Daphne."

"What?"

Aaron filled Pasquale in on what had transpired in NYC over the past day.

"This is definitely a first," Pasquale responded. "We've never heard of her working outside of Europe or Africa. I wonder what changed her MO?"

"That is the million-dollar-question. So, what can you tell me?"

"Officially or unofficially?"

"Both."

"Well officially, I cannot release any information without going through proper channels, and the Daphne case is still very much ongoing. Unofficially, we've been stumped since you left France. Honestly, beyond the signature toxin cocktail and the occasional veiled photo, we have nothing. Any chance you had better luck with security footage?"

"Nope. She always seems to know where all the cameras are located. She definitely does her due diligence before taking on a job."

"Hmm... With your permission, I'm going to inform my superiors about this recent development. Unofficially, check your email. I've sent you a little something while we've been chatting."

"Officially, I look forward to hearing from your agency through the correct channels. Unofficially, thanks."

"You'll be hearing from me soon." With that, Pasquale disconnected the call without even saying goodbye.

Aaron looked at his phone and found an encrypted file had been sent to his FBI email address. He forwarded the email to Frank.

"Frank, I got a document from Interpol, unofficially. Let's look."

Frank motioned for Jasika to join them, and they opened the file. It was password protected. "Damn! A lot of good this is going to do us."

"Don't fret, Frank. I know Pasquale pretty well. I'm betting the password is '*levrette*'."

"Huh?"

"*Levrette*. It's the French word for doggy-style."

"Are you kidding me?"

"Pasquale has a dark sense of humor, and it was his favorite position."

"Dear God," Frank said. "It's just a day for you and your exes."

"We never dated. We fooled around a couple of times, but we realized we were not compatible on any front. I can't believe I'm discussing my sexual history again today."

Aaron spelled out the French word as Frank typed it into the computer. Immediately, a PDF document over one-thousand pages opened on the desktop.

"Damn, it's long," Frank said. "I'll print the document, and we can divvy it up and start reading."

"Sounds good," Aaron responded. "I need to check in with Chief Barling or she'll have my hide."

Aaron grabbed his phone again and dialed into the FBI field office.

"Chief Barling's office," a chipper voice answered.

"Hello, Caroline."

"Agent Massey, to what do I owe the honor of your call today? I didn't realize bestselling authors were still slumming it with the likes of us," she joked.

"Hardy-har-har. You know I could never get too far away from you. Besides, I'm still on the payroll."

"That you are."

"How are Jack and the girls?"

"My husband is doing great. And Carly and Hannah are teens now. I can't believe how quickly they age."

"Wow, I remember when they were born. Hard to believe that they're teenagers."

"They do grow fast." There was a sudden pause before O'Donnell said, "So, I'm betting this isn't a social catch-up call. How can I help?"

"Is Chief Barling in?"

"She is. She has asked not to be disturbed. Is it urgent?"

"I wouldn't ask you to patch me through if it wasn't."

"Sounds good to me. Let me check with her first."

Aaron heard the soft clicking sound as he was placed on hold. An audio recording about the FBI's importance and history played while he waited.

"This better be good, Agent Massey," Barling said into the phone, a clear edge to her voice.

"I wouldn't have asked to speak to you if it wasn't important." Aaron filled Barling in on what had transpired over the last twenty-four hours.

"Damn! Why does this shit always seem to follow you?"

"I'm lucky?"

"Don't be glib, Agent Massey."

"Sorry, ma'am."

"I guess it makes sense to have you liaise with the NYPD on this one because of your background with the case and connection to Interpol. Don't make me regret this. I want to see you in my office at nine a.m. tomorrow morning for a briefing."

"Yes, Chief. I'll be there. Have a good day." Aaron heard the click on the other end of the line. *She didn't even bother saying goodbye. Oh well, time to get to work.* Aaron walked back to Frank and Jasika's desks. The two had printed the document and were already going through the pages.

Frank motioned for Aaron to pull up a chair and start reading a stack he'd set aside for him.

# Chapter Thirteen

The three of them spent the next couple of hours poring over their respective stacks. Frank thought his eyes were going to pop out of his head. After reading the same paragraph for the third time, he realized he needed to take a breather.

"Anyone need to take five?"

"Dear God, yes," Jasika said. "I've found my eyes glazing over twice in the last ten minutes."

Frank looked at Aaron, who didn't even seem to have heard them. "Aaron, you need a break?" he asked, nudging his shoulder.

"Wha—?"

"Break. Do you need a break?" Frank asked, drawing out each word.

"Yeah, I could take a break."

Jasika barked out a short laugh at the confused look on Aaron's face.

"What's so funny?" he asked, finally seeming to get caught up with the other two.

"You were lost in those files — and I mean lost." She smiled, shaking her head. "Okay, pretty boys. Viva La Coffee?"

"Sounds like a plan," Frank agreed.

The three of them grabbed their coats, headed out of the precinct and made their way around the corner to their favorite local coffee shop. The shadows from the tall buildings were causing temperatures to drop again in the late afternoon. Frank put his arm around Aaron to share body heat.

"So not fair," Jasika said, noting Frank's gesture. "I'm the small one of the group. Here you two, big, strong men are huddled together to get warm while we're walking."

"Want to snuggle between us?" Aaron joked.

"Even if that were my fantasy, it ain't gonna happen. I'm too good for both of you."

Thankfully, the shop was right ahead, and Frank didn't feel the need to respond to that. He opened the door and held it for Jasika and Aaron. They stood in line, and Aaron offered to pay for all their coffees. *He knows I have money. Why does he always have to pay? It makes me feel like some kind of kept boy. And I'm the older one, dammit!* Frank and Aaron had discussed this issue in the past, but Frank didn't feel the need to rehash it now in front of Jasika, so he let it slide and said, "Thank you," instead.

After they had their coffees, they huddled at a table in the corner of the room. Thankfully, no one else was hanging out in the coffee shop. Once everyone was settled, Frank asked, "So, what has everyone learned this afternoon?"

"I'll start," Jasika said. "Honestly, not a lot. I had the first three-hundred-something pages of the document.

There was a lot of information about past crime scenes and Daphne's MO, but so much of it was conjecture and not solid evidence."

"Jasika, you're right there," Aaron acknowledged. "I found the same thing in the next set of pages. Their best guess is that Daphne is French and may have had a student exchange experience in Africa. However, the connection to Africa is tenuous and only exists because Interpol knows she'd killed a couple of African warlords when they'd visited France. The French Intelligence Service hadn't even known the warlords were on French soil until she'd killed them."

"I noticed one peculiar story," Jasika said. She looked at the guys, and Frank gave her a nod to go on. She told them about one of Daphne's hits that had gone completely awry. The killing had involved a poisoning case. After the killing, Daphne had apparently learned that she had been given faulty intelligence. As a result, Daphne had killed an innocent person. When she'd found out, Daphne killed the man who had employed her.

"The real kicker to the story is that Daphne sent a fruit basket and an apology letter to the Paris police," Jasika said, clearly mystified by this unusual turn of events.

"She did *what*?" Frank questioned.

"Yep, she sent a gift basket. The note was short and simple. *'Sorry for the betrayal of your trust. The situation was rectified. Daphne.'*"

"Wow, that's ballsy," Aaron noted, a look that crossed between shock and admiration. "She's clearly very sure of her skill set. This also tells us something about her as a person. She sees herself as an 'avenging angel' type."

"What do you mean?" Jasika asked.

"Think about it. Her hits are mostly despicable people. And when she makes a mistake, she kills the person for guiding her down the wrong path—then apologizes to the police. It's almost like she sees herself as helping them. But that doesn't make killing Danielle Tebbutt make sense. She *was* the police. And from what I know about her, she was one of the straightest arrows I've met in policing."

"Any chance she could have changed or had a checkered past coming back to haunt her?" Frank asked.

"Frank, I know you need to ask, but I've known Danielle for years. She was a class act. Policing was her life. She would have found it dishonorable to get a speeding ticket. I can't imagine why she would be Daphne's target."

"What about a copycat?" Jasika questioned.

"Like I told Hays, I seriously can't see how. We never released information about the daphne petals left on the victims. And that fact never made it into any news reporting that I know of."

"I doubt it too," Frank said. "I had the last part of the document dump. A lot of the forensic information has matched with what we saw yesterday. And, as we all know, Interpol has not made her MO readily available beyond a handful of people directly involved in the investigations."

"In retrospect, I'm kind of shocked Pasquale was so willing to send us the file," Aaron said in agreement.

*So, where does that leave us?* Frank thought to himself. *Nowhere. We have a lot of information and nothing to go on. For all we know, Daphne has already left the country.* "Well, let's get back to the precinct and put what we know on the whiteboard. Maybe when we see it there, we'll notice some connection we're missing."

They put on their coats, got refills for the road and made their way back out into the cold. The walk back to the precinct was quiet, and the precinct was pretty subdued. Frank, along with Aaron and Jasika, set up shop in an open conference room and started mapping out what they had on the case. After a couple of hours, Frank looked at his watch and called it a day. "There's nothing else we can do right now. We have a ton of information but no motive, nothing linking Tebbutt to any of the previous murders and no idea what Daphne will do next—if anything."

"It's true," Jasika noted. "Hell, she could have been on the first plane back to France or Africa long before we identified Tebbutt."

"She had a good twenty-four-hour window where you guys had a Jane Doe," Aaron agreed. "If the different agencies weren't always so secretive with each other, maybe you could have identified Tebbutt faster. I wish I'd known she was getting in yesterday early for the conference and staying at the Sofitel. Perhaps I could have put two and two together somehow last night."

"Aaron, this isn't on you," Frank said putting his hand on Aaron's shoulder. Frank stared into Aaron's eyes to make sure the man was listening before he continued. "It's not on us. It's on this Daphne character. But like I said, we're spinning our wheels here. Let's regroup after we've had a night to decompress."

# Chapter Fourteen

Aaron and Frank made their way back to the condo. Bully was happy to see them. His little tail wagged back and forth, and he made little whining noises as Aaron got out of his jacket.

"I'm going to take Bully for a quick walk. It will be good for him and help me clear my mind," Frank said as he walked over to let him out of his crate and began to help the little guy into his harness, which was no easy feat since Bully was a jumble of excited wiggles.

"When you get back, we can he reheat the leftover Chinese from Saturday?"

"Sounds like a plan to me."

Aaron walked over and leaned into Frank, kissing him on the lips before Bully pulled Frank toward the door.

"I get it. I get it," Frank said, looking down at the dog. "No playtime for the adults until you're taken care of." Bully tilted his head sideways in an impatient look. "We'll be back in about fifteen minutes. As cold as it is outside, I'll be amazed if he makes it around the block."

Bully pulled Frank out of the condo. *That dog is a spoiled little guy. I can't imagine not having him around. He was the perfect addition to make this place a home for us.* Aaron sighed wistfully before heading into the bedroom.

He changed out of his work clothes and put on a pair of jogging shorts he liked to wear around the house, topping the outfit with an FBI sweatshirt that had seen better days. He also threw on his favorite slippers. Frank thought they were ugly as sin, but they were so comfortable. Frank had made Aaron agree to never wear them outside the apartment.

Aaron puttered around as he waited for Frank to get back from walking Bully. It wasn't too long before he heard the door open and the clear sound of paws scurrying across the marble floor in the kitchen.

After giving Bully a treat, Aaron and Frank sat down on the couch. Aaron let out a little sigh as he settled into Frank.

"What was that about?" Frank asked.

"Today was just a long, crazy day—from being sexually molested by my naked ex to losing a long-term colleague."

"Want to talk about it?"

"Which part?"

"Any of it."

"Not right now. I'm still processing. I want to say how sorry I am about Jonathan this morning. He never acted like that at all. I mean, he was always a bit selfish and into himself, but I don't know what happened... That's not the man I knew."

"Well, California will do that to a person, I hear."

"Don't blame an entire state for one asshole's behavior. We don't want the rest of the United States blaming New York for Donald Trump."

"That's former President Trump." Frank snickered. "And you're right. They shouldn't blame the whole state—just blame Queens."

"Asshole Trump has a better ring to it." Aaron laughed.

The two pulled the leftover Chinese food out of the oven and sat to have a nice, quiet evening together.

"Don't forget to set the alarm, so we can make it to the gym on time," Aaron reminded Frank from the bathroom.

"On it! Oh, and I got a text from Logan during intermission. He says Daryl Davenport was nice in *The Post*."

"Ben's show is really that bad?" Aaron asked, coming back into the bedroom.

"Apparently. Logan said he'd be surprised if the show lasts past the week. He overheard some guy in the box office talking about how bad ticket sales were."

"Well, I'm sure Ben will bounce back. He has that personality. He'll find a new project he can sink his teeth into."

"Actually, I had an idea," Frank hesitated. Aaron leaned his head out of the bathroom with a quizzical look on my face. "Now, don't say no until you listen first."

"Now, I'm both scared and intrigued."

"Well, you know how we lost April."

"Who?"

"April, the wedding planner?"

"You mean Amber."

"Okay, so we lost Amber. What if we asked Ben to do it?"

"Are you kidding me!?"

"Aaron, I wouldn't ask you to consider this if I didn't think it was actually a good idea. Don't roll your eyes at me just yet. Hear me out. Ben was a party planner for years before getting his big break. Besides, I don't even know if he'll do it, but this could be an outstanding arrangement, assuming his show goes bust and closes, which it looks like will happen in a matter of days. Planning our wedding would give Ben something to do, which would protect Logan's sanity. And you wouldn't have to worry about the wedding plans, which would protect my sanity. It's a win-win."

Aaron took a second to process Frank's idea before saying, "I'm not sure how I'm supposed to take that, future Mr. Massey."

"Well, future Mr. Schultt, you can take it any way that keeps you happy." Frank said the last part seductively as he pulled Aaron on top of him. Frank looked up into Aaron's eyes and ran his hand down the side of his face. He used his fingertip to trace around Aaron's lips. Aaron closed his eyes and parted his lips as Frank placed just the tip of his finger inside. Immediately, Aaron gently sucked on it. Frank slipped his hand under Aaron's sweatshirt, feeling his muscles before stopping at his pec to roll one of Aaron's nipples between his fingers. Aaron groaned as he continued to suck on Frank's finger, taking it deeper in his mouth. Aaron's weight pressed down on him as their aching arousals demanded immediate attention.

The ringtones on both of their iPhones went off almost simultaneously.

"Well, fuck!" Aaron said as he rolled off Frank and reached for his phone. "This can't be good."

Frank reached over to his side of the bed, grabbed the phone, held it in front of his face, his head still resting on his pillow and saw the call was from dispatch. "Detective Schultt."

"Detective Schultt, please hold."

Aaron answered his phone then walked out of the bedroom while raising his voice as he talked to his caller.

"Frank, this is Chief Hays."

"Chief, how can I help you this evening?" Frank asked, bolting up in bed. *Fuck! He never calls me at home.*

"I wanted you to hear it from me first. I'm betting your fiancé is getting a similar call."

"Really?"

"Yes. Now, stop interrupting."

*This can't be good.* "Go on, Chief. Sorry…"

"As I was saying," the chief started, letting out a gruff huff, "we have another body. I got off the phone with Dr. Ramos. She's convinced this victim is related to the French cop's case."

"Okay?" he responded, urging the chief to continue.

"You're going to have a lot of eyes on you now. Everything must be by the book."

"Always, sir."

"No information gets slipped to anyone beyond the team."

"Yes, sir." Frank wasn't sure where the chief was going with this conversation.

There was a pause on the other end of the line before the chief continued, "The victim is a high-profile target. Do you know Penelope Cristillo?"

Frank thought for a few seconds before saying, "The name sounds familiar, but I can't place it."

"She's the wife of the Director of the FBI, Donald Price."

# Chapter Fifteen

"*The* Donald Price? *Director* Donald Price? Aaron's *boss* Donald Price?" Frank spat out in rapid succession.

"Pull yourself together, Schultt, and keep your wits about you. But yes, the Director of the FBI's wife has been assassinated on American soil. Dr. Ramos thinks the method of murder was the same as the French police officer's yesterday," Chief Hays said into the phone.

"Well, fuck," Frank cursed under his breath. "Sorry, sir. I shouldn't have—"

"'Well, fuck', is right. You've found yourself at the center of another shitstorm."

Frank wanted to laugh because he'd never heard Chief Hays mutter a single cuss word in the many years he'd worked for him. Frank paused for a second and pulled himself together.

"Thanks for the heads-up, sir."

"You're welcome, Detective. Now get your ass to Lincoln Cent—"

The chief broke up for a second, and he could hear him talking to someone else in the room where he was. "Detective, turn on your television. It has already hit the air."

Frank said goodbye, hung up and grabbed the remote control for the bedroom television. Immediately, Jenny Mace's image was on the screen. "In breaking news, we have a new video from the murder that happened at Lincoln Center this evening. Warning, the following is not appropriate for all viewers."

The screen turned black. A tall, elegant woman in a black tulle gown with raven-black hair in an updo was standing on a podium discussing the importance of NYC's foster care system. She paused, took a drink from the water glass and continued. Suddenly, she wobbled behind the podium, knocking over her glass as she collapsed to the ground. An older, distinguished-looking man with white hair ran to her aid. In the last shot before the screen went to black, the man turned his head, yelling for help. The turned head was just enough to clearly see Director Donald Price's face as the image paused and zoomed in on the man.

Frank sat transfixed, and he barely noticed Aaron come back into the room, watching from the doorway.

Jenny Mace appeared on the screen looking somber. "Yes, viewers, if you recognized the gentleman in the video, that was the Director of the FBI, Donald Price, who ran to the aid of the fallen woman. We can also confirm the woman who died was his wife, Penelope Cristillo, heiress to the medical equipment manufacturing empire built by her late father, Juan Cristillo."

The screen immediately started playing a short biopic about the Cristillo family. It then focused on the charity work of Penelope Cristillo after her father had passed. Frank learned Cristillo's passion for the foster care system was because her father had been a foster kid before making his millions. It was a true immigrant rags-to-riches American story.

After the piece ended, Mace said that the weather was after the next commercial. Frank turned off the television and looked at Aaron.

"Did you know her?" Frank asked.

"I'd met her once or twice. Did you know her?" Aaron replied.

"What do you mean? She was married to your boss."

"Yes, but apparently her father had a close working relationship with your father."

"What?" Frank responded, utterly taken aback.

"You didn't know?"

"Know what?" Frank responded, still very confused.

"Your parents and the Cristillos run in the same circles."

# Chapter Sixteen

Aaron and Frank had their clothes back on within the next ten minutes and were out of the door. "Should we hail a cab?" Aaron questioned.

"Nah, we're, what...seven blocks from Lincoln Center. We can probably make it there in under fifteen with no problems at this time of night — probably faster than finding a cab," Frank replied. The two set off heading north on Columbus Avenue. When they were about three blocks away, Frank could see the familiar flashing of red and blue lights against the dark night sky.

At the barrier tape, Frank caught the attention of the officer-in-charge of the scene. "Detective Frank Schultt and Supervisory Special Agent Aaron Massey," he said. "You should be expecting us."

"Yes, Detective Schultt and Special Agent Massey. Dispatch radioed to be on the lookout for you."

"How bad is it in there?" Frank asked.

"It's not pretty. Half of the super-elite of the city were at this charity gala tonight. I'm sure glad it's not one of my guys who caught this case."

"Thanks for that."

"Hey, just being honest here," the officer responded in his thick Brooklyn accent. "It's a veritable who's who in there. The mayor and her husband, the commissioner and his wife, etc...."

"Fuck!"

"Yep. Now you know why I'm glad it's not one of my guys who caught this case. It's a veritable clusterfuck of suits and ties."

"Well, thanks for at least getting the scene cordoned off."

"Least me and my boys could do for you, Detective. Take care of yourself. I'm glad I'm not the one stepping into the vipers' den."

After ducking under the tape, Frank and Aaron walked through Josey Robertson Plaza, heading toward David Geffen Hall, the home of the New York Philharmonic. *Glad the Fountains aren't on right now. This place would be a skating rink.* As they got closer to David Geffen Hall, Frank could see lights on the atrium and many guests milling around inside. Patrol officers were blocking the exits. *We need to make sure everyone's name is taken, then free these people quickly. We don't want people hanging around the crime scene for too long.*

Frank and Aaron walked up the steps. He let Aaron take the lead this time, giving him a brief nod in his direction, "I'm Supervisory Special Agent Aaron Massey, and this is Detective Frank Schultt."

"Thank God. The crowd is getting rowdy in there," the young female officer responded, her breath coming out of her mouth in smoky turrets.

"How so?" Aaron asked.

"Let's just say that I'm glad I'm out here preventing people from entering, and not in there stopping people from leaving. We've had a couple of officers who have already been pulled out because things started running a bit hot. Nothing physical, mind you, but definitely a shit-ton of cussing."

"Not surprised," Frank acknowledged. "You can't have that many mukity-mucks in one place without at least one of them threatening to call in their lawyers."

"If only it were just one. See that group over there?" the officer asked, pointing off toward the sidewalk between the subway line and the steps into the Jose Robertson Plaza. "That's where the bottom-feeders are being kept at bay."

"Who did an officer have to piss off to get stuck with that duty?" Frank joked.

"Thank God, not me," she said, shaking her head. "Anyway, have a good night, Detective. Good luck." She opened the door and let them into the hall.

Frank immediately heard his name being called from somewhere within the glass foyer of the building. He swiveled his head and watched Richardson making his way toward him. "Follow me, gents. The body's this way." Aaron and Frank fell into step behind Richardson as he led them through the lobby.

"Where was the group meeting?" Aaron asked as they walked.

"They were in the Lincoln Center Kitchen. The hall itself doesn't have banquet facilities."

Richardson led them around a group of guests who were still carrying their wine glasses. As they approached the restaurant, Frank saw the door was propped open with a uniformed officer standing outside. As they approached, the officer took them in before recognizing Richardson then opened the door for them.

"About time you boys graced us with your presence," a voice came from somewhere within the room.

"Mariella, where are you?" Frank asked.

"Let Richardson guide you by the hand. He'll get you here."

Frank jokingly extended his hand to Richardson, who shook his head with a clear *yeah, I don't think so* at Frank.

"Sorry, Mariella. Aaron would get jealous," Frank responded as Richardson led them through the restaurant to where the meeting had been set up.

"What are we looking at here?" Aaron asked as they approached.

"Well, the decedent was at the podium when she collapsed." Mariella stood as she was speaking and walked them through pretty much exactly what they'd seen on the video. "At least, that's what the eyewitnesses told us."

"You don't know yet—" Frank said.

"Know what?"

"Jenny Mace already released a video of the murder."

"How the fuck did I not know that?" Mariella questioned, looking at Richardson.

"Don't look at me. It's the first I'm hearing about it."

Frank looked between Richardson and Mariella, seeing their tempers rise because they had not been informed about such a critical piece of information. "Sorry to break that one to you. I'm sure it's already on their website," Frank said, pulling out his cell phone and asking it to search for it. Once he found it on YouTube, he handed it over to Mariella, who watched intently, pausing periodically and double-checking her own notes as she walked back through the scene. After a couple of minutes, she was ready to start their conversation again.

"Okay, boys. Thankfully, that changes nothing about what I knew."

"Well, that's good," Aaron replied.

"With one major exception." She rewound the video and watched it again. A puzzled look crossed her face.

"What's wrong?" Frank asked.

"Where's the water glass?"

"The what?" Frank asked.

"The water glass." She held the phone to Frank and replayed the section where the victim had taken a drink before her collapse. "The water glass... It's not here."

"Well, that's definitely a problem," Aaron said.

"Do you think it was picked up by a staff member or someone who tried performing first aid?" Frank explained. "We know the director was here, so I'm betting his detail was with him. I seriously can't imagine no one tried to render first aid. Maybe they picked it up and placed it somewhere out of the way?"

"Frank, you think a bunch of elite members of the Goon Squad—no offense, Aaron—are going to accidentally handle a piece of evidence right after their director's wife died?"

"Yeah, it's definitely unlikely. That means between when Cristillo died and now, someone either picked up the glass and placed it somewhere accidentally or someone purposefully took it. And since there was a perimeter around the body when I got here, I seriously doubt anyone took the glass by accident."

Frank glanced at Aaron, who seemed to be pondering the information. "Either a member of the director's body team was part of this, or someone slipped it out of here right under their noses without being seen," Aaron replied. "In either case, that's not good."

"Richardson, any chance this place has internal videos?" Frank asked.

"Nasab is already looking at them, but they aren't designed for internal security within the restaurant. There are a few cameras in the building. Okay, a lot of cameras in the building, but most of them aren't focused here. They're focused in the hall."

"Any chance everyone gets funneled through the hall at some point?"

"Sorry, Frank. The restaurant has its own entry and exit points for the staff. It's entirely possible to get in and get out of here without ever being on a clear camera."

"Couldn't be easy, could it?" Mariella said with a sigh as she handed Frank back his phone.

"Never is," Richardson agreed. "But anyway, Nasab is checking the footage just in case. He's getting recordings for the past couple of days. We'll have someone comb through them, but I seriously doubt anything will pop. We'll let you know if it does."

"So, Mariella, why did you think this case is related to ours?" Frank said.

"At first, I wouldn't have even considered it. Let's face it. We have no way of knowing if this was murder. However, the foaming at the mouth is very reminiscent of what we saw Saturday. I can't be completely sure it's the same combination, but I took a sample of the foam, so we'll know for sure once we run toxicology. *But*, I'm also seeing the same subconjunctival bleeding in the eyes. It's definitely different from I would expect to see on a normal corpse. The blood vessels also drained and pooled in the eye, which isn't normal." Mariella paused for a second then turned to Aaron. "I hear you knew the victim. I'm so sorry for your loss."

"Thanks," Aaron said. "It's definitely a huge shock for a lot of people, myself included. As for the eyes, can you show me what you're talking about? I didn't see the original autopsy."

Mariella leaned over the body, took out her pocket light and a large magnifying glass to make looking into the eye easier. She then pulled back the eyelids on the body, shining the light into the victim's eyes. "See the larger red splotches there? You can see where the blood is pooling. Again, this isn't something I normally see. I've seen it with a couple of infections over the years, but never with something like this. Between the foaming at the mouth and the subconjunctival bleeding, I'm pretty confident we're looking at the same method of murder."

Frank thanked her for the information and told her that once she was ready to transport the body, she was good to do so. He asked her to email him the autopsy results if anything unexpected appeared. He didn't think he and Jasika needed to attend the procedure if it was the same poison. Before she left, Frank asked Mariella one last question. "What about a puncture mark? On Saturday, the toxin was delivered with a puncture mark."

"Didn't find one yet," she responded. "Again, she's not on my table. And I didn't find the puncture mark until much later on the other corpse, so it's possible I haven't seen it yet."

"It's also possible there isn't one," Jasika said, arriving. "Sorry for being so late. Had to catch a ride into the city from Queens."

"Anytime we have to go out to the NYPD Forensics Laboratory for something, it always takes forever," Richardson replied.

"And, Frank," Jasika said, "the police commissioner would like to speak with you when you get a moment."

"Thanks, Jasika. How's he looking?"

"He doesn't look pissed off — if that's what you're asking."

"Yeah, that's pretty much what I wanted to know. But before I go speak to him, you were saying something about there not being a puncture wound."

"Yes, one thing we know from the report we read is Daphne has used a variety of delivery methods over the years," Jasika noted. "She has used hypodermic injection, food-drink poisoning and she even once aerosolized it. There are probably a half-dozen techniques she has used, so it's entirely possible she didn't leave a puncture wound."

"Damn!" Mariella said under her breath. "I'll give three points to Slytherin for potions making. Well, boys, I could lie and say it's been fun... But it's time for this lovely young woman and me" — gesturing toward the victim as she removed her latex gloves — "to head to my lab. I'm sure I'll be talking to you soon." She spun on her heels and motioned for a couple of techs to come help her load the body into the OCME truck that was waiting outside the building somewhere. Mariella oversaw the techs as they placed the victim in a body bag, strapped her to the gurney and wheeled her away.

With the body removed, Frank, Jasika and Aaron headed toward the front door of the restaurant. "Okay,

I'll talk to the commissioner. Jasika, talk to the first officer on the scene. And Aaron, see if you can find Director Price, and do what you need to do there." Aaron nodded his head, understanding what Frank was asking. Frank opened the door, and the three fanned out to perform their respective tasks. Before any of them had made it more than a few steps, the NYPD Commissioner and Chief Barling walked up. Frank motioned with his hand for Jasika to go, that he'd handle this. Before Frank could say anything, Barling pulled Aaron away saying, "Agent Massey, may I have a word?" Barling made it sound like a request when it was clearly anything but.

"Detective Schultt."

"Commissioner Diaz," Frank said, focusing his attention on the man wearing a black tuxedo standing in front of him.

"Let me make this brief, Detective. Your chief will run point, but if you need anything — any resources your precinct doesn't have — come directly to me. I want this solved quickly."

"I understand, Commissioner."

Commissioner Diaz turned to leave before stopping and pivoting back one more time. "And, Detective, don't let your *relationship* with Agent Massey be a problem. I know the FBI likes him, but I don't like it when the feds poke their noses into the NYPD's business. You make sure the collar stays in-house."

"I understand," Frank said, slowly nodding his head. *Fuck, a jurisdictional pissing match, and I'm stuck in the middle.* When the commissioner was out of earshot, he took a deep breath and let it out before heading off to find Jasika.

# Chapter Seventeen

Barling led Aaron by the elbow to a secluded nook in the atrium. She had a look of determination, and Aaron suspected he wouldn't like where this conversation was headed.

"Agent Massey... Well, I guess we can barely call you that now."

"Sir."

"Don't *sir* me. You know as well as I do that you're being kept around by the Bureau for publicity only. It's not like you can do any genuine work outside of consulting at this point. Between your teaching job and being an *author*" — she said the word like it was some kind of detestable disease — "I'm surprised we bother giving you a paycheck."

"That's so not fair. It's not like they gave me much of a choice in the matter after how high-profile The Twelve-Day Killer case was."

"I'm not saying I blame you...completely. But let's just say, if I had my way about this, you wouldn't be working for me at all. Hell, if I could pull you off this case, I would." Aaron started to say something, but Barling raised her hand and continued, "I was going to tell you this first thing in the morning, but things have...escalated. I'm stuck with you. The director still has faith in you, even if I don't."

"With all due respect, this is pretty unfair."

"I don't care. You stepped right into the middle of probably the highest-profile case in the US right now."

"Trust me, I know. I would argue it's not just a high-profile case in the US. It's going to be all over Africa and Europe in the next few hours."

"What do you mean?"

Aaron told Barling about everything that had transpired since their phone call earlier that afternoon. He didn't explain how he had gotten ahold of the Daphne dossier, and Barling didn't ask. "Of course, all this is in the report we planned on finishing before our meeting in the morning."

"For fuck's sake. I had a vague idea of who this Daphne character was from discussions at an international policing symposia I've attended, but I had no idea how dangerous this woman is. Are we sure it's a woman?"

"I would say we're ninety-five percent sure it's a woman. Let's face it. No one's ever survived meeting her, so we can never be completely sure."

"How did she get into the US?"

"We still don't know. We hit a bit of a brick wall with DHS. We're hoping they'll force the TSA to be more compliant tomorrow."

"Trust me, they'll be more compliant. If they don't play ball, we'll force their hand in the morning." Barling gave Aaron another once over before saying, "It's time to talk to the director."

\* \* \* \*

Frank wormed his way in and out of partygoers who were now being interviewed by several detectives he recognized. The Chief of Detectives had apparently called in reinforcement to help with this case. *I'm sure she's around here somewhere. Seems like everyone with a title is walking around this clusterfuck.* Just as soon as he thought it, Chief of Detectives Amanda Gleason stood in his way, wearing a cocktail dress.

"Detective," she said.

"Chief Gleason. How can I be of service?"

"I'm sure you've already talked to your own chief and the commissioner already," she guessed as Frank nodded. "I'll tell you the same thing they told you. Solve this, solve it fast and, if you need anything, reach out. And I mean anything. I can already tell this one stinks more than New Jersey in the summer. There are already a lot of moving pieces."

"That there are, sir. That there are."

"I received a cryptic email from someone at Interpol about getting information to me tomorrow. What's that about?"

Frank read in the Chief of Detectives about everything that had happened, including the less formal document they had received that afternoon. "I'm betting you'll be officially getting that document tomorrow, sir."

"I'll forward it to you as soon as I get it, just in case it's not the identical dossier Agent Massey's contact sent you earlier."

"Thanks, sir."

"And, Detective…Frank, tell me immediately if you run into any problems working with Agent Massey."

"Sir?"

"Frank, working with one's partner can be difficult in the best of times. And we don't exactly work under the best of circumstances. I understand why the FBI wants him on this case. He has a unique set of attributes that makes him valuable for this. I'm worried about this case, obviously. But it's also my job to worry about the mental health of *my* detectives," she noted, looking him straight in the eyes.

"Understood, sir. If I ever suspect the case or my relationship are not at one-hundred percent, I'll come in for a chat—off the record."

"Perfect! Now, about how much longer do you think you'll need everyone here? I want to go home, myself. These fucking heels are killing me."

Frank and Chief Detective Gleason had a long relationship history. They had gone through the academy together. He'd known her before she'd even come out. Hell, he knew her when she was still married to a guy. The two had even been partners for a brief stint years ago before she had been tapped to take on more senior-level leadership duties.

"Where's your wife?" Frank asked.

"Samantha's around here somewhere. Last I saw her, she was huddled with the police commissioner's wife, trying to come up with their own theories about who killed poor Penelope."

"So, you knew the victim?" Frank questioned cautiously.

"Socially. Samantha knew her better than I did. I think they met through a few of the police auxiliary groups."

"Anything I should know about the victim?"

"Honestly, I couldn't tell you much. There are many more people in here who knew her better than I did. Heck, I'm sure your mother knows her better than I do, and she's around here somewhere," she said before her eyes grew, realizing what she'd just said.

"My *mother* is here?" Frank questioned.

"Fuck!" Chief Gleason said. "Sorry, Frank. Maybe I should have led with that one. But yeah, she's around here somewhere. A small contingent from Schultt Pharmaceuticals was attending the benefit." Amanda knew all about Frank's relationship — or the lack thereof — with his parents.

*I'm kind of amazed my mom is friends with someone who hangs out with a known lesbian. The shock. What would her society friends say? But then, I'm guessing everyone in my mom's social circle knows that I'm gay by this point.*

Frank let out another sigh. "Well, fingers crossed that we don't accidentally run into each other. She's the last person I want to handle tonight."

"Sorry, Frank. Really, I am sorry."

"Well, Chief, time for me to get back to work."

\* \* \* \*

Barling and Aaron walked to another corner where Director Price was sitting with Mayor Olivia Rhinehart and her husband. Barling walked right up to the table, but Aaron hesitated before joining. Aaron stood back watching, not wanting to intrude on a highly intimate moment by barging into the conversation.

"Director Price, I'm sure you've met Supervisory Special Agent Dr. Aaron Massey in the past," Barling announced.

"Agent Massey — or should I call you Dr. Massey?" Price questioned.

"Please, sir, just call me Aaron."

"Fine, fine," Price said, nodding.

*He clearly hasn't processed everything. He looks like he's keeping it together, but there's something about how he's holding himself. He's still very much in denial. I need to tread carefully.*

"Director Price, first, let me offer my condolences for your loss. I know words cannot represent what this means to you but know that myself and the Bureau will do everything in our power to catch this Daphne and bring her to justice."

"Damn right you will. And I don't need platitudes. Despite what you may think, Agent, I don't need to be handled like a grieving victim," Price growled. "I want this dog found and put down."

"I'm with you, Don," Mayor Olivia Rhinehart said. "This murder is an affront to the US and a war on democracy. She should be treated like an enemy combatant."

Aaron stood there for a second, not sure what to say. Thankfully, Barling saved him. "I can promise you that Agent Massey will have every tool at the FBI's disposal. No rock will go unturned. We will bring this assassin to justice."

"Good, good," Price said, shaking his head. "What do you need, Agent Massey?"

"Director, we can definitely use a bit more staff to help sift through the evidence as it comes in."

"I'll have O'Donnell work on ops at the Bureau," Barling said, referring to her trusted assistant.

"O'Donnell would be a significant addition to the team, but I think we're still going to run ops out of the precinct."

"Why?" Barling responded.

"Because that's where the case originated. Also, their conference room is state-of-the-art now, so there's nothing they don't have tech-wise that we could get at the FBI."

"It's only *tech-wise* because you gave it to them," Barling said as she narrowed her eyes.

"I helped, but it was mostly my publisher. They wanted to thank the precinct for the unfettered access I had during the investigation and while writing the book," Aaron said, a bit more defensively than he'd intended.

"What else do you need?" Price asked.

"I could use a dedicated tech person. Is Julian Rummy available?" Aaron had worked with Rummy on many cases and trusted his tech skills.

"Agent Rummy is currently on assignment in Austin," Barling notified her boss.

"I don't care where he is," Price chastised. "He'll be back tomorrow morning," making it clear the issue was not up for discussion. "As for keeping the investigation in the NYPD, we can keep the face of the investigation there." Price shot Barling a look that clearly said that part of the conversation was over. Aaron watched as Price then refocused his attention on him, "But, and this is a pretty fucking big *but*, if you need anything—and I mean anything—skip the bureaucracy at the NYPD and come directly to me."

"You mean *us*, sir?" Barling questioned.

"I. Mean. *Me*," Price said, his face a blank slate of emotion as he stared Barling down. "Agent Massey," he said again, looking Aaron square in the eyes, "I expect you to keep me informed about the investigation, but also make sure Barling gets copied on everything."

"Understood, sir."

Price looked away and took a drink of the water sitting before him. Aaron realized the conversation was over, so he didn't wait to be dismissed. He nodded his head at everyone without saying a word and left. *Guess I need to go find the others.* Aaron walked through the crowd and finally spotted Jasika.

He caught her attention and motioned for her to join him over to an empty piece of glass that functioned as an outside wall.

"How did your conversations go?" Aaron inquired, and Jasika took a moment to fill him in.

"So, what did we find out?" Frank asked, approaching Aaron and Jasika.

"Well, Aaron found out his boss hates your boss."

"Which boss?" Frank asked.

"Well, Barling and your commissioner somehow go way back. Let's say there's no love lost there."

"I was wondering what was going on. Something definitely seemed off to me, too," Franked noted. "I also ran into the Chief Detective."

"She's here? I didn't see her interviewing anyone," Jasika said, swerving her head around to see if she could spot her.

"She's not working. Well, allegedly not working. She was here for the fundraiser with her wife."

"Oh?" Jasika questioned, seemingly not sure what to say.

"Oh, it gets better. Her wife was friends with the victim…and my mother."

"Your *mother*?" Aaron and Jasika gasped at the same time.

"Apparently, mommy dearest is somewhere in this building."

"Whoa," Aaron said, his eyes wide, looking into Frank's face.

Frank could tell Aaron was trying to find some sign of emotion on his face, but he wasn't ready to have the conversation with him.

"Holy fuck!" Jasika let out.

"Honey, are you okay?" Aaron finally asked.

"Aaron, I haven't been near that woman in almost two decades. This isn't the time for a family reunion. I have enough on my plate without opening old wounds that have been closed for a long time."

"We're going to talk about this later," Aaron said flatly. "But I agree. Personal shit must take a back seat right now." Frank nodded in agreement before Aaron continued. "Basically, my marching orders were simple. Solve the case, and solve it fast. I was also told if I needed anything, I should bypass the NYPD and get it directly from the director."

Frank let out a little laugh. "That's rich. The commissioner said the same damn thing to me about bypassing my own chief and the FBI." Frank let out a huff before finishing his thought. "We've dropped ourselves into a heavy-hitter pissing match this time."

Aaron, Jasika and Frank continued their conversation for a couple of more minutes before deciding they didn't need to talk to anyone specifically tonight, as long as the other detectives took statements. Within fifteen minutes, the place was empty. Frank had managed the whole evening without running into his mother. He thought he had seen her at one point, but a junior detective from somewhere Uptown had needed something from Frank, which had diverted his attention. When he'd looked back, the face in the crowd was gone.

By a little after three in the morning, Aaron and Frank were ready to head back to their condo. Jasika called one of her friends who lived in the city and asked if she could crash there instead of heading back to Queens.

"Jasika, you know you can always stay with us. We have a bed in the home office. Any time you need to use it, just let us know."

"Thanks, I'll keep that in mind. I already texted my mother and let her know I'm staying in the city tonight. I'm so glad she helps me with Ginny. I don't know how I would get through all this without her support. I'll see you around nine-thirty?"

"Hmm… Make it ten," Frank replied. "We've had a long night. And I suspect we have a few more long days ahead of us."

# Chapter Eighteen

At eight-thirty the next morning, Aaron and Frank dragged themselves out of bed. Aaron jumped in the shower first while Frank checked his phone for any messages. The first one he read was from Logan.

*Frank, saw your text this morning. Ben says hello and missed ya guys at the gym. Call me later.*

Frank shot off a quick response.

*Yeah, long night at Lincoln Center. Just getting up.*

Frank thought about what else he should tell Logan about what had happened the night before. He gave the crib notes version.

*So, long story short. This whole situation is a political clusterfuck. Oh, and apparently, my mother was friends with the victim. Didn't run into her last night, but I heard she was there.*

Frank let out a sigh and set about reading his email messages. Well, it was less about reading his email messages than triaging the important ones and deleting any that he didn't want to deal with right then. One email was a link to the typed witness statements from the night before.

*Wow, those detectives put in some overtime last night getting these back to me. I guess we'll divvy up the transcripts when we get into the precinct and see if anything stands out. I doubt it, but it's worth a look.*

Frank continued to scroll through his emails, but nothing stood out as immediately important.

"Honey, I'm out of the shower."

"Thanks," Frank responded before putting his phone down.

"Anything new I should know?"

"Nope. Just a bunch of information for us to sift through once we're in the office."

"Well, get cracking. I have a suspicion we have a long day ahead of us."

With Frank in the shower, Aaron picked up his cell to see if there was anything he needed to deal with. *Spam, spam, spam,* he thought as he bulk deleted a bunch of emails. He glanced over the official file from Interpol that had been forwarded from Barling. He checked the PDF to see if there was anything different from the one Pasquale had sent him the day before. *Nope, same information. Same number of pages.* He forwarded the email to Frank and Jasika, just to have the official copy. He then sent it to O'Donnell and Rummy to read them in.

Once he was sure there were no emails that needed his immediate attention, he switched to his text messages to see if there was anything there. The first message was from Jonathan Fetty.

*It was good running into you yesterday. Let me know when you can get together for coffee.*

Aaron pondered what he wanted to answer but decided to not respond for the time being. He also wondered how Jon had his cell phone number. The second text message was from Rummy.

*Not sure what strings you pulled, but I was on a flight from Austin that left at six a.m. local time — seven a.m. where you are. I should land at LaGuardia at ten, so I will roll into the precinct by eleven, depending on how bad the traffic is.*

Aaron looked at his watch. *Nine a.m., so he's definitely mid-flight, but I might as well respond.*

*Thanks. We're planning on getting there around ten ourselves — late night here — so we'll see you when you get there.*

*Hey, thanks for the heads up.*

*You can text in the sky?*

*In-cabin Wi-Fi, baby! Can't imagine flying without it these days.*

*The joys of modern travel. Anyway, I sent you a file. Did you get it?*

*Yep, I was glancing through it while I was sitting here. Anything specific I should look for?*

*We read through it yesterday, so just familiarize yourself. We'll talk when you get here. Always good to get another pair of eyes on it.*

*Will do! See you in a couple of hours. I'll probably run it through a few algorithms to see if some data crunching makes anything stand out.*

*Perfect!*

With the emails and texts checked, Aaron threw on a suit he had hanging in the closet. He was getting his tie on when Frank stepped out of the bathroom. *Damn! He's gorgeous when he's freshly clean and butt-ass naked.*

"Anything I need to know?"

"Nah, was checking my emails and texts. Rummy should be at the precinct by eleven. Also, we got the official Interpol report on Daphne."

"Anything not in the one we read yesterday?"

"Nope, it's the same document as far as I can tell. I forwarded it to you, Jasika, O'Donnell and Rummy, just to keep everyone in the loop officially."

Aaron watched Frank walk over to his dresser and fish around for a pair of underwear before deciding on a pair of boxer briefs. He then pulled out a button-down shirt and a pair of dress slacks from the closet before getting dressed.

"What do you want for breakfast?"

"Uhh, hadn't even gotten that far," Frank muttered. "I guess a protein shake and coffee."

"On it!" Aaron walked out into the living room, grabbed a shake from the fridge, walked back to the bedroom and tossed it to Frank. "Hey, I'm going to take Bully out real fast."

"Okay. I should be ready to go by the time you get back."

Aaron grabbed Bully's harness and the pup's tail wagged with excitement. "Come on, little man. Work with me here. I can't get the harness on you when you're constantly wiggling." Aaron finally got it on Bully and headed outside.

At ten a.m., the building was pretty quiet, so he didn't run into anyone on the way down. When Aaron got to the lobby, he noticed a few snowflakes in the air on the other side of the glass wall that fronted the building. *Winter in New York*. The dog looked at the snow and tried to sit in the lobby. "Come on, Bully. You've got to go potty," Aaron cajoled while tugging lightly on Bully's leash. Finally, the pup stood and gave Aaron a look of displeasure, but he let Aaron take him outside.

Bully wasted no time going to the bathroom at his usual spot. Aaron pulled the poop bag from his pocket and cleaned up after his dog as soon as he was done. Bully decided being outside was no fun and started pulling Aaron back toward their building. Thankfully, they were in a bit of a rush, so it was nice that Bully didn't feel the need to smell everything along the way. When Aaron entered their condo, Frank was in the kitchen, finishing his shake.

"Hey, you two are back fast."

"Yeah, it's snowing outside. Not much, but enough that Bully had no desire to waste any time this morning."

Frank looked at the bulldog, who cocked his head to the side. Frank squatted and helped Bully out of the harness, and he immediately flipped onto his back so

Frank could give him a quick belly rub. "So, you ready to go?" Frank asked, looking at Aaron.

"Yep," Aaron replied. "Just need to grab my bag."

"I'll get Bully into his crate."

Aaron nodded, went back into his office and grabbed his leather attaché case. "Okay, ready?" The two slipped into their coats, and Aaron slung his bag over one of his shoulders and around his neck. "Let's do this."

# Chapter Nineteen

After a quick stop at Viva La Coffee, where they had opted for a box of coffee, five cups and all the sugar packets and cream that the team could use, Aaron and Frank made their way to the precinct. By the time they arrived there, the snow had become steadier. It was hardly a blizzard but enough to make things a bit wet, since nothing stuck to the ground.

Once in the bullpen, Aaron put his attaché case on Frank's desk and noticed the conference room light was on. Frank sat at his desk to read a few more emails, so Aaron took a moment to see what was happening in the conference room. He opened the door and found O'Donnell and Jasika already plugging information into the electronic whiteboard.

"Look who the cat dragged in," O'Donnell said.

"Good morning, Caroline. When did you get here?"

"I was here at nine."

"I'm so sorry. I didn't even think to text you. We were going to start late this morning because of the late night."

"Not a problem, Aaron. It gave me a chance to get set up and start reading over the case materials. Oh, and thanks for the email this morning. This Daphne character is definitely a slippery one, isn't she?"

"That's the understatement of the year," Aaron sighed. "Anyway, I'm glad you could join us."

"I'm glad to get away from the Princess of Power for a few days," Caroline joked.

"Oh my God, I totally forgot that's what you call Barling," Aaron laughed. "It totally fits, though."

"Yep! So, where are we?"

Caroline, Jasika and Aaron hashed out what they'd learned so far. Once Frank got to the room, the team plugged in as much information as they had into the whiteboard. They had just finished getting the basics entered when there was a quick knock on the door and Rummy came strolling in, his rolling bag in tow.

"Made it," Rummy chirped. "Wasn't too sure once we got to the city. You never know what to expect when it snows. Thankfully, the FBI had a car waiting for me and everything. Talk about a first-class act. So, what have I missed?"

"Not much," Aaron replied. "We've been inputting as much information in the whiteboard as possible."

"Great! Saves me the time on data entry."

Over the next hour, the team had discussed the case and pieced together all the information they had. Rummy sat in the corner and tried to find any links between Danielle Tebbutt and Penelope Cristillo. He'd also run a text analysis program against all the witness statements to see if anything jumped out.

Caroline had begun making phone calls to coordinate information between Interpol, DHS, the FBI and the NYPD. Thankfully, Director Price was true to his word, and everyone had seemed much more cooperative this morning. Once she had the full flight manifests, Caroline had combed through the lists.

By early afternoon, the group had more information but not any more leads. "Okay. It's one. Let's see where everyone is," Aaron said. "Jasika, what have you found out?

"Well, we know Daphne has a history of taking out African warlords. I checked in with a contact at the United Nations to see if anything was going on there we should know about. As far as they know, no one fitting Daphne's usual target profile is in the city. Admittedly, it's not like a lot of warlords advertise when they get here."

"Caroline?" Aaron asked.

"So, we finally have full inter-agency cooperation, which has been very helpful. I have a contact at DHS who is coordinating passenger manifests with customs to see if anyone could fit the bill. We're looking for similarities between Daphne, the image from the Sofitel and what we got from Interpol. Hopefully, we'll get something, but only time will tell."

"Rummy?" Aaron said, turning to look at the man hunched over his computer in the corner of the room.

"So, my basic text analysis of witness statements showed nothing unusual. Mostly no one saw anything out of the ordinary before Cristillo started her presentation. I also checked the restaurant employees' witness statements, and they didn't have anyone new working last night. All employees working at the time were long-term employees. And none of them have left the US in the past few years, so I seriously doubt it's someone who worked for the restaurant."

"What about the guest list for the benefit?" Aaron questioned.

"Still running through that, but it's a who's who of people in the city," Jasika said. "As you already know, the guest list included major politicians, actors, models and other deep-pocketed donors. From what I can tell, everyone was accounted for, and no one was there who wasn't on the list. However, many corporations sponsored tables at the benefit and not everyone who sat at one of the tables was on the original guest list. I'm cross-listing the witness statements with the guest list right now."

"Frank?" Aaron asked, looking at his fiancé.

"Nothing much on my end. Been running down some leads from yesterday, but everything is a dead end."

"Well, this isn't getting us—" A sudden knock at the door broke his attention.

Jasika got up from her chair and opened the door. A patrolman stood there with a gigantic flower bouquet.

"These were delivered for Agent Massey." The officer looked at Aaron. "Why are you getting flowers here?"

"Beats me." The officer handed the bouquet to Jasika, who closed the door with her foot.

"What the hell?" Aaron cursed. He stared at the large vase, then he noticed something. Among the flowers was one he recognized—a daphne.

# Chapter Twenty

Aaron jumped out of his chair and sprinted out of the conference room. Running out of the bullpen, he stopped at the front desk and asked the desk sergeant, "Did you see who delivered those flowers?"

"Yeah, it was from the flower shop around the corner. I get stuff for my wife there all the time."

Without saying a word, Aaron bolted out of the precinct. He had just made it outside when Frank caught up to him. He grabbed Aaron's arm before asking, "What's going on? Stop for a second. Talk to me."

"The flowers. The bouquet has daphne flowers in it."

"You could tell that?"

"Trust me. We spent a lot of time looking at those flowers when I was an FBI legal attaché working with Interpol in Lyon. Heck, at one point, I could even tell you the specific genus of the flowers."

"Okay, so where are you going?"

"The desk sergeant said the order came from the flower shop around the corner."

"You don't think she's there?"

"No, but maybe the store owner can remember something about the order. I'm betting she doesn't get calls for daphne every day."

"Want me to come?"

"Nah, go back and tell the others what's going on. Sorry about the abruptness. I was taken aback and hoping the delivery guy was still somewhere close. Didn't even think the florist would right be around the corner. I'll go there and be back soon."

With Frank now caught up, Aaron turned on his heels and started toward the corner. When Aaron reached it, he realized he had no idea what direction he was heading in. He looked to the left and to the right. He saw a green bin in front of a storefront with bouquets of fresh flowers. *Might as well go there.* Aaron walked over and opened the door. A small bell above the doorway chimed as he walked into the florist.

"Aaron Massey, if I live and breathe. Twice in two days."

Aaron didn't even need to look to recognize that voice. "Jon, what are you doing here?"

"What am *I* doing here? If I didn't know better, I'd say you were stalking me," Fetty replied.

*You wish, buddy. You wish.* "That's not exactly an answer, though. Is it?"

"You always were good with the cat-and-mouse routine."

"Yes, but I never quite knew who was the cat and who was the mouse."

Jon raised his eyebrows in a mock 'who, me?' impression, like something out of an awful movie from the nineteen-forties. Aaron stood there with his arms crossed, staring Jon down, waiting for an actual response.

Jon sighed. "If you must know," he said, rolling his eyes, "I am ordering an arrangement for one of my authors who sold a multi-million-dollar deal. We're all excited. And that's just the book deal. Wait till I see what I can get for the movie rights. And you, what are you doing here?"

"Official FBI business."

"The FBI has a flower division now? Yas, Kween!" Now it was Aaron's turn to roll his eyes. "Oh, come on. Don't be such a stick-in-the-mud. You're wound tighter than girdle on a three-hundred-pound drag queen."

Aaron stared at Fetty. He looked the same, but this was most definitely not the man he had at one point dated and thought that he'd loved.

"But really, what are you doing here, Aaron? Buying flowers for that hot fiancé of yours?"

"I'm here on official FBI business," Aaron said again, which was followed by an awkward silence.

A voice from the front of the shop cut through the invisible tension, "Mr. Fetty, your basket is ready."

"I guess that's my cue to skedaddle." Fetty turned and walked toward the front of the store. Aaron followed because that's the direction he needed to head. *Did he just say 'skedaddle'?* At the front of the store, Fetty pulled out his card and paid for a giant basket of flowers and other goodies. It had a blown-up 'congratulations' balloon right in the middle of everything. "It's perfect. She's going to love it. Thanks, doll. You've been a real gem."

Aaron watched him, realizing what had changed about Jon was that he seemed more like a plastic Ken doll than an actual human. Everything about him, from his shined shoes to his perfectly combed hair, just seemed too put together.

"Darla, this is my friend Aaron," Jon said adding more emphasis on the word 'friend' than Aaron was comfortable with. "He's in the FBI."

"The FBI? What can I do for you?"

"I need to ask you questions about a recent order," Aaron responded, pulling out his badge and showing it to the woman. He glanced sideways at Jon before glancing back at Darla. "Is there somewhere we can talk privately?"

"Yes, I have an office in the back. This way —"

"Supervisory Special Agent Aaron Massey, ma'am. I'm sorry I didn't have time to introduce myself properly."

"Well, you two have fun. I've gotta jet." Jon picked up the enormous basket and brushed by Aaron, stopping for a second and leaning in to kiss him on the cheek. *What the fuck!? If I wasn't in public, I'd probably deck you. Good thing Frank's not here because you'd already be laid out on the ground.* Darla motioned for Aaron to follow her to the back.

"How can I help you, Agent Massey?" Darla asked as she ushered Aaron into a cluttered office. She stopped to remove a binder from a chair and motioned for Aaron to take a seat as she sat in the opposite chair. *This room is definitely not set up for office visits.*

Aaron pulled out his small notepad and a pen. "I'm sorry. I didn't get your full name either."

"I'm Darla Flowers. And before you ask, that's not a joke. That's my birth last name."

Aaron jotted a note. "Mrs. Flowers —"

"Ms. Flowers,"

"Ms. Flowers, my mistake. Well, I received a delivery from your flower shop maybe twenty to thirty minutes ago."

"You did?" Darla thought for a second. "Right. I sent Ed over with the bouquet."

"Ed?"

"Ed's my delivery guy. Was there a problem with the delivery? With Ed?"

"No, nothing like that. It's just" — Aaron paused as he tried to put the right words together — "the bouquet had a unique flower not exactly common — "

"That's right. You were the one who got the daphne arrangement. I don't get too many requests for those. Thankfully, I have a nursery I've ordered from before in Oregon that grows them."

"Really?"

"How long does it take to get a shipment in?"

"I can get them in under twenty-four-hours."

"So, when was this order placed?"

"Let me check." Darla walked over to the computer that was sitting in the room's corner and slid behind the keyboard. In a few clicks, she had opened a web browser and was reading through her notes. "It looks like the order originally came in four days ago."

"Four days ago?" That was before Tebbutt's flight had even landed.

"Yep, it looks like they ordered it online. We received an updated order yesterday to split the arrangement into two. I delivered the first arrangement to the Lincoln Centre Kitchen yesterday evening. I sent the second one to Aaron Massey. That's you." Darla continued to stare at her computer screen before adding, "Oh that's right, I also received an updated request just this morning to change the note in the card." She then read the updated message that was sent with the flowers.

"Thanks for the information. Any chance you have the credit card on file?"

"Nope. Sorry. It's run through a web portal, flowerorders.com. We get a transfer of funds and the order. All the processing is done through the website, but I can give you the number I have on file for them."

"That would be very helpful."

"Can I ask why you're asking about the arrangement? I've never had the FBI show up after delivering a bouquet, so this is new for me," she said, swiveling around in the desk chair before standing.

Aaron stood as well. "I'm sorry. I cannot talk about why we're curious about this order. I can say that it's in my official capacity and not as someone who received the bouquet from a mysterious person."

"I'll take your word for it, Agent. If you ever need flowers, you know where to find me." She followed Aaron back into the main store. "Have a great day," she said with a gigantic smile.

"You too. Mrs. — oops, *Ms*. Flowers."

# Chapter Twenty-One

"Frank, what was that about?" Jasika questioned as he entered back into the conference room.

"The flowers. They're daphnes."

"They are?" Jasika asked and she stared at the bouquet with a more intense gaze. "Well, I hope no one was planning on having them for lunch."

Frank pushed the bouquet to the side. As he did, a small blue envelope fell out. Frank looked at the envelope and debated whether he should open it. Jasika caught him staring at it. "Should I?"

"Well, unless Daphne is his secret lover, I don't think he'll mind."

Before Frank opened the card, he had Rummy take several photos using his camera phone to document the evidence. Frank walked out of the conference room over to his desk and pulled out an evidence bag and a pair of latex gloves. He flipped open his phone and called the Geek Twins.

"Hello, Frank. How can I help you this fine afternoon?"

"Nasab, we had a bouquet delivery at the precinct for Aaron."

"Don't tell me you're a jealous boyfriend."

"Yeah, but of the person who sent the flowers? They're from Daphne."

"What?"

"Yep. I'm about to open the envelope."

"Did you document—?"

"Don't worry. Agent Rummy is here, and he took photos for me."

"Perfect. Dust the card for prints. Rummy can send them to me. On second thought, have Rummy run them using his fancy equipment. He gets things turned around faster than we can."

"One benefit of being a fed is that they have nicer toys," Frank joked back.

"I'll make sure Rummy forwards the results. We'll also lock the bouquet down until one of your team can come and cart it away for further analysis."

"Sounds good. I'll see who's going to be out in your direction."

"Great, talk to you soon." Frank put his phone back in his pocket as he walked into the conference room. "Rummy, please forward Nasab anything you find. Do you have a print kit on you?"

"Do I have a print kit on me? Yeah, I have one. I travel with a small lab in my carry-on."

Rummy turned his bag on its side, opened it and found a tackle box that included all kinds of things Frank wondered how TSA let through security. Rummy handed his iPhone to Jasika to keep taking photos as Frank opened the card. Thankfully, the envelope wasn't licked shut, so he could quickly sift out the card without tearing anything. The card was a light purple color.

*Dr. Massey, it's so good to see you again. Was surprised to see you arrive last night with Detective Schultt. Is he the handsome NY Detective you spoke of in your last book? Here's to our game of cat and mouse!* À la prochaine — *until next time, Daphne.*

Frank's iPhone vibrated in his pocket as he was finishing reading the note. He stepped out of the way and let Jasika take more pictures before he answered the phone. He glanced at the caller ID as he answered.

"Aaron, what did you find out?"

Aaron recounted his interview with Darla Flowers. Frank could hear the sounds of the traffic, *so Aaron must already be on his way back.* "Hey, can you hand your phone over to Rummy?" Aaron asked "I have a phone number I need him to reach out to."

"Sure, he was about to dust the card that came with your flowers."

"The flower owner told me about the message."

"Don't worry. Everyone is following protocol right now. We've photographed everything and dusted the card for prints."

"Honestly, don't bother. The florist handled everything. The flowers themselves were never touched by Daphne."

Frank waited until Rummy found one set of prints on the card. The lettering was done electronically, so he was betting the prints would belong to the florist who'd handled the order.

He handed his cell phone to Rummy. Rummy jotted the phone number from Aaron then passed it off to O'Donnell, who was already sitting in front of a laptop.

Frank stood back and watched Agents Rummy and O'Donnell quickly maneuver to get information. O'Donnell picked up her cell, and Frank could hear her talking to someone at a third-party online order processing company.

"There have been no immediate hits in our system for the prints. Admittedly, it's a fairly limited system, so that's not too surprising."

"Rummy, Aaron mentioned talking to" — he glanced at his notes — "Darla Flowers, the florist shop owner. I'm betting those are her prints. Aaron also told me the order was placed online, so Daphne never interacted with anyone directly."

"Figures," Rummy said.

"Also, a second bouquet was sent last night to the party at the Lincoln Center Kitchen."

"And no one saw them?" Jasika said.

"Not that we know of. I'm going to text Richardson and see if he can go through the photos he has to see if there are any similar flower arrangements."

"Frank," O'Donnell said as Aaron returned. Aaron's face was still red from the frigid February air outside. "The purchase was made from an iPhone belonging to Danielle Tebbutt."

"What?" Aaron and Frank said in disbelieving unison.

"What's the phone number?" Rummy asked from behind his own terminal.

O'Donnell read off the number, and Rummy ran his fingers across the keys on his laptop. Frank walked over to see what he was doing and looked at a black screen with a ton of type and Rummy's fingers running at one-hundred miles per hour across the keyboard. In less than thirty seconds, he piped up, "The iPhone's SIM card is still activated—and it's on the move."

"Where is it?" Aaron asked.

Without skipping a beat, a map of the theater district popped up on the main whiteboard with a red circle. The dot was definitely moving, but it was moving slowly and systematically.

Jasika pulled out her phone and called dispatch, asking for a squad car in the area to find the vehicle. While Jasika was patched into several patrol cars, the group watched as the red dot turned the corner, headed down Seventh Avenue turning onto Forty-Fourth Street. It would drive down four or five blocks then turn back to the next street. It was making a zig-zag ride through the city.

"Who does that?" Aaron asked. "It's slow enough to be a person, but why?"

"Not who," Jasika said, getting off her phone. "It's what. A city garbage truck is making a late-day pickup. Should the patrol cars stop the truck?"

"Yes," Frank responded. Jasika asked the patrol cars to stop it and take necessary precautions. The group watched as the red dot came to a standstill around Forty-Seventh Street between Sixth and Seventh Avenues.

Jasika put her phone on the table, turning on the phone's speaker. After a couple of minutes, a voice spoke through the phone, "Detective Torv, this is Officer Raymond. The truck has been pulled over to the side of the road. When the driver opened the back, well, ma'am, there's a mangled leg."

"We're on our way," Torv responded without waiting.

# Chapter Twenty-Two

Because of its proximity to the station, Aaron, Frank and Jasika walked the few blocks to the scene. Before they got there, the street had been cordoned off. The three flashed their shields, signed in and ducked under the police tape.

In front of them was a large garbage truck. Frank walked to the truck, peered inside the back and said, "Yep, definitely a leg."

An officer approached them. "Detective Torv?"

"That's me. Office Raymond?"

"Yes. And over there's my partner, Officer Dereck Rigolino," Raymond said, pointing at a man who was talking to the sanitation truck crew.

Frank walked over to Officer Rigolino and made introductions. The officer told Frank how the garbage truck crew had no idea there was a body in the truck. One man kept saying, "*We threw in the trash. I didn't even notice the body*," repeatedly. Clearly, the sanitation truck worker had been thrown for a loop.

"It's his first week on the job," Rigolino explained conspiratorially with Frank.

The other workers tried to console the guy, but he slumped to the ground. "Let's get these men some coffee." Frank pulled out his wallet and gave Officer Rigolino twenty dollars. "Would you mind?"

"Sure thing, Detective."

Frank stood waiting for forensics and the ME truck to arrive. *Hanging out on a frozen street in New York in February. Ain't my life glamorous?* He glanced over to see what Jasika and Aaron were doing. They were milling around. Frank looked up to see Chief Detective Gleason ducking under the police tape, so Frank headed in her direction.

"Detective Schultt."

"Chief Detective Gleason."

"What do you have for me? I picked up the tail end of the conversation with the on-scene officers. When I heard there was a body and you were involved, I figured I should come to see what you needed."

"Right now, not much. We're waiting for Mariella and the Geek Twins to get here."

"They're en route," Jasika said, walking over to Frank and Gleason.

"Detective Torv," Gleason said with a bow of her head.

Frank and Jasika let Gleason know everything that had gone on that day. By the time they'd caught her up, the ME van and the Geek Squad had parked down the road and were unloading. They made their way to the barrier to see if Mariella or the Geek Twins needed any help with the equipment.

"Hello, all! You need to stop giving me work to do," Mariella said, stepping out of the van. "Fuck, it's cold out here!" she said, looking around. "Amanda! I didn't know they sent you an invitation to this party?"

"They didn't. I'm a regular party crasher."

"So, where's my body?"

All three, almost in unison, looked toward the garbage truck. "Fuck me!" Mariella groaned. "Please tell me I'm not going to wade around in there. I just got my nails done."

"Well, we can see a leg," Jasika noted. "Fingers crossed the rest of the body is attached and you can easily fish it out."

Before long, the Geek Twins, along with their intern, Dana Ramirez, were decked out in disposable protective coveralls and rummaging around in the back of the truck. Nasab and Richardson were handling the body as Ramirez took pictures.

"I found a hand," Aaron heard Richardson say from within the bowels of the truck.

"So, that makes two hands, a foot and most of the torso. God, this one is a mess," Gleason said to no one in particular.

*Better those people than me*, Aaron thought to himself.

Mariella stood close enough to the garbage truck to yell directions, but far enough away that she didn't have to get the stench on her.

"Wait a second. You found a hand?" Aaron asked. Turning to Mariella, he said, "Any chance we can get the hand and print it?"

"If you must," Mariella said with a sigh. "Normally, I just show up and cart the body back to autopsy."

Richardson beckoned Mariella over then gave her the hand after Richardson placed it an evidence bag. Mariella reached into her pockets and pulled out a pair of latex gloves, slipped them on and took the hand from Richardson.

"Let's go back to the truck and get this hand printed." Mariella looked around for a second. "Where's Frank?"

"I haven't seen him for a while. Not sure where he is."

"Damn. I'm doing my best to keep all my hand job jokes to myself."

Aaron just groaned and shook his head. "What are we going to do with you?"

"Let me do my job?" Mariella said with a wink as they got to the truck and she pulled out a toolbox and print kit. She swiftly inked and printed the hand. So far, all they knew was that the victim was an older Black male.

"Perfect," Aaron noted. "You're really fast at printing."

"I've had a little experience over the years," Mariella said as Aaron took a few photos of the print with his phone.

"I'm going to send these to Rummy," Aaron said. "Wait! You've never even met Rummy before, have you?"

"Only if his first name is Gin."

"Nope, Julian. He's the FBI tech guy I like to use on my cases. He's a wiz on the computer. He's the one who found the moving iPhone in the truck."

"Ahh, so that's how you found me a dead body."

Aaron filled Mariella in on what had happened since Frank and he had arrived at work that morning. He then texted the pictures to Rummy, asking him to run them through their databases. Within a couple of minutes, Rummy texted him back.

*I have a hit. Your bad day is about to get worse.*

*Worse than a dead body in a garbage truck?*

*Try an African warlord dead in a garbage truck.*

*WTF?*

*The print came back through our system as one General Kader Nibombé – the current dictator of Togo.*

*Start pulling a dossier together. Be back soon.*

*On it! O'Donnell's already calling Barling and Price. Once they give the go-ahead, she'll contact the State Department. This shit show just keeps getting better.*

Aaron looked up from his phone and noticed Mariella looking at him. "Why do I have a strange feeling you're about to make my day worse?"

"Because I already have an ID on the vic."

"Wow, that's fast."

"He was in our system. Let's find Frank and Jasika, and I'll tell you all what I found out." Aaron and Mariella found Frank and Jasika huddled in the open door of the coffee shop. Mariella gave them a little grief about trying to stay warm while she and Aaron were out solving the crime. Aaron then told them what he'd found out from Rummy. He also pulled up a website that provided some necessary biographical information about General Nibombé. *Thank you, Wikipedia.*

"Wow, this guy sounds like a grade-A dick!" Mariella said.

"How the hell did he even get into NYC?" Jasika questioned.

"O'Donnell is checking in with the State Department, so hopefully we'll have some answers on that soon," Aaron explained.

"You all having a pow-wow and forget to invite us?" Richardson chided as he strolled toward the group.

"You," Mariella demanded, "stay at least ten feet away from me at all times. I can already smell you."

"Well, you'll be glad to know we've found the head. All we're missing now is the other hand."

"Yippee," Mariella said as she twirled her middle finger in a slightly obscene gesture. "Guess that means it's time to load the body parts into my truck. It was good seeing all of you again. I'm going to go suit up. I'll call you once I have a better idea of what happened."

"I'm going to bet it was the bullet hole in the head?" Richardson tossed out.

"Way to bury the lead," Jasika said.

"I wanted it to be dramatic," Richardson said with a wink. "I'll also say we found the murder weapon. It was underneath the victim's torso."

"A gun?" Aaron asked. "Not very Daphne-like."

"Actually," Jasika explained, "she has used a gun in a couple of cases linked to her. Specifically, she likes a Beretta 3032 Tomcat Inox."

"Score one for Detective Torv," Richardson said, marking one mark in the air as if keeping a tally.

"I'll also bet it had a homemade suppressor attached."

"Score two for Detective Torv."

"The Fed Boy is getting spanked!" Mariella chided before walking away to get ready to load the body into the ME truck.

Aaron rolled his eyes as Jasika said, "I got lucky. My part of the report had those little tidbits of information."

"Last thing before I go," Richardson said. "I should also note we found a flower in the victim's breast pocket."

Jasika looked at Aaron. "This one's yours."

"That will be most assuredly be daphne. It's her trademark."

"Aaron, any chance the gun will be traceable?" Frank asked.

"Doubt it," Jasika jumped in. "The last two times she used a gun, she stole it straight from the manufacturer. The gun itself was completely clean before the hit. Then she disposed of the gun with the body, like she did here."

"I'm betting that information wasn't released to the public, so it strengthens the connection to Daphne," Frank said.

"Maybe, maybe not," Jasika said. "Sure, the public wasn't informed, but who knows how many people outside of Interpol were told that information as part of the investigation."

"I'll have O'Donnell check in with the Beretta factory in Brescia, Italy, to see if they've had a missing shipment in the past few months," Aaron said, pulling out his phone.

Everyone stared at Aaron, and he got an uncomfortable look and said, "What?"

"How do you know where Berettas come from off the top of your head?" Jasika questioned.

"I got to tour the place when I was working over there. It's a state-of-the-art facility. Pretty damn cool, actually."

Aaron took a beat as he glanced over at the garbage truck and watched Nasab, Richardson and their intern finish the dumpster diving. Nasab caught Aaron looking at him. "Aaron," he yelled across the street, "tell Frank to check his email. The tox report from last night was sent to his inbox."

Aaron glanced at Frank. "Did you get that?"

Frank pulled out his cell phone and read through the report. "Blah, blah, blah… This is pretty much what we expected, based on the MO. Well, here's something unexpected. The lily of the valley component was *C. majalis var. Montana*. Apparently, Daphne switched out her usual plant for the US version."

"That means she's cooking here in the US," Jasika reasoned.

Without skipping a beat, Aaron pulled out his phone. "Rummy, I have a new search for you. I want you to cross-reference three things and see if anything pops—lab equipment purchases and rentals, facility rentals and purchases, and French names."

"She's cooking in the US?" Frank asked.

"She needs a place to do this," Aaron explained. "If she's French like we think, she had to have arranged this before getting here, so she probably set it up under a French corporate name."

"Makes sense to me, but what about—?"

"Uh-huh," Aaron said, putting his ear back to the phone while grabbing out his pad and pen. "You have a location in Brooklyn rented two months ago by someone named Pierre Lemaitre. Get me the address."

"Who is Pierre Lemaitre?" Jasika questioned.

"A famous French crime writer."

# Chapter Twenty-Three

After divvying up phone calls, Aaron, Frank and Jasika began the quick walk back to the station. On their way, they all pulled out their phones and begin organizing a breach of the warehouse. Jasika called in the address to the NYPD Emergency Service Unit to let them know they were needed for a tactical breach. Aaron coordinated with the Bureau of Alcohol, Tobacco, Firearms and Explosives. And Frank coordinated the search warrant by chatting with ADA Popova. He went into his phone and found the number for the District Attorney's office. *Hopefully, she's still there*. He hit the call button.

"Manhattan District Attorney's office," a voice chimed on the other end.

"Hello, this is Detective Frank Schultt with the NYPD. I need to speak with ADA Popova."

"Let me see if she's available, Detective." The voice clipped off the line as a standard voice recording started playing, extolling the virtues of the DA's office and the need for citizens to help law enforcement ensure a safe and secure NYC.

"Detective Schultt, missed you at autopsy this morning."

"Long night, ma'am."

"So, I heard. What can I do for you?"

Frank got her up to speed on what had transpired that afternoon, starting with the flower delivery through to the tox report.

"So based on this additional information, what do you want from me?"

"We want a search warrant for the warehouse in Brooklyn. If Daphne is cooking her poison locally, we believe finding the lab could lead to finding and stopping her."

"Let's get real, Detective. The FBI triangulation search is interesting and may prove fruitful, but it's flimsy at best. You technically have zero eyes on anyone in the building committing an actual crime. You have no reason to suspect this location is being used for criminal purposes other than a series of hunches that may or may not be right."

"You're right, ma'am. We know this is a long shot, but it's one we think we should take." Silence. *Is she still there?*

Finally, after what seems like a few minutes but was probably only thirty seconds, Popova responded, "Any chance you have a friendly judge who would be open to this type of search?"

"I have one I can call. If you support the search, I know she'll issue an emergency search warrant." Frank was once again met with silence.

"Technically, we could issue the warrant using the Patriot Act and suspected terrorism. Daphne killed the FBI Director's wife," Popova pondered aloud. "Those parameters give us a bit more wiggle room. How long before you need the warrant?"

"An hour?"

"That puts us at about five p.m. I can track down a federal judge I know and have him issue this one. It's definitely easier to get a warrant through the Patriot Act here—less red tape. I'll call you when the warrant is in hand."

"Thank you, ma'am." Frank heard the familiar sound of an ended call before he got the words out of his mouth. *Definitely not one for social graces, is she?*

\* \* \* \*

After everything was coordinated, the team checked out a sedan from the pool, threw on their bubble light and headed out to Brooklyn. Frank looked out at the passing landscape and was glad it wasn't snowing anymore. *At this time of day, it should take them maybe thirty minutes to get there, assuming the bridge cooperates.*

With Frank behind the wheel, they shared how their relative phone calls had gone. Frank explained the warrant's situation. Jasika told them the ESU was mobilizing and would set up a parameter one block away from the address. "They'll call me when they have a command station in place. We'll be coordinating with ESU-Seven from East Brooklyn."

"ESU-Seven?" Aaron questioned.

"Emergency Service Unit... It's what the NYPD calls its highly skilled SWAT teams," Frank responded. "What about you, Aaron? Anything to report?"

"Rummy got in contact with the rental agent."

A taxi cut in front of them, and Frank hit the brake hard to avoid clipping the taxi. He looked to his right and noticed the stunned pedestrian the taxi had swerved to avoid running over. The pedestrian was eating a sandwich and was cussing up a storm at the cab that was already speeding away.

"Sorry about that. Everyone okay?" If they weren't in such a hurry, Frank would have thrown the car in park, issued the pedestrian a citation and lectured him on being more aware of his surroundings and the right of way. After checking that everyone was okay, he continued their drive. "Again, sorry about that. You were saying something about a rental agent?"

"Yeah, umm…" Aaron looked at the notes he'd jotted while talking to Rummy. "We know the building was rented directly by Pierre Lemaitre. Big surprise… A female in her mid-twenties to early thirties rented it. We also know the social security number used to rent the building belongs to a Freddy Jessup, who's been dead for about four years."

"How did the rental agent let that one slide?" Jasika questioned. "When I got my apartment out in Queens, they ran every check under the sun. I half expected them to ask for a body cavity search before I signed the rental agreement."

"Well, apparently, in the warehouse business, due diligence isn't as necessary as expedience," Frank guessed. Frank glanced in the review mirror at Jasika, who looked at her phone before answering.

"Detective Torv."

Frank listened to a one-sided conversation Jasika had with the ESU Lieutenant in charge. Once finished, she gave him an address, and Aaron plugged it into the car's navigator.

# Chapter Twenty-Four

Frank parked his vehicle behind a mobile command center after flashing his shield to ESU members manning the perimeter. Getting out of the vehicle, Aaron, Frank and Jasika did a quick stretch before they were approached by an officer in tactical gear.

"Detective Torv?"

"That's me," Jasika responded. She then introduced Frank and Aaron.

"If you three will follow me." The officer showed them into the mobile command center.

"Detective Torv?" An ESU officer greeted them upon entry. "I'm Lieutenant Tucker. Here's what we have so far." Tucker explained they were already linked to the NYPD counter-terrorism surveillance system. "We have a couple of Mavic Pro Quadcopters in the air. You can see their footage in real-time here," Tucker said, pointing to a monitor built into the side of the truck. In front of the monitor, there was a small computer station operated by a technician. Frank could hear the man coordinating the drone efforts and camera feeds from several ESU personnel helmets.

"What have you seen?" Frank asked.

"Well, we've seen a few people coming in and out of the building. Facial recognition software pinged a couple of people who have existing warrants, so there is definitely some kind of criminal behavior going on there."

"Interesting…" Aaron pondered. "Not quite sure why Daphne would work with known criminals. That's definitely not like her."

"Speaking of your suspect," Tucker continued, "a woman in her mid-to-late twenties was seen entering the building about five minutes ago."

"What did she look like?" Frank asked.

"We couldn't get a good look. She was pretty bundled, so the drones couldn't get a shot of her face."

Just then, Frank's phone vibrated. "Excuse me," Frank said to the group. "Detective Schultt."

"Detective," ADA Popova said. "I have the warrant in hand. I'm sending it to the email address I have on file. Please let me know if you get it."

Frank glanced at his phone and scrolled to his email. The first message was from the ADA, and the attached PDF was the signed search warrant. "Thanks! Got it."

"Let me know what happens after you execute the warrant. I'll be on my cell phone. I've already texted you the number."

*And she hung up. Definitely not one for small talk.* "We have the warrant." Lieutenant Tucker asked to see it, so Frank forwarded it to him.

After Tucker read through the parameters of the warrant, he said, "Wow, this warrant is broad. How did you manage to get this so quickly?"

"This case is tied to the case of the assassination of the FBI Director's wife," Frank said. "Apparently, that's enough to put this search squarely with the Patriot Act."

"Interesting," Lieutenant Tucker said. He picked up a microphone and explained the warrant to his team. After finishing, he turned to the technician. "Everyone in place?"

"Yes, sir."

"On my mark..." the lieutenant said. "Execute."

Frank watched the helmet camera feed from ESU officers as they approached the building various entry points. On the monitors, Frank's focus shot between four helmet cameras plus the two drones' bird's-eye views—one in front and one in back of the building. With so much visual information on the screen, it was hard to figure out where to keep focus. Once all the officers were in place, the lieutenant ordered the breach of the structure.

The officers entered the ground floor of the warehouse from four different locations. The camera movements were jerky, and Frank could hear shouts of 'NYPD', followed by short bursts of gunfire. Watching the breach was like watching a chaotic gun battle in a movie. There was so much happening that it was hard to figure out who was who in all the chaos.

One drone suddenly caught his attention. "Lieutenant, is that smoke?" Frank pointed out in one of the drone's feeds.

Tucker leaned in to get a better look and ordered the drone pilot to get in closer. Not only was there smoke, but there was also fire leaping out of the window. "Order an evacuation *now*!"

The technician gave the order, and officers backed out of the building. Frank zeroed in on one of the helmet feeds when a sudden flash of light happened before the camera went dark. The roaring sound of the explosion hit the command center.

# Chapter Twenty-Five

Everyone in the command center raced outside to see a giant ball of fire growing in the distance. Without thinking, they all started running toward the warehouse to see if anyone needed help. Frank heard Tucker calling in ESU's medical squad and fire teams.

The scene unfolding in front of them was thankfully not as bad as Frank had feared. The few extra seconds the drone footage provided them had allowed all the officers to safely exit the building. A few were sitting on the ground cradling burned arms or bloody cuts, but no one looked like they were fatally injured. One of the ESU personnel handed Aaron, Frank and Jasika latex gloves and emergency medical kits. The three set about triaging where they could until the ESU medical team arrived on the scene.

One thing permeating the air was the acrid smell of rotten eggs. *What is that smell?* Frank was helping an officer when he overheard someone else talking about it. He wasn't sure where the conversation originated, but what he caught was the phrase *"meth lab."*

Aaron surveyed the scene around him and was very glad things weren't worse. He couldn't say the same for those inside the building. From what he could tell, the only ones who made it out alive were the ESU squad members. Thankfully, most of the injuries Aaron had seen were pretty minor. He'd seen one officer with a pretty large piece of glass sticking out of leg, but it looked like the glass had missed an artery, based on the amount of bleeding Aaron was seeing. Still, the man's fellow officers were already applying a tourniquet to stem the flow of blood.

Aaron put on his latex gloves and helped where he could, but his help wasn't needed for the most part. After a few minutes, he found Frank and walked over to him. "Any idea what happened?"

"I heard an officer mention the rotten egg smell could be meth-related."

"Oh yeah, it's definitely meth," an officer broke into their conversation. "I worked in NARCO for six years before joining ESU. It's a pretty distinctive smell."

"Thanks!" Aaron responded. "I seriously doubt this is our case."

"Why?" Frank questioned.

"I don't see Daphne working with a bunch of meth heads. It's not her style. She's known to be a lone wolf. We have no images of her for a reason. Working with a group of meth heads would definitely expose her in a way that makes no sense."

Once the scene was secure and the ATF was en route, the lieutenant told them they could file their reports from their home offices and ESU would take it from there. Aaron, Frank and Jasika made their way back to their sedan and headed back to Midtown.

Aaron checked his messages on his phone and read a text from O'Donnell. She'd contacted Beretta. Sure enough, a shipment of Beretta 3032 Tomcat Inox had gone missing six months earlier. He thought about calling Pasqual Bosc to see if he had any information on the missing shipment but decided not to, since it was past midnight in France.

He shot off a text to O'Donnell, telling her and Rummy to head home for the day. He'd call them if anything happened before nine a.m. the next morning. "I told O'Donnell and Rummy to go home for the evening."

"Probably a good idea," Frank said. "I know Rummy's had one hell of a day traveling and doing all the work for us."

"Yep. I told them we'd see them at nine tomorrow."

Aaron noticed him glance in the review mirror, getting Jasika's attention. "What do you think? Call it a day when we get back to the station?"

"Yeah, it's been a long one. And there's not much we can do, so it makes sense to me. Besides, it would be nice to get home at a reasonable hour and spends some time with Ginny and Mom for a change."

Once back at the station, Frank called ADA Popova and told her about the meth lab explosion. She wasn't happy that it wasn't their case, but taking out a meth lab was still a win in her book. After that conversation, the trio returned the car and said their goodbyes. Aaron and Frank walked back to their condo, holding hands and huddling close together to keep each other warm. They picked up some Indian takeout before heading back to the condo. Aaron glanced at his watch. *We might actually be in bed before ten for a change.*

# Chapter Twenty-Six

It felt good to feel the consistent rhythm of his feet pounding the treadmill the next morning. Frank might not be a morning person, but he was always a bit off if he didn't get his morning exercise in before heading to the precinct. Even though he was there with Aaron, Logan and Ben, he found the solitude of running a great way to wake up. It was almost as good as coffee…but not quite.

Frank noticed all four of them had their headsets in, so he motioned for Logan to see if he wanted to talk. Logan removed his and left it dangling around his neck while he kept running.

"So, how was Ben's show the other night?"

"Honestly…" Logan looked to make sure Ben couldn't hear him before he continued. "Like I said in our texts yesterday, it was as bad as you'd warned me, if not worse. Everything about the show was just horrible."

"Sorry to hear that."

"Don't tell him I told you, but today's show is the last one before they close. It hasn't been announced to the public yet, but the producers informed the cast last night."

"Ouch." Frank then spent a few minutes catching Logan up on everything from Lincoln Center to the meth lab the evening before. He could easily hold his conversation with Logan, so he increased the incline a bit to at least work his lungs a bit more.

Aaron and Ben both noticed Logan and him having a conversation, so all of them ended up unplugging their headsets.

"What are you biddies talking about?" Ben queried between breaths.

"Just catching up on what's going on in our lives," Logan said. He then looked at Aaron. "Sorry to hear about your wedding planner."

"Wedding planner?" Ben asked. "What happened to Amber? Spill the tea?"

Frank looked at Aaron, who had a slightly bemused look on his face. *Fuck! He probably thinks I planned this after the conversation we had a couple of days ago.* Frank tried to give Aaron his best 'not my fault' look.

"Well, Amber is having a rough pregnancy and won't be able to finish the wedding planning for us," Aaron said, jumping into the conversation. "Not sure what we're going to do at this time. She gave us a list of names, but these past few days have not exactly left us with much time to contact anyone."

"Really?" Ben asked. "Well, you may not know this, but I used to be an event manager and worked all kinds of weddings from big to small."

Aaron did his best to look shocked. "I had no idea."

"Yep. And as it so happens, I have some free time coming up. Between us and the walls, my show was killed by the tabloid press, so we're closing early. It's sad, really. The Tony voters won't even get a chance to see how amazing the show is. So, I don't have any jobs lined up, and I would be glad to step in."

Aaron looked to Frank, and Frank gave him an 'it's up to you' look. "Sure," Aaron responded. "Why not? I'll give you Amber's information when we get back to the locker room so you can contact her and see what she's already finished."

"Amazing!" Ben chirped. "How big are we making it? If you want it under five-hundred, there are some amazing locations in the city. If you're going larger than that, we'll need to see which theaters are either empty or can be available for an afternoon ceremony."

For the first time, Frank looked over and saw Aaron had met his match in the bridezilla department. Frank hadn't seen Ben this excited about something in a long time. He shot Aaron a quick glance and mouthed "thank you," and Aaron reassured him with a slight smile. Aaron began to look like a deer in the headlights as Ben started rattling on about all his ideas.

"Aaron Massey! Fancy meeting you here," an all-too-chipper voice cut through Aaron and Ben's wedding planning.

Frank recognized Jon Fetty. He sounded like fingernails on a chalkboard.

"I hope you got what you needed yesterday from the florist," Jon told Aaron, leaning against the railing in front of Aaron's treadmill.

*What the fuck? Aaron didn't tell me about that.*

"Jon, you know I can't talk to you about an ongoing investigation, so don't even try to squeeze something out of me. Anyway, I hope your client enjoyed her gift basket."

"She did! In fact, I can't talk too long because the bidding for the movie rights starts this morning at nine. Should be exciting. So far, all the major studios appear to be ready to make bids. It should make for a fun time. Toodles!"

*Toodles? Who says that?*

"Oh, and, Aaron, I almost forgot to mention yesterday that I found out Penny, Aaron's agent," Fetty said, turning to Frank as if Frank didn't know who Penny was, "is looking to retire, and so there's going to be a shuffling of her clients. With any luck, I may be your new agent, which would be amazeballs. And just in time to auction off the rights to your latest book to Hollywood. I hear that there have already been a few inquiries at the agency."

Frank practically snarled when he heard that. Thankfully, only Logan noticed and shot Frank a quick 'get it together' look.

Frank could tell from Aaron's expression that this extra information made Aaron uncomfortable, even as Aaron tried to mask the look of shock with a then-smile.

"Interesting news," Aaron said.

*Aaron didn't exactly say it was good news, just interesting. I still don't like this asshole.*

"Well, anyway, gotta get my workout in before heading to the office. I'm sure you'll be hearing from me soon. We still need to get coffee. Who knows? Maybe we'll be getting coffee as agent and client. Wouldn't that be just gorge!" Jon spun on his heels and headed over to a stair climber machine.

Without waiting for Frank to ask, Aaron told the story about the run-in with Jon the day before. Frank trusted Aaron, but he definitely didn't trust Jon. After listening to the story, Frank grumbled some kind of acknowledgment before putting his headset back in his ears and turning on the treadmill's television.

He flipped through the channels and settled on the early morning news on WNTV. Immediately, Frank regretted that decision. On the screen, Jenny Mace was interviewing someone from General Kader Nibombé's staff. "Aaron, turn on WNTV," Frank said over the audio in his ears. Aaron flipped on his own TV screen and started watching.

"*This is a horrible day for Togo,*" the man began. "*I'm calling on the UN to sanction the United States for withholding information that there was an assassination plot against my country's beloved leader.*"

"*You're telling me that US authorities knew of the assassination plot and purposefully withheld this information?*"

"*Precisely.*"

"*Do you think the US was behind the assassination?*"

"*Either the US or the French, maybe both. According to a security brief I received yesterday evening after my beloved leader was killed, the US authorities knew the international assassin known as Daphne was on a killing spree in the US.*"

"*Whoa,*" Jenny replied, clearly surprised. "*Say that one again.*"

"*According to the brief my embassy received last night from the United Nations Department of Safety and Security, the assassin known only as Daphne killed two people in this city before murdering General Kader Nibombé in cold blood.*"

"*What other murders?*"

"*You should know. You reported on the murders of both Danielle Tebbutt and Penelope Cristillo.*"

"*Viewers, you heard it here first on WNTV. We have an internationally known assassin working on US soil. Why haven't the authorities released this information to the public? I may not have answers yet, but I can guarantee you WNTV will sort out this story. And now, we must take a commercial break. When we get back, we'll hear all about the snowy day ahead of us."*

"Well, fuck!" Frank exclaimed then quickly realized he had practically yelled it when a couple of other gym members turned their heads in his direction. He mouthed 'sorry' to the ones who could see him.

"Easy there, tiger," Jon Fetty said as he walked past Frank. "You don't have to act so happy to see me!"

"The world isn't always about you, Mr. Fetty," Frank responded, not even attempting to hide the venom in his voice.

# Chapter Twenty-Seven

After finishing their runs, Aaron needed to talk to Frank. From the way Frank had been pouting after their run-in with Jon that morning, Aaron knew it wouldn't be a fun conversation. In the shower, Aaron had a lot of time to think about what had happened. *If he weren't so damn jealous and threatened by Jon, my running into him wouldn't be a big deal in the first place. Frank should trust me. He should know by now that I'm not one to fuck around on him.* The more he thought about it, the more frustrated he grew at Frank. *Frank's the one acting like a childish ass. Why am I the one who has to seek the Almighty Frank's forgiveness when I've done nothing wrong?*

By the time Aaron had finished his shower, he was ready for a fight, because Frank needed to learn that the world did not revolve around him and his insecurities. Aaron did his best to stay pleasant as they said their goodbyes to Logan and Ben. He waited for Frank to say something. Instead, Frank ignored him entirely and pulled out his phone.

*Whatever… If you don't want to talk like an adult, two can play this game.* Aaron pulled out his phone and started checking his messages. There was one from the director asking how the UN had gotten hold of the information and who had authorized its release. Aaron composed a quick response saying he had no idea who told the UN anything. He mentioned the US State Department knew about the general's death—per protocol when dealing with the death of a foreign diplomat on US soil. He copied Barling on the email, as well.

He then texted Pasquale to ask him if he knew anything about the Barretta shipment that had gone missing. He received a text back saying Interpol was aware of the situation, but no one had any idea Daphne was involved. They figured it was a usual gun-running operation, so not too much time and energy had been put into the theft.

Frank muttered something about getting a cab because of the snow, so he stood out in the street and hailed one. *Honestly, I hadn't even noticed the snow yet.* Aaron kept running through his texts and emails, but nothing was popping as something he needed to immediately deal with.

Aaron and Frank got into the cab without saying a word to each other. Frank told the driver where to take them then leaned back to start playing with his phone again. *Why did I get him that? He's totally an addict now!*

Within minutes, the car was turning the corner and pulling up to the precinct. The mob of people outside took Aaron by surprise. Protestors were out front with signs reading, 'Death to American Imperialism', 'The CIA Killed General Kader Nibombé', 'Justice for Nibombé', and other sayings. *How did they put this together so quickly?* Aaron looked out and also saw several reporters standing around talking to the demonstrators.

When the cab pulled over, Frank pulled out his credit card and paid the cabby. Aaron exited the car holding the door for Frank as he slid across the back seat to exit on the curbside with Aaron.

"Thanks!" Frank said under his breath without even looking at Aaron.

Aaron was about to have a witty comeback when a bright light was suddenly cast in his face. "Agent Massey, what is your role in this?" Jenny Mace asked, thrusting a microphone in his face.

"Ms. Mace, what is the 'this' you are referring to? I'm not even sure what's going on here. As you can see, we just arrived."

"Don't play coy with me, Agent Massey. I know both you and Detective Schultt have been actively investigating the international terrorist known as Daphne."

"Jenny," Aaron said with a sigh, "you know I cannot and will not speak officially about an ongoing investigation. There are media liaisons at both the FBI and NYPD who would be more than happy to talk to you."

While Aaron was being accosted, Frank went around her and headed into the precinct, avoiding any interactions with the protestors out front. Aaron smiled as Jenny tossed more questions his direction, which he easily deflected. He was thankful that the NYPD had already erected a barrier preventing the protestors from blocking the door or traffic. *Gotta love how efficient they are when it comes to a protest.* He quickly said his goodbyes and slipped behind the barricade before entering the station.

# Chapter Twenty-Eight

Frank wasn't sure what he was mad at by the time he got to his desk. He was pissed at Jon for always flirting with his fiancé, and he was pissed at Aaron for not stopping it. *How had he not told me about his run-in with Fetty yesterday? Is he ashamed of me? Afraid I'm going to do something rash to Fetty if I found out?* Frank admitted he probably would have decked the guy if he had come and hugged Aaron again while naked. *There are some things a man just can't let pass.*

Frank busied himself with the paperwork he needed to deal with. Jasika rolled in shortly after Frank had sat down, and Aaron came in and headed right to the conference room. Jasika noticed that Frank and Aaron were avoiding each other.

"I don't want to know," Jasika said to Frank as she headed into the conference room. Frank followed here and was only a little surprised to find O'Donnell and Rummy were already inside working.

"Frank," Rummy called out, "I received the autopsy report for the general. Apparently, your ME and," he began, while glancing at his notes, "someone called Ropova were there last night."

"Popova," Jasika responded. "It's ADA Popova. She definitely wants to be involved in every aspect of this case."

"What did the report say?" Frank asked.

"Nothing too unexpected, based on what you told us yesterday afternoon." Rummy glanced at his notes and began reading again. "A small caliber gunshot penetrated the right frontal area of the cranium. Bullet fragments were pulled from the right occipital lobe during autopsy."

"That's what we expected," Frank said. "Anything else?"

"Nothing that seems to be of any importance. Your ME asked me to thank you, and I'm quoting here, 'For sending me some crispy critters' last night."

Aaron, Frank and Jasika all started laughing.

O'Donnell looked at Aaron, Frank and Jasika. "You are definitely three peas in a pod — a sick pod, but a pod nonetheless."

Frank sat in a rolling chair, pulled out his phone and read the ME's report for himself. Jasika was already doing the same thing.

Aaron looked at them and said, "I'm going to see if I can get ahold of Bosc and see if he has any ideas."

Aaron pulled out his cell phone and went into the bullpen to sit at Frank's desk while making the call. It was about four p.m. in France, so it was a good time to call to see what was going on there.

"Aaron, good to hear from you again so soon. How is your case?"

"Not sure if you've heard, but we have a dead African warlord sitting in our morgue right now."

"I am familiar with said warlord. I saw the information coming over the newswire a little bit ago myself."

"What can you tell me about General Nibombé?"

"He was a murdering genocidal asshole who killed anyone who opposed him. The world will be a better place with him gone."

"Tell me how you really feel," Aaron responded sarcastically. "He was that bad, huh?"

"He was that bad and then some. Honestly, I was amazed no one had already — how would Hollywood put it — 'put a cap in his ass'. Don't get me wrong. There have been attempts, but no one had succeeded."

"Any idea what happens now in Togo?"

"They'll get another murdering genocidal asshole to lead."

Aaron half snorted at that one. "Any idea who is the most likely candidate?"

"Most likely," Bosc explained. Aaron could hear Bosc shuffling through his notes over the phone. "My intel is putting the probability of General Gassing Grunitzky as the next leader."

"Can't say I've heard of him. Admittedly, Togo is not exactly a country I spend a lot of time thinking about."

"Ahh... You Americans rarely spend *any* time thinking about *any* other country but your own."

"Hey, totally not fair," Aaron said, sounding offended, before adding, "even if it's pretty accurate."

Bosc barked out a laugh on the other end of the phone. "You were always an odd duck compared to your countrymen, Agent Massey. I guess that's why I like you. Most Americans bore me."

"Anything else I should know?"

"Unofficially, it wouldn't surprise me if Grunitzky had paid Daphne to kill Nibombé. Officially, they were like brothers. But these were more like brothers in the Cain and Abel sense."

Aaron could sense that Bosc wasn't telling him everything, so he prompted him, "Tell me what you're not telling me."

"You were always perceptive. Again, unofficially, the men basically hated each other, but neither could directly assassinate the other. It was—how do you Americans say it—'mutually assured destruction'. We don't know what it was, but Grunitzky couldn't touch Nibombé, and Nibombé couldn't touch Grunitzky. Maybe it was blackmail? We don't know. Perhaps now that one of them is dead, it will come to light."

"Interesting." Aaron's head ran in circles, mulling over all the distinct possibilities that could get two powerful men leery enough not to kill each other. "Out of curiosity, Pasquale, why would Daphne take the hit to kill one tyrannical warlord by the next warlord, who is waiting in the wings?"

"Again, I'm not sure if this is the case. Nibombé was a special kind of horrible. He was the type of dictator who had 'free elections' where he won in a landslide vote of ninety-eight percent. You know, because one-hundred percent of the vote would look fishy."

"Ahh, yes, pretend democracy. The West smiles and nods our heads when it serves us and our geopolitical goals but condemns it when it doesn't."

"But what do you expect when the country's top exports are petroleum and gold?" Bosc responded.

"Those are two things the West will often turn a blind eye for. As long as they're exporting to us, we look the other way."

"Well, if you hear anything else, call me."

"I will. And if you get any intel we need over here, we always welcome reciprocity."

"I will, as well. Have a great rest of your day."

"*Au revoir*," Bosc replied before hanging up.

Aaron slipped the phone back in his pocket, spending a minute swiveling back and forth in Frank's chair. *Why do I feel like we're missing something here? Sure, there are many pieces on the board, but I still don't think we're seeing what's actually going on. Something doesn't feel complete.* Aaron stood and stretched a second before sighing and steadying himself to go back into the conference room. *Put on your professional face, Aaron. For now, Frank — Detective Schultt — is a colleague you need to talk to.*

Frank looked up from his phone as Aaron strode back into the conference room. Aaron had a no-nonsense look Frank recognized happened when Aaron had turned off his emotions and was all-business.

"Agent Massey," Frank said, "what did you learn from your contact at Interpol?"

Frank caught the sideways glance between O'Donnell and Rummy. *Fuck! Why did I do that?*

"Well, Detective Schultt," Aaron replied, drawing out the word 'detective' while he spoke. Aaron told the group what he had learned on the phone with Bosc. Frank read between the lines that there was more to the story than Aaron was telling them. Just as Aaron was wrapping up, there was a commotion out in the bullpen.

"François Schultt? Where are you?" a deep voice bellowed in an off-European-sounding accent.

# Chapter Twenty-Nine

Frank opened the door and saw a tall, bulking Black man standing in the bullpen. He was surrounded by a group of men who were clearly armed, which had a lot of cops uneasy. A few had drawn their weapons, aiming at the intruders who were aiming right back.

Chief Hays strode out of his office. "What's the meaning of this?"

"Who are you?" the tall Black asked.

"This is *my* house," Hays said. "So, who are *you*?"

Frank found Aaron by his side with his hand hovering over his service weapon. "Well, this should be interesting," Frank muttered to him.

"My name is General Gassing Grunitzky. As of this morning, I am the new President of Togo," the man replied, staring Hays down.

"And what, President Grunitzky, do you want with my detective?"

Grunitzky's eyes narrowed on Aaron and Frank. "Agent Massey and Detective Schultt, I have evidence you need to see." Slowly, he dipped his hand into his suit jacket, removing a small USB drive that he slowly held up for everyone to see. "I have a video I would like to show both of you before releasing it to your media at a press conference. Out of courtesy, I am showing you first."

Frank looked to Chief Hays for some kind of marching orders. At first, the chief stood there warily eyeing Grunitzky. Then the chief nodded his head to Frank before he turned and walked back into his office. With the chief leaving the bullpen area, the tension in the room quickly dissipated.

"General Grunitzky, if you would follow us?" Frank asked. Frank led the bulking figure down a narrow hallway to a secondary conference room. Rummy followed, with his laptop and a small projector in tow.

"General, if you'd be so kind as to provide Agent Rummy with the USB stick," Aaron said. "I'm sorry about the death of your president. I'm sure you two were very close." Frank watched to see what kind of reaction that last sentence would get, because Frank sensed the statement was a fishing expedition on Aaron's part. *Probably trying to figure out the real nature of Grunitzky and Nibombé's relationship.*

The general nodded his head and responded, "Thank you. It is a significant loss for my country. I can only hope I am as effective a leader as he has been."

*This is one smooth-ass motherfucker.*

"As for the USB, there's only one file on here. We made this copy especially for you."

Rummy accepted the USB stick from Grunitzky and inserted it into the laptop. Frank shot Rummy a quick look of concern. Rummy responded, "Don't worry. It's an air-gap computer, so there are no network interfaces—either wired or wireless." Frank walked to watch over Rummy's shoulder as the USB stick showed a single mp4 file while Rummy ran his fingers over the keyboard.

"What are you doing?" Frank asked.

"I'm running a quick virus scan. Then I'll partition a section of the laptop hard drive and transfer the file to that, so we can give the president back his USB stick."

Rummy worked quickly. In a matter of seconds, the video was playing from the small projector he'd attached.

The video was grainy, but it was of Nibombé in what looked like a bar. Nibombé sat on a couch being served drinks, and there were a couple of women performing personal lap dances. Frank realized quickly that it wasn't a bar. He was looking inside a suite at an upscale hotel. The video fast-forwarded and all the girls were gone. Nibombé's head swiveled as if he'd heard something. Nibombé stood and walked off camera. When he came back into frame, there was a new woman with him.

"Where's his security?" Aaron asked.

"He never let security into his hotel suite when he was going to have *company*," stressing the word to make it clear to everyone that Nibombé was seeing a prostitute. "That's one reason I always made sure we discretely record his sessions. When he went missing, I immediately went to the suite to retrieve the footage."

"Anyone else know that the camera was there?" Aaron asked.

"Of course not. Not even Nibombé knew the *lengths* I went to protect him."

Frank turned his attention back to the video. The woman started a striptease as Nibombé loosened the silk robe he was wearing. Underneath, the warlord wore a matching pair of boxer shorts. The woman said something to him and he smiled. She then ran a finger down the man's chest, twirling her long nail along his stomach. Nibombé leaned in and whispered something in her ear before drawing her in for a kiss. She tossed her head back in a look of ecstasy then used her tongue to lick one of his ears, whispered something before grabbing her small red clutch. Seductively, she turned around and bent over, thrusting her ass in his face. When she popped back up, she spun around holding a gun. Without any hesitation, she fired two shots into his torso and one to the front of his skull.

"Whoa! She's a pro," Jasika said with a soft whistle.

"As you can see, Agent Massey and Detective Schultt, we have evidence that a Black female was responsible for this assassination. I believe the bulk of intelligence you've had about Daphne pointed to her being a French citizen. Based on our own analysis, we believe she is probably African born and not French. She may have lived in France, but she has used this misdirection for many years."

"Just because she's not white doesn't mean she's not a French citizen," Aaron noted.

"True. But something about how she completed the assassination seems less French than African."

"From what you saw in the video, which is clearly something we're not seeing, you can deduce that she was trained in Africa?" Frank asked.

"Very perceptive, Detective Schultt. And before you ask, no, I won't tell you what we see in the video. I will only tell you she is *not* a French-raised individual like your Western police agencies have assumed."

Frank pondered what that could mean to the case, if anything. "Whether she's a French assassin or an

African assassin, she's still in the US killing people. What does it matter?"

"Detective, it matters a great deal. Our worlds, our cultures, our methods and our reasons are very different in Africa. In fact, each African country is as different from each other as you Americans are from the Europeans. Yet, you *Westerners*," Grunitzky said, his voice dripping with disdain, "always clump us together. You never take the time to notice these differences and their importance."

"I didn't mean to offend you," Frank said.

"No offense, Detective. I'm used to the ignorance of the West when it comes to the internal workings of Africa—probably like we are ignorant of the differences here in the US between New York and New Jersey."

Jasika laughed out loud at that one. "I'm sorry. I wouldn't go around NYC saying that in many places."

The general studied Jasika in a puzzled fashion. "You must be Detective Torv. I thought you would be taller."

Jasika started to say something in response, but Aaron jumped in first. "Well, General... I mean *President* Grunitzky, thank you for bringing this to our attention. We'll definitely study this video further."

"You are most welcome."

"And, sir," Frank inquired, "what hotel did this take place in?"

"The president was staying at the Sofitel. Interesting how your first murder took place right on the hotel's front steps."

# Chapter Thirty

Frank excused himself, stepping out into the corridor as he pulled out his cell. He swiped his phone on before saying, "Mariella," into the phone. After a couple of rings, the line picked up and he heard, "NYC Medical Examiner's Office."

"Mariella, it's Frank."

"What can I do for you, sugar tits?"

"I didn't know you checked out my pecs?"

"Why wouldn't I? I may not get to touch them, but I can still stare at them longingly." Frank chuckled into the phone before Mariella continued. "I'm guessing this isn't a dirty phone call. But in case you're wondering, I'm in blue scrubs and a hairnet," she said in her best Eartha Kitt's Catwoman voice. She even added a purring sound for emphasis.

"Anyway, Ms. Cat, we have a line on where the Nibombé murder took place."

"Just a second. Yo, Geeks, get in here," Mariella yelled a little too loudly, causing Frank to pull the phone away from his ear on instinct.

"Damn, woman, you trying to make me go deaf?"

"Sorry. I don't know the power of my own lungs some days." Mariella put down the handset as she turned on the speakerphone. "You're in luck. The Geek Twins were dropping some things off for a different case."

"Hey, Frank," he heard both Nasab and Colin say into the speaker, almost in unison.

Frank explained what had transpired over the last hour. Mariella told Frank she didn't need to head over to the scene since she already had the body, but the Geek Twins said they would go to the Sofitel and start processing the suite. Once the call was finished, Frank headed back into the conference room to find Aaron and Grunitzky still verbally jousting.

"Why did you feel the need to bring us the video today when you could have done it last night when you found out President Nibombé was dead?"

"To be honest, our internal security team had a discussion about whether we should release the video. We didn't want to disparage the name of our president. But, of course, I want to help your investigation find this evil killer and finally bring her to justice."

"Really?" Aaron responded, clearly not buying Grunitzky's altruistic pretense. "And how did that interview this morning with Jenny Mace help our investigation?"

"Oh, you Americans are so sensitive. In my country, that was business as usual. We always shake hands with someone while we stab them in the back with our free hand. It's in my political interests to look like I'm helping you while clearly being ahead of you. My country needs to trust its new leader, after all." With that, Grunitzky stood and made it clear that his time there was done. "It's been a pleasure meeting all of you. Now, if you don't mind, I have work to do at the UN to ensure a smooth transition of power back in Togo."

No one in the room made any effort to stop him. Technically, based on the Vienna Convention on Diplomatic Relations, there was nothing they could do to stop Grunitzky from leaving. They couldn't even force him to sit for an interview without having the State Department involved.

Once his entourage had left the building, the entire team regrouped back in their conference room where they were joined by the chief.

"I don't trust that man," the chief said. "I may not have been on the street in many years, but that guy is only doing what's in his best interests."

"Agreed, Chief," Frank responded. "I would bet my week's salary he orchestrated the 'protest' out front, along with the media coverage, so they would see him coming to the station."

"Frank," O'Donnell said, "you're more on the button than you'd guessed." She turned her laptop around to the group where they watched Grunitzky on the front steps of their precinct, already telling the media out front how his security squad had just delivered a video to the NYPD showing who had killed his beloved president.

"Turn that nonsense off," Chief Hays growled. "I dislike my precinct being used as a photo-op for a megalomaniac. I'm going to have to go play politics with the commissioner's office now. Get this wrapped up, Schultt and Torv." Hays didn't wait for a response before heading out of the conference room, taking out his anger on the poor door as he slammed it shut behind him.

"Well," Aaron probed. "Now what? Rummy, think you can render a composite image of the killer?"

Rummy was typing away on his keyboard, practically oblivious to what had transpired in the room. Aaron was about to repeat himself when Rummy suddenly looked up and said, "I could if this video hadn't been doctored."

That phrase was enough to stop the entire room in their tracks, and their combined heads swiveled in his direction. "Doctored?" Jasika was the first to get out.

"Yep, I thought something was fishy when we were watching the video in the other room. I couldn't quite put my finger on it, but something was off." Rummy sent the video to the larger screen in the room. He replayed the video, slowing it down. He finally stood and walked to the board, pointing to a specific frame. "Right here. Did you see that?"

"I have no idea what I'm supposed to be looking at." Frank grumbled.

"Let me play it back for you. Watch the shadows." They all watched it again.

"Nope, still not seeing it," Jasika said.

"Is this like one of those three-dimensional images you have to stare at for an hour before you finally see the hidden message?" Aaron questioned.

"Let me slow it frame-by-frame." Rummy rewound the video, and they watched it in slow motion.

Frank was about to give up when he saw something that didn't look right. "Was that it?"

"It was," Rummy acknowledged.

"What did you see, Frank?" Aaron asked.

"Play it back, Rummy," Frank directed. He walked to the board and pointed out what he saw as it flashed again across the screen. "Watch the light on her face.

You'll see that just for about a second, the shadow on her face is wrong. It flips." Frank showed them how in one frame, the shadow of the killer was shown on the left side of her face, then it flashed to the right side of her face and back again to the left side.

"I'll be damned," Jasika thought out loud. "I don't think I would have seen that in a million years if it hadn't been pointed out to me. How d'you catch it, Rummy? Fancy software?"

"Nope. I worked a case a couple of years ago involving what are called 'deepfakes'. I got good at looking for the indicators." Rummy broke into an explanation about deepfakes—or video and audio recordings that had been altered to seem like the real thing. "Some deepfakes are funny. There's a whole genre of superimposing Nicolas Cage into every movie role imaginable—Princess Leia, Rose in *Titanic*, scarecrow in *The Wizard of Oz*, etc. But many lonely, sad men have taken their favorite Hollywood actress's face and mapped it to the face of a porn actress and released the video, making it look like the actress had filmed a sex tape."

"Is that legal?" Jasika asked.

"Depends on where you are," Aaron responded. "Hollywood has been using this technology for years in movies. But as more and more people have access to the means to do it, anyone and their at-home studio setup can create one of these. As is often the case, the legal system is woefully behind the times on this matter."

"Exactly," Rummy said. "There are clearly some cases that are more clear-cut than others. But right now, different states have different laws. You can sue someone who created a deepfake of you without your permission in California and New York, but there are no such laws in many other states."

"As is often the case with emerging tech law," O'Donnell chimed in. "The technology is far faster than the legal system."

"While this lesson is interesting," Frank acknowledged, "where does this actually leave us?"

"Honestly," Aaron admitted, "we're back where we started."

"Aaron, not necessarily," O'Donnell responded. "While you were entertaining our new general friend, I got in contact with Pasqual Bosc at Interpol. I mentioned Grunitzky and whether they'd ever heard of anything about Daphne being from Africa."

"And?"

"Bosc remembered he had heard it as a theory tossed around at one point." O'Donnell paused for a moment to look down and flip through her notes before continuing. "The gist of the theory was that she had grown up in one of the former French provinces in West Africa, of which Togo is one."

"So, you're telling me," Frank jumped in, "our little dictator wannabe friend may have been telling us the truth?"

"About the possibility that Daphne is West African?" O'Donnell responded, looking at Frank. "Quite possibly. That Daphne is the murderer of General Kader Nibombé? Debatable."

"Debatable?" Jasika asked.

"I'd bet General Grunitzky saw an opportunity to take care of Nibombé. Daphne was already in NYC, so he could have used it to his advantage. Most African warlords are familiar with the Daphne lore, so it wouldn't be too difficult to fake."

"So, it's entirely possible Nibombé's murder and the murders of Cristillo and Tebbutt aren't related?" Frank asked.

"It's definitely possible," O'Donnell responded.

The additional information lay heavy in the room as everyone absorbed what they'd learned and tried to make sense of all the moving parts. Frank watched Aaron slip into a chair at the desk as he started writing on a legal pad. After about a minute of silence, Aaron finally spoke.

"O'Donnell, I think you should call Director Price and Chief Barling and give them a heads-up on the video and our analysis." Aaron paused again, clearly not sure if he wanted to say what was on his mind. Frank saw the moment when he finally decided. "Also, let them know there's a strong possibility that Grunitzky was involved with—if not orchestrated—Nibombé's murder. We want nothing getting out yet, but I think the director should call State and have them open some back channels to people in the Nibombé administration without raising red flags about our suspicions at this point. We have zero evidence of wrongdoing."

# Chapter Thirty-One

Frank took the opportunity to give Chief Hays the heads-up while O'Donnell filled in the FBI. When he knocked on his door, he heard the chief grumble something, so Frank thought he'd been invited in. The chief looked up in surprise. "I said not now," Hays barked while listening to someone on the phone.

"Sorry, Chief. I misheard you through the door."

Suddenly, the chief's attention was diverted back to the phone, and Frank turned to leave the office when he heard the chief mention the video. Frank hesitated, looked at his boss, got his attention and whispered, "I have new intel."

"Just a moment," Hays spoke into the phone. "This had better be good."

Frank explained what they'd discovered on the video. Hays put his phone on speaker and told the commissioner that Frank was standing right there and had Frank re-tell them what they'd learned. Once Frank had given them the new information, Frank was summarily dismissed to get back to work.

Frank walked back into the conference room and found Aaron hanging up the phone. "I just got off the phone with the Geek Twins. They're at the Sofitel already. They said to come on over when we can," Aaron said.

"I told the chief. He was talking to the commissioner, so I filled them both in. I guess we should head off to the Sofitel."

"How do we get out of here without being seen by the mob out front?"

"There's an old back entrance that leads us to an alleyway that's gated. Unless you work in this building, you'd have no idea the alley is part of the precinct," Frank responded.

"Keeping secrets from me?"

"I guess that makes two of us who can keep secrets." As the words flew out of his mouth, Frank regretted them. He watched Aaron stiffen. "Aaron, I'm sorry. I shouldn't—"

"Whatever, Frank. We're working. Just keep it professional." Aaron didn't wait for a response. He picked up his coat and looked at Frank. "Are you and Jasika coming?"

Frank wanted to respond flippantly but held his tongue for a change. *Why the fuck did I say that? I hadn't even thought about our argument. It just came out. Fuck, fuckity, fuck, fuck!*

Frank looked over at Jasika, who had already put on her jacket. She looked really uncomfortable in that moment. "Let's get this show on the road," she said.

Jasika and Frank led Aaron through the alley and out of the side gate before heading over to the Sofitel. Thankfully, the hotel wasn't far from the precinct, so they could walk there faster than they could get a car and drive. As soon as they were outside, Aaron was on his cell phone. Frank overheard him having a conversation with Jenny Mace. Aaron wanted to know if she had the video yet. Jenny wanted to know if they were heading to the Sofitel again. *Apparently, she knows about the video and the Sofitel already.* Aaron was pretty adept at handling Jenny, Frank realized. He was perfectly affable without actually divulging any pertinent information. *He can be so fucking charming, which is why people open up to him. Hell, it's what got me out of my funk.*

When Aaron, Frank and Jasika arrived at the Sofitel, the hotel hadn't been locked down yet. Anyone could come in and out of the building with no one saying anything. He pulled out his phone and called dispatch to have them send uniformed police to stand at the entryway and ID people coming in and out. "Only people with room key cards, employees with badges or other officers should be coming into the Sofitel while we're still seeing what's going on here." When he was finished with that call, he turned and said, "Jasika, I'm going to head back to talk to the security guy, to let him know we're going to help tighten security for a while. Why don't you and Aaron head up to the room Richardson gave us on the phone?"

"Excuse me, sir. Can I help you?" a voice chimed from the check-in desk.

Aaron and Jasika headed off toward the elevator bank. He spun and nodded politely at the young woman behind the desk. "I'm Detective Frank Schultt, NYPD." He flashed his shield, pulling out his note pad and checking his notes before continuing. "Is Harvey MacMahon working today?"

"Yes, sir. He's back in our security suite. Someone else from the NYPD is already with him."

"Pale white guy or Middle Eastern guy?"

"The white guy," the desk agent responded.

"Perfect! Can you let me through?" Frank asked, motioning to the side door next to the desk clerk. The clerk quickly let him pass and started to give him directions, but Frank said, "I remember. It's my second time seeing your head of security this week," as he walked on, hurrying to the security office. *I've lived years in this city and never ventured into this hotel. Now I'm visiting twice in one week.* The door to the suite was ajar, and Frank could hear Richardson's voice through the crack. "You guys leave the door open for me?" Frank asked as he came in.

"Good to see you again, Detective Schultt," MacMahon said as Frank entered the room. "I was showing Richardson here how to navigate the hotel's surveillance system."

"It's a pretty sweet operation," Richardson bragged. "It's one of the nicer ones in the city. There are hidden cameras on every floor covering entry and exit points, along with remote site backup for thirty days. We've been tracing the hitwoman's steps."

"Perfect!" Frank exclaimed. MacMahon pulled another rolling chair for Frank to sit on as the group scanned through the video. They began by locating the time when the woman entered the hotel room. Thankfully, they had a time stamp on the video Grunitzky had given them, so they could find the woman and watch her enter the room pretty quickly. The three then traced her back through the elevators into the basement where she exited the public restroom in her black cocktail dress, her bag slung over her shoulder. Rewinding, they watched a woman in a maid's uniform enter that same restroom.

"Can you trace that maid's movements?" Frank asked. Without skipping a beat, Richardson shifted between cameras. The woman had walked in right off the street. No one had even glanced at her as she walked into the hotel and went downstairs. "We know how she got in. Let's figure out what happened afterward," Frank said.

Richardson went back to the shot of the woman going into the penthouse suite and tracked her again when she left it. She had gone back to the basement, then to the restroom and exited again as the maid. They watched her look around for a few minutes until she had found a cleaning cart, which she grabbed and headed back to the elevator. Next, the woman and the cleaning cart had gone back to the room in the hotel. About fifteen minutes later, she had exited the room, hung the 'do not disturb' sign on the door and took the cleaning cart back to the first floor. On the first floor, she had retreated into a back hallway that took her to a door next to the shipping entrance.

"Do you have a camera outside there?" Frank asked. He watched as MacMahon stepped in and helped Richardson find the exterior camera. They then watched as the woman had put her bag on the ground and hefted a large and very heavy shower curtain into the dumpster.

"Well, now we know how he ended up in the garbage truck," Frank noted almost absentmindedly. At that point, the woman had pulled out a cell phone, made a call and left the alley.

The whole execution and cleanup had taken a little over an hour. *She never looked panicked or pressed for time.*

*Not once did she look at her watch or a clock?* Something about the scene seemed off to Frank.

"Richardson, did you notice how none of the video cameras caught her face?"

"I was thinking the same thing."

"Mr. MacMahon," Frank said, "could she be one of your regular staff members? She looked like she knew the place pretty well."

"She could have cased the joint," MacMahon noted. "But yeah, it's entirely possible she works for the hotel. It's not like we can see anything here."

Frank ran through the video images he'd watched repeatedly in his head, looking for any details pointing them in the right direction. After a couple of minutes going forward and backward through the videos, it suddenly dawned on him. *The bag!*

"Richardson, can you enlarge her bag?"

"Definitely possible. Let me see if I can find a good shot where it's visible." Richardson scrolled through the feed until he found an image that showed her wrist clear enough. Richardson enlarged the bag enough to see the famous Hermes logo imprinted into the delicate leather.

"That's either a damn good fake or that's a twenty-thousand-dollar Hermes Birkin Bag," MacMahon noted.

Frank turned and looked at him, "When I was at the Fifth Precinct, I worked on the Knockoff Squad. A lot of knockoffs get filtered through Chinatown. You get good at spotting the real thing. Admittedly, without inspecting the bag, I can't know for sure, but it looks pretty real in the picture. That looks like a gold Togo leather bag with white contrast stitching and two twenty-four-karat gold locks."

"Why would someone bring a twenty-thousand-dollar handbag to kill someone?" Richardson asked.

"I don't have the foggiest idea," Frank admitted.

# Chapter Thirty-Two

Aaron had seen his share of expensive suites over the years. The room had a large bedroom with a king-sized bed, a living room space, an office and one-and-a-half restrooms. From the twenty-ninth floor, the view out of the window was a nice one. Admittedly, the view was just of more buildings, but it was still a great vantage point to see people working in offices across the street.

"So, anything we need to know, Nasab?" Jasika asked, snapping Aaron back to the moment.

"Honestly, this place is pretty clean. Even based on what we saw in the video you guys forwarded us, the couch General Nibombé sat on was spotless. Nothing jumps out under ultraviolet light at all."

"Well, the killer was clearly a neat freak," Jasika said.

"True, but we'd still see some kind of discoloration because of the cleaning, unless they cleaned everything top-to-bottom so that everything was discolored evenly. That would take a team of people days to pull off. There's nothing here."

"Did you check out his office?" Aaron asked.

"There's nothing in the office that seems out of the ordinary, but we found a bag with a laptop shoved into a drawer in the desk. Someone had broken into the safe, but they apparently didn't catch the laptop wedged in the drawer."

"Want me to have Rummy come over and take a crack at it?"

"Officially," Nasab advised, "that would violate protocols. Unofficially, he can do it a lot faster than our team will. I've seen that guy work magic before."

"Sure thing, Nasab. I'm going to step out into the hallway and call him." Aaron nodded at Jasika as he pulled his phone out of his pocket before heading for the door. As he opened it, a young maid was standing there. She was pretty, Black and she screamed in his face. At first, Aaron was afraid he'd startled her, but she spun quickly and began running down the hall toward the stairs.

"Jasika! We've got a runner. Have Nasab call Frank. Let's go."

Jasika came tearing out of the room and quickly caught up to Aaron. The stairwell door slammed closed as he and Jasika raced down the narrow hallway. Entering the stairwell, they could hear pounding feet below them, and they took off. Aaron yelled, "FBI, stop!" but the fleeing woman kept going. *Didn't think that would work. Never does! Still, I've gotta legally announce myself.*

Jasika lagged behind, and Aaron heard her pulling out her phone as she called Frank. "Frank, we have a runner in the south stairwell going down." Aaron kept going but Jasika yelled after him, "What does she look like?"

"Maid, mid-twenties, Black female," he replied as he bounded down more stairs and turned before heading down the next flight. Below him, he heard a door open and close. "She's left the stairwell," he yelled to Jasika.

\* \* \* \*

Richardson pulled the live feed with the help of MacMahon, and the three men actively searched for the woman in the maid's outfit. They finally caught sight of a woman wearing a maid outfit on the seventeenth-floor heading toward the north stairwell.

"That's not one of our uniforms," MacMahon noted when they found her on the video feed.

"Jasika, north stairwell, seventeenth floor. I'm going to climb. Hopefully, we can box her in." Frank turned to MacMahon. "How can I get to the north stairwell?"

"Out the door, to the right. You'll see the T-intersection, take another right and you'll see a door. Go through that one and right across the hall is the north stairwell entrance," MacMahon replied.

"Richardson, call my cell if anything changes." Frank didn't wait for a reply before he darted out of the room to find the stairwell. *God, I hope I get those directions right.*

\* \* \* \*

Jasika and Aaron kept going down their stairwell, now being directed by Richardson on Jasika's cell. "She's slowed down and trying to catch her breath," Richardson informed them. "In two more flights, exit the stairwell and enter the northern one. I'm going to help time this so you two and Frank can box her in between flights."

Aaron and Jasika followed Richardson's guidance and could hear him doing the same with Frank. At the appropriate time, Richardson told them the suspect had stopped in the stairwell to catch her breath. Jasika and Aaron exited their stairwell and made it across the plush carpeted flooring to the other one to wait for his signal. They heard Richardson tell Frank to enter the northern stairwell. Aaron could hear Frank yell, "NYPD, *stop!*"

Aaron didn't wait to be told by Richardson what he needed to do. He threw open the stairway door, unholstering his weapon as he entered. A Black woman was already moving up toward his landing. Aaron braced himself for a fight, but the woman seemed to lose all steam at once. She took two steps back, slumped in the stairwell's corner and broke into tears. *Definitely not what I was expecting,* Aaron thought, trading a glance with Jasika, who shrugged. Aaron let Jasika approach slowly before helping her stand, turning her around, frisking her for any weapons and handcuffing her.

The woman was clearly scared out of her mind. She kept shaking and crying. Aaron noticed her shoes first. When Jasika lifted the woman off the ground, he noticed one sole of her shoes was almost worn through. Whoever this woman was, she was clearly dirt poor.

In cuffs, Jasika led the woman out of the stairwell and into an elevator. In the lobby, she handed off the woman to a set of patrolmen and asked them to transport her back to the precinct. Frank called Richardson to make sure he had everything he needed before suggesting they head back to the precinct.

"We have a date with an international assassin," he noted dryly.

"Really? Did you just say that?" Jasika looked at him. "What's next? You going to remove your sunglasses à la *CSI Miami* style?"

"Hey, what's wrong with my David Caruso impression?" Aaron joked as they headed back out into the snowy afternoon.

# Chapter Thirty-Three

The walk back was pretty quiet, and Frank could tell that the tension between him and Aaron would be a problem if he didn't resolve it soon. But Frank was stubborn, and he knew Aaron could be relentless when he thought he was right. He shot Aaron a few sideways glances that he was sure Aaron noticed. Of course, Aaron did the same. By the time he looked at the young woman in the maid's outfit sitting in the interview room, he was ready to get the show moving.

"Jasika, you're with me," Frank said. He watched as Aaron thought about saying something but didn't. Instead, Aaron walked into the observation room without saying a word. *Well, that just happened. Damn him! He's such a baby about this. Why wouldn't he tell me? I don't understand why this is happening. I have a right not to have my boyfriend hugged by a hot naked guy in the gym locker room and not be upset when he 'forgets' to tell me he bumped into him the next day. Okay, Frank. Get your act together.* He caught a sideways look from Jasika, who gave him an 'are you okay?' look. "I'm fine."

"Really? You're not acting fine."

"Let's get this over with." Frank looked at her. He pleaded using his eyes for her to accept his words over how he looked. "I promise, my head's in the game."

"It had better be." Jasika opened the door to the interview room and walked in. They had cuffed the suspect to the table. She went over and uncuffed her before offering the woman a bottle of water.

Frank watched the entire exchange to see how the woman would react. The young female didn't seem like the stone-cold killer he'd seen on the video, but he knew looks could be deceiving. Frank looked at Jasika, and they sat like a pair of synchronized swimmers in perfect unison. Jasika kicked off the interview with the most basic questions.

"What's your name?"

"My name is Reine Avla," she began in a clipped accent.

"Age?"

"I'm twenty-four years old."

"Why don't you tell me what happened back at the hotel?"

Avla sat there for a moment, composing herself. "I've lived in the United States for five years now. I fled from Togo and am becoming a US citizen."

"Why did you flee Togo?" Frank asked.

"My mother and me — she came to the US, too — and we fled my father." Tears pooled in the corners of her eyes as she continued the story. She came from the Tchamba people in Togo who had fairly strict, outdated views of women. Her father had promised her mother years before that his daughter would never be cut like she had been as a teenage girl. "The Tchamba still practice female genital mutilation."

"Oh, wow!" Jasika let out before quickly recovering.

Frank was also taken aback but kept his thoughts to himself. "Okay, but that still doesn't tell me what you were doing in the Sofitel today," Frank said in his most calm voice. It was the voice he used when he had a suspect he was afraid would have a mental breakdown if he didn't use a soft touch. Some suspects needed the stick, some suspects needed a carrot and others just needed someone to hear them.

"I'm getting to that, sir," Avla started again without looking at Frank. "My mother and I fled to the US and, with the help of a nongovernmental agency, applied for asylum. My father had promised me to a member of his tribe, but the man wouldn't marry a woman who wasn't 'pure'." Avla must have caught Jasika's look of disgust and added, "Their words, not mine." Avla continued her story by explaining that when her mother found out what her father had planned, she'd arranged for her and her daughter to be smuggled out of Togo. They thought they had disappeared into the world without a trace. "We haven't seen my father or any of the men from my people since we got to the US."

"Okay, but there's still a piece we're missing here," Jasika said.

"I know. I'm sorry. I don't know how to tell the story. My head is all jumbled."

"Take a break, have a drink and tell us what happened. We're not in any rush," Frank reassured her. "We want to know why you killed President Nibombé."

"I didn't. That's what I'm trying to tell you."

"We have you on vid—"

"I don't know how that is. I mean, I don't know how they made that video, but it's not me."

"Okay, so you're telling me the video is fake?" Frank asked skeptically. She looked at him for the first time. Her eyes pleaded with him to understand. "Why do you think the video is fake? I mean, why would someone from Togo implicate you in the video?"

"That's what I'm trying to tell you." Avla gripped the sides of her temples and started massaging herself as if the gesture would help her arrange her thoughts more clearly.

Under the interview table, Jasika brushed the back of her hand against Frank's thigh. They'd used this gesture before to let the other know when they had an idea during an interview.

"Reine, let me see if I have this right," Jasika probed. "You and your mother fled to the US to avoid you being a victim of female genital mutilation?"

"Yes."

"How did you end up on the videotape that was released to the public?"

"I don't know. I wasn't there. I couldn't have been there. I was working last night."

"Is there any way for us to verify you were working?" Avla immediately looked crestfallen. "Okay, right there. Something went through your head, and you didn't tell us something. What was it?"

"I had a client last night."

"Client?" Franked interjected, confused.

Jasika took a deep breath. "Let me guess. You work as an escort, Ms. Avla?" The woman didn't answer, but she nodded her head up and down slowly. "Who do you work for?"

The woman didn't respond, but her eyes grew huge at the question. Frank realized they'd hit another wall, so he signaled to Jasika that he was going to start questioning again.

"It's okay, Ms. Avla. We're not with Vice. We're not here to arrest you for sex work."

"No. Not a prostitute. *Never* a prostitute," Avla said determinedly. "Some of the other girls? Yes. But I don't do those kinds of jobs. I only take dates with rich men who want companionship."

*I've heard this line before. Not going to push this one. Probably doesn't want to admit to being a working girl because it could have consequences on her and her mother's immigration status.*

"During the day, I'm finishing my master's in fine arts at New York University," Avla said. "At night, I take dates to help pay for my education and our rent."

"Okay, so you're taking care of your mother on your income?" Jasika asked.

"She works, but it's hard to get a good job in this city as a green-card holder. Even with our work visas, most employers don't want to be hassled with non-citizens."

"Okay, so we've veered a bit off-topic," Frank admitted, trying to get the interview back on track. "Last night you had a date with a client. Would this client verify your story?"

"Probably not," Avla said knowingly. "I don't even know his actual name. I call him Jack...or Mr. White. I don't think either of those are real."

"Well, that definitely puts us in a bind. We can't corroborate your story."

"I know," Avla said, shaking her head looking at the wall, trying to form what else to say. Suddenly, her face lightened and she looked at Frank. "The show I saw... The theater may have had cameras." She told Frank and

Jasika she'd seen a play the previous night at the Vivian Beaumont Theater.

Frank knew he didn't need to signal Aaron to have Rummy get the security footage to corroborate her story. *I'm still missing something here.*

"So, for argument's sake, we find out that you were most definitely at the theater last night," Frank said. "Why would someone create a fake video of you killing someone?"

"I don't know. All I can think of is my father did this somehow."

"Your father?" Jasika asked. "Is he that powerful in Togo?"

"He's not. But the man I was supposed to marry is." Avla quickly filled in several missing blanks in the story. President Nibombé belonged to the Tchamba people, so most, if not all, of his US entourage were Tchamba.

"I get it," Frank said. "Anyone in Nibombé's inner circle could want to frame you for fleeing?"

"I don't know how they found us. We've been so careful. I'm not on social media. We changed our names."

"I think I have an idea," Jasika claimed. "Let me ask you a question first. How do you get your dates?"

"The woman who runs the agency vets them, then tells us where and when to go."

"I see where you're going with this, Detective Torv," Frank said. "I bet the woman who runs the escort service has some way of showing your potential dates what you look like. She may even have a website where your pictures are displayed."

Avla's face tried to mask the horror at the realization that it might have been her job that put her in the situation.

Jasika continued. "I'm betting someone you didn't want to see your picture saw it when they were looking for a date. That person told someone in Nibombé's inner circle, and that's how you became targeted with the video. The pieces fit. Of course, this is all guess work because we have no evidence of this."

The phone in Frank's hand vibrated. He flipped it over and read a text from Aaron.

*We have her on camera before the show, during intermission and after the show. The story holds up.*

"Well, Ms. Avla, you're in luck," Frank said. "I was informed your story checks out. You were not anywhere near the Sofitel at the time of the murder two nights ago."

A quick look of relief flashed over her face, making Frank glad she wasn't the murderer in this case. "Now, just because you didn't commit this crime doesn't mean you're completely off the hook here. We still need to get to the bottom of why you were chosen for the faked video. We also need to find out who created it."

"Wait a second," Jasika said suddenly. "Who do you work for?"

"I cannot say. If she knew it was me, then…"

"Detective Schultt, can I speak with you in the hall?" Jasika asked, standing.

Frank shot her a questioning look but said nothing as he stood and exited the room the room with her. When they closed the door, Aaron joined them.

"What are you thinking, Jasika?" Aaron asked.

"I have a theory. It may be one crazy-ass theory, but the pieces may fit."

"Tell us," Frank said.

"What if the same agency that sent those girls to President Nibombé's suite is the one she works for?" Jasika questioned.

"It would explain how they found her," Aaron noted.

"It still seems like a pretty far stretch. I mean, why would they target a girl who ran away to avoid being butchered?" Frank asked.

"That's the piece of the puzzle I'm still figuring out," Jasika admitted. "She mentioned her people are the same as those of President Nibombé. We know it wasn't Nibombé himself, but what if it was someone else here in the US who purposefully set her up?"

"Who are you thinking?" Frank asked.

"Only one man seems to have enough clout here to make something like this happen."

"General Gassing Grunitzky," Frank said.

# Chapter Thirty-Four

Frank texted Rummy and asked for a picture of Grunitzky, and almost immediately he texted Frank back with one. Jasika and Frank went back into the interview room and showed Avla the picture. He didn't even need it confirmed. Fear washed over Avla's face when she Grunitzky's picture.

"Okay, so I'm still missing something here," Frank pondered aloud. "We know you didn't kill President Nibombé. Why were you at the Sofitel?"

"I saw the video of me on TV. I went hoping to find something to prove my innocence."

"But how did you not know Grunitzky was in town?" Frank kept going.

"How would I? I never thought I would see my betrothed again."

"Aw, fuck," Jasika let out. "Not where I thought this was going."

"How did you not know?" Frank asked. "He's been on a few different news shows. Heck, he's been on a lot of television today."

"I don't know. When I saw my face on TV, I kind of panicked. I didn't want my mother to worry, so I turned off the television and told her I had class."

"That's very strange, especially since he's the one who released the video." Frank could almost hear the gears in his head click as it all fit together.

Frank stared at Jasika, who was scrunching her lips, clearly rolling the thoughts around in her head. He was in the same state, not sure what to do next. He told Avla they'd be back and offered to have an officer bring her in something to eat. He needed to get the team together for a tête-à-tête.

After five minutes, he had all five of them— including O'Donnell and Rummy—back in their conference room going over the information they'd gotten from Avla's interview.

"So, here are the pieces we have," Rummy asserted. "We know Avla was pledged to Grunitzky. We suspect Grunitzky saw the picture of Avla when he arranged the call girls for President Nibombé. He probably faked the video given to the press to kill two birds with one stone—killing Nibombé and getting revenge on the woman who'd left him at the altar."

"If I were a betting woman," O'Donnell stated, "I'd bet that he's responsible for Nibombé's murder. All the pieces definitely point in that direction."

"All this is well and good," Aaron said, "but this is looking more and more like a wild goose chase that's completely unrelated to our original one."

"You're probably right there," Frank noted. "I think Grunitzky orchestrated this because he saw the opportunity to blame Daphne, kill Nibombé and punish Avla."

"Yes," Aaron said, "but is that enough to get him convicted of anything?"

"Probably not," Jasika admitted. "But it may be enough to get a judge to hold him while we dive deeper."

"Only one problem," O'Donnell stated. "He has diplomatic immunity. We can't even hold him for anything."

"Dammit!" Jasika said. "You're right. If only he wasn't here on a diplomatic visa."

"That's it!" Aaron exclaimed. "We need to have the Togo government rescind his diplomatic immunity. If they do, he'll be a foreign national in the US with zero protection."

"On it," O'Donnell said. "Let me contact someone at State and get their take on this situation."

"If State doesn't work out, I'll use some international contacts as a backup," Aaron said.

"All this is great," Frank said, "but we are still far from a slam-dunk case against this guy."

"I may be able to help with that," Rummy added. "Once your video-impersonation victim in there told you it wasn't her on the video, Aaron asked me to go back through the vid and look for any further indicators that it was a deepfake. Now that I know what I'm looking for, that shadow I found earlier today is far from the only problem."

"And Grunitzky told me he was the only one who knew about the recording," Aaron noted. "At the very least, we have him for tampering with evidence. It's not necessarily enough to get him indicted, but maybe enough to get a warrant."

"But he has diplomatic immunity," Frank reminded everyone.

"Not necessarily," O'Donnell said, hanging up her phone. "My contact at State says the current Togo regime is running scared of a Grunitzky presidency. And technically, they're the ones in charge right now. Unless Grunitzky commits a coup in the next few hours, Togo may be more than happy to pull Grunitzky's diplomatic immunity. Hell, from the sound of it, they'd be happy to pull it if he had a parking ticket."

"So, there's no love lost there, which fits into what we got from Bosc this morning," Aaron reminded them.

"I guess it's time for us to call our bosses," Frank said.

* * * *

Within a couple of hours, the Togo government was unofficially more than happy to pull Grunitzky's diplomatic immunity, which gave the NYPD and the FBI authority to arrest him and his bodyguards and hold them for questioning and possible prosecution in the murder of President Nibombé. But they needed a warrant first. Frank called Judge Kahl.

"Hello?"

"Janice, it's Frank."

"Hello, Frank. It's a bit late for a social call. What's up?"

Frank ran through the entire story, along with the evidence. "Okay, slow down there, cowboy. You're only going to get one chance at this. Convince me. What's the actual evidence?"

"What we know is the video was tampered with and faked. General Gassing Grunitzky previously told us he was the only one who knew about the camera. So, he would be the only one who had access to the camera to edit the video he provided the US."

"At best, you have a tampering with evidence charge — not murder."

"But is it enough to get him into custody so we can get access to his things?"

"Ultimately, the Togo government would have to be on board before you could enter their embassy to retrieve evidence, assuming that's even where the general kept it," Kahl responded.

"Is it enough to get the warrant?"

"If we were dealing with a US citizen, the warrant would already be signed. But we're not. I will not violate the Vienna Convention on Diplomatic Relations on a hunch."

"But—"

"Even if it's a real good hunch, Frank, you're not there yet."

"Okay, I'll let the team know."

Frank was disappointed, but Kahl was right. They needed something that tied Grunitzky to the murder more clearly.

# Chapter Thirty-Five

"Well, we're in a bit of a standstill for the moment, so we might as well call it a night," Aaron suggested. They wrapped things up with Reine Avla, and had FBI agents place both Reine and her mother in temporary protective custody.

Everyone in the conference room nodded their agreement and started shutting down their individual workstations. Aaron watched Frank out of the corner of his eye. *What am I going to do about you?* He and Frank had some seriously unresolved issues from the past few days, but Aaron wasn't sure if he was in the mood to deal with it all tonight. Aaron said goodbye to his coworkers as he put all his materials in his attaché case and slid into his black wool trench coat. He knew the cold February evening was going to be pretty bad once he stepped outside of the warmth of the police precinct. He slipped his phone out of his pocket and texted his best friend, Judith.

*You home tonight?*

*Sure am. Why?*

*I need some place to think.*

*That sounds ominous. What's wrong?*

*Can we talk about it when I get there?*

*Sure. I'll order pizza and have the wine opened.*

*Wine! That's precisely what I need right now. And lots of it!*

Aaron left the precinct with Frank to avoid making any scene in front of the rest of the crew. Once they were alone on the sidewalk, Aaron turned to Frank. "I'm heading over to Judi's for a while."

"Okay, when will you be home?"

"I'm not sure." Aaron scrunched his face, trying to figure out what he should say to Frank. "Honestly, I'm not sure if I'll be home tonight." Frank's eyes grew large in shock. Before Frank could say anything, Aaron continued. "Please, don't. I'm too tired to hash this out right now with you. I need some alone time. Give Bully a hug from me."

Without waiting for a response, Aaron crossed the street and turned the corner. *Don't look back. You know if you look back, you'll give in and go running back to him.* Aaron took a deep breath and let the frigid air burn his lungs before exhaling his warm breath in a foggy haze in front of him. He saw a cab coming in his direction, so he hailed the taxi to get to Judi's apartment near Astor Plaza.

"Good evening," Aaron said as he entered the cab and shook off the cold. "One-Hundred-Twenty-Eighth and East Twelfth Street. It's The Nathaniel if you're familiar with the area."

"Sure thing, boss," the cabbie replied, switching on the meter as the cab pulled out into traffic.

Aaron stared out of the window at the passing sights. Thankfully, the cabbie did the smart thing and went over to Third Avenue before heading south toward the East Village.

* * * *

Frank stood stunned for a second as he watched Aaron disappear around the corner. *What the fuck?* Frank barely realized what was happening before Aaron was already out of sight. He stared in silence for a few seconds, not sure what he was supposed to do. *Do I run after him? Does he even want me to run after him? I doubt it. Not from the way he just took off.*

Frank headed toward their condo. He barely even noticed what was going on around him. Magically he made it to their block without stepping out in front of a speeding car. He'd been on complete autopilot while his brain was running a thousand miles per minute. He ducked inside the local deli and grabbed himself something to eat because there was nothing sitting in the fridge. He opted for a salad and a sandwich.

He entered their building and was glad to see no one was in the lobby. He wasn't in the mood to deal with anyone tonight. He made his way over the elevator bank and rode up still in a daze.

Bully was happy to see him. His little butt wagged, and he tried clawing at his crate to get to Frank. "Hey there, boy. You ready to go for a walk?" Bully did a little hop in his crate, so Frank let him out and was immediately jumped on. *Well, it's nice that someone's glad to see me.* He retrieved Bully's harness off the kitchen table. The dog walker had left a note telling them she'd been there twice that day. Frank looked at and read the message, *"Hey, Aaron and Frank, wanted to let you know Bully went out around eleven a.m. and again around five p.m. He's already been fed, so don't let him fool you into wanting a second dinner. As usual, Bully was a proper gentleman."* The note was signed, *"Rose, the dog walker."*

With Bully now in his harness, Frank left the apartment and took the dog for his evening potty break.

* * * *

After getting buzzed up, Aaron knocked on Judi's door and was let into her apartment. Judi's apartment was the definition of New York City cozy. It was over six-hundred square feet and cost her right under five grand a month to rent. Judi's Peek-a-Poo, Gypsy, came over to Aaron for a good sniff and a head scratch, clearly smelling Bully all over him.

"Perfect timing... The food beat you by a couple of minutes," Judi said as she laid out plates on her small kitchenette table.

"Good. I didn't realize how hungry I was until I smelled the pizza."

"Hope you don't mind, but I went with straight pepperoni. From the sound of your texts, it didn't seem like a fancy pizza kind of night," Judi said as she handed Aaron a glass of Sangiovese.

"Thanks!" Aaron sat at the table, took a first sip of the wine and smiled inwardly at the medium-bodied red. "Nice... What is it?"

"It's a two-thousand-sixteen Querciabella Chianti Classico. It's a ninety-five percent Sangiovese and five percent Cabernet Sauvignon from Tuscany."

"Look at you, Ms. Wine Expert."

"Hardly! When I asked for an excellent red wine a couple of weeks ago, the clerk droned on about this wine forever. By the time he'd finished, I would have sworn he owned the vineyard."

The two engaged in casual chitchat through most of the dinner. Aaron enjoyed the relaxed nature of his conversation with Judi. She always put him at ease. After dinner, Aaron helped her with the dishes then poured them another glass of wine, finishing the bottle before they retreated to her living room.

"So, you ready to talk?" Judi asked.

"I guess so," Aaron replied before delving into the story of the past couple of days and his relationship with Frank.

* * * *

Bully was not a happy camper outside because of the cold. He did his business quickly then dragged Frank back toward their building. The lobby was still empty and quiet. *Guess people want to hunker down on a frosty night like tonight.*

Once back in the condo, Frank took off Bully's harness and sat on the couch with his dinner from the deli. Bully whined for a second, so Frank bent down and helped him onto the couch. Bully eyed Frank's food longingly, but realized he wouldn't get any scraps from Frank, so he dozed off instead. Frank loved listening to Bully's little snoring sounds. There was something so peaceful about a snoring dog nestled next to him.

After dinner, Frank took out his cell phone. The slight move made Bully open one eye. Once Bully was sure Frank wasn't going anywhere, he closed his eyes again and was quickly snoring once more. *I wish I could fall asleep as quickly as you, Bully.* Frank had hoped he'd have a text from Aaron, but wasn't too surprised when he didn't. He texted Logan instead.

*Hey, you around?*

*Yep! What's up?*

*I'm not even sure. Let's just say Aaron went to Judi's for the night.*

*What happened?*

*Aaron's ex happened. That's what.*

*You're still harping on that?*

Frank wasn't sure how he should respond to Logan. Logan wouldn't pull any punches if he thought Frank was being an ass.

*You still there? Need to talk?*

# Chapter Thirty-Six

Aaron lay on the couch with his head in Judi's lap, looking at her face and trying to figure out what was going on inside her head. "Okay, so we both know Jon was always a bit much, but he's definitely gotten more out there since he's come back from California," Aaron admitted. "I don't get why Frank is so obnoxious about this."

Aaron had spent the last forty-five minutes going over what had happened with Frank, Jon and him over the past few days. He loved Frank, but this toxic masculinity of Frank's and the need to 'claim' Aaron as his own had been a bit over-the-top—even for Frank. When Aaron had finished pouring out his soul, Judi took a sip of the tea she made once the wine was gone. Aaron watched the gears in her head running as she decided what she wanted to say.

"You're not exactly known for your subtlety, either," Judi admonished. To further her point, Judi started listing all the times Aaron had done things in relationships himself that were clearly borderline stalkerish or out of control. "Let's face it. You're both deeply passionate people. It's so blatantly obvious you care about each other. So, he's a little protective. I would be too if a naked woman walked up and hugged my man."

"Well, when you say it like that—"

"Don't get me wrong, I don't think the way Frank handled the situation was any better. You both need to learn to communicate what's going on inside your little noggins better."

\* \* \* \*

"Okay, Frank. Try to see things from Aaron's point-of-view," Logan cautioned. Logan had hopped in a cab and come over to Aaron and Frank's condo, even though Frank had insisted it wasn't necessary. Frank had grabbed Logan a beer from the fridge, and they had sat on the floor leaning against the couch. Bully was lying between both of them, stretched out just enough so he had one paw touching each of them.

"You're taking his side?!" Frank asked with a bit of tension in his voice.

"I'm not taking sides here. I'm laying out the facts—"

"That's lawyer-speak for 'I'm taking his side'."

"No, that's Logan-speak for 'shut the fuck up, Frank, and listen to me for a moment,'" he responded, cocking his head to one side to emphasize that Frank was acting like a petulant child. Frank took the hint and shut up. "As I was saying, think about things from Aaron's POV. One, he didn't ask Crazy Fetty to come back to New York. Two, he didn't ask Crazy Fetty to act all flirty at the gym. Three, he didn't ask Crazy Fetty to hug him without his clothes on. Four, he didn't intentionally run into Crazy Fetty at the flower shop. Five, in your own admission, it's not like you had time once he got back from the flower shop to discuss anything beyond the case. Hello, you had a dead African warlord in a garbage truck—"

"But—"

"Umm…still not finished," Logan continued. "So, maybe Aaron should have mentioned something when you two got home that night. I'll give you that. You didn't exactly instill confidence in him that you wouldn't knock Crazy Fetty out the next time you saw him."

"In my defense, I haven't hit Fetty once. Thought about it a thousand times, *but* never followed through."

"And with that statement, I rest my case," Logan retorted with a roll of his eyes.

Frank absent-mindedly scratched Bully behind his ears while taking a swig of his beer. *God, I know he's right. Why am I so jealous? I never acted like this with Adam. Admittedly, Adam didn't have a Crazy Fetty from his past. But then, we all have pasts.*

"So, what are you going to do?" Logan asked, gently breaking the silence.

Frank looked at Logan for a minute, mulling over the options he had. "I need to talk to him. I need to be honest about my feelings," Frank said, rolling out the word 'feelings' with as much sarcasm as he could interject.

"I get it. You're not a *feelings* person. But guess what? It's not all about you at this point. I know you're a bit out of practice on the relationship front, but being honest with your fiancé about what's going on inside that little head of yours is important." Logan tilted his bottle of beer up, finishing his last swallow. Frank raised his bottle, asking if Logan wanted another one. "Better not. I still need to get back to Ben. He's still a bit bummed about the whole flop—again. Thankfully, that little side-gig of yours, planning your wedding, has kept him busy."

"Really? We barely talked about it at the gym."

"You know how he gets when there's a new project. He's like Bully with a new squeaky toy," Logan joked as he squeezed Bully's back paw, which elicited a single wag of the tail. "So, there's another reason you need to make up with Aaron quickly. I need this wedding to go off to keep Ben busy!"

Frank snorted at that one. "I see how you are. Always got an ulterior motive when it comes to my love life."

"Exactly. Your relationship woes need to get settled to prevent my relationship woes," Logan wiggled his eyebrows at Frank. "Anyway, reach out to Aaron and let him know you want to have a heart-to-heart."

Logan handed his empty bottle to Frank and got off the floor, stretching. Bully looked at Logan, sighed and got up too, doing his favorite doggy yoga positions. Bully looked at Frank expectantly, "Yes, Bully, it's time to go for a quick walk." Turning to Logan, Frank said, "I might as well walk you out."

The two put on their coats and got Bully ready to go out into the frigid night air. They were quiet riding the elevator. Once outside, Frank and Logan hugged goodbye. Bully pulled Frank toward his favorite potty spot, so Frank absently let Bully tug him along. While Bully was doing the potty circle dance, Frank pulled out his phone.

*Hey, babe, sorry I've been such an ass these last couple of days.*

Frank paused, waiting to see if Aaron would text back immediately. After not getting one back quickly, he shot off another text.

*So, out with Bully for his nightly potty. He misses you. I miss you. We really should talk.*

This time, he got a response fairly quickly.

*I agree. I'm not coming home tonight. Not about you, just had a bit too much wine with Judi.*

*I understand.*

*Give Bully a big hug from me.*

*Will do.*

*Probably not going to make it to the gym in the a.m. Let's meet for breakfast at Viva La Coffee at eight?*

*Sounds like a plan. See you then.*

Frank stared at the text, not sure what he should type next. He had so many things he wanted to say right then, but he'd have to wait until they were face-to-face to really say those things. He went with something simple.

*Love ya.*

*Love ya too!*

# Chapter Thirty-Seven

Frank barely slept. He tossed and turned all night, trying to figure out what he was going to say to Aaron when they met up the next morning. He hoped going to gym would calm his nerves, but even the endorphin rush of exercise didn't squash his anxiety.

Frank arrived at Viva La Coffee at about seven-forty-five and found a cozy table in the store's corner that would allow him and Aaron some privacy. He ordered Aaron's favorite drink and had it ready for when he got there. While waiting, he nervously scrolled through his email messages to see if there was anything he needed a heads-up about before going into the station. Nothing popped as immediately important.

He opened *The New York Times* app on his phone and scrolled through the list of articles about crime. A politician's best friend had been arrested on federal cyberstalking charges. New research showed that Black people were still more likely to be stopped by NYPD Officers. *Fuck! When is that nonsense of racial profiling going to stop?* He flipped the page and read about the latest scandal rocking the governor's mansion in Albany. As he aimlessly flipped through the paper, he caught a headline reading *Schultt Pharmaceuticals Stock Already Soaring in Anticipation of Product Unveiling.* Under the headline, he saw a picture of his mother. *She has aged well*, Frank thought to himself. He skimmed the article. The company was on the verge of releasing a new product that was all 'hush-hush', but anticipation of its unveiling later that week had already started having a positive impact on stock prices. *I really should tell Aaron about my shares.*

When Frank's grandmother had passed, she had left him shares in the family business that no one knew about. Frank's lawyer oversaw their day-to-day functioning under a pseudonym so that his parents wouldn't know he owned stock. Even though he took precautions to keep the family business at arm's length, he wondered if his parents knew somehow. He owned enough shares that he could retire early if he played his cards right. Despite his grievances with his parents, he still trusted their brains and business acumen.

"What ya reading?" Aaron said, slipping into the chair opposite Frank.

"About my parents' company," Frank said. Aaron raised a knowing eyebrow at Frank. "Yeah, I know. I'm not known for talking about my parents or their company much."

"That's an understatement," Aaron said compassionately. "You don't need to now, either."

"No, I need to. That's half the fucking problem. I keep everything bottled inside and never say anything about anything." Frank watched Aaron take a sip of his coffee. He noticed Aaron hadn't even asked him what it was, because Aaron knew Frank would get him the right drink. "So, let me tell you a story." Frank spent the next twenty minutes spelling out everything that had happened between him and his parents when he'd come out. He even told him about his grandmother's trust and his stock options. "I mean, they're not worth a ton of money, but they will definitely help us when we decide to retire."

"I like that."

"What?"

"You talking about us in the long term. I know opening up is hard for you, and it definitely comes in stages, but I want you to know I see us for the long haul, too," Aaron said. Frank smiled and reached across the table to grab Aaron's hand. Aaron grasped it back, giving it a quick squeeze. "However, we, like any couple, have issues we're going to have to work through. For me, I need to think about how you see things. I didn't want you to worry about Jon because there was nothing to worry about."

"But—"

"I know. I know," Aaron said, shaking his head and averting his eyes. "I'm sure on some level I liked the attention. We all like attention. But I don't want to be in a relationship with anyone but you. And I don't want to have sex with anyone but you. I need you to know that about me. I know I can be a huge flirt. I've been using it to my advantage for years. Hell, it's how I've been successful in my career. I'm well aware of the doors my pretty face and perfect teeth have opened for me. If I'm not getting my way, I pop on the 'killer Aaron smile and charm'. I don't even realize I'm doing it half the time. It's so ingrained in me."

"And I like that it's ingrained in you," Frank said. He sighed and tried to form the words in his head before speaking. "I need you to know on some level I'm afraid of losing you. I'm afraid all this is going to end. Between losing my family then losing Adam, Dr. Weintraub thinks I have an innate fear of intimacy because I'm afraid of getting hurt."

"Frank, we all have a fear of being hurt." Aaron absently rubbed his thumb over the back of Frank's hand.

"I need you to know I love you," Frank said. "God, you have no idea how much I love you. And I know I suck at saying and showing it at times, but I would be lost without you."

"I love you, too. But part of loving someone is trusting them and being open with them."

"I do trust you," Frank quickly interjected. "I don't trust Crazy Fetty."

"Crazy Fetty?" Aaron asked with a sly smile.

"Umm, yeah," Frank drew out. "It's kind of what Logan and I have been calling him behind your back."

Aaron let out a burst of laughter and quickly covered his mouth. Aaron got himself under control before saying, "Crazy Fetty, eh? Well, it definitely fits. Trust me. I spent half of our relationship trying to diagnose him, and that was before he went to Hollywood."

"And?"

"Well, never diagnose a partner. But he had narcissistic tendencies already in development before he left New York. As you can tell, those have clearly been enhanced by his time on the West Coast. He doesn't understand the concept of boundaries. He acts without thinking. He's hyper-impulsive and says or does whatever he feels like saying—consequences be damned. For his job, being an impulsive narcissist has served him well. As a person, it's left him a bit of a fucking mess."

"And you knew this and still dated him?"

"He was fun. He was the party boy to end all party boys. And for a while, it was fun to move in those circles." Frank scrunched his face, not sure what circles Aaron referred to. "You know the ones I'm talking about. The 'Gay-List' or the 'A-Gays of New York'. They're all about living life large and beyond their means."

"Yeah, never really been my scene."

"I had my stint, then I grew tired of it. It had affected my professional and personal judgment. You can't live on three hours of sleep for long before it impairs you. I had crashed once for twenty-four hours and missed a critical bust. I had almost been terminated. Someone pulled some strings for me and had me reassigned as the FBI legal attaché working out of the US Embassy in Lyon."

"Oh!" Frank responded as his eyebrows shot up. "I always assumed that was something you wanted."

"It was definitely not in my original career plan. But I'm thankful someone saw my worth and forced me to change my scenery for a few years. Once I was out of the city, it was amazing how much clearer my perspective on life and my relationship with Jon had become. We had talked about doing the long-distance relationship, but we both knew it wouldn't last. We ultimately broke up one night through FaceTime."

Frank took a sip of his coffee as he processed this additional information. *Why didn't Aaron tell me about this before? Probably because he tried to keep that part of him in the past. Can't blame him for that.*

"So, I do *so* solemnly swear," Frank declared raising his three fingers like a Boy Scout, "to work on my jealousy issues. And to work on being more open and communicate what's going on in my head so it doesn't fester."

Aaron repeated the gesture and responded, "And I do solemnly swear to be open and not hide things from you when I think I'm trying to 'protect' you. And, I swear to not let the sun go down on an argument between us again. If there's a problem, I'll provide us a safe space where we can be open and honest with each other, even if things are rough."

"I like that one," Frank said, nodding. "I know this doesn't fix everything, but I definitely think it's an impressive start. Dr. Weintraub would be so proud of me for acting like a big boy with 'big-boy' feelings."

Aaron smiled and rolled his eyes jokingly at that last statement. "I think she's good for you, Frank."

"And speaking of Dr. Weintraub. She thinks it would be a good idea if I invited you to one of our sessions. You don't have to —"

"I would be honored. I think the safe space of therapy could be great for both of us. All it can do is improve our already-loving relationship."

Frank smiled and leaned across the table to kiss Aaron. Placing his hand on the back of Aaron's head, he leaned their foreheads together before saying, "Again, I'm so sorry about being such an ass these past few days."

"Water under the bridge. Let's make sure we learn from this and never let it happen again." Frank released Aaron, and as he did, Aaron glanced at his watch. "Well, I guess it's time to head into work. Shall we go?"

"That we shall." Frank picked up a to-go box of coffee for the group, along with cups, sugar, stirrers and cream before leaving. With the bag of supplies in Frank's hand and the box of coffee in Aaron's, they held hands as they left the coffee shop, huddled against each other as they walked to the precinct through the blistery morning cold.

# Chapter Thirty-Eight

Frank sat at his desk and noticed a padded envelope left there. He set it aside as he booted his computer and scrolled through his email list. Nothing much caught his attention. There were a few requests for information about the case from the higher-ups. Joanna Gleason asked if the task force needed any new resources. He shot her a quick email, letting her know they were good at the moment. He summarized what they suspected about Grunitzky's involvement with the Nibombé assassination. Almost immediately, she responded with a one-line question that was sent from her iPhone. "Do you need to hand that case off?"

Frank thought about the question for a moment before responding. "Nah, I can't help shaking the feeling there is still some kind of overlap. Not sure what it is. If I'm wrong, I'll let you know." After hitting send, he looked up to see Jasika settled at her own desk. "Didn't even hear you come in. Anything new on your end?" Frank questioned.

"Nope. Just reading the full forensic report from Mariella and the Geek Twins. Nothing stands out as surprising, given what we know." She paused for a moment before starting again. "I take that back. Just found out the Beretta we found with Nibombé was not part of the shipment that went missing earlier this year. In fact" — she skimmed over her screen before looking up, snorting and continuing — "the serial number belongs to a batch that was purchased by the — drumroll please — Togo government."

"Interesting," Frank said.

"What's interesting?" Aaron asked as he approached and put his hand on Frank's shoulder.

"The gun used to kill Nibombé was purchased by the Togo government," Jasika responded.

"Interesting, indeed," Aaron responded. "Still not quite enough to get a warrant for Grunitzky, but it's definitely one more nail in that guy's coffin."

They caught each other up on other details of the case. Beyond the gun, nothing major had come in overnight. "Well, we might as well go update the whiteboard in the conference room with the gun info," Jasika said. Frank stood and started heading that way. But before Frank could step away from his desk, Jasika asked, "Frank, who's the package from? A new secret admirer?"

"Don't know. Didn't even open it yet. I got sidetracked." Frank grabbed it and took it with them.

The five task force members sat around the room. They updated the whiteboard with all the information they'd garnered over the previous twenty-four-hours. Frank sat back, eyeing the board. *As often happens at this point in a case, there are definitely a lot of empty spaces and missing information.* He kept trying to find some kind of pattern that would make all the disparate parts make sense, but nothing seemed to click in his head. Absently, he picked up the package and opened it. There was a folded sheet of paper inside, so he slipped it out and read it.

*Dear Daphne Taskforce:*
*I'm sure you're well aware by now, I did not kill President Kader Nibombé. I was, however, approached to handle that job. They provided me information about his 'extra-curricular' activities at the Sofitel. I hope the following helps with your investigation.*
*Daphne*

"Umm, Rummy. I need you to get your fingerprinting kit."

"What is it, Frank?" Aaron asked.

Frank read the note to the group while Rummy put on his latex gloves and dusted for prints. Once Rummy was done with the envelope, Frank looked inside and found a USB stick. "She also sent a present," Frank said as he upended the envelope and the drive hit the table. Rummy quickly printed the USB drive, but it was clean.

"Wow, she's brave," O'Donnell responded almost admiringly.

"Brave or brazen, not sure which," Aaron noted. "Either way, this should be interesting."

"Okay, so there are a ton of prints on the exterior of the envelope, which is not surprising," Rummy said. "As for the letter, I'm only seeing one sent, which are almost assuredly Frank's. I'll cut up the envelope to see if there are any interior prints, but she's always so clean I'm not expecting anything. She's definitely good at covering her tracks. I'm going to run all the prints, but I seriously doubt any of them are hers."

Frank had to agree with Rummy's assessment. "So, shall we see what's on the USB?"

Without responding, Rummy pulled out his air-gap laptop and plugged in the USB stick. After scanning the stick for any signs of viruses or other potential evidence, he told the group the USB one contained a single .mp4 file. All five of them looked up at the screen as he hit play on the video. The video was a different angle of the assassination of President Nibombé — and this one told a very different story.

# Chapter Thirty-Nine

Aaron sat transfixed by the video, as did everyone in the room, as the woman shot President Nibombé. The angle was an overhead shot, so he still didn't get a great look at the female assassin. However, there were definitely a few significant differences. Following the gunshot, the screen had panned to a side door as three people walked out. The first two he recognized as members of General Grunitzky's entourage from the previous morning. The third figure had been General Grunitzky himself. *Got you, motherfucker!*

"Whoa," Rummy said in a low voice. "Didn't see that coming."

Aaron watched as Frank pulled out his phone and spoke the name 'Kahl' into it. "Is this one faked?" he asked, looking at Rummy.

"It's always possible, but I won't know until I've dissected the images. But, if I were a betting man, I'd bet this is legit."

"Why?" Jasika questioned.

"The camera angle, the shadowing, the smoothness of the panning and a few other details would be pretty hard to fake. That's not to say it's impossible, but it would be hard. You'd need an outstanding special effects team to pull off a fake like this."

Aaron nodded in understanding. Rummy replayed the video multiple times, and Aaron searched for additional details with each viewing. In the background, he listened to Frank describing the video and the gun's information to Judge Kahl. *We shouldn't have a problem getting that arrest warrant now.*

Frank quickly outlined everything they'd learned over the last hour. "So, do you think this provides enough to arrest him now?"

"Do you trust this Daphne? What are her motives?" Kahl asked.

"I don't know enough about her to trust her or her motives. What I know is she has some kind of honor code she's historically worked by, so sending this video seems to fit into that code of hers."

Frank could practically see Kahl sitting in her chambers playing with the cord on her phone as she thought about the information he'd supplied. "Officially, you've got your warrant to execute the arrest of any non-embassy residents that are known to be direct associates of General Grunitzky. Unofficially, I would hold off on calling State. I doubt they'd stop you, but it's definitely easier to get them on board when he's already in custody."

"Thanks."

"Don't thank me, Frank. Just make sure the case sticks. You know going after a foreign dignitary is dicey. All this ultimately hinges on whether Togo will revoke his diplomatic status. If that doesn't happen, then State will cry holy hell and the US will make an enemy of the new President of Togo."

"I get it."

"I'm sure you do, but this isn't policing as normal. This is international politics. If this blows up in your face, there will be no saving you or anyone associated. I want you to know what you're stepping into."

"Thanks. I trust my team. I'll let everyone know about your warning." Kahl said her goodbye and promised to sign the warrants once she received them from Frank's group. With that part of the plan taken care of, Frank told them what Kahl had said. He gave the team all one last chance to bow-out in case he was steering the Titanic right into a Grunitzky iceberg. Thankfully, everyone was on board with the plan.

"I'll start in on the warrants," O'Donnell said.

"Great," Frank replied. "Rummy, can you find Grunitzky?"

"Sure. Give me about twenty minutes and I'll have a general idea of where he's located."

"I'm going to go give Hays a heads-up." He spun on his heels and exited the conference room as everyone set off on their immediate tasks.

Hays' office was shut, but the light inside shown through the blinds on the door window. Frank rapped three times on the door and waited for a response. "Enter." Frank did precisely that. Hays was shuffling through a bunch of paperwork on his desk. "What can I do for you, Detective?"

Frank broke into a rundown of everything that's been going on. Hays put his hands under his chin in a steeple as Frank laid out his conversation with Kahl. "I'll be honest, Detective. I'm not too keen on keeping

State out of this right now, but I'm going to trust Judge Kahl's reasoning. Here's what I'm going to do. When you leave my office, I'm going to call the commissioner and tell him what you've told me. Unless instructed otherwise by the commissioner, I will not inform the mayor's office until you are apprehending the general." Frank waited for more elaboration. "Let's face it. The mayor's office is a sieve. As soon as anyone there hears about the raid, people in Washington will know within minutes. As such..." the chief continued, but suddenly took a deliberate pause. A look of careful determination swept across his face before he began speaking again. "As such, I recommend having someone call State as soon as the warrants are served. Heck, I would have the person call the State Department right before you give the 'go' order."

Frank easily read between the lines. Just in case the State Department threw a hissy fit about the warrants' execution, they had to be read in but not until the last possible second. That way, State couldn't cry foul for not knowing, but they also couldn't do anything about it.

The chief looked back at his paperwork, indicating the conversation was over. Once back in the conference room, Frank got up-to-date status reports from everyone, while also telling them what he'd been told by the chief.

"Funny enough," Aaron admitted, "Barling basically said the same thing to me. She's going to call Director Price but doesn't plan on alerting anyone else until the warrants are served."

"I guess that's why my chief and yours get paid the big bucks to play politics," Frank responded. "I'm glad

I get to do my job without having to be so Machiavellian in every move I make."

"Look at you, using big, fancy words," Jasika heckled.

"I have degrees, you know," Frank retorted.

"So, I hear," Jasika said playfully. "Just don't see you using them very often here. Anyway, I have the ESU on standby. Once we know where Grunitzky is, they'll establish a mobile command post and support the arrest."

"Why did you call ESU?" Aaron asked.

"You remember those bodyguards the general had when he strolled in here with his video. I figured overpowering them with personnel and weaponry was the smartest way to go."

"Also, I just emailed the warrants to Judge Kahl's office," O'Donnell told the group.

"So," Rummy jumped in, "I have a location for Grunitzky. Apparently, our dear leader is enjoying some nicer parts of New York City at the moment." Frank could hear the sarcasm dripping from Rummy's voice.

"Where is he?" Aaron asked.

"A place you and Frank have definitely never visited…The Executive Club."

"Dear God," O'Donnell said. "Could he be more cliché? I'm an evil African douchebag warlord. After I've committed murder and mayhem, let's go to a strip club."

# Chapter Forty

Aaron, Frank and Jasika made their way to the staging area once the ESU was ready. Instead of going into the club — which posed several problems because the Togolese would have possible hostages — they planned to wait until Grunitzky and his entourage left. The problem with this was that they had no way of knowing how long it would take for Grunitzky and his minions to depart.

"I have an idea, but you're not going to like it," Aaron said. All the eyes in the mobile command unit swiveled in his direction. "We know Grunitzky is constantly keeping tabs on things in Togo, which I bet he's still doing. What if we planted a fake news story about a coup in Togo? He'd head to the embassy for an official briefing immediately."

"Interesting idea," Frank said. "How are we going to plant a fake news story, though?"

"Our favorite reporter?" Aaron said, more as a question than a statement.

"Dear God, no. You know Mace will want something in return."

"True. But, if it gets Grunitzky out of there with no civilians put in harm's way, it's worth it." Aaron looked to Frank, who just grunted his consent. Aaron stepped out of the command center, pulled out his phone and dialed the Mace's number.

"Jenny Mace," the chipper voice on the other end of the line said. "How can I help you, Agent Massey?" Without skipping a beat, she added, "While I have you on the phone, would you like to comment officially on Daphne's involvement in the murder of President Kader Nibombé?"

"Blah, blah, blah, you know I can't comment on an ongoing investigation."

"A reporter's gotta try."

"So, as to your first question, I need a favor."

"Those don't come cheap, you know?"

"And I have something you'll want, exclusively, if you help us."

"I'm listening."

Without giving too many details away, Aaron told Mace that he needed a fake news story about Togo's coup. "In exchange, once we have President Kader Nibombé's murderer in custody, you'll get the complete story before anyone else even knows it has happened."

"Sure. But it has to come with an on-air interview."

"Jenny—"

"Gotta have it. You're asking me to put my journalistic integrity on the line with no information. I'm going to need a big-time interview to smooth over any ruffled feathers this fake story may cause. And let's face it. It's already twelve-twenty, so I only have a few minutes to convince my boss to let me cut in during the noon-time news."

Aaron sighed before saying, "Fine. Here's what I need the story to say," he continued before dictating the key points that needed to be made within the story. Once he and Jenny hammered out the specifics, she told him the report would be live on their news in the last segment and on the website in under ten minutes. "Thanks," Aaron said.

"Don't mention it. I look forward to our interview," she said and hung up the phone.

Aaron leaned against the trailer's wall and took a deep breath. *Sometimes you have to get in bed with the devil to avoid turning the world into hell.* He collected his thoughts, pushed himself off and reentered into the command post. He looked at the ESU leader. "We should have a news article online in about five minutes. Once Grunitzky is outside, have your team move in. Make sure everyone knows his bodyguards will be armed and dangerous. Your team needs to pat them down thoroughly. Look for all kinds of weaponry and other hidden tools."

\* \* \* \*

They watched the takedown from the command post, which was executed to textbook perfection. Frank thought the video would make a great case for how to confront, disarm and take into custody people who are armed and dangerous. All-in-all, everything went according to plan. No one was shot. Once Grunitzky's men saw they were outgunned, they quickly laid down their weapons, agreed to be handcuffed and were placed in a large prisoner transport van. Grunitzky was placed in the back of a patrol car and sent ahead to the precinct. Frank called to give the desk sergeant a heads-up, who agreed to have Grunitzky processed and waiting in an interview room before the team got back to the station.

"Well, that was entirely too easy," Jasika muttered under her breath as the mobile command unit rolled away.

"Oh, you just had to say that?" Aaron responded, shaking his head slightly. "You know the other shoe is going to drop now," he chided.

"Okay, you two," Frank cut in. "Time to get back to the station. We have a president-wannabe waiting for us." Frank ushered the Jasika and Aaron into their sedan before heading back. Frank played over everything in his head, trying to put any missing pieces together before he questioned Grunitzky. Frank had learned a long time ago that it was best to be as informed as possible when interviewing someone. He wanted to make sure he had more information than the prisoner thought he did.

The ride was short and quick in the early afternoon traffic, so getting back to the station only took a few minutes. At the station, news reporters were milling around outside. Frank noticed one reporter obviously absent from the fray was Jenny Mace. Of course, she didn't need to be there because she had an exclusive coming to her from Aaron.

Once Aaron, Frank and Jasika got past the reporters, saying their customary "no comment" to anyone who tried to shove a camera or microphone into their faces, the relative calm of the precinct was welcomed. The desk sergeant nodded his head and let them know their prisoner was in interrogation two. They'd just entered the bullpen when O'Donnell stepped out of the conference room and started walking toward them. She had a phone to her ear, saying goodbye when she met them.

"State knows. They're not happy."

"Big surprise. And we figured someone would let them know once we told the mayor's office," Frank reminded her.

"True, but our back-channel communications with the Togolese government have been unexpected. They want Grunitzky."

"Whoa," Aaron said. "They're going to let him keep his diplomatic status and get away with it. What happened to Nibombé's people? They were supposed to ensure Grunitzky stayed here."

"That's just it, Aaron. Nibombé's people want Grunitzky's head." O'Donnell quickly explained that as soon as State had been notified, Togo's ambassador had been contacted to let her know the arrest was happening. Instead of revoking Grunitzky's diplomatic status, the Togolese government has asked for the general's extradition to stand trial in Togo.

"Well, that's one angle we hadn't even considered," Aaron admitted.

"Oh, it gets better," O'Donnell said. "I just got off the phone with Pasquale Bosc. Apparently, the woman who would be the likely next President of Togo…" O'Donnell trailed off as she looked down at her notes, finding the woman's name, "Prime Minister Hadiza Akakpo, would rather Grunitzky stay in the US. It's basically a Togolese pissing match at this point between two disparate political factions. If Grunitzky comes back, Nibombé's people will seize control after Grunitzky is executed."

"Okay, for those of us who failed geopolitics in school, they have a president and a prime minister."

"Basically, the president is the Chief of State and the prime minister is the Head of the Government. The president appoints the prime minister from the parliamentary majority. Apparently, in the last election, Nibombé kept his presidency, but Parliament went to a different party. Out of the that party, Nibombé saw Hadiza Akakpo as the weakest member, so he elevated her to prime minister," O'Donnell explained.

"This is making my head ache," Jasika said.

"So, let me get this straight," Aaron said. "There are two political movements underfoot, and depending on what happens to Grunitzky, one takes over Togo?"

"Pretty much," O'Donnell replied.

"Well, fuck," Jasika grumbled. "What does our government want?"

"I'm still waiting on that phone call." As if almost on cue, O'Donnell's ring tone started playing the theme song from *She-Ra*. "Oh, the Princess of Power calleth," she joked before hitting the answer button on the screen. "O'Donnell."

Frank listened to the one-sided conversation. It became apparent that this one would last longer than a minute, so he took the break to run to the restroom. Aaron followed suit. At their separate urinals, Aaron joked, "You know they're going to wonder what we're doing in here together?"

Frank snorted. "Just tell them we were adjusting our makeup." They zipped their flies and washed their hands.

Aaron quickly looked around the restroom to note that no one was there, so Aaron spun Frank around, pushing him against the wall. Frank let out a little '*oof*' as his belly was pressed against it. Aaron leaned into him, his taut stomach pressing into Frank's back. Aaron brushed the side of his neck with his jaw before nibbling on Frank's earlobe. Aaron's growing member was pressing into Frank's ass, so he responded by arching his back and grinding deeper into Aaron's crotch. He whispered into Frank's ear, "This is for later."

Aaron's weight disappeared from Frank's back, so he turned around and looked at Aaron, whose erection was clearly visible through his pants. Aaron buttoned his coat, making it so even Frank couldn't tell his cock was still standing at attention. Frank leaned forward and kissed Aaron. "That's *so* not fair," he said, pointing to Aaron's hidden erection. "I'm flying at full mast here."

"You should probably get control of that before you come back to the conference room," Aaron said, smirking before turning and leaving the room.

*What got into him? Cocktease much?* Frank let out a sigh, looking at himself in one of the bathroom mirrors. "Down, boy! Not the time to play. Play? Yes! Just not now." He took a couple of deep breaths and splashed cold water on his face, focused on the cooling sensation of the water as blood rushed out of his cock. Once he was put back together, he left the restroom and headed to the bullpen.

# Chapter Forty-One

By the time Aaron returned, Jasika and O'Donnell had retreated into the conference room. He opened the door as O'Donnell was getting off the phone.

"That went on forever," Jasika said.

"I was only gone for a couple of minutes," Aaron said. Jasika spun her chair, obviously startled.

"Dear God! I didn't even hear you come in," Jasika squealed.

"I'm quiet, like a ninja," Aaron quipped.

"Okay, you two, playtime's over," O'Donnell teased.

*Playtime didn't even get started.* Aaron sat down at the table, still thinking about what had happened in the restroom with Frank. *What got into me?* He replayed the movie in his head, but his erection was growing again, so he swung himself under the table before unbuttoning his jacket.

Aaron refocused his attention on her as O'Donnell continued, "After all that, the State Department is leaving it to us to make, and I quote, 'the right decision' for the United States'."

"In other words," Aaron cut in, "they don't want to be the ones left holding the bag if everything goes sideways."

"Bingo!"

Frank opened the door and walked into the room. Aaron had finally gotten himself under control, but seeing Frank framed in the doorway made his blood rush south again. *Down, boy!* Aaron grabbed a legal pad and positioned it in front of himself casually as he stood. "Who's ready for an interview?"

Frank and Jasika agreed to conduct the interview, so Aaron, O'Donnell and Rummy entered the observation room.

\* \* \* \*

"Gassing," Jasika said as she entered the room. Frank and Jasika decided to let her conduct most of the interview because of Grunitzky's apparent low view of women. Also, Frank knew that avoiding his honorific title of 'general' or 'president' and calling the man by only his first name would definitely piss Grunitzky off.

Grunitzky didn't respond. He eyed Frank and Jasika as they sat on the other side of the table. "Is this how you interrogate people in your country?"

"Not an interrogation, Gassing. We're going to have a polite conversation," Jasika said with a sickly-sweet smile.

"In my country, I'd have you strung up, hanging from chains with electric cables dangling from your genitals already."

Frank began to say something, but Jasika placed a single finger on his thigh under the table. "If you're trying to get a rise out of me, it won't work. There's nothing you can say I haven't heard a thousand times before, or worse, since I've been a cop." Grunitzky let out an acknowledging grunt, so Jasika continued. "Gassing, I assume you've been read your rights. And from what I was told by the desk sergeant, you waived your right to counsel. Is that correct?" Grunitzky grunted again. "For the record, please say 'yes' or 'no,'" as she motioned to the two cameras in the corners that were recording the interview.

"Yes, I am informed. And yes, I have not requested a lawyer for this *interrogation*."

"Thank you. And again, this is an interview between professional law enforcement officials." She glanced at her notes before continuing. "That's basically what you did in Togo? You were head of President Nibombé's security, after all."

Grunitzky gave a quick nod, saying nothing. He was good at keeping his face blank. *I'm betting he's been on both sides of his country's interrogation techniques. He has this assurance that nothing we can do in here can get to him.*

"Great. So now that we're having a polite conversation, here's what we know." She laid out the evidence.

"These are all interesting speculations," Grunitzky said after Jasika stopped. "But where is your evidence?"

"Thanks for asking," Jasika said, in a tone that suggested she'd forgotten that evidence was necessary. "Why don't I show you a quick video." She pulled out her phone and showed Grunitzky the video of him entering the penthouse suite at the Sofitel immediately after the president had been assassinated.

"Where did you get this?" Grunitzky growled, the stillness in his face breaking for the first time since they'd entered the interview room.

"Oh, and before you ask, this one is not a fake, unlike the one you gave us."

Grunitzky bolted out of his chair. Frank had seen the twitch in the man's muscles milliseconds before he'd stood, so he was already on his feet, putting himself between Grunitzky and Jasika.

"Sit down, Grunitzky," Frank said, opting to use the man's last name. The man stared into Frank's face, and Frank stared right back. *Come on. Do it! Take a swing at me. Give me a reason to knock you on your ass, you smug prick.* Slowly, Grunitzky lowered himself back down.

"I want to speak to my consulate."

"Sure," Jasika said. "But before you do, you may want to know that they are itching for that phone call. Hell, they want us to handcuff you and extradite you back to Togo."

"They know," Grunitzky muttered, his eyes widening. Frank watched the moment Grunitzky realized his lifelines were disappearing.

"Yes, they want you," Jasika started in again. "But, we're not sure what to do with you just yet. Give me one reason *not* to hand you over to your countrymen. I'm betting there'll be a nice showy trial then a public execution on television." Jasika paused, looked at her notes then looked at the man, staring him straight in the eyes. "You wouldn't be the first former presidential bodyguard to be tortured and killed by your government, now would you?"

Grunitzky looked at her and diverted his eyes to Frank. "I want a deal. I have information your government may want."

"I'm a cop. You know that shit's above my paygrade. Thankfully for you, we have some people behind that mirror representing the federal government who may be inclined help you. But this *information* of yours is going to have to be damn good."

# Chapter Forty-Two

*What is he thinking?* Aaron questioned as Frank held out hope of a deal to Grunitzky. Aaron looked at O'Donnell. "Ready for this?"

"What? You want me to go in there? I haven't interviewed a suspect in years. You realize that, don't you?"

"Caroline, take a deep breath," Aaron said as he demonstrated the slow in and out motion of deep breathing. "I have complete faith you can handle this. Most of what you're going to be doing is making phone calls to relevant people while we're in there."

Aaron watched for Caroline's reaction. She nodded her head a few times, pulled out her phone and gave Aaron a 'let's get this over with' look. Aaron left the interview observation room and knocked twice on the door. Frank answered it.

"For the record, I'm Special Agent Aaron Massey and this is my colleague Special Agent Caroline O'Donnell. We're both with the Federal Bureau of Investigation, so we're here representing the US federal government. What do you have to offer us this evening, General?" With a quick glance at Frank and Jasika, Aaron said, "You two can leave us now. We'll take it from here."

*God, I hope they realize what I'm doing.* Frank looked at Aaron and responded, "Sure thing," as he picked up his materials. As he left the room with Jasika, Frank nodded, saying, "Agents."

With that nod and the use of the word 'agents', Frank showed he knew exactly what Aaron was up to.

"So, General, tell us what you have," O'Donnell said.

"First, tell me what you can offer."

"General," Aaron said, rolling out the 'l' for added emphasis. "You know, as well as I do, that's not how a negotiation works when you don't have the upper hand."

"But don't I?"

"Not really. You have two plays. One, I say goodbye and escort you to a plane, and you fly home where you will be tortured and executed. We both know that's what your government will do."

"True," Grunitzky agreed, nodding his head. "But if I leave, you'll never know the intelligence I have collected about Daphne."

"You're assuming we don't already have it," Aaron smirked. *I need to keep this guy talking. The more in control he thinks he is, the more likely he's going to let something slip.*

"You don't. If you did, we wouldn't be having this conversation. I'd already be on a plane to Togo."

"Okay, so let's say we don't have this intelligence. How good is it? You know who she is? Where's she staying? Her favorite perfume? The reason she's here?"

Aaron threw the perfume in before the last question to see if he could get a reaction to it. He was rewarded with a slight wrinkling of Grunitzky's brow in recognition. "So, you know why she's here?"

"I did not say that."

"No, but your face did. You're used to using brute force and violence to get information out of people. We both know information gained from violence is often highly unreliable, because people will lie and say anything to make the pain stop." Aaron watched for a reaction. Not getting one, he continued. "You see, I think your best bet at this point is to relinquish your diplomatic status and plead guilty to conspiracy to commit murder and accessory to murder after the fact in the death of President Kader Nibombé. You'll spend the rest of your life in an American prison, but at least you'll be alive. And we both know our prisons are a hell of a lot nicer than the ones you run in Togo."

"Can you get my wife and daughter out of the country?"

"Your *what*?" Caroline blurted out. Turning to Aaron, she said, "We don't have any information about him having a wife and daughter."

"You wouldn't. Let's say very few people know about them. It was the only way I could protect them."

"Okay, I'm confused," Aaron admitted. "How long have you been married?"

"Almost a decade. We got married shortly after my daughter was born."

"Wait a second. What about Reine Avla?" O'Donnell asked.

Grunitzky rubbed the side of his pointing finger with his thumb while he searched for the right words. "I never intended to marry Avla or to harm her."

"Then why implicate her in President Nibombé's murder?" O'Donnell questioned.

"That was not my doing," he said. "I never directed my men to edit the video like that. I didn't know it had happened until I saw the video with you. One of my men had been tasked with getting prostitutes for the president. This underling had recognized Avla as my bride-to-be who fled Togo. Unbeknownst to me, this man had taken it upon himself to edit Avla's face into the video after the fact."

"Can this man corroborate your story?" Aaron asked.

"Not anymore," the general said. Something about how he said made Aaron realize there was another body out there somewhere. "Besides, I've known where Avla and her mother were all this time. I never intended her any harm. Her fleeing made my life easier."

Aaron could tell that the general was experiencing genuine remorse about Avla. All his bravado over the past few days had evaporated. Instead of acting like a crazed animal trapped in a cage, Grunitzky let the weight of decisions bear down on his current predicament.

Aaron nodded at Caroline, who stood and walked out of the room. As she did, she pulled her phone to her ear and immediately connected with someone on the other end.

"Tell me about them?"

"Who?"

"Your actual wife and daughter."

Grunitzky explained that his wife was a member of a different tribe in Togo. To avoid controversy, they had not been publicly married. Grunitzky's father would have disowned him if he'd known about the marriage, which is why he had kept pushing women like Avla on to him. "My wife is innocent, as is my daughter. My wife thinks I'm a banker."

"Your face is on the news all the time in Togo. How does she not know who you are?"

"Her village is remote. They don't have a television. I come and go as I please, and no one there asks questions. Hell, I'm one of only two people who own cars within fifty miles of her village."

There was a sudden knock on the door and O'Donnell entered. Aaron looked at her and she nodded her head once then exited again.

"Okay, here's our offer. You will plead guilty. You will go to jail for the murder of President Nibombé and we will get your family out of Togo. Now, your turn?"

"How do I know I can trust you to follow your word?"

"You don't. I have no ill-will toward your wife and child if, as you say, they are completely innocent in all this. They'll have wonderful new lives here in the United States with new names and identities. However, you can never contact them."

"What?"

"It's for their safety," O'Donnell noted. "If they know who you are and where you are, they could still be used as political pawns by your enemies. With us, they will have new lives and new identities. I will make sure you get pictures of them both before they're relocated within the US."

"I'm not a trusting man, Agent Massey. If you break your end of the bargain, no prison will be strong enough to hold me back from hunting you."

"Are you threatening me?" Aaron said, tilting his head slightly. He put his hand out toward the two-way mirror. *I hope Frank sees my hand and doesn't come busting in here as some kind of hero.*

"I'm not threatening you. A threat is a demonstration of intention. I do not 'intend' to kill you, but I promise you will die at my hand. So not a threat, but a promise. I want to make sure that we both understand each other."

"Threats aside, I believe we have ourselves a deal. So, what do you know?"

"Get me my cufflinks."

# Chapter Forty-Three

*Cufflinks?* Frank thought to himself. *Why does he want his cufflinks?* "Jasika." Frank turned to her.

"Already on it," she responded as she left the room. Frank continued to watch the interview. He stood down when Aaron had motioned for him not to freak out about Grunitzky's threat. Aaron was competent. Aaron was a capable field agent with a lot of experience under his belt, but that didn't mean Frank had to like it when Aaron was threatened. But Frank had to respect him enough not to barge in every time he thought Aaron needed him.

*Aaron isn't someone I need to protect.*

*Whoa, was that a breakthrough? I mean, I know that I couldn't protect Adam. Is that why I'm such a jealous asshole when it comes to Aaron? I love him — God knows I do — but I'm probably smothering him. Things were never this difficult with Adam. I never felt the need to protect him. I'm trying to protect Aaron because I couldn't protect Adam. Dear God, Weintraub's going to have a field day with this. Hell, she probably already knows that's what I'm doing, but I have to be pigheaded and figure things out for myself.*

Frank was lost in his own thoughts and didn't even realize it when Jasika came back into the room. She knocked once on the glass.

"Good. My partners have your cufflinks. Why did you need them?"

"Let me tell you a story," Grunitzky responded. "Almost two years ago, President Nibombé became hyper-paranoid that someone was out to kill him. Let's face it. You don't get a reputation like Nibombé's without leaving a trail of bodies and even more angry families and friends. He wanted to know who was going to try to kill him. He became obsessed with the idea that the famed Daphne was going to assassinate him in his sleep. He wanted me to investigate her. Unlike Western security forces, we'd always believed Daphne was West African. We're not sure where in West Africa she was from, though, because there are sixteen countries in the region."

"So, you started an investigation? I thought you hated Nibombé."

"Not initially. When I began working as his chief of security, I had respected and admired Nibombé. However, over time, he had become increasingly paranoid. Many in his inner circle had become targets of his conspiracies, so he had them killed. I would have been killed, too, but I had some very incriminating videos of him. You'll find those videos on the cufflinks."

Frank turned and looked at Jasika. "On the cufflinks?"

"Let me see those," Rummy said from his perch against the back wall. Rummy had been so quiet that Frank had forgotten he had even been there.

"Nice," Rummy said when he received the cufflinks. "These are Thomas Ford Octagon diamond cufflinks with a sapphire center. If I'm right," he said as he pushed on the sapphire and twisted it slightly as a small USB stick revealed itself, "these things are like sixty-K easily."

"Damn," Jasika responded. "Imagine walking around with sixty thousand dollars' worth of jewelry on your wrists."

"More to the point," Frank said, "what's so important that he keeps it on a sixty-thousand-dollar USB stick?" Frank walked over to the glass and rapped once on it, focusing his attention once again on Aaron and Grunitzky.

"I'm going to assume," Grunitzky said, "that the rapping sound on the window was your people finding the USB hidden inside my cufflinks." Grunitzky tilted in the chair to look straight at the glass, almost as if he were staring straight at Frank, which was impossible since it was a one-way mirror. "Please be careful with those cufflinks. As part of our agreement, I'm going to ask that you make sure those get to my wife and daughter." Aaron began to say something, but Grunitzky summarily cut him off with a quick wave of his hand. "Of course, after you've pulled all the useful information off them, I want my family to have them. They're quite expensive, so the money they can get from them will help them get settled here in the US. I also have an account in the Cayman Islands I want them to have access to."

"Why are you telling me this?" Aaron asked. "You know we'll secure the account and your family won't see any of it."

"I will give you access to one USB. Suppose you want to see the information on the other one. And trust me, your government will want to see that information. I'll need a separate deal for that one."

*So that's what this is all about. Whet the government's appetite and make us beg for more.*

"And don't worry, Agent Massey," Grunitzky said, looking at him. "The information you are seeking is on the one I plan on unlocking for you. After all, I keep *my*...promises." Without skipping a beat, he rattled off a twenty-digit alphanumeric password. Frank heard the stream of lowercase and uppercase letters, numbers and symbols fly by.

"Did you get all of that?" Frank asked, looking to Rummy, who was on the floor with the USB plugged into his secure laptop.

"We're in."

At that moment, Aaron and Caroline joined them, likely to see what was on the USB.

"Could you have broken the code without the password?" O'Donnell questioned Rummy.

"Not a chance. These use a Rivest-Shamir-Adleman encryption algorithm with a four-thousand-and-ninety-six bit key. I mean, technically, in theory, any encryption can be broken with enough computing power and time. We might break a one-thousand-twenty-four bit key in the future, but we're nowhere near breaking the four-thousand-and-ninety-six bit key. Sure, at some point, but not soon."

\* \* \* \*

After their interview, Aaron had Grunitzky taken down to lockup. The team decided to officially reprocess the general under an assumed name. The FBI didn't want anyone in Togo to know Grunitzky was still in US custody until certain matters were taken care of. Aaron spent a good chunk of the rest of his afternoon pushing to make sure Grunitzky's wife and daughter were put on the list of top military priorities.

With the operation underway to extract Grunitzky's family, Aaron finally had time to skim through the material from the cufflink. The rest of the team was already plodding their way through the materials when Aaron started. There was a ton of information about the running of the Togolese government. The corruption documented on the cufflinks would throw most of the Togolese government out of power if this information became public. Heck, most of the neighboring countries would lose their ruling powers too.

"Caroline," Aaron inquired, "can you hold off on telling State about the nature of the data? I don't want them sending in the NSA as soon as they know what's on these cufflinks."

"Understood," Caroline said with a mischievous grin. "I know how to stonewall people. Besides, I don't want them to know how good Rummy is. The FBI doesn't want to lose him."

Aaron glanced at his watch. It was already six p.m. He'd checked in with the dog sitter, and she'd already taken Bully out twice and made sure he had dinner. He reached for the box of coffee and found it empty. "Damn!" he said, mostly to himself.

"What's wrong, honey... Agent Massy?" Frank corrected himself, grinning sheepishly.

"If you two get all lovey-dovey and cutesy in here, I'm going to lose my lunch," Jasika said, making a barfing sound.

"So, *dear*," Aaron said, winking at Jasika, who mimed gagging, "we're out of coffee. Think we'll be here for a few more hours? Looks like it."

"Holy shit!" Jasika exclaimed. "I'm talking full-on 'padre christening a turd on a stick' shit! Frank, you need to see this."

Frank went to hover over Jasika's shoulder. The image was a photo of five people—Danielle Tebbutt, Penelope Cristillo, a young Black woman he didn't recognize and his parents.

Without thinking, Aaron said, "Daphne murdered two of the people in this picture. Did you know Tebbutt and Cristillo knew your parents?" Aaron stared at Frank as he shook his head, his mouth agape. "Frank...earth to Frank."

"Sorry. I got lost there for a moment," Frank responded as if waking from a dream. "What did you ask?"

"Frank?" Aaron asked, placing his arm on Frank's shoulder and looking him straight in the eyes. "What do you know about your father's death? I'm grasping at straws here, but could Daphne have killed him?"

"No," Frank said hurriedly. "I mean, I don't know. I don't know. I haven't known my parents or their associates since they disowned me."

Jasika opened a few more files and found the autopsy report for Gaétan Schultt, performed by the NYPD. "Damn! Grunitzky has your father's autopsy file."

Aaron took a quick peek at what Jasika had found before gently saying, "Frank, you don't need to look at this." Aaron steered Frank to a chair and grabbed him a bottle of water. Frank looked like he was utterly shocked on the verge of a meltdown. "Just breathe," he told Frank, stroking the top of his back.

"The ME ruled it a heart attack, so a complete autopsy wasn't deemed necessary," Jasika said as she skimmed the report. "The ME noted one thing that stood out. She found a flower in the breast pocket of your father's jacket — *daphne mezereum*."

Frank took in a visibly deep breath and slowly let it out. "This could be nothing," Aaron said.

"You don't believe that any more than I do," Frank responded.

# Chapter Forty-Four

Frank sat there, his eyes barely focusing, his mouth open, just staring into space. A rush of feelings he'd bottled up over a decade ago flooded in like a dam cracking. And he didn't have nearly enough fingers to stick in all the holes opening to keep it from washing over him uncontrollably. Things were happening around him, but he sat there in a daze. He wasn't sure how long he sat. *Minutes? Hours?* "We need to send someone to watch my mom."

"Frank," Jasika whispered from somewhere off to his left, "we already have a patrol car there. She was at the condo in the city and not the estate in Connecticut."

The words rushed over him and set his mind at ease, but he still couldn't focus his mind on what was going on around him. He piped up, "I think I need to go home." As the words rushed out of his mouth, he realized Aaron was already putting his jacket on him.

"It's okay, Frank. I'm right here. I'm going to take care of you. You've had a bit of a shock."

* * * *

The walk home seemed to help Frank get back to his normal self, but that didn't mean Aaron wasn't still worried about him. They hopped in and out of the deli down from their building before heading home. Thankfully, Bully had already been fed, but he needed to go for a quick walk. With Frank eating, Aaron put Bully in his harness and took him outside.

Heading back into the cold air was definitely not something Aaron was dying to do, but Bully liked his routines, so going outside once they got home was a must. The buzz in his pocket snapped him out of his ruminations about that afternoon's events. "Aaron Massey," he muttered into the phone without checking the caller ID.

"Aaron, it's Temperance Barling. I have Director Price on the line, too. Give me a status result. What happened after you took General Gassing Grunitzky into custody?"

"Sorry about the delay. It's been a bit of a rollercoaster of an afternoon." Aaron proceeded to break down Grunitzky's arrest, the deal with State and the information on the one cufflink he'd given them access to. "If he's to be believed — and I have no reason to think he's bluffing — the second cufflink is definitely something the US will want access to."

"Any idea what he's trying to get out of this?" Price asked.

"I'm betting it's going to be his family, money, relocation, protection and no jail time. He seemed pretty sincere about his desire to protect his family. If that's his primary motivator, then that seems his likely course of action." Aaron expected Barling or Price to say something, but the phone went silent for a second.

"Massey, you still there?"

"Yes, Director Price."

"Good. Stay out of State's way. They're not the happiest group of people right now."

"Trust me. We've already moved on and—oh shit," Aaron said, realizing he'd forgotten to tell them about the picture. "Sorry, sirs. I realized I left out a critical piece of information."

"What is it?" Price asked.

"In the stack of materials we started going through from the cufflink, there was a picture that connected your wife and Danielle Tebbutt."

"Really? I had no idea their paths had crossed."

"Until we saw the pic, we had no evidence that they ever had. But there were other people in the picture as well, Gaétan and Darlene Schultt and an unidentified Black female."

"Gaétan and Darlene Schultt? Of Schultt Pharmaceuticals?" Price asked.

"The same, sir. And, for full disclosure, they are Detective Frank Schultt's parents."

"*What*? Gaétan told me his son had died years ago."

"More like disowned," Aaron said, trying to keep his temper in check, realizing what Frank's father had been telling people.

"Barling," Price interjected, "did you know about the connection?"

"Yes, Director Price. I've known who Detective Schultt was since the serial murder situation last year. We put together a dossier on Detective Schultt when we created that task force..." Aaron heard the trailing off in Barling's voice. She might as well have said, "*It was in the report you never read.*"

"Interesting," Price said. "Well, since we're trading information. Penelope and Darlene Schultt were in college together at Wellesley. I got to know the Schultts about a decade ago when I married Penelope. The Schultts attended the wedding. We also had a few social and professional dinners in Washington. Remember that before I met Penelope, she had been working as a pharmaceutical lobbyist on Capitol Hill."

Aaron found it interesting how the director was throwing out tidbits of information about his personal life as if everyone should know these things. Admittedly, two powerful DC insiders didn't get married too often, so Aaron was sure it was a bit of a circus when it had happened. Realizing that the director had stopped talking, Aaron asked, "Did Cristillo ever work for Schultt Pharmaceuticals?"

"Not that I know of," Price responded. "It's entirely possible, though. Before becoming a lobbyist, she worked as a sales rep for a few different drug companies. Why?"

"Nothing concrete," Aaron said. "Honestly, I have a ton of ideas floating around in my head. My goal is to have a conversation with Darlene Schultt tomorrow. I'm hoping she'll be able to fill in some missing pieces."

"Does Detective Schultt need to be pulled from the case?" Barling questioned. "I know he's your fiancé, but objectively, what kind of conflict of interest are we dealing with?"

Aaron took a deep breath and looked at Bully who was tugging on his leash to head back to their building. "I'll be honest. The picture was a bit of a shock for Frank tonight, especially when we tossed around the idea that his father's death may not have been natural."

"Yes, but should he be pulled?"

"Chief Barling, I have no reason to believe Detective Schultt cannot execute his job at this point. If I worry this case is too much for him, I will not hesitate in asking for your help in getting Frank reassigned. With that said, I think he'll be fine by tomorrow morning."

"That's good enough for me," Price said, putting a clear end to that discussion. "Well, I want this wrapped soon. Do you need anything? Equipment? Personnel? Anything?"

"Director, I think the task force works smoothly at this time. Both Agents O'Donnell and Rummy are priceless additions. I think adding anyone else would complicate matters."

"Fine," Price said. "I want a report on my desk as soon as your interview with Darlene Schultt is over. I want to know what her thoughts are."

"Yes, Director. She's definitely on the top of our agenda for tomorrow morning."

The three quickly said their goodbyes, and Aaron immediately texted O'Donnell.

*Hey, did you get in contact with Darlene Schultt or one of her people?*

*Yes. I spoke to her assistant. She'll be at the precinct by noon. She had an eight o'clock breakfast meeting.*

*Heaven forbid an international assassin impede that.*

*It's some charity breakfast with the governor.*

*Of course, it is. Nothing is ever easy for us.*

Aaron thought for a second about what he would say next, waiting to see if O'Donnell would respond. After a second, he shot off another text.

*First thing in the morning, start looking for a connection between Penelope Cristillo and Schultt Pharmaceuticals.*

*On it. What are you thinking?*

*Nothing concrete. Just something the director said made me wonder if this was an inquiry path we should explore.*

*Makes sense when you think about it. Three of the five people in the picture are connected to Schultt Pharmaceuticals.*

*Oh, and anything you find related to the Schultts, bring it directly to me.*

*I understand completely.*

Aaron was glad he didn't need to spell it out to O'Donnell. Frank might be too close to this, despite what he'd said to Price and Barling. Frank spent most of his adult life trying to forget about his parents and their lives, so finding out they were at the center of one of his murder investigations could be a bit much. *I just want to make sure we don't break him.*

# Chapter Forty-Five

Frank stared at himself in the mirror after working out at the gym. Thankfully, Aaron had set his alarm and gotten both of them there. He hated skipping the gym more than one day in a row because it was good for both his mental and physical health. Frank's mind was still a bit of a jumbled mess after the day before, but he was in a much better state than when he'd left the precinct.

After getting home the previous evening, Frank had curled up on the couch and was fast asleep before Aaron and Bully had gotten back to the condo. He had woken around one a.m. and had found Aaron fast asleep in their bed. *I must have been dead to the world. Bully's not exactly the quietest of housemates when he gets back from walking. Can't believe they didn't wake me last night.*

He glanced over at Aaron, who was shaving in the mirror next to him, his towel securely fastened around his hips. *How did I get so lucky to get you in my life?* Next to Aaron, Ben was a chatterbox of wedding plans. He'd only been on wedding planning duty for a couple of days and already had done more than Amber had in the first few months. *Apparently, having a D-list celebrity, ex-party-planner-cum-wedding-planner opens doors.*

Logan missed their morning gym routine because he had some kind of charity function and had to go by the firm before heading to the event. *Lawyers keep such odd hours.* Frank slipped behind Aaron and swatted him on the backside. Aaron gave him a dirty look before going back to his conversation with Ben.

"I've been checking out venues," Ben said. "There's the Liberty Warehouse, the Foundry, the New York Public Library, the Brooklyn Botanic Garden. Do you want an indoor or an outdoor wedding?"

"Slow down, Ben," Aaron said, rinsing his razor off in the sink. "We're not even sure how large we want the ceremony to be. Shouldn't that factor in?"

"Of course, it does," Ben said. "I'm planning for a minimum of five-hundred guests."

Aaron's jaw dropped. *Wow!* Before Frank could get dragged into that conversation, he headed to his locker to get dressed. Frank slipped into his usual detective get-up and got ready for the day ahead of them. Even though he hadn't talked to Aaron about last night yet, he had a pretty good suspicion he would come face-to-face with his mother at some point in this investigation. He was still trying to steel himself for that inevitability.

\* \* \* \*

Even though Aaron and Frank had slept in the same condo, exercised and walked to the precinct together, Aaron hadn't asked Frank how he was doing. He had heard Frank when he woke around one a.m. and had been surprised when Frank hadn't joined Bully and him in bed. Aaron figured Frank probably had needed to work things out on his own.

As Aaron and Frank entered the precinct after picking up a fresh box of coffee from Via La Coffee, they headed right toward the conference room where the light was already turned on. As usual, O'Donnell had beaten everyone there and was already set up and raring to go.

"Aaron, I'm glad you got here. I found a link between the two victims and Darlene Schultt." Aaron shot a sideways glance to see how Frank would respond. O'Donnell didn't notice and plowed right along. "So, as we already know, Cristillo and Schultt went to Wellesley College together. What took me a while to drag up was that Danielle Tebbutt spent a semester abroad at Wellesley, which overlapped with Cristillo and Schultt. Now, this is far from anything beyond a coincidence at the moment, but at least we have some kind of link."

"So," Frank began, the mental gears in his head visibly whirling as he pieced his thoughts together, "you think Daphne is killing people who went to Wellesley?"

"Not necessarily," O'Donnell admitted. "But we at least have some kind of common link between our two current victims and your mother, giving us a potential line of exploration."

"Maybe," Frank said. "Honestly, I'm the last person who would know anything about my father and mother."

"Frank," Aaron began, taking in a deep breath and letting out. "I'm wondering if this isn't somehow tied back to Schultt Pharmaceuticals—"

"What?"

"Wait... Hear me out. I talked to Director Price last night." Aaron caught the look of surprise on Frank's face. "I got a call when I took Bully out to go potty."

"Who went potty?" Jasika asked, coming into the conference room.

"Aaron took Bully to go potty," O'Donnell helped.

"So, Bully is doing his business," Aaron said exasperatedly, "and I received a phone call from Price and Barling."

"Barling was on the call, too?" Frank questioned.

"Yes, both of them were on the call. We are *so* getting off track here."

"What track would that be?" Rummy asked as he came into the conference room.

"Dear God!" Aaron exclaimed. "From the beginning...this time, no interruptions," Aaron said, making sure everyone held his eye contact and nodded in agreement. "Okay, last night I received a phone call from Director Price and Chief Barling. They wanted a report about Grunitzky's arrest and what was happening with State. By the way, they told us to stay as far away from that mess as possible, but that's beside the point. So, while I was talking to Price, I asked him about his wife's relationship with Frank's parents." Aaron continued to recall the conversation to the room. "After the phone call, I texted O'Donnell and asked her to look for any connection between Cristillo, Tebbutt and Frank's mom. One direction was Wellesley, and the other was Schultt Pharmaceutical."

"That's it?" Frank asked.

"That's it."

"What about the other woman in the photo? Do we have any idea who she is?" Frank asked no one in particular.

"Sorry... I ran facial recognition software and didn't get a hit on her yet," Rummy said. "But, assuming she's an international citizen and not a US one, that could take weeks to get a match. We may get one from Homeland Security if they give us access to the international flight customs photos, but that's still a question mark."

"Umm...Aaron?" Jasika inquired.

"Yes, Jasika."

"I think I may have the answer you're looking for." The focus in the room swiveled in Jasika's direction. "Okay, so when I first got assigned to this precinct and to Frank specifically, I did my homework. Frank had been a known hothead, and my pairing with him had seemed like a quick way to kill my career. Sorry," she said, looking at Frank.

"Hey, I can't disagree with you. I was a bit of a mess back then."

"But anyway, I had done some digging around. And I went down a dark Google black hole, learning all kinds of stuff about Schultt Pharmaceuticals. I remember something about a clinical trial that caused international uproar in—"

"Gabon," O'Donnell said at the same time. All the heads swiveled in O'Donnell's direction. "There was a report from the files we found on the cufflink yesterday. I remember thinking the random news article seemed out of place in the mix, so I googled that last night myself." She pulled out her phone, hit a few keys and said, "Rummy, I sent you the link."

Rummy plugged his laptop into the projector and displayed the article for everyone to see. Aaron skimmed through it. Basically, the Gabonese government accused Schultt Pharmaceuticals of knowingly conducting a drug trial in Gabon and not in US because of the potential side effects for a drug named iXotix. iXotix prevented specific cancer cells from growing in mice. Unfortunately, the drug had the opposite results in humans, causing cancer cells to grow faster.

"What's the connection with our victims?" Frank asked.

"Well, I don't know about Tebbutt," O'Donnell admitted, "but I found an article that noted Penelope Cristillo was someone who had helped Schultt Pharmaceuticals get permission from the Gabonese government. The clinical trial took place," she said as she looked at her notes, "in the Albert Schweitzer Hospital on the bank of the Ogooué River, which runs through a tropical rain forest in Western Gabon."

"And fun fact," Rummy added. "Albert Schweitzer established the hospital in Gabon during the First World War back in nineteen-thirteen. He was known for treating people like humans, which was not common in those days."

"You're totally reading from Wikipedia," Jasika joked.

"I was not reading from Wikipedia, merely summarizing what they wrote."

"Rummy," Frank began, "could you run a search through all the files we downloaded from the cufflinks looking for the word 'Gabon' or 'drug trial'?"

"Sure thing. Give me a second," Rummy said as his fingers flashed over the keyboard. "Boom!" The keyword search appeared on the room's display screen. Rummy started scrolling the information quickly.

"Whoa, slow down," Frank said. "Go back a couple of lines. I thought I saw something."

Rummy obliged and slowly scrolled backward through the list.

"What did you see, Frank?" Aaron asked.

"Gerald Nesbitt. That name sounds familiar to me."

Rummy hit a few keys, and the obituary for a short, portly man filled the screen.

"I knew him," Frank admitted. "I'm pretty sure he worked for my father."

The obituary said nothing about Schultt Pharmaceuticals, but it mentioned his time in Western Africa where he and his wife had adopted a child. Once everyone read the article, Rummy went back to scrolling through the data. A few seconds later, he stopped on another article about Nesbit. He opened the article and found the transcript of a speech Nesbit had delivered in Paris at a pharmaceutical convention on the lessons learned from the Gabon drug trials.

"Frank," O'Donnell said, "Nesbit worked for Schultt Pharmaceuticals and oversaw those trials. I googled an old press release from Schultt Pharmaceuticals when he died. Thank God, the Internet keeps all."

"Okay," Frank said. "What do we know about the Gabon drug trial?"

"Let me find out," Rummy replied. "I'll look in these files. O'Donnell, keep googling. Hopefully, between both of us, we'll have a better idea."

"Hey, Frank," Jasika piped up. "I ran Nesbit through the files we received from Interpol. He's not on their official list of people suspected to have died by Daphne."

"Let me call Pasqual and see if he knows anything," Aaron chimed in. "It's about four p.m., so he should be in his office."

Aaron stepped outside while the other three kept tossing around ideas and looking into Gabon. Aaron got Pasqual on the phone, who admitted he had never heard of Nesbit. Nesbit also didn't appear in Interpol's databases. Pasqual promised to reach out to one of his contacts at the Paris Police Prefecture to see if there was anything in their database.

Aaron slipped back into the conference room. Frank looked at him and asked, "Get anything?"

"Nesbit doesn't appear in any Interpol database. But since he died in Paris, he may be in a French Police database. Bosc promised to reach out to a friend with the Paris police and get back to me. Anything new in here?"

"Everyone is so focused on Daphne as a contract killer, but what if we're looking at two different types of hits?" Frank asked.

"You mean two different killers?" Aaron responded.

"No, more like two reasons for a person to kill. What if one set is her regular contract work and the other is some kind of revenge?"

"Interesting idea. Go on."

"Most of her regular hits are big-time, known African warlords with a ton of enemies. Then, out of nowhere, we have a couple of random killings in the US. These don't seem to fit. And, if, by chance, Nesbit is another victim, along with my father, then Daphne has been hunting this group of people outside of the African warlords for a few years."

"The pieces may fit," O'Donnell reasoned. "But right now, we're flying on a lot of conjecture and not too many facts. We also must entertain the thought we're being purposefully led down a rabbit hole by Grunitzky."

"I don't think so," Aaron said. "Well, I think you're right about the conjecture part, but I didn't get a sense Grunitzky was playing with us. He seemed genuinely worried about protecting his wife and daughter. I think he may be playing with the information on the other cufflink, but that's up to State to deal with."

"I trust your judgment, Aaron," O'Donnell said. "But we still need to keep that possibility in our heads."

"Umm, Frank," Jasika blurted. "I tried to get ahold of someone at the Schultt estate, both here in the city and in Connecticut, I haven't been able to get anyone to answer the phone. Should I send uniformed officers to check out both places? You know, just in case."

"Don't bother," O'Donnell said. "She's hosting some kind of charity breakfast at The Pierre this morning."

"I totally forgot about that," Aaron said. "I just remember she'd be in around noon. I'd forgotten the reason." Aaron suddenly realized he hadn't told Frank about that. The deer in headlights look on Frank's face froze him in place.

# Chapter Forty-Six

"What did you say?" Frank asked. He tried to keep his cool, even though he wanted to yell at someone or hit an inanimate object.

"After last night's findings, we put in a polite request to interview the CEO of Schultt Pharmaceuticals about her relationship with two of our victims. Well, now what are we up to...like, four victims?"

"Three maybes and the fourth is a definite possibility," Frank said coolly. "So, Dr. Schultt agreed to come for an interview?"

"Yes, well, I didn't talk to her directly. I arranged it through her assistant," O'Donnell said, looking down at her notes, "Percival Pettyfer. He informed me she would be here between eleven-forty-five a.m. and noon, depending on the traffic. He sounded very British and uptight."

Frank barked out a laugh. "You are very right on both fronts. Very British, and uptight doesn't come close to explaining him."

"Frank," Rummy called from his corner in the room. "I found a copy of the invitation for today's breakfast. Someone snapped a shot and put it on social media."

The elegant invitation suddenly filled the front screen. "I request your presence at a benefit for orphanages in West Africa. Your hosts for the event will be Dr. Darlene Schultt of Schultt Pharmaceuticals and Mr. Jonathan Fetty, literary agent at A-Star Talent."

Frank didn't realize he'd made a growling sound until everyone in the room was staring at him with their eyes wide.

"Frank," Aaron said, "you need to calm down."

"What is that fucking asshole doing with my mother?"

"I don't—"

"For those of you who missed this one, Fetty is Aaron's douchebag ex," Frank groused.

The silence in the room was overwhelming. Frank finally looked at Aaron. "I know this has nothing to do with you, but I need to calm down. I'm going for a quick walk."

With Frank out of the room, the team looked to Aaron for insight into what the hell had just happened. Aaron told them the complete story, starting with the gym to the flower shop. "So, Frank is not exactly Fetty's best friend by any stretch of the imagination."

"You don't think he would actually harm him?" O'Donnell asked.

"I definitely wouldn't want to see Frank and Fetty in a dark alleyway at night, but Frank knows how to keep it together. He's been working on that for a few years."

"Right, a few years," Jasika responded a little too quickly.

"For now, let's keep digging and see what we can find. I think the more information we have when we interview Dr. Schultt, the better off that's going to go." With that, they all set about pulling materials together for their interview with Dr. Darlene Schultt.

* * * *

Frank was visibly shaking with anger as he stepped out of the precinct into the cold air. He was halfway down the block before he realized he'd left his jacket in the conference room. *Just when I thought I'd gotten over Fetty, here he is, popping his head up again. He's fucking whac-a-mole. I'd like to whack him a few times. And with my mother, no less. What the fuck? What the actual fuck?*

His feet were on autopilot. He wasn't even sure where he was going. But before he knew it, he found himself back inside Viva La Coffee with a latté in hand. He wanted to talk to someone, but he didn't know who to talk to. Logan was at his charity breakfast. He shot him off a quick text.

*Please don't tell me you're with my mother and Crazy Fetty at The Pierre?*

*Okay. I won't tell you that.*

*You are, though, aren't you?*

*Yep! In my defense, I had no idea.*

*No idea?*

*Office set this up, not me. It involves one of the partners. I was just invited. Trust me, so not my idea. I'll call you later.*

Frank picked up the phone and called the only person he could think to call.

"Hello?"

"Polly?"

"Yes," the voice on the other line paused for a second. "Oh, Frank. How are you doing, honey?"

"I'm doing," Frank said with as much pep as he could fake. "Is Janice there?"

"Let me see. She was on her way out."

Frank heard Polly call out her name. There was a sudden rustle on the phone before a second line picked up. "Polly, got it!" Janice Kahl said before adding, "Judge Kahl."

"Hey, Janice."

"Frank, how are you doing today? Please don't tell me you need another warrant signed? I got a bit of a talking to about the one yesterday, not that I really give a fuck. The warrant was good. State's mad and feels the need to mark their turf."

"No, no warrant today."

"What's wrong? And don't bullshit me. I can tell from the tone of your voice that something's wrong."

"Two words…my mother," he said with zero emotion.

Frank heard the intake of breath on the other end of the line. "Where are you? This seems more like an in-person conversation." Frank provided her the address, and she said she'd be right over.

For the next fifteen minutes, Frank sat in the corner of the coffee shop. His mind was racing a thousand miles per hour. He kept reliving that morning. He remembered moments from his teen years. He relived the moment he'd heard about his father's death. He sat there with the little hamster wheels inside his head churning in overdrive. He was so lost in his thoughts he didn't even hear when Kahl sat.

"Earth to Frank," she said, snapping her fingers at him. "You in there?"

"Oh, sorry. I didn't even see you come in."

"Didn't see me come in. Didn't see me put my coat over there. Didn't see me get my coffee. And didn't see me sit. You were off in Frank-land, where it is clearly a dark and dreary day."

"You don't know the half of it."

"Then tell me. You mentioned your mother on the phone. What happened?"

Frank sighed, took a drink of his lukewarm coffee and spilled his guts. He started with the Fetty incidents all the way to seeing the invitation. Kahl sat there sipping on her chai tea, listening. She nodded her head and periodically asked for more detail when Frank hadn't been the most forthcoming. Kahl always seemed to know when Frank was holding back.

"Wow, sounds like you've had a few rough days."

"After yesterday morning's conversation with Aaron, I thought things were on the right path. But then, out of nowhere, my mom pops into the picture and she's with Crazy Fetty. I just lost it."

"Did you yell at anyone or hit anything?"

"No," Frank said, like a child being scolded for getting in trouble at school. "I kind of just...left."

"Has Aaron texted you?"

"Yes."

"Have you responded to any of them?"

"I told him I was okay and would be back in a bit after I cleared my head."

"Well, at least you let him know you were okay. That's a step in the right direction." Kahl took another sip of her tea before adding, "Let's face it. Not too long ago, you would have gone out and done something destructive, not brood like some kind of hipster in a coffee shop."

Frank barked out a laugh. "Me, a hipster? Good lord, no."

"I should also admit something, Frank," Kahl said. Frank raised his eyebrows at her before she continued. "I've heard of Fetty."

"You have?" Frank asked, wearily eyeing Kahl with one eyebrow raised.

"Not like that. I wouldn't even call him an acquaintance. It's just, NYC is a small town in some circles. From what I understand, he is a seriously conniving, back-stabbing prick who does anything to get his way. It may not be easy, but stay out of his warpath."

"He's basically throwing himself at Aaron," Frank interjected. "What should I do? Just let him steal Aaron away from me?"

"Wow, did you hear yourself?" Kahl asked, her nails clicking on the table. "First, Aaron's a big boy. He doesn't need protecting. Second, if Aaron is stolen away from you that easily, then he was never yours— and we both know that's not true. I've watched you together for almost a year. He's truly in love with you. You need to stop playing these mind games with yourself, Frank. If anyone is going to drive Aaron into the arms of another man, it's going to be you."

Frank shot Kahl an angry look but then softened his face. "I know you're right. I'm so afraid of losing him."

"Just don't lose him. Don't push him away. Besides, people in this city hate Fetty. But more than hating him, they fear him—kind of like how people fear your mother."

"Then there's my mother..."

"You knew you'd run into her eventually—maybe not on this case, but eventually you'd be in the same place at the same time."

"Yeah, I was kind of glad that didn't happen the other night at Lincoln Center. I wasn't ready for it."

"Well, this time, you know when and where she's going to be. More than that, she's coming onto *your* turf."

"True," Frank sighed. "When did you get to be so smart?"

"I've always been this smart. You just haven't always been ready to listen. I learned a long time ago not everyone is ready to hear what a person has to say. Sometimes, you need to let them grow until they're ready to hear you." She reached out, grabbing Frank's hand. He held it for a moment, looking at her in the eyes. "Okay, you can let my hand go. The last thing I need is someone seeing me in here and ruining my reputation as the toughest judge in the city."

Frank let out a little laugh shaking his head. "Thanks for killing the moment, Obi-Wan."

"You're right. I'm your fucking Obi-Wan—and don't you forget it." Kahl quickly glanced at her watch. "Look at that. It's almost eleven. I have court at noon. I know you need to get back to the precinct. I can have my driver drop you off."

"Thanks, but I think I'm going to buy another box of coffee for the team as an 'I'm sorry I'm an asshole most days' apology."

Kahl smiled at Frank. "And don't worry about your mother, Aaron or even Crazy Fetty. Aaron loves you, and that's what really matters. You've got to learn to trust that love."

After standing and helping Kahl back into her coat, they said their goodbyes. Kahl's driver pulled up a minute later. She opened the door, turned to wave goodbye one last time before slipping into the car and heading off to court.

Frank smiled and got himself back in line. He needed that brief conversation with Kahl. She always seemed to know how to knock some sense into him when he was pigheaded. On his way back to the office, he definitely noticed the chill this time. *How I didn't freeze to death earlier is beyond me*, he wondered as he walked with a cold, splintering wind at his back. It felt like tiny icicles were being lodged into the back of his neck.

Lifting the plastic bag of cups and sugar packets, Frank checked out his watch. *It's eleven-twenty, giving me about forty minutes to mentally prepare.* As Frank rounded the corner, there was a limo parked illegally outside the front of the precinct. *Great, the Ice Queen or one of her henchmen is already here. If I'm lucky, it's just some VIP from State who has come to chew everyone out.* Entering the building, Frank braced himself for whatever muckety-muck graced their presence. He walked by the desk sergeant's desk and nodded his help before heading into the bullpen.

He hadn't rounded the corner before he heard the clipped sound of his name.

"François."

# Chapter Forty-Seven

Aaron sat in the conference room preparing for the noon interview when there was a knock at the door. An officer ducked her head inside the room. "Detective Torv?"

"Yes," Jasika responded, glancing up from her laptop. "What can I do for you, Officer…?"

"Shelby, Patricia Shelby."

*Ahh, look at that. Jasika has a new friend…or a fan.* Aaron studied the young officer's face, trying to get a bead on the officer's facial expression. He could tell that it was admiration and not familiarization, so Jasika probably hadn't met the young officer before.

"Yes, Officer Shelby?"

"Yes, so sorry, sir— I mean ma'am."

"Either is fine, but you can call me Jasika," she said, letting the younger woman off the hook on formality. "So, what can I do for you?"

"There's a woman and her assistant here to see you." Officer Shelby looked at a notepad she was carrying and read, "A Dr. Schultt and a Percival Something-or-other. She says she has an appointment."

Aaron glanced at his wrist. *She's early. This will be interesting. I wonder if this is a power tactic. Most power players show up late to keep you waiting, but some do like to be early to throw you off balance.*

"She wasn't supposed to be here till noon. She's like an hour early," Jasika said, looking down at her watch. "Want to join me?" she asked Aaron.

"Do I have to?" Aaron queried. "Not so sure I'm ready to meet the future mother-in-law yet," he noted with a sense of sarcasm.

Jasika turned toward the young officer and said, "Tell Dr. Schultt we'll be right out, Officer Shelby. She can wait a minute."

Officer Shelby exited the conference room with one last look over her shoulder at Jasika.

"What was that?" Rummy asked from his corner of the room. "Does Officer Young One have a crush?"

"Shut it, Rummy," Jasika teased with a half-smile. "It's not my fault some are drawn to greatness."

Caroline O'Donnell lifted her coffee cup. "Here, here!"

"I wish Frank was back," Jasika said. "I don't know if I'm ready to meet this woman."

"There's power in numbers," O'Donnell said. "And let's face it," she said, swiveling her head back and forth in a conspiratorial manner, "we're all curious about Dr. Heartless."

"How long did it take you to come up with that one?" Rummy asked.

"I thought about Madam Heartless or Sinister Schultt and even Betty Bitch, but I figured I'd be nice and stick with her honorific."

Aaron rolled his eyes. "You love your nicknames."

"Nicknames have power," O'Donnell said matter-of-factly. "I read an article that people in subordinate positions use nicknames to get a better grip on their environment and the people who wield power over them."

"Interesting psychological theory," Aaron noted.

"Me? I find them more fun and definitely easier to remember than people's actual names," O'Donnell admitted.

"So, let's do this?" Jasika asked the group.

They all stood, put back on their jackets and did a quick once-over on each other to make sure everyone was presentable. Aaron realized how much they were stalling. "She doesn't bite. She may drug us, but she won't bite." Turning to Jasika, he prodded, "You take the lead. We'll follow."

"*Thanks*," Jasika said, drawing the word out with an abundance of sarcasm.

She led them out of the office and through the bullpen to the tiny reception area. It was New York City, where they rarely wasted space on reception. As soon as Aaron noticed the smartly dressed woman whose back was turned to the desk sergeant, looking out of the window, he started analyzing. *Okay, so she's put together. Nothing is out of place. Her assistant is holding her bag. He's used to be subservient, which follows what Frank has told me about the guy.* Darlene Schultt stood like a statue with her arms crossed. She impatiently drummed her fingers on her forearm, rolling her dark red nails over and over again.

"Dr. Schultt," Jasika stated. "I'm Detective Jasika Torv." Dr. Schultt turned slowly, dragging her eyes up

Jasika, starting at her feet. "I have with me FBI Agents Massey, O'Donnell and Rummy."

"I see." Dr. Schultt's voice came out clipped. "And François?"

"Detective Schultt," Jasika corrected with a hint of a smile, "will join us shortly. Please follow me."

"Come, Percival." Dr. Schultt beckoned to her assistant, who dutifully followed like a lapdog following his master.

*Wow, what kind of fucked up sadomasochistic relationship is this? I could write a whole research article on just that one interaction.* Aaron followed last, watching the group walk back into the bullpen. The group had gotten back into the bullpen when Dr. Schultt looked over Aaron's shoulder and said, "François."

"Mother," Frank responded from behind him.

# Chapter Forty-Eight

Aaron sidestepped Frank's mother and turned so he could see them both. "Dr. Schultt, it's nice of you to join us this morning. I had the appointment down for noon. Glad you could get here *so* early. I hope my absence didn't keep you waiting long," Frank ground out as if talking to a complete stranger.

"Indeed," was all she said in return, eyeing Frank wearily. "So, I haven't got all day. What can I help you with, Detectives? Agents?"

"Aaron," Frank said, "why don't you show Dr. Schultt to interview room one."

"If you'll follow me," Aaron said. With a wave of her hand, Dr. Schultt and her assistant immediately followed Aaron.

"Jasika, why don't you show Mr. Pettyfer to interview room two."

Dr. Schultt's assistant stopped in his tracks. "Me? What do you need me for?"

"François, is this necessary?" Dr. Schultt questioned with a raise of her eyebrow.

"Yes. This is very necessary. Your name has come up as a person of interest in an assassination plot that's already led to three deaths on US soil. So yes, this is necessary."

"Hmm...intriguing. Go along, Percival. Play nice with Detective Torv. Tell her anything she wants to hear. We have no secrets." With that, she gave a brief nod to Aaron, showing she was ready to follow. Jasika shot Frank a side glance that basically said, 'What the fuck?'

Frank followed the group until their guests were seated in their interview rooms. He went into each observation room and knocked on the glass to get their attentions, letting them know he wanted to huddle in the hallway. Once the entire group had gathered, he began. "Aaron, I want you to interview my mom. I know this is going to be awkward. You okay with this?" Frank asked.

Aaron nodded and said, "I'm sort of looking forward to it."

Frank narrowed his eyes at Aaron but didn't say anything. Instead, he turned to Jasika. "You good with interviewing Pettyfer?"

Jasika nodded.

"Rummy, I want you to observe my mother's interview. And, O'Donnell, observe Percival's. I want a second pair of eyes watching both of them. I'm going to float back and forth." Everyone nodded in agreement. Frank continued, "Aaron, remember that my mother is a control freak. Allow her to think she's in control while you steer her in the direction you want her to go. As for Percival," Frank said, turning his attention to Jasika, "he's a fifty-eight-year-old gay man who probably hasn't been with a man in decades. I'm sure you witnessed how my mother treats him. He responds better to a stick than a carrot. Use the threat of talking to my mother. Remember that she told him to tell us anything, so use it against him."

"Got it."

Frank let out a sigh. "Let's do this." Before they headed off to their various interview rooms, Frank asked, "Aaron, can I talk to you for a minute real fast before you get started?"

"Sure," Aaron responded, hanging back as the other three left them.

"I'm so sorry about earlier. It was one thing to deal with my mother, but the shock of Fetty being with my mother made my head spin."

"I get it," Aaron said. "But these jealous tirades need to stop, okay?"

"Agreed. But this wasn't a jealousy thing. It was like, suddenly, two supervillains teamed up together to ruin my morning. My brain wasn't ready to process it. Thankfully, Janice talked me off the ledge."

"You spoke to Judge Kahl?" Aaron asked, drawing his eyebrows together.

"Yeah, she met me for coffee, and we talked. She's the only person I talk to these days who knew me before my parents disowned me. You know that. Anytime my mother gets involved in something, Kahl always has a fresh perspective because she knows her. She also knows about Fetty. Apparently, he's getting quite the reputation around the city."

"Really?" Aaron replied, his voice slightly elevated. "That's definitely a story I want to hear later. For now, let's get through this interview." Aaron wrapped his arms around Frank. The two quickly kissed before

Aaron turned and entered the interview room with Dr. Schultt.

Frank looked at the two doors, took a breath and went into the observation room of interview one. He closed the door and nodded to O'Donnell. "Anything interesting yet?" O'Donnell quickly told him Aaron had just begun laying out what they'd learned.

Frank observed Aaron's skillful navigation of what had been happening over the past few days. His mother sat passively, listening to the information. *Always the analytic one. She's clearly digesting the information and making her own connections.* "I'll be right back." He nodded to O'Donnell.

He quickly entered the other observation room to see how Jasika was faring. "So, how are things going in here?" Frank asked Rummy.

"Please, you should have told me how much fun this was going to be. I would have popped some popcorn. All Jasika needs is a cat of nine tails, and she'd have the whole Dominatrix thing down."

"I told you. Percival is some kind of gay sadist who buckles under powerful women," Frank said absently, looking into the interview room. Jasika had opted to stand in the corner, looking down on Percival. The height differential definitely made her seem more in control. Plus, she kept firing off questions in rapid-fire and glowered when Percival's answers weren't quick or to the point.

"If this whole 'police thing' doesn't work out for her," Rummy joked, "she definitely has a second career as an actor or Dominatrix."

"That she does." Frank looked at Rummy. "Don't tell her I told you this, but she's definitely grown into her own over the past few years. When she first became a detective, I wasn't sure if she could handle it, but I have no worries about her now at all. Anyway, I'm going to go check on Aaron. If you need me, come get me."

"Will do."

# Chapter Forty-Nine

Dr. Schultt let out an exasperated sigh. "Please, get to the point, Agent."

"Dr. Schultt, please allow me to finish telling you about the case. There are a few facts I need to lay out still."

Dr. Schultt rolled her eyes. She was clearly not used to being under someone else's control. "So, you and François? When's the wedding?"

Aaron blanched at those questions. He was definitely not ready for her to play mother of the year during the interview. It took him a few seconds to gain his composure. "Maybe you should ask Frank those questions."

"Why? I'm asking you," she said with a grin that could rival the Cheshire Cat.

"Because this is neither the time nor the place to play future mother-in-law. Two of your close friends and husband have been killed by a notorious international assassin."

"Excuse me?" Dr. Schultt replied with the first crack in her demeanor. "My husband died of natural causes."

"Yeah, about that," Aaron began. He laid out what they'd learned about Gaétan Schultt's death and the daphne flower found in his jacket that had gone unnoticed by the medical examiner at the time because there was no reason to think there was foul play. Aaron tried to watch her face while he laid out the evidence, but she had quickly regained her composure and sat stockily, absorbing the information.

"If what you say is true—"

"It is."

"Then may I ask if you consider my life to be in danger? Two of my close friends and husband have been killed by this assassin. Should I be worried?" Dr. Schultt questioned, choosing her words delicately.

"We have no actionable intelligence your life is in immediate danger. However, the lack of intelligence doesn't mean you're not. Based on the circumstantial information we have here, we can't discount you're on Daphne's list."

She leaned back in her chair, absorbing the information. "How did you piece all this together?"

"For obvious reasons," Aaron said, "I can't tell you about our intelligence gathering process, but we received information leading us to you. Specifically, we found a picture linking you to the other assassinations." Aaron pulled out the photo of the Schultts with Tebbutt and Cristillo. Aaron stared at Dr. Schultt's face, hoping to see some expression. *Damn, not even an eyebrow twitch. She's either pumped full of Botox or one of the steeliest women I've ever met.* "Who is the other woman in the photo?" Aaron asked, tapping the young

Black woman. "We haven't been able to identify her yet. We want to make sure she's safe as well."

"That's Dr. Christelle Perillo. She's on the research and development team at Schultt Pharmaceuticals."

Aaron jotted the name on his legal pad and kept going. "What can you tell me about Daphne?"

"The person? Nothing. The plant? Any responsible biochemist should have a working knowledge of homeopathies. In fact, we have a new over-the-counter product set to be unveiled today that uses trace amounts of daphne to help with rheumatism."

"What else can you tell me?"

"Normally, I'd require you to sign a nondisclosure agreement before I'd tell you anything." Aaron started to object, but Dr. Schultt simply waved him off and kept going. "But these are extraordinary circumstances and the unveiling is this afternoon, so I'm not worried about divulging a little information to the FBI ahead of schedule."

"Go on."

"We've been developing this product between the Westchester Plant and our research lab outside of Paris."

"Really?"

"I wouldn't lie to you, Agent Massey," she responded. "And before you ask, Dr. Perillo is the head researcher on that project."

Frank stood in the observation room as Aaron questioned his mother. When she mentioned the name Dr. Christelle Perillo, he shot Rummy a quick text to see what he could find about the researcher. He then slipped the phone back into his pants pocket before turning his attention back to the interview that was happening on the other side of the one-way mirror.

"So, how long have you known Christelle Perillo?"

"She's been on our research and development team for almost a decade."

"How did she join Schultt Pharmaceuticals?"

"Why are you so interested in Dr. Perillo?"

"She's just a new piece to the puzzle, so I'm trying to fill in as much information as possible."

"Well," Dr. Schultt said, "my husband first met Christelle when she was a teenager. We were working on a drug trial in Gabon."

"Gabon?"

"Yes, it's a relatively unheard of Western African country to people in the West. We were testing a cancer vaccine that…had unfortunate side effects."

"Go on."

"Well, Christelle's intellect impressed Gaétan. He created a scholarship to send her to school in Paris. When she finished her doctorate in biochemistry, she immediately came to work for the company."

*Holy shit! I think my mother just broke the case*, Frank realized.

"Is Dr. Perillo in New York currently?" Aaron asked. "We want to make sure she's safe too."

"She got to the US last week to help with the rollout in Westchester. I don't know where she's staying, but I'm sure Percival knows. He keeps track of those types of details for me."

Frank pulled out his cell phone and texted Jasika.

*Find out from Percival where Dr. Christelle Perillo is staying.*

# Chapter Fifty

Aaron continued his line of questions until he heard a quick rap on the observation window. "Well, I think we have everything we need."

"Be honest, Agent Massey," Dr. Schultt said quietly. "How worried should I be?"

Aaron took a second to parcel out his thoughts. "I don't know. I wish I did. There are still a lot of moving parts and missing pieces to this puzzle."

"Thank you for your honesty."

"I'm going to get the NYPD to step up your security for the next couple of days, just in case."

"No need. I'll contact my private security firm and let them know about the increased need for personal security."

"You have a personal security firm?"

"You don't build a multinational pharmaceutical empire without making a few enemies along the way. We try to do everything above board, but not everything pans out the way we hope it will."

"Like Gabon?" Aaron quickly threw out.

Aaron said nothing but nodded his head, indicating for Dr. Schultt to continue.

"Yes, Gabon was a series of small miscalculations that quickly added up to a disaster, not the brightest moment in the corporation's history. Despite what some gossip columnists wrote, we had no idea iXotix was going to cause problems. All the preliminary testing was so positive. We had no idea it would speed the development of human cancer cells."

Aaron kept his demeanor noncommittal, but he remained internally skeptical of Dr. Schultt's retelling of how Gabon had gone down. "Well, Dr. Schultt, thank you for your time. We'll keep you apprised of any developments as they occur."

Aaron stood and Dr. Schultt did the same thing. They were almost to the door when Aaron turned his head and said, "One more question?"

"Yes?"

"Jonathan Fetty?"

Dr. Schultt chuckled. "That little weasel." She reached out and gently touched Aaron's hand. "You're definitely better off without him."

Without saying another word, she sidestepped Aaron and opened the door. Aaron stood there slack-jawed for a second. *Did that really just happen?*

Frank had Aaron escort his mother back to the waiting area before going to check on Jasika's interview. With his mother out of the hallway, Frank and O'Donnell stepped into observation room two. Frank went to the one-way mirror and lightly rapped on the window to get Jasika's attention. She quickly exited the interview and joined the group.

Jason Wrench

"What's up?" she asked when she got into the room. Frank quickly read her in on what they'd found out from his mother. Jasika told Frank that it aligned with what he had been told by Percival.

"Oh yeah, got your text," Jasika said. "Percival didn't know where she was staying. He assumed it was somewhere up in Westchester since it would put her closer to the manufacturing facility up there."

Aaron walked into the room. "It's getting a bit crowded in here. What did I miss?" Frank performed a quick recap of what Percival had been able to tell them so far. Jasika periodically chimed in, adding more details she'd been able to draw out of Percival during her interrogation.

"Sorry to interrupt," Rummy said, butting into the conversation, "but I have something for you. I was able to get Dr. Perillo's passport photo from TSA. I didn't go through proper channels. I happen to know someone over there who owed me a favor."

"Get to the point," Jasika said. Her tone of voice had everyone's attention swivel in her direction. "Sorry... I didn't mean to use my 'don't fuck with me now, Percival' voice on you." There was a sudden pause as everyone stood there stunned for a few seconds before everyone burst into laughter.

"Anyway, I've been playing with this new software a friend of mine created. Basically, it compiles images and tries to make a three-dimensional form. It's far from perfect."

"As Jasika said, get to the point already," O'Donnell said.

"Touchy," Rummy said with a grin. "Okay, so basically, I tried to create a three-dimensional composite of all the images ever taken of Daphne that we have access to." He turned the laptop toward them, and they all saw a vague-looking Black female.

"Doesn't tell us much," Aaron noted.

"True, but when I compare it to the biomatrix scan of the passport photo, it's a decent match. Again, far from being something admissible in court, but I'm pretty sure Dr. Perillo is our Daphne."

Frank gave Aaron a quick glance before saying, "We were already leaning in that direction. Your 'evidence' definitely gives us more to go on."

Aaron turned to Jasika, "Could you go ask Percival about Dr. Schultt's schedule today?"

"Why not ask her?"

"Well, from what Frank's told us, she probably doesn't have any idea where she's supposed to be. That's Percival's job."

Jasika shrugged her shoulders and headed back into the interrogation room.

"What are you thinking, Frank?" Aaron asked, turning his attention to Frank.

"Not sure yet... We know the announcement of the new drug is today. If I wanted to make a loud, public statement, I think I would make it there."

"That assumes your mother's a target," O'Donnell added.

"True, but I would be surprised if she's not," Frank said with little emotion behind his voice. "Something about all this seems like Daphne—well, Perillo—is building up to assassinating my mother."

Jasika entered the observation room and informed them Dr. Schultt was supposed to be back at The Pierre for the big unveiling of the new drug in the Edgewood Room for the announcement at three p.m.

"We're going to need my mother's help."

# Chapter Fifty-One

The entire team was ushered into the back of Dr. Schultt's limo and took off toward The Pierre. Frank had quickly explained their suspicions. At first, Dr. Schultt hadn't been convinced. But after a little nudging, she had agreed to let them accompany her to the hotel. Frank had suggested the team would meet her there, but she had insisted they all pile into the limo since it was there and ready to go.

The limo pulled outside a service entrance at The Pierre. Everyone exited the vehicle then meandered through the bowels of the hotel until they got to the rotunda in the lobby and took the stairs down into the Salon. It was next to the Wedgewood Room, where the press conference was scheduled to happen.

"Did you have your breakfast in here, too?" Frank asked.

"No, we were upstairs in the Grand Ballroom. I thought the Wedgewood Room would be better for this press conference."

*And by 'I thought', she means Percival thought.* Frank's mother wouldn't bother herself with the event's details. That's what Percival was for.

As they entered the Salon, a chipper voice said, "Wow! The gangs all here. Let the party begin."

Frank looked over to see Jonathan Fetty sitting on a chair in the Salon, reading his iPad.

"What brings the FBI and NYPD to a simple pharmaceutical press conference?" Fetty asked.

"Mr. Fetty," Frank said, "unfortunately, we cannot divulge any information to you. At this moment, we are here on a need-to-know basis. And, let's face it, you are the last person who needs to know." *Straight and to the point. And I don't even feel like hitting him. Good sign!*

"Oh, and if you post seeing us on social media," Aaron said, "'I will have you arrested and brought up on federal charges of obstruction of justice."

"Well," Fetty replied in a huff, "I can tell I'm not wanted in here. The temperature dropped twenty degrees when you all walked in. I'll go read in the lobby." Turning to look at Dr. Schultt, he said, "Darlene, I'll be back for the press conference."

Dr. Schultt walked over to Fetty and gave him a brief hug and kiss on the cheek. Frank was close enough that he heard his mom whisper in Fetty's ear, "Jonathan, be a dear. Stay out of Aaron and François' lives. If I hear that you've tried to break Aaron and Frank up again, I'll make sure you can't even sell books to independent Harlequin romance presses." The smile on Darlene's face as she pulled away was not friendly. It was the smile of a predator just waiting for her prey to make the wrong move.

Frank did his best not to smirk when Fetty's eyes widened at the threat. Without saying another word, Fetty scurried out of the Salon.

"So, now what?" Dr. Schultt asked.

"Now, we get set up in the Wedgewood Room," Aaron responded, then directed Rummy and O'Donnell to set up the equipment for monitoring.

Frank turned to his mother and said, "I need to make sure someone is with you at all times during the press conference."

"I'll do that," Percival chipped in.

"Sorry, Percy," Frank said, using a nickname he was aware that Percival despised. "But I need to make sure that person is armed."

"I'll stay with her, Frank," Jasika said.

"François—"

"Frank, Mother. I haven't been François in fifteen plus years—not since, well, you know."

"I am sorry about that," Dr. Schultt began. "You know how your father could be."

"You can't blame this on him. You let it happen. You let him disown me. You stood idly by," Frank said rapidly. *Keep it together, Frank. Not the time. Not the place.* He took a deep breath. "Maybe one day we can have this conversation, but now is not the time." Without skipping a beat, Frank walked away saying, "I'm leaving you with Detective Torv. Please, just do what she tells you."

\* \* \* \*

Frank stood at the back of the Wedgewood Room as various dignitaries and media personnel arrived. Jasika was still with his mother, and Aaron found a seat in the back row on the left-hand side of the room so he could watch the comings and goings. Rummy had gotten in touch with the hotel's security team and situated himself in their control room so he could check the hotel security feed in real-time. O'Donnell seated herself on the front row and pulled her chair askew so she could watch the room from the diagonal vantage point of Aaron. Frank leaned against the back wall of the room next to the table of glasses and a water cooler. People came in and got themselves drinks, but no one paid him much attention. *It's amazing how people just overlook security.*

He scanned the room, and nothing seemed out of place. He watched as Jonathan Fetty entered. Fetty swiveled, caught sight of Frank then Aaron, and got as far away from both of them as possible. *I wonder why he's here in the first place? This isn't exactly a huge literary event. I must ask him afterward.*

# Chapter Fifty-Two

At precisely three p.m., the Ballroom lights dimmed and two screens set at the front of the room began playing a video. It explained the Schultt family legacy and the creation of Schultt Pharmaceuticals. From its earliest days as a small old-country style medicinary when his great-grandparents had immigrated to the United States, to when his grandfather had earned a degree in chemistry from New York University with a specialization in pharmaceutical chemistry, the video told his family's story right up to his father's passing and how his mother had taken the reins of the corporation.

The video ended with a quick montage of images from the pharmaceutical company's history and finished with a picture he'd never seen before. Frank vaguely remembered taking the picture on the day he had graduated from Yale, hours before he'd come out to his parents. He was dressed in his cap and gown with his parents on either side of them. His mom had been genuinely smiling. His father had looked both proud and happy. The video ended by reading out the text that was superimposed over the image, "Bridging Healthcare from the Old World to the New World, From Our Family to Yours."

The crowd burst into enthusiastic applause. Frank said into his headset, "If anyone cracks a joke about my hairstyle fifteen years ago, they're gonna get a shoe up their ass."

"Sure thing, mullet boy," Rummy said over the earpiece.

"Anyone see anything?" Frank asked, ignoring Rummy's jab.

Everyone chimed in with a quick "no" or "nope".

"We're coming into the room via a backdoor near the front of the room," Jasika noted.

As the lights went up, his mother was standing behind a lectern on the raised dais in the room's front. "Thank you, thank you," she started. The audience took their cue and sat. A few photojournalists took photos of her behind the lectern. "I want to thank everyone for joining us today as I announce the release of our latest, groundbreaking medication, Nannixile. Before I jump into why Nannixile is an amazing new drug that received FDA approval after three peer-reviewed studies, I want to play mother for a second."

*She's not. Oh, dear God, please don't.*

"Many of you have made the connection between the Schultt family legacy and my amazingly talented son, Detective François — Frank — Schultt of the NYPD." She motioned toward him in the back of the room. "I am a very proud mother, even though we have been estranged for many years. Some of you may have even heard the nasty rumor that my François had passed away many years ago. I want the world to know I love my son and am very proud of him."

*Holy shit, she just did.* He felt like a deer in headlights as everyone was staring at him. A few flashbulbs lit as his picture was taken. He smiled sheepishly and raised one hand.

"Oh, you're never living this one down, babe," Aaron said in his earpiece.

"So much for maintaining my anonymity," Frank muttered back.

Frank then watched as she pointed to Aaron. "I also want to welcome Frank's fiancé, FBI Special Agent Massey, to the Schultt family. Many of you know him from his international bestselling books, *Blood Money* and the upcoming *Twelve-Day Killer*. Aaron dear, please stand."

Aaron stood from his seat in the back of the room. He looked at Aaron and mouthed, "I'm sorry," and he saw Aaron's response of, "It's okay."

Out of the corner of his eye, Frank saw Jonathan Fetty slinking around the outside of the chairs, making his way toward the exit. Frank sighed internally, afraid Fetty was going to make a scene. But he walked toward the door, trying to look as inconspicuous as humanly possible while all the attention was on Aaron and Frank.

As Aaron and Frank stared at each other, a solitary figure walked into the Wedgewood Room. She was dressed in a navy-blue business suit, her hair swept back in a tight bun on her head.

Frank yelled, "Christelle Perillo, you're under arrest!"

# Chapter Fifty-Three

Frank heard Rummy swear, "Fuck, she came out of nowhere," into his earpiece over the rumble in the room as people stared nervously at the scene unfolding in front of them.

Frank watched Christine do a quick mental calculation of the situation and made the only play she had. She took a hostage. Of course, the closest hostage to her was Jonathan Fetty. She pulled a gun from a small clutch purse and shoved it into Fetty's side, spinning him around so his back was pressed to her as she slowly began to drag him from the room. Aaron and Frank, guns drawn, began their approach.

"Please do not move any farther, or I will shoot him," Perillo said smoothly, glancing between Aaron and Frank. "As you both know, I don't like hurting innocents, but I will if I have to."

*Shoot him. He's not that innocent*, Frank thought. He wanted to say it out loud, but opted for, "You don't want to do this, Dr. Perillo."

"Just let him go," Aaron said. "He has nothing to do with this."

"You're right, of course, Agent Massey," Perillo responded. In one swift motion, she pointed her gun at Fetty's leg and fired. The gunshot and Fetty's piercing scream reverberated around the small space, which was all the distraction Perillo needed. She shoved Fetty away from her, closed the door and was gone.

Aaron and Frank made their way to the closed door as the room erupted in panic around them. Both quickly sidestepped Fetty as a stranger ran to him and started performing first aid. Frank could hear Rummy's voice, but his ears were still echoing after the gunshot. "The Salon is empty. You're safe to proceed."

"Where is she now?" Frank called.

"Running up the stairs to the lobby. I called Emergency Services, but they are a couple of minutes out."

"O'Donnell, secure my mother and wait for the EMTs," Frank yelled over the noise in the room.

"Jasika, Aaron, you're with me," he barked and took off after Daphne.

He shoved a few reporters out of his way as he barked, "NYPD, out of the way." Aaron and Jasika were doing the same thing.

Frank ran across the Salon and bounded up the stairs three at a time as he heard Rummy say, "She just exited the front of the building." Frank felt his blood pumping even harder as he pressed on.

When he entered the lobby, he shouted, "NYPD," at the hotel security guard in the lobby who was just getting concerned.

"Caught her heading north on Fifth Avenue. I have no more eyes on her."

"Call for backup and eyes in the sky," Frank said between breaths.

He exited the front of the building and caught sight of Perillo as she pushed someone out of her way and crossed a side street. A cab barely missed hitting her at the intersection as she ran. In typical New York fashion, the cabbie rolled down the window and was yelling obscenities at her as she fled. Perillo paused for a moment and turned her head in his direction. Catching sight of him, she continued running down Fifth Avenue again.

Seconds later, Frank paused at the same intersection. He held out his shield to the cabbie who was still yelling a series of obscenities. Jasika and Aaron caught up to him and they all kept running.

"I don't think this was planned," Frank huffed out between breaths. "It looks like her only plan is to outrun us." Frank found himself very grateful for all those early mornings on the treadmill.

"I think you're right," Aaron said.

Finally, Frank saw Perillo look back and see they were running after her. She crossed Fifth Avenue heading west on Terrace Avenue.

"She's cutting through the park," he heard Aaron say to no one in particular. Aaron caught the look Frank gave him as they hit the corner. "Rummy patched my headset into my phone."

"Frank, Frank, can you hear me? It's Rummy?" a voice suddenly chirped in his ear. He'd forgotten he still had the earpiece in until Rummy began talking again.

"Can't talk. Chasing the suspect," Frank said between clipped breaths.

They crossed Fifth Avenue slowly as they had to stop oncoming traffic. "She got lucky and crossed with the light," Jasika said. They made it across safely and took off again.

"Just got a report from an officer in the park. He saw a woman in a business suit running down East Drive. When she saw him, she took off back down Terrace," Rummy said.

They all immediately started after her again. "We have a patrol coming in from the West along Terrace, hoping to box her in," Rummy let them know.

Frank realized Perillo had thirty to forty-five seconds on them, but that's all she needed to get lost in this city.

"A patrol car just saw her cut into The Mall, heading toward Bethesda Terrace."

"I bet she's heading for the bridge. That's the only crossing point. Let's try to box her in," Aaron said, taking off down East Drive to circle behind the Loeb Boathouse.

Frank trusted Aaron's instincts, but he didn't like him running off alone.

Frank and Jasika picked up their pace, trying to gain ground on Perillo. Frank could tell both of them were losing the adrenaline rush and wouldn't be able to keep up this pace for much longer. They rounded the corner into The Mall, not taking time to examine the ornate structure of the arched columns leading to the Angel of the Water in the Bethesda Terrace fountain. At the base of the fountain, there was an older gentleman who was helping a woman stand.

The older man heard Frank and Jasika run into the Terrace. He pointed wildly to his right. "She went that way!"

"Thanks!" Jasika yelled as they took off running again.

As they headed down the footpath toward the Bow Bridge, there were only a few footprints in the fallen snow, so it was easy to see the marked heel of a woman's pair of flats. Frank motioned for Jasika to slow as he unholstered his service gun, whispering, "Follow the tracks?"

"Aaron wanted me to tell you that he's past the boathouse and on the back trail leading to the bridge. His cell reception was getting funky, and I lost him after that," Rummy said in his ear.

"Got it," Frank whispered back.

He and Jasika continued down the path. Frank only heard the occasional sound of a small animal scurrying through the surrounding trees and the crunching of snow under their feet.

"Heads up! We have officers coming East down the Cherry Hill path too. Unless she diverts from the trail, she's got nowhere to go."

"Rummy, thanks. Turning you off now. Need to focus," Frank said as he pulled the earpiece out and motioned for Jasika to do the same. "Couldn't concentrate with him constantly yapping in my ear."

"Tell me about it," she whispered back.

They rounded the corner, losing their tree cover as they heard the unmistakable sound of someone fleeing over the wooden planks of the bridge. Frank and Jasika took off running and got to the bridge's foot before Perillo had gotten halfway across.

Frank yelled, "NYPD, *stop!*"

Frank and Jasika started crossing the bridge as Perillo turned to face them. She held one of her signature Berettas in her hand and leveled the gun at them.

"Please, do *not* come any closer. I may not kill both of you, but I will shoot your partner, François," swiveling her gun at Jasika. "Now, please, let me go. No one has to die today."

"Not gonna happen," Frank said as he took one more step closer.

"The next step you take will be her last. You should know enough about me by now to know I don't joke around."

"Why'd you do it?"

"Be specific. I've done a lot of things in my life. Many I'm proud of, some I'm not."

"Okay, let's start with why you killed my father?"

A thin smile turned the corner of her lip. "Bravo. Finally, someone figured that out."

Frank caught Jasika trying to take a step closer, but Perillo quickly lowered her gun and fired one shot into the bridge a couple of yards in front of Jasika's feet, sending splinters in all directions.

"Detective Torv, you see, I've done my homework too, so please do not try that again. I have no desire to kill anyone today. I know you're an excellent shot. Maybe your skills rival mine, but I don't feel the need to find out. Do you?" She kept her gun focused on Jasika, but she looked at Frank. "Your father killed my parents."

"What?"

"I'm sure you've heard about the Gabon trials by now?"

"Yes."

"Well, my parents were test subjects. I watched as cancer ravaged their bodies. When I was orphaned, I was so glad your father came to my rescue and saw to my education. I trusted your father. But when I began working for Schultt Pharmaceuticals, I got access to internal documents showing your father knowingly allowed the trials to happen, despite evidence his drug had serious side effects in humans. He violated the trust I'd put in him in a way I couldn't forgive."

"Whoa," Jasika said under her breath.

"Whoa, indeed."

"So, you killed him?" Frank asked.

"Him and everyone who knew about it. It has taken me some time, but Cristillo was the last."

"What about my mom?"

"Your mom?" Perillo said, a clear mark of confusion crossing her face.

"Why were you planning on killing her?"

Perillo barked out a quick laugh. "I have no intentions of killing her. As I said, I had no intentions of killing anyone today. I love your mom. Besides, she's the one who blew the whistle on the Gabon trials."

"She did *what*?"

"Oh, you have much to learn about your mother, dear François." She swiveled her head down the path to the other end of the bridge. "It's been a pleasure, but I must run."

Frank heard the creek of a wooden plank on the other side of the bridge. So did Perillo as she spun her head and saw Aaron at the other end of the bridge, his gun leveled at her.

Out of nowhere, she had a second gun in her hand — one raised in each direction of the bridge.

A sharp noise sounded from next to Frank. At first, Frank thought Perillo had shot Aaron, but in that split-second moment of panicked fear, Perillo spun around and toppled over the side of the bridge. There was a crunching sound as her body hit the frozen water beneath it.

Next to him, he heard the spent casing from Jasika's pistol as it clanked off the wooden plank.

Frank dashed to the last spot where he'd seen her before she'd gone over. A spattering of blood painted the side of the bridge crimson where she had been moments before. He looked at the river, seeing if he could see her.

The hole where she punched through the ice was already freezing back over. Frank heard footsteps on the wooden plans and Aaron slipped his arm around Frank as Aaron whispered, "You okay?"

"I think I'm going to be."

# Epilogue

The next month was a whirlwind of activity for Aaron and Frank. With all the press at his mother's press conference, the hunting down of Daphne garnered a lot of international attention. The police searched all twenty-two acres of the Central Park Lake looking for Daphne's body. The NYPD even sent in a cold-weather divers team, but they didn't find the body. Officials believed she might surface once the lake thawed later that spring, so they planned on keeping an eye out. Frank had his doubts. There was no evidence that she survived the fall, but the lack of a body definitely made him wonder.

The story was on the front page of *The New York Times'* website for a few days. Frank got a big kick out of how Jonathan Fetty became a news story instead of being the one behind the scenes planting them. It amazed Frank the amount of dirt reporters pulled up on Fetty while he was in the spotlight. Not enough to kill his career, but definitely enough to take him down a few pegs. Daphne's shot had grazed Fetty in the upper thigh through muscle, missing arteries. In the after-action report, Frank had noted the gunshot was definitely meant to scare and throw the room in confusion instead of killing Fetty. But, getting shot in the leg has a way of giving people an epiphany. Aaron and Frank ran into Fetty at the gym a few weeks later. He looked better, and Jonathan apologized profusely for acting like an ass the previous month. In fact, he invited Aaron and Frank to have dinner with him and his new boyfriend—a nice, young doctor he'd met while he was in the hospital. Frank had no desire, but Aaron thought it would be good for them to heal old wounds. Surprisingly, Frank liked the new and improved Fetty, though he still called him 'Crazy Fetty' when talking to Logan.

* * * *

"Hurry up," Ben told Frank. "We are at T-minus ten minutes and counting."

Frank stared at himself in the mirror, adjusting his bowtie for the hundredth time. He couldn't believe he was getting married...again. He had to admit he looked damn good in his tux, and he couldn't wait to get out of it later that evening. They'd booked The Love Room at the Library for the next two nights before they would board a plane and head off to Bora Bora, where they'd be spending ten days at the Sofitel's Bora Bora Private Island.

"I'm ready whenever you are," Frank told Ben. "Ben, before this gets going, I want to say thank you again for managing all this. You've done an amazing job."

"You are more than welcome. It's been fun for me, too. And I know I may have gone a bit overboard on the wedding planning," Ben admitted, "but I couldn't let two of my favorite people have any old wedding. I wanted one that would make the papers."

Frank smiled. The wedding had definitely grown. In fact, they'd ended up booking Gotham Hall to accommodate the five-hundred guests who were attending their nuptials.

A quick rap on the door and Logan and Jasika came into the room. "You decent?" Jasika asked.

"Never decent, but fully clothed," Frank responded.

Jasika walked into the room and let out a low whistle before saying, "Well, look at you. You look sharp."

"You don't look half bad yourself," Frank noted. "I don't think I've ever seen you in a dress and heels."

"Don't get used to it. These shoes are killing me."

"So, you ready for this?" Logan asked.

"As ready as I'm going to be. Have either of you seen Aaron yet?" Frank asked.

"What? Afraid he's going to leave you at the altar?" Jasika joked.

"Hardy-har-har," Frank said. "No, just curious to know how he's doing."

"He looks amazing," Logan admitted.

Logan began to describe what Aaron was wearing, but Ben quickly cut him off. "Do not tell the groom what the other groom looks like. It's bad form." Logan began to say something, but Ben held up a finger and listened to someone talking into his earpiece. "We're a go."

Frank took a deep breath as Ben led him and his half of the wedding party to a side door near the front of the

Ballroom. Frank could hear the voices over the chamber orchestra inside. He took a deep breath.

"You got this," Logan said, patting him on the back.

Frank smiled sheepishly and nodded. *Keep it together, Frank. You want this. You need this. Just enjoy the day.* Frank looked over and saw Ben muttering into his earpiece.

"Cue the music," Ben said. Immediately the sound of Pachelbel's Canon in D Major started playing. "Okay, best man," Ben said, "you're up." Ben opened the door for Logan, and he walked into the ballroom.

Frank heard the hushed sounds as Logan entered the room. If everything was going to Ben's plan, Judith Wright was entering from Aaron's side room. Aaron had Judi and his two sisters on his side, while Frank had Logan, Jasika and Ben. Ben had not wanted to be part of the wedding party, but finally agreed when he realized it would be unbalanced if it was two and not three.

"Jasika, you're up."

Jasika entered the ballroom.

"Okay, Frank, I'm going to head in. Once I do, count to forty-five and enter — just like we practiced."

"Got it."

"And just because I'm going in does not give you permission to run off. I've spent too much time and energy on this to have the bride fly the coop at the last second."

"I promise. I'm not going anywhere."

Ben smiled then entered himself, and Frank began his countdown. After forty-five seconds, Frank entered the ballroom as everyone rose to their feet. The room was set up with fifty round tables and a raised stage at the front. With everyone standing, Frank couldn't see

Aaron until he climbed the stairs. Frank had gone with a traditional black tux, and Aaron was wearing a navy-blue tux with a black lapel. Frank was gobsmacked at how amazing Aaron looked. *Damn! That thing is tailored within an inch of its life to highlight Aaron's amazing assets. Speaking of assets, I wonder how amazing his ass looks. Whoa, keep it together, Frank. Save that for tonight.* As much as Frank loved seeing Aaron in his tux, he couldn't help but smile at what it would look like when it was on The Library's floor later.

When Frank finally stood in front of Aaron, he muttered, "You look amazing."

"Right back at ya," Aaron responded with a wink.

Frank couldn't help but smile. *Keep it cool. Keep it cool.* But Frank couldn't. Aaron was absolutely glowing, and it brought joy to Frank he had never experienced before. It took all his self-control not to rip his soon-to-be-husband's clothes off right then and there.

The ceremony went on as planned. Frank stared into Aaron's eyes through the whole thing. When it was time to say their wedding vows, Frank was suddenly brought out of his happy haze.

"Frank, I choose you to be my husband every day. From when we wake in the morning to when we go to sleep at night, I will cherish and love you. We will laugh, cry, scream and grow as a couple. I will be your partner, friend, confidant and whatever else you need me to be. I give you my trust. I give you my love. I give you myself. Whether we experience good times or stressful times, I will be there for you through it all."

Frank did everything he could to hold it together, because he had to get through his vows. The officiant turned to Frank and he began.

"Aaron, how lucky am I to call you mine? I'm madly in love with you. I promise my love for you will continue to grow each day. I trust, appreciate and respect you. I promise to share my thoughts, fears, joys and love as we build our lives together. Today, surrounded by our friends and family, I choose you to be my husband. You helped me believe in myself and love again. I am the person I am today because of your love. In your arms, by your side and in my heart, I know there is no mountain we cannot climb if we do it together. I am honored to be called your husband." Frank took a deep breath and saw a tear forming at the corner of Aaron's eye. *Thank you, Ben, for helping me write that.*

Judge Janice Kahl had Aaron and Frank exchange their rings. With their new wedding bands in place, Kahl concluded the service, "Aaron Massey and François Schultt, before these witnesses we have heard your promise to share your lives in marriage. You have sealed this promise with the exchange of wedding rings. We, your family and friends gathered in this space, bear witness and respect the pledge you have made to each other. By the power vested in me by the State of New York, it is my pleasure to introduce you to the world as Aaron and François Massey-Schultt. You may now seal this ceremony with a kiss."

A loud applause filled the room as Frank grabbed Aaron's head and brought his lips to rest against his new husband's. Maybe the kiss was too long or maybe it was too short. Frank didn't care. As long as Aaron was at his side, he knew he could weather any storm before them.

The rest of the evening was a whirlwind of food, toasts, dancing and congratulations from everyone.

Aaron's family was all there and so was Frank's mother, so it was fun to see both sides of the family finally meeting.

When the reception finally wound down, Ben ushered Aaron and Frank outside to a waiting limo to whisk them away to The Library. Ben had already checked them into the room before the ceremony, so all they needed to do was go straight to the Love Room when they arrived.

Frank used the keycard to enter the room and lifted Aaron to carry him over the threshold, laughing as he did it. The room was as he imagined. A copy of Dr. Ruth's *The Encyclopedia of Sex* leaned against the bedroom mirror. Rose petals were strewn across the bed. A bottle of Champagne was on ice waiting for them. On the marble tabletop underneath the window was an enormous vase of flowers.

Frank did a double take when he saw the vase. "Is that?"

"What?" Aaron asked as he was slipping out of his tux jacket and undoing his bowtie.

"The vase," Aaron turned to see what Frank was talking about. "Is that daphne?"

"Exactly what I was thinking," Frank said. He walked over to the vase and picked up the card sticking out of the arrangement.

*Dearest Aaron and François Massey-Schultt. Congratulations on your nuptials. It was truly a beautiful ceremony. I wish you both the best.*
*Christelle Perillo.*

# Want to see more from this author? Here's a taster for you to enjoy!

# Up on the Farm: Finding a Farmer
## Jason Wrench

## Coming Summer 2022

### *Excerpt*

I glanced down at the Rolex watch my granddad had given me when I finished my MBA a few years earlier. It's not one of the crazy expensive ones. Of course, I had to google the price after Granddad gave it to me. At the time, it was worth around ten grand. So, nothing to sneeze at, but still on the lower end of the Rolex world. I've thought about upgrading it a couple of times but can't bring myself to do it. Sure, I can afford a more expensive one. Between my day job working on Wall Street and my trust fund, I can afford almost anything I want.

I guess I should say my 'former' job on Wall Street, since that's what I'm celebrating tonight—my getting fired. I wasn't fired for cause or anything. My firm had scrolled back its trading arm in the US to focus on overseas markets. Thankfully, Granddad taught me to squirrel away money. I'd been taking my skills on the trading room floor of the Stock Exchange and turning them into my private nest egg. There was something satisfying about having an account with seven figures that hadn't been given to me by my family. At least the firm had waited until the Tuesday after Memorial Day to fire my ass. So, here I was on June first, drunk out of my mind.

I stared down at my empty glass, which was supposed to be filled with two shots of Belvedere Single Estate Lake Bartężek Vodka. I was about to raise my hand and order another one when I caught sight of my watch. I didn't realize it was this late already.

"Dudes, it's ten-thirty," I said, looking at my two drinking companions.

On my left was my best friend in the universe, Grayson Jackson. Grayson and I had met when we were attending The Quad Preparatory School in Manhattan. And with a seventy-five-thousand-dollar a year price tag, The Quad opened the doors to go anywhere we wanted. We'd both ended up at Harvard, for the fun of it. After making it through our undergraduate years barely sober, I had gone off to their MBA program, and Grayson had gone to law school. Now, we were both single, hot, wealthy guys in their late twenties getting everything we ever wanted out of life. We've lived by the 'work hard, play harder' motto our entire adult lives.

On my right was Avery Addington, my sort of on-again, off-again lover or fuck buddy. He's a couple of years younger than me. I met him on a dating app and figured it would be a onetime hookup, but he ended up sticking around. I call him my 'on-again, off-again boyfriend' because I don't know what the hell we are. Hell, I don't know if we even *are* at this point. We're not exclusive, that much I know. God, the idea of being in a long-term relationship practically brings me heart palpitations — and not the good kind. I like my freedom. I enjoy doing what I want to do when I want to do it. If I find a hot guy at a bar and I want to fuck him senseless in the back room, then I'm going to take him into the back room, bend him over and show him the best time of his life. And while I'm an admitted slut, I am on PREP and play safely…most of the time. And despite my use of protection, I get regular checkups to make sure I have contracted nothing. Shit happens.

"It's already ten-thirty?" Avery slurred. "How long have we been drinking?"

I found myself with my mouth open, on the verge of responding, but I honestly did not know what time we'd gotten here. I tilted my head to the side and glanced at Grayson, because I knew he'd know.

Grayson rolled his eyes. "You texted me about four, and I got here about five-thirty. You said you'd just gotten here, which I figured meant you had at least thirty minutes on me already. Based on this, you've been here drinking for six hours," he said with emotion of a forensic accountant. Oh, I should have mentioned that Grayson also got a master's in accounting after law school from NYU. He works for the Manhattan District Attorney's Office in accounting crimes — or something like that. Honestly, when he talks about numbers, I daydream. I enjoy making money and can tell you all about bulls and bears, but when it comes to the day-to-day math part, I tune out. I like the game of making money, the strategy of making money — hence, why I have an accountant who handles my books.

"I don't feel drunk." I heard myself say right before I started touching my forehead. "But I can't feel my forehead."

"Okay," Grayson grumbled. "I hate to be the adult in the room, but I have work in the morning, so I've gotta get out of here. Can you two make it home?"

"Your place or mine?" I asked Avery.

"Yours. It's closer."

"We can call my car service." *No worries.*

Grayson shook his head and grabbed my phone off the table. "What are you doing?" I asked.

"I'm calling your car service."

"But we're not ready to leave yet," Avery whined.

"Yeah, I think you two are."

"But, Dad," I complained.

"I've gotta go," Grayson said flatly. "And I'm not leaving you two to your own devices. To keep my conscience clean, I'm putting you in a car and sending you on your way. What you do after that is up to you."

I thought about objecting, but I knew Grayson was right. I'd had my pity party and would have to get up and join the world of the unemployed the next morning. Thankfully, between my granddad's and my contacts, I was sure I wouldn't be unemployed for too long. Honestly, I don't understand why some people stay unemployed for so long. It's like, why don't they use their personal and family networks to get a new job? It's not like it's that difficult.

Grayson got up and put his suit coat back on.

"How can you wear a suit in this heat?" I questioned.

"Don't you wear a suit to the office?" Grayson asked.

"Oh yeah," I said, as I tried to stand and realized my eyes were going in and out of focus. Grayson reached out and steadied me until I got my feet firmly planted below me. "Whoa, maybe I've had too much to drink."

"You think?" Grayson asked.

Once I was fully standing and the lightheadedness had passed, I helped Avery to his feet and the three of us exited the bar and grill after paying our tabs. I did not know how much this little evening was going to cost me. I'd handed over my American Express Black Card and given my signature. I'd worry about the expense later.

Thankfully, my car service arrived right as Grayson's Uber did. I shuffled into the car, sliding over so Avery could get in. Once Avery closed the door, the driver took off. I put my arm around Avery and rested my head on his shoulder. I felt his arm sneak around and pat the side of my head as he leaned down and planted a kiss on the top of my head.

*Why aren't we dating?* I thought to myself, as I was almost on the verge of falling asleep.

"We're here," the driver said.

"Thanks. That was fast," I muttered as I unentangled myself from Avery, who had fallen asleep.

"What?" Avery said as I jostled him awake.

"We're at my place."

"I must have fallen asleep."

"Well, duh," I said, reaching over him to open the door.

I nudged him out of the car and followed before lightly closing the door. I stared up at my apartment building, noticing all the lights in the windows were turned on.

I walked into Twenty Exchange, where I have a two-bedroom apartment. For its location and proximity to Wall Street, Twenty Exchange is an ideal apartment complex for the up-and-coming business type in Manhattan. Not only is it in the heart of Wall Street, but it also caters to an exclusive tenant list. When I decided I wanted to live there, I had my granddad pull a few strings to get me to the top of the list for new two-bedroom apartments when they opened up, which wasn't often. But here I am, four years later and I'm still living here, paying my four-thousand-dollar-a-month rent. Maybe one day I'll break down and buy a condo in the city. But for the time being, I'm okay with renting. I've always liked the idea that I could choose to move at the end of my lease if I wanted to.

The doorman opened the door for us with a polite bow of his head. "Good evening, Mr. Devereaux."

"Good evening, Jack," I responded. "How are the kids?"

"They enter the first grade this year," the uniformed man responded. He had the look that all proud fathers get when they realize their kids are growing up much faster than expected.

"Wow! Already... I can't believe it," I said with a smile. "Well, good night."

"You, too, Mr. Deveraux."

Grandad had taught me early in life to always respect those people in service positions. He was a whiz at remembering names, birthdates, anniversaries and all kinds of other facts. Me? I was happy I could remember someone's first name and maybe one or two details about their lives, but I tried.

Avery and I made our way to the elevator banks. I pushed the button, then leaned against the wall to make the marble around me stop spinning. *I haven't been this wasted since my first year in college.*

I heard the ding of the door and sort of spun myself into the elevator and hit the button for the fifty-fifth floor. Avery was leaning against me by this point as the elevator doors slid shut.

The ride up was smooth and uneventful. When the elevator opened onto my floor, Avery and I stumbled out and made it the few feet to my door. I whipped out my key card and let myself into the apartment.

"I'm going to get a bottle of water?" I asked Avery. "You want one?"

"Yeah, we should definitely hydrate after all this alcohol. I'm going to take a leak first."

I didn't watch him make his way to the bathroom, but I heard him as he bumped into one wall and tried to apologize to it.

I made my way into the kitchen, opened the fridge door and pulled out a bottle of Berg, a bottled water company that harvested water from fifteen-thousand-year-old icebergs. Each twenty-four-ounce bottle cost something like sixteen-dollars, but I liked it and loved the conversation starter it provided me when I was drinking one at work. I could always talk about saving the planet and our melting icebergs while I was drinking one. Trust me… The irony wasn't lost on me.

I twisted off the top and took a swig, savoring the crisp taste before swallowing. I leaned against the fridge, took a second sip and noticed that my answering machine light was blinking. Okay, I know what you're thinking. Who has an answering machine in the twenty-first century? Well, I do. And it's connected to my home line. I know… Who has one of those in this century?

I'd broken down and gotten myself a home line and answering machine when I had to work from home for six months during the pandemic. I could have done everything through my cellphone, but I figured having an actual phone with a headset attached was going to make my life easier while I stared at the four-monitor terminal I'd set up in the spare bedroom. I lived in the one bedroom, and the second one had become my home office. I figured the only people who ever stay over with me sleep in my bed, so I didn't need a spare room. Besides, a spare room seems like an utter waste of space. Who needs to have a bedroom that is only used when they have company over? I don't get that. If someone is coming for a visit, I'll put them up in a luxurious hotel, not my apartment. Again, I like my space.

I walked over to the flashing red light, put both of the water bottles on the island separating the kitchen from the dining area and pushed the button.

*"Dale, it's your granddad. I heard through the grapevine that you were let go from your firm today. I'm sorry to hear that, but I think it's the perfect opportunity to talk to you about the family business. Why don't you show up at my office tomorrow morning at seven a.m. for breakfast?"*

*Well, fuck!*

"How the hell does he already know?"

"Who knows what?" Avery asked, coming into the kitchen. I picked up one of the bottles of water and offered it to him. I turned around, leaned my hip against the island, screwed off the cap on my bottle again and took another swig.

"My granddad. He already knows about my being let go today. I swear he has spies that watch my every move."

"You don't think he'd actually do that, do you?" Avery questioned, scrunching up his face in an expression I couldn't read.

"No. It's a figure of speech. In reality, Granddad knows too many people in this town. I can't say that I'm too surprised, though, but I wish I'd been the one to tell him. You know?"

I glanced over the clock on the microwave, and it read eleven-twenty p.m. "Dear God, I have to be up in five hours."

"Five hours?"

"If I'm going to get to his office by seven a.m., I'm going to have to get up at four-thirty to hit the gym."

"Why not skip tomorrow?"

"Because you don't look this amazing by skipping the gym," I said. I attempted to wink at Avery, but I'm sure my wink probably appeared more like some kind of facial spasm. "Let's just crash."

I grabbed Avery's hand and led him down the hall to my bedroom. I wished I could text my granddad and say I wouldn't be able to see him in the morning, but I knew that when you're summoned by my granddad, you show up—whether you like it or not.

\* \* \* \*

I was enjoying a pleasant dream that involved me and a team of cabana boys when the dance version of *I Am What I Am* roused me out of my sleep.

Next to me, I heard Avery grumble, "Dear God, you *are* gay."

"Shut it," I replied as I pulled myself from under the sheets and turned off the phone. "Go back to sleep."

I leaned over and kissed him once on the forehead before I put my legs over the side of the bed and started wiping the sleep from my eyes. *God, I hate mornings.* Okay, in reality, I hate being awake. I love to sleep. If sleep were an Olympic event, I would absolutely get behind devoting my life to training for it. Sadly, our world doesn't work that way, so I planted my feet on the floor and walked over to my dresser. I rummaged around, quietly finding my workout clothes before grabbing my sneakers and slipping into the living room. I closed the door behind me so I wouldn't wake Avery again when I turned on the lights. Avery was already snoring away—not obnoxious snoring, just a gentle, even pattern that I found comforting and cute.

I went into the bathroom and relieved myself before slipping out of my night clothes and hanging them on the back of the bathroom door. Next, I put on my workout clothes. I was wearing a night-blue tank top and a pair of two-in-one running shorts. I loved the shorts because they provided me the support for my junk with compression shorts stitched inside. One pair of shorts to rule them all... I went back into the living room and slipped into my sneakers.

I then grabbed a water bottle and glanced at myself in the mirror that I have hung in the hallway. *Dear God, pasty much?* I'm a white boy. And when I say white, I mean that I'm practically translucent because I'm so white. There are people out there who look at the sun and magically have a gold tan. I am *not* one of those guys. I can spend the entire summer slathered in olive oil on a beach and I would become a crispy critter reminiscent of a blackened lobster. I simply do *not* tan.

When I used to spend summers out in the Hamptons as a child, my friends would joke that my skinny white body blinded them next to the pool. They also joked when I applied the highest-strength sunscreen possible. When I was in middle school, I spent the day at a friend's pool and didn't think about applying sunscreen to my feet. I couldn't wear shoes for a week because of how burned the tops of my feet had gotten that day. After that incident, I have always applied sunscreen liberally and often any time I had to be out in the sun.

I may not be able to control how white my skin is, but I can definitely control how defined my abs are, which is why I grabbed my water, phone, AirPods and key card before heading off to the gym. I rode the elevator down to the nineteenth floor where the gym and sun deck were located, then I let myself into the gym and flipped on the light switch. Although the gym was technically open twenty-four-hours a day, no one was in here at four-fifty in the morning. I wished I didn't have to be.

Thankfully, the gym was state-of-the-art and contained a range of cardio machines, weight machines and free weights. I put my AirPods in and picked out a treadmill. Today was a chest day, so I needed to get warmed up. I would start with twenty minutes of running, followed by thirty minutes of chest pumping and another twenty minutes doing more cardio.

I opened my favorite music app and selected an appropriately upbeat dance station as I hopped on the treadmill and started running.

By six-fifteen when I was finally leaving the gym, there were probably a dozen other residents who were now exercising in the pre-dawn hour. I'd forgotten to bring a towel with me, but I used the same paper towels used to clean the equipment to at least tamp off the worst of my sweat. Thankfully, the gym was air conditioned, because I thought even at this early hour it was going to be hot and humid outside. *The joys of summer in New York.*

I rode back up to my apartment and let myself back inside. Since I'd left, Avery had gotten out of bed and let himself out. Again, we may be friends and regular sex fiends, but we were hardly joined at the hip. I wasn't surprised that he'd gone or that he hadn't left me a note. I figured I'd text him at some point later in the day.

I threw my gym clothes in the laundry. The cleaning lady who came in daily to care for my apartment would wash and fold my dirty clothes and have them sitting on my bed when I got home from work. *Probably need to decide whether that's an expense I need, now that I'm out of work. Nah, that's a decision for another day.*

Before jumping into the shower, I called my car service and asked to be picked up at six-forty-five. I hated doing this to my car service last minute, but they were always very accommodating. Sure, I could have used an Uber like Grayson does, but they were not as reliable as my car service. And with my granddad expecting me at seven, I needed to make sure I was on time. With the car taken care of, I slipped into the bathroom and took a quick shower.

Finally feeling like a human, I slipped into a slim-fitting blue suit with a light blue button-down shirt and a gold tie. I liked how the blue made my hazel eyes pop in the mirror as I was tying the tie. Once I was in the suit, I put some product in my hair and got it to stand the way I liked it. I was going for a clean-cut but slightly tossed style. I know my granddad hated my haircut, but it was what all the gorgeous guys on Wall Street were doing, and I love to follow the latest trends in businesswear and fashion. If I didn't look like I'd stepped out of a Tom Ford catalog, then I hadn't done my job in the morning. Half of being good in business was looking the part. I learned a long time ago that people who are hot and smart get much further in life than those that were just either hot *or* smart. And thanks to my gifted genetics and premier education, I was fucking gorgeous and a highly intelligent businessman.

After stare-fucking myself once more in the mirror, I smiled at what I saw and grabbed my attaché case before leaving the apartment. I glanced at my watch, and it was already six-forty, so it was time to head downstairs and catch my car.

The ride down was uneventful, and a couple of other residents joined me in the elevator. One guy was in his exercise clothes. I nodded in his direction.

"Going for a morning jog?"

"Yep, want to get out there before it's too crazy hot."

I smiled and nodded knowingly. *What is his name? We fucked once after seeing each other at a club — or was it someone's party? I honestly don't remember.*

I exited the elevator then walked to the front door. My car was pulling up as the doorman opened the door for me.

"Good morning, Mr. Jessup," I said, nodding to the doorman.

"Have a pleasant day, sir," the older gentleman said.

I walked to the curb and opened the door to the black sedan.

"Mr. Devereux," the driver said, recognizing me from previous trips. "Where am I taking you this morning?"

"I'm heading to the Bush Tower, Carl."

"Which entrance?"

"One-hundred-thirty-second West and Forty-Second Street."

"Sure thing. We should be there in ten minutes."

I peeked down at my watch. It was already six-fifty. *Great, I'm going to be late.* "Any way you can shave a minute off the trip?"

"I know a couple bypass routes at this time of the morning. Shouldn't be a problem, sir."

"Great. I'm meeting with my granddad, and he is the king of punctuality." The driver nodded at me and kept his eyes on the road. I pulled out my iPhone to see if there was anything I needed to deal with.

*Hey, D. Got home last night. Checking in to see if you're okay.*

I quickly responded to Grayson.

*Hey, G. All is good. Got summoned to G-Dad's this morning. He's already heard... Sigh... Will text after my seven a.m. meeting.*

There was also a quick text from Avery.

*Went home to get ready. Had fun last night. Totally need to do it again. Preferably some time when we aren't so wasted all do is pass out when we hit your bed.*

I turned off my phone. *I'll text him later.* I leaned my head against the black cushion and closed my eyes for the rest of the ride.

* * * *

The black sedan slowed down, and I opened my eyes. We were pulling in right behind my granddad's black limo. *Perfect timing.*

"Thanks," I said as I opened the door. "I'll call the agency when I'm done. I don't know how long that will be."

"Not a problem. If it's not me, one of the other drivers will be glad to come get you, Mr. Devereux."

I put my foot on the curb, grabbed the inside door handle and hoisted myself into a standing position outside the vehicle. I closed the door and nodded goodbye to my driver, who wasted no time heading back into traffic.

I walked a few paces to my granddad's limo and rapped on the window three times lightly. The driver's side door opened, and Franklyn, dad's long-term chauffer, came out into the morning air.

"Good morning, Master Devereux."

"How many times am I going to have to tell you to call me Dale?"

"As many as you like, Master Devereux," the old man said with a sly smile.

We'd been playing this little game for years. Franklyn Jackson was an old-school chauffer. He was part driver, part body man, part confidant and probably filled more roles than my granddad's secretary did. They definitely don't make them like him anymore. Admittedly, my generation preferred using car services instead of a single car and driver. It's easier to always have a car and person on standby whenever you need them.

There was a light rap on the inside of the window and Franklyn moved around me to open the door. With it opened, he reached one hand in to help my granddad out.

"I won't be needing you again until around one, so go do what it is you do when you're not driving me around this town," my granddad said to Franklyn.

"Will do, Mr. Deveraux. If you need me, have your secretary call and I'll be here in minutes."

With that and a nod to me, Granddad started walking toward the front door of the Bush Tower. My granddad's offices were on the fifteenth floor of the building's thirty.

My granddad isn't one for small talk, so we basically walked into the building then rode the elevator to the fifteenth floor in silence. The Devereux Farms corporate headquarters were simple by New York standards. They leased half the floor, and the other half was leased by a Chinese corporation, which was rarely seen on the floor. In fact, I'd only run into people from the Jīnróng Corporation twice in all the years my granddad had leased the space.

We walked into the primary office, which was still quiet at five minutes after seven. The rest of his workers wouldn't be in until eight-thirty and nine. My granddad liked this time before the rush of people came into the office to get a lot of work accomplished. He might not be a skilled conversationalist with me, but he was definitely the epitome of the old IBM 'management by walking around'. He knew everyone who worked in the corporate offices and was known to drop by to see how things were going. In that respect, Granddad's ability to know his workers and know his business always amazed me.

I followed him into his primary office.

"Good morning, Mr. Devereux—and good morning, Dale. Well, isn't this a pleasant surprise," a chipper voice from an older woman in a neat teal business suit said as I walked into the office. Molly Frone has been my granddad's personal assistant for as long as I'd been alive. She was one of the first people outside the immediate family who'd held me as a baby. For that reason, she always seemed way more like family than she did my granddad's assistant. "Let me get a look at you."

I did a little spin and a pose. "Well, if this business thing doesn't work out, you can always have a second job as a model. Shall I call a couple of modeling agencies and set up appointments? I have a few connections," she said with a wink.

"I don't think we're there yet," I said. "But trust me... After the day I had yesterday, I may be a couple of days away from taking you up on that offer."

"Oh, let me show you what your grandfather bought me for my birthday," Molly said, gesturing for me to come over to her desk. She looked from side to side conspiratorially before she opened the top drawer on her desk. Just inside, in the pencil tray, sat a two-inch toy gun.

"Okay?" I asked. "What am I looking at? He bought you a model gun?"

"Not a model," Granddad said, "but rather the Swiss Mini Gun."

"It is, it is," Molly said with glee. "I've always wanted one. The gun shoots real ammunition."

"I never knew you were a 'gun nut', Molly," I admitted.

"Oh, I'm not like one of those card-carrying crazy people or anything. I just love antique or interesting guns. I've been a collector for years. And your grandfather gets me a new and unique one every year for my birthday."

"Well, happy belated birthday. And don't go shooting your eye out with that thing."

"I would never!" Molly looked almost scandalized by the prospect of shooting herself, clearly missing my *A Christmas Story* reference.

"Well, we've got items to discuss, Molly," Granddad interjected. "Come into my office, Dale." He then turned to Molly. "Will you bring in breakfast in about ten minutes?"

"Yes, sir." Molly walked over to a phone and dialed a number. I heard her put in the order before leaving to go pick it up.

My granddad's office was old school—all dark cherry wood and a lush midnight blue carpet. The carpet was something that should be in the Oval Office at the White House, except Granddad's carpet had the Devereux family crest embroidered into it.

"Just out of curiosity, how much does something like that cost?" I asked my granddad as I sat down in a leather chair on the opposite side of his desk.

"Roughly six-thousand Swiss francs."

"So essentially, sixty-five hundred US dollars, then," I replied after converting the sum in my head.

"Good to see your time on the floor of the New York Stock Exchange hasn't dulled your currency knowledge, my boy."

"And speaking of the stock market, I guess you heard about my being let go."

"Yes, yes I did. I was sorry to hear about that."

"Not half as sorry as I was."

"If it's any consolation, their letting you go had nothing to do with your performance or perceived value to the firm itself."

I didn't bother asking my granddad how he knew that. I've learned over the years that granddad has his fingers in so many pies and knows half the 'who's-who' of New York City. I wouldn't be surprised if he'd talked to the firm's CEO last night and given him a piece of his mind. He would never tell me he'd done that, though.

"Well, as much as I'm sure this is a blow to your ego, I don't think it's necessarily a bad thing."

That caught my attention. I hadn't expected him to say that. I had expected him to say many things, but that wasn't one of them. I expected him to blame me for choosing the firm when he had been opposed to them. I expected him to blame me for choosing to go to Harvard instead of Columbia. I expected him to blame me for not being so indispensable at work that they'd fired everyone else first.

"How so?" was all I said.

"Well, I've done a lot of thinking about life and you in the past year. I think it's time we discuss what you want for your future."

"Granddad, I'm only twenty-nine. Can we have the future talk when I'm in my thirties — or maybe my forties?"

He cocked his head and eyed me for a second. I could tell he was trying to figure out how to make sense of what I'd said.

"It's just...I'm not ready to settle down yet. I don't know if I'm the getting married and having children type—"

"Oh, dear God," he said with a huff. "I'm not talking about that. I'm talking about your future with Devereux Farms."

My eyes grew with the realization at what he was saying. "Granddad, I don't know if I want to work for Devereux Farms." *Well fuck, that just flew out of my mouth.*

"Excuse me?"

"I want to make my own way in the world. I want to make my own decisions in business without knowing you're ten steps away watching over me."

"And?"

"And I enjoy working on the stock market. I like the thrill of trading. I don't know if I'm meant to work in an office like this one."

"What's wrong with an office like this one?"

*Fuck.* "There's nothing wrong with your office. I don't know if I'm ready for a traditional nine-to-five office-type job yet. I like the interaction with people I get on the stock-room floor. I enjoy having more control and flexibility over my life and schedule."

I was about to continue listing all the reasons I couldn't work here in the corporate offices when a knock on the door interrupted me.

"Enter," Granddad said. He still eyed me as Molly opened the door, rolled in a breakfast spread and started putting it out on the board room table my granddad kept in the corner of the room for important business meetings. I watched as Molly laid out placemats to prevent anything from scratching the wood's surface. I wonder if they'd ever removed my crayon artwork from under the table that I'd done when I'd been a kid?

As soon as Molly left the room, my granddad motioned to the table. I walked over with him. We both slipped out of our suit jackets and hung them on the backs of our chairs before sitting down. I placed the linen napkin in my lap, then removed the cover of the plated breakfast.

My granddad likes his hot breakfasts, so I wasn't surprised when I saw a plate of scrambled eggs, bacon, sausage links, toast and fresh fruit staring back at me. *Thank God I ran this morning.*

"Coffee?" I asked my granddad.

"Yes, please." I picked up the carafe, poured him a cup and handed it to him.

He took the cup of coffee, and I poured my own as he said, "I have cancer."

# About the Author

Jason Wrench is a professor in the Department of Communication at SUNY New Paltz and has authored/edited 15+ books and over 35 academic research articles. He is also an avid reader and regularly reviews books for publishers in a wide number of genres. This book marks his first full-length work of fiction.

Jason loves to hear from readers. You can find his contact information, website details and author profile page at https://www.pride-publishing.com

PUBLISHING

Sign up for our newsletter and find out about all our romance book releases, eBook sales and promotions, sneak peeks and FREE romance books!